Soul of a MARINE

BOOK THREE WOUNDED WARRIOR SERIES

Patty Campbell

ISBN: 978-1-68046-727-7

Published by Satin Romance
An Imprint of Melange Books, LLC
White Bear Lake, MN 55110
www.satinromance.com

Published in the United States of America.

Cover Design by Ashley Redbird Designs

Chapter One

Master Sgt. Misty Beachy, USMC (ret), pressed her fingers against her eyes and moaned. She looked forward to hosting the kids from the local continuation high school about as much as she longed for a root canal. Not that she'd ever had one thanks to her parents spending a fortune on her teeth while she was growing up, but she was best friends with a former Marine who'd recently undergone the gruesome procedure and was still whining about it.

"Continuation High School." She sighed. Most of the kids there were one step away from juvie. She understood teenage rebellion. At thirty-three she wasn't so far removed from that period of her life. She'd joined the Marines when her big brother got killed in Afghanistan, nearly destroying her parents. At the time she thought she was doing it to make them proud. *How self-centered is that?* She smirked at her young cluelessness.

What she'd accomplished was to make them sick with worry that they'd lose their only other child in the middle-east for no good reason. And she'd come pretty damn close to making their anxiety a self-fulfilling prophesy in Iraq eleven years ago.

"Quit acting like a baby, Beachy," she chided herself between clenched teeth. "If you can handle a bunch of testosterone loaded

1

Marines at a forward operating base in a war zone, you can handle a half dozen sneering, self-destructive loser kids for an hour."

"Talking to yourself again, boss?"

"Kiss my ass, Jeremy."

"No fraternizing allowed. Says so right in the employment contract, but if we both quit our jobs, I'd be happy to oblige." She couldn't help smiling at her sunny young assistant. How he could remain cheerful day after day of working under her supervision was a mystery.

She wrinkled her nose. "I'm not a child molester." He was barely twenty-one.

"I have this thing for older women."

"You're very annoying, Jeremy."

Instead of answering her accusation, he grinned bigger.

Beachy sighed and shook her head. This kid always looked like he'd just opened up a Christmas gift and discovered Santa had left the exact thing he'd been asking for, right down to the brand name and model number. A happy boy in a rangy man's body. He had an annoying habit of making her smile, when she was enjoying a moment of self-indulgent funk.

"Your favorite high school kids are here, boss. Time to put a smile on your doll face, and a sparkle in those big brown eyes."

She rose from her desk with weary resignation, flashed an obscene and very un-ladylike gesture before grinding out, "You're fired."

Jeremy laughed. "Again? That's the second time today."

"Go line up the dogs. It's a shame we're teaching them to sniff explosive and contraband instead of attacking a pack of kids only their mothers could love."

"Don't be too sure. I doubt some of them still have mothers." He went toward the kennel and Misty took a deep breath, tucked a wisp short blond hair behind her ears and pasted a smile of greeting on her face. Might as well get on with it.

An hour later

The snarly blonde girl whose face seemed eerily familiar asked, "What's

2

that one's name?" She pointed to a flop-eared beagle bouncing with eagerness to get out of his kennel and join the teenagers.

Misty looked over shoulder. "Oh, that's Happy."

"So why's he locked up? Did he break the rules?" Her comment was directed at a fellow student who cracked his first grin of the morning. Hands in the pockets of his low-slung tattered jeans, he slouched and lagged behind his schoolmates. Stringy hair hung over his eyes, but not far enough to hide the silver ring in the corner of his pierced right eyebrow.

The kid reminded Beachy of a private once under her command in Iraq. She had no idea why Joey Hamilton had joined the Marines, except maybe to stay out of jail. By the time they returned from deployment he was one of her most reliable soldiers. The guys in his billet laid the nickname Boozy on him because he drank too much. Most of the Marines in the unit had stayed in contact over the years and Boozy was Joey again. Had a job, a girlfriend and was working on a degree in computer forensics. Misty Beachy was proud of him. Glad she'd had something to do with turning him around.

She hoped somebody would help this young man with some good direction for his future.

A couple of these kids looked hopeless. She faced the girl. "Happy is being retired from the service. He has trouble concentrating on his job and would rather play with every human, adult or child, he encounters in the commission of his duties."

The girl snorted. "So, what'll happen to him?" Her demeanor said...Like-I-care.

"He'll go to a shelter. Hopefully he'll get adopted before they have to euthanize him."

Misty loved the little mutt, but he was hopeless as a sniffer. He belonged in a home filled with rambunctious children.

Like balloons filling with too much helium, the girl's eyes expanded. Her sullen expression, the one she'd spent a lot of time perfecting, suddenly melted away, replaced by a look of any normal teenager who'd just seen somebody run over a kitten. Her next question squeaked out on a high note, "They'll kill him?"

Well, well, well. There's a sweet little girl hiding under the façade of snarky boredom. "It's a possibility. I hope it doesn't happen."

"I'll adopt him."

"It's not that simple."

"Why not?"

The teacher escorting the group stepped through the door. "Time to get on the bus, gang."

"No! Wait!" Panicky as a bird caught in a net, the girl turned to Misty. "Why not?"

The teacher touched her shoulder. "Sorry, it's time to go Ms. Hawk. We have to be back on campus before lunch."

Misty pulled an official Customs Bureau business card from her shirt pocket and handed it to the girl named Hawk. She knew a man named Jack Hawk. Maybe this kid was related to him. Her eyes were the same odd color, and the shape of her jaw looked familiar. That's what had been bothering her for the past hour, why the girl looked so familiar. "Take this. Call me later and I'll try and explain the process to you. What's your name?"

She grabbed the card. "Ellen Hawk."

Unbelievable. This girl was Hot Stick Hawk's daughter. Had to be. She was the right age. They lived in the area. Jack was currently stationed at Camp Pendleton.

The group cleared out. Misty checked her watch, picked up her office phone and entered a number from memory.

"Hello?"

"Santos? Misty Beachy here. Is Mac home?"

"Yeah. Hey, Dad! It's the Marine lady on the phone."

"Hey, Mis. What's up?"

The sound of her best friend's voice always warmed her to her bones. "So, it's Dad now, is it?"

"My sweet boy started calling me Dad when we all drove to Vegas the day I married his mother. He was my best man. Great, huh?"

Misty knew how much that meant to Mac but didn't comment. "You still at home whimpering about your root canal?"

A soft chuckle brushed her ear as if he were in the room. "Yep, but I've been informed by my gorgeous pregnant wife that I've used up my sympathy quota. I've been ordered to go back to work tomorrow. The better part of valor would be to follow her orders."

"You're right on that score, Mac." Misty pictured McPherson's wife, Graciella. He'd fallen like an anvil off the back of a bouncing pickup for that woman. Physically, Graciella couldn't have been more different from Misty. Exotic, willowy, dark hair and eyes, nearly as tall as Mac. Cluny McPherson was Misty's best pal. A fellow Marine who'd briefly been her lover so many years ago in Iraq. Misty had never been *in* love with Mac, but to this day she measured every man against him, and they all came up wanting. He was her best friend in the world, and probably knew her better than anyone.

"I know you didn't call me to ask about my dental work, Sarge. Not that I don't love hearing from you. How about heading up this way sometime soon?"

"Maybe. The reason I called was to ask you whether that woman who married the hot undertaker still has that no-kill animal shelter in town."

"She does. They just put on a big expansion. Dempsey and I got the building and plumbing contracts."

"Hey, didn't Gunny Dempsey and his wife recently have another kid?"

"Marla had twin girls. They've got three girls and a boy now. Gunny's of the opinion they should go for one more boy, to even the odds."

Misty couldn't imagine ever having one child let alone four. "I can't imagine."

"Why did you ask about the shelter?"

"I've got a dog who flunked out of the sniffer program. He'd make a great family pet and I don't want to send him to one of the shelters down here. They only hold them for about thirty days. Do you think she'd take an out-of-town happy beagle?"

"Are you kidding? Why do you think she expanded the facility? She won't turn away a single dog or cat. Do you want me to call her and ask?"

"Would you? If she'll take him, I'll drive up there next Saturday. I'll check on you and Gunny and all your kids. It's kind of hard when the men I used to boss around are now taking orders from different women. A blow to my overblown ego, especially when they're able to do it without carrying a side arm."

Mac's laugh was like a swallow of good whiskey. Fiery and mellow at the same time. "I'll give her a call and let you know, Mis."

"Thanks. If I don't answer, leave me a text, or Jeremy will take a message for me on the office phone. Gotta run."

"Hope to see you next weekend, sugar-lips."

"Careful, the wife might be listening."

"She's cool." His voice was directed away from the phone briefly. "Aren't you, baby?" He was back. "I'll call you."

It was time to grab a bite while she had the chance. Misty slung her bag over her shoulder and shouted. "Jeremy! I'll be about an hour. You want me to bring you back anything?"

He walked in holding a sandwich and pointed at his full mouth. "I'm good," he mumbled through tight lips. Deep dimples creased both cheeks.

He must have a dozen girlfriends, Misty thought and shook her head. *If I were ten years younger, I'd be all over you, Jere.* "Okay, then, back around one." She left the office and went to the Jeep parked out back. When the dogs spotted her they broke into a chorus of happy barks. She'd never been a dog person until she'd seen Queen, Mac's service dog, calm him out of a PTS episode. Her admiration for them took off like a hot rocket and spurred her into her present job with the Customs Bureau.

She hoped she'd be driving her old Jeep north to Spring Grove and Simi Valley over the weekend with Happy on the seat next to her.

* * *

In spite of the coolness of the afternoon, Misty and Jeremy glowed heat and exhaustion by the time they called it a day. The dogs were super smart and they all had special abilities. Some were better at sniffing out drugs and others were super keen on explosives. A few of them probably should have gone into K9 Warrior training. They could sniff out a bad guy a quarter mile away, whether or not he had any kind of contraband on his person.

"Buy you a cold beer, boss?" Jeremy retrieved his keys from the drawer of the desk they shared. No frills, everything basic in their drab government office.

"Isn't your girlfriend anxiously waiting for you to call?"

"You're my only girlfriend, boss." His dimples deepened when he grinned. "At the moment anyway."

It only took a second for her to make up her mind. "I'll meet you at Brazos, but we're going Dutch as usual."

"I'll take what I can get." Jeremy left through the rear door, turning off the back office lights as he went.

Misty took a minute to clear off her desk then go outside to check the kennel lights and gate locks. She waved at the night security guard as she drove past the kiosk on her way to the main road.

Brazos always had a healthy contingent of sailors and marines hanging on the bar and playing pool. She was very comfortable in the company of men. Especially military men. The more the better. Her with only one guy always turned out to be bad news.

The owner of Brazos, Jake McKillan, played nothing but Mexican music in his jukebox. On Saturday nights he had a Mariachi band to entertain his customers. A dance floor was cleared in the center of the rustic, noisy room and a full contingent of Mexican cooks cranked out the most delicious food this side of the border. Tonight he'd only have nachos and dips available, but the beer would flow cold and continuously from bottles and taps and cans.

She parked her car and went inside. Jeremy hailed her from across the room and pointed to a chair he was resting a foot on to keep anyone from taking it or sitting down. He'd already ordered two bottles of Corona, and Jake's wife, Guadalupé set a large plate of nachos on the table.

Misty touched the woman's arm. "Thanks, Lupe. Those look good. How about an order of guacamole and a bowl of your homemade salsa to go along with it?"

The short, plump, stunningly exotic beauty grinned, threw her long braid over her shoulder and nodded. "Pronto for you, Missy."

"Gracias."

Jeremy lifted his foot off the chair and Misty plopped down with a grateful sigh. "I don't know what it is about those loser-kids that wear me to the bone. Two hours with them and I'm ready to drop."

"Loser kids?" The familiar deep voice came from behind. Without being asked, Hot Stick Hawk plopped in the chair next to her and put his sweating beer bottle on the table then helped himself to a handful of nachos. He tipped his head to Jeremy whose smirk oozed amusement, and then took a deep swallow of icy beer.

Very few things ever embarrassed Misty Beachy, but being caught bad-mouthing his daughter did the trick. The heat level in her chest shot up so fast her ears burned. "Sorry, Jack. I wasn't talking about Ellen. It's just...um...sometimes those kids...from that school... they..." Better to clam up before she jammed her foot down her throat any farther.

"I get it." He tapped the neck of his beer bottle against her nose. "Relax."

What was it about Jack Hawk that always set her teeth on edge? He was a stand-up guy, a fellow Marine. They went way back. Jack had been there to save their asses in Fallujah when it counted. One of the top A-10, close air-ground support pilots in Iraq at the time.

What was it? He never uttered an opinion, but she was sure he didn't like women in the military. Mac said he was old school, but the guy couldn't be more than forty-five at the most. How could that qualify for old-school?

"I hear you met Ellen today." He stared at her with eyes not gray and not brown. They darkened when he discussed something strategic and serious and got lighter when shooting the bull in a mess hall. Jack had never made a move on her, but he had a way of making her feel soft and feminine when she needed her steel in the company of her Marines. As a major he'd outranked her by a mile, but he'd always maintained a professional military attitude at the FOB. He may not have been in favor of women in the military but had always treated her like a fellow soldier.

"Look, Jack, I'm mortified you heard what I said. I wasn't singling out Ellen. I have so little patience with slackers. Those kids drive me to the edge. Ellen isn't as tough as she pretends to be. I didn't know she was your daughter until a couple of minutes before they left this morning. I apologize. Let me buy you a beer."

"You already did. I told McKillan to put this on your tab." Hawk's smile was special. He seldom flashed it, but when he did, it was dazzling and sincere.

Misty pointed an accusing finger at Jeremy. "If I find out you were in on this, you're fired."

"I gotta go." Jeremy pushed back his chair. "Three firings is my quota for one day. My mother will be so disappointed in me. Again." He snagged his denim jacket off the back of the chair and headed to the door. "See you tomorrow, boss."

Hawk's gaze followed his slim back. "Nice kid."

"I don't know what I'd do without him."

"Ellen thought he was 'steaming hot.' Her words."

"Does she say stuff like that to annoy you?"

"Too often. She likes to test dear old dad."

"I don't know how parents do it. Cripes. My brother and I were the worst. I'm surprised my parents ever got any sleep, worrying about whether we'd end up in jail or not." Misty pictured some of the stunts she and Bill had pulled. Bill was her hero. He'd pulled her ass out of the fire more times that she could count. When he'd been killed in Afghanistan all she wanted to do was join the Marines and get revenge on as many bad guys as possible before one of them got her first.

* * *

Beachy had to be the most fascinating female Jack had ever encountered. Not that he encountered many in his line of work. He never did figure out his ex-wife. They'd been married for fifteen years, but with his deployments, had probably spent less than three years total under the same roof. Now Ellen. Another story. There had to be a vengeful god out there who delighted in torturing men. Make them love their women so much they'd be willing to die for them, but never giving them a clue as to what made them tick.

The play of emotions on Beachy's face added to the mystery of her. They flitted from saucy to deep sadness in a flash. Her expressive brown eyes had always appeared oversize in her pixie face. Shit, she didn't look much older than Ellen, but he knew she had to be in her early thirties.

Do the math.

She'd joined up in her twenties, done three tours in the middle-east, then rose in rank to master sergeant. She'd probably still be active duty if she hadn't been seriously wounded in that last convoy ambush while she and her men were heading back to Baghdad, returning home.

Aware of the rumors that swirled around her and Cluny McPherson, Jack figured they were the only two people in the world who knew what, if anything, happened between them over there. McPherson was a good man. A quiet man. He and Misty had remained friends ever since then. Had to be going on eleven or twelve years by now. She had a relaxed way about her when with McPherson. It said a lot about what may have occurred between them.

"I'm retiring." *Whoa, where'd that come from?*

The surprise on her face couldn't have been faked. He doubted she faked any emotion. Hide them, yes. Fake them, no. "When did you decide to retire?"

He picked up his beer and took a swallow, pressed the sweaty bottle to his forehead and chuckled. "Just this minute. I'm as bowled over as you are."

"Jesus, Jack. You can't make a decision as big as retiring from the military just like that."

"Appears as if I did."

It was time for him to put some distance between himself and Misty Beachy. He couldn't be in her company for very long before getting that buzz, that tug. Silly. Dangerous. The last thing he needed was another female complicating his existence. Ellen was more than he could handle at the moment. He shoved back his chair with a loud scraping squeak. It mirrored the loud scraping squeak echoing deep down in his belly where it had no business being in the first place.

Time to haul ass.

"Jack," she called to his retreating back.

He raised a hand and kept walking.

Chapter Two

Misty finished her beer while brooding over Jack's startling revelation. Jack retiring? On the spur of the moment? Hawk had been a Marine pilot all his adult life. What would he do now? She'd call Mac to ask him what he thought of Jack retiring. He knew Hawk better than she did.

"Hey, babe. You look lonely." A fresh-faced young sailor sat in the chair recently vacated by Hawk and another sailor took Jeremy's empty seat.

"Is that right?" What did these two children think they were doing hitting on her? "You boys place a bet on which one of you I'd go home with?"

To his credit, the sailor across from her blushed and stared at the floor.

"Hey, no!" The baby-faced blond on her left declared. "We're just being friendly."

"Look, *boys*. I'm way too old for you, I've put in a long day, a friend has just told me he's retiring from an illustrious military career way too early, and my co-worker bugged out and left me with the check. So maybe you better look for greener pastures."

Shy Kid cocked his head. "I'm surprised they didn't card you. How old are you?"

"Smooth move. Your pick-up lines need work. But if you want to sit here, shoot the bull and finish these nachos and chips, be my guest. The next round of Corona is on you."

She barely got the words out of her mouth when the kid grinned and signaled the barmaid. "Maybe you can give me some pointers. I haven't had much luck lately."

"I can't imagine why." She turned to Baby Face. "What's your excuse?"

"I don't have one." He shrugged. "I just picked the prettiest girl in the room and here you were, all alone."

Misty pointed to Shy Kid. "His pick-up line is a little better than yours, but not by much." She lifted the fresh beer to her lips and took a swallow to keep from laughing then set the bottle down and eyed them one at a time. "My name is Misty Beachy, I'm a retired Marine Master Sergeant. I served three tours in Iraq, and was released after getting wounded in an ambush outside the forward operating base in Fallujah. I was in high school when you were still in diapers. Are we clear?"

"Clear." Baby Face's posture stiffened.

Shy Kid, his mouth hanging open, nodded. "I thought you were about twenty-three."

"Good answer. Let's finish our beers and nachos so you boys can get home by bedtime. You can tell me about the dozens of broken hearts you left back home."

They were nice kids, and she enjoyed the next hour with them. Her heart went out to lonely young servicemen, feeling their oats and denying their homesickness. She'd seen battle hardened Marines wipe a tear staring at a photograph or reading a letter from the girlfriend dumping him. Or, opening a box from Mom.

They stood, respectfully, when she announced her departure. She walked to the bar and settled the tab. "Those two kids have had enough to drink, McKillan. Time to cut 'em off."

"Gotcha. I'll get them out of here before the shore patrol shows up. You coming in Saturday? I got a new band for the night."

"Got someplace else to be, but you'll see me before too long. Semper Fi."

"Backatcha. Thanks for looking out for those boys."

Once she'd distanced herself from the glare of city lights she could appreciate the velvety black night and balmy air of San Diego. She rolled down the windows of the Jeep and let the wind pound her ears and blow hair around her face. A million stars reflected off Balboa Bay.

Next Saturday she'd be on this road, driving even farther north, through L.A. and into Ventura County. She'd catch up with Mac and his family and Dempsey's growing brood. Happy would be sitting on the passenger seat enjoying a new adventure, a silly grin on his hairy muzzle. She chuckled when she pictured his big soft brown ears flapping in the breeze. Another soldier retiring early. Somebody would want him. He'd end up in a good home.

* * *

Friday night

Instead of driving to Spring Grove Saturday morning as she'd planned, Misty sat in the passenger seat of Jack's car, Happy breathing down her neck from the back seat, heading north on the San Diego Freeway.

He'd called her Thursday to say he planned to visit a private aviation company in Van Nuys that had offered him a job as flight instructor. "I'm gonna check it out. Ellen is camping in Joshua with my sister's family for the weekend."

Misty gave Hawk a tentative yes then spent a couple of frustrating hours doing paperwork and making phone calls to get permission to take Happy and place him in the Simi shelter. Once the task was done, she figured it would have been easier if she'd lied and told them their *government property* had died.

She called Mac to see if he'd heard back from the shelter. The minute his home phone rang, she realized he'd be at work and should have called his cell. She was about to disconnect when Graciella answered.

"Hello," her faint but discernable accent unmistakable.

"Graciella, hello, Misty Beachy here. I wanted to talk to Mac and realized after I'd entered your home number that he'd be at work. I hope I'm not disturbing you."

"Not at all. Cluny's at the dental surgeon's office, so his cell phone is off. Is there a message you'd like me to pass on to him?"

Misty hesitated, then decided to plunge right in. "You probably know I asked him to call the shelter in Simi to see if they'd take Happy."

"Oh, yes, he did call them, but the owner was out of town for a few days and the woman who answered didn't have the authority to grant permission. She'll be back the middle of next week."

"Dammit!"

"Oh, dear, I hope that won't be too late for the dog." Genuine alarm in Graciella's voice echoed in Misty's ear.

"No. It's just... I was planning on bringing him up tomorrow night. Jack Hawk offered to drive us Friday night and take me home on Sunday. I'll call him and let him know we won't be making the trip."

"Misty, bring him. We'll be happy to keep the dog until next week. If it doesn't work out you can retrieve him later. You're welcome to stay here with us too. We've still got an extra bedroom, for the moment." Her words were punctuated by a soft chuckle.

"I couldn't stay with—"

"Of course, you could. We're having the Dempsey's over for dinner on Saturday. It will give us all a chance to catch up."

"Well, uh." Misty marveled at Mac's wife. It had only been a couple of years ago that she and Mac had nearly broken up because Graciella had found Misty's hair brush and a couple of other things of hers in Mac's guest bedroom. Graciella and her son, Santos, had moved to Mac's house temporarily. Mac had insisted the police couldn't protect them until the man who'd accosted her was in custody. Graciella had stumbled on Misty's carelessly left behind belongings, having no inkling of her and Mac's past.

"Misty, we don't have to rehash the past."

"Um, you're having the Dempseys for dinner? Aren't you due to deliver soon?" The woman was carrying Mac's first child. She'd never known him to be so happy and contented. Graciella and her son had changed his life dramatically, his PTS episodes now rare and incidental.

"I have another month to go, but you'd never believe it the way I lumber around like a rhino. I have a lot of energy despite how I look." She laughed. "Cluny swears I'm still beautiful. Love is blind."

Misty wouldn't know about blind love. She'd never been in love. Mac was her best friend and she loved him, but it wasn't the same. There was no chance she'd ever experience the kind of love Mac and Graciella had. *I'm bad news.* She'd managed to spoil any budding relationship she'd had in the past ten years. She was on her road to becoming a cranky old maid. She'd perfected cranky, so old maid was inevitable. She'd do the men of the world a great service if she'd just stay away from them.

"Okay, if you're sure it's all right with you…and Mac."

"Are you kidding? He'd love a nice long visit with his best friend. Plan to stay Friday night and Saturday. Invite Jack Hawk to join us for dinner on Saturday night."

"I'll do that. Thanks. See you tomorrow night."

Now, she and Hawk were about halfway there. They'd arrive before nine o'clock. Still early enough for a brief visit before bedtime. She glanced at Jack. Except for the gray in his hair, he hadn't changed much in the last dozen years. A man of average height and size, and physically fit. Attractive even, when she looked at him objectively. She didn't know what it was about him that had always made her uncomfortable, unsure of herself.

"Do I pass inspection?" He gave her a sober look.

Heat rose from her neck to her scalp. He was the only man who could make her blush nearly every time they were together. "I was just thinking I'd like to kill you."

"Have at it, but maybe you should wait until we're not on the freeway doing seventy."

"How do you do that, Hawk?"

"Do what?"

"Set me on edge. You've never liked me, have you?" She turned her head and stared out the side window. His not-gray-not-brown eyes were downright unnerving.

"Is that what you think?"

"Isn't it obvious?"

He clamped his lips together and blew a breath through his nose and shook his head like she was some kind of clueless idiot. Then he turned those eyes on her.

"What!" She slapped her knee. "You're doing it again!"

"What the hell am I doing, Beachy? Explain it to me."

If she could explain it to him she would. She couldn't explain it to herself. Instead she growled through clenched teeth, "Never mind." The next two hours would be torture.

* * *

Shit. So, she thought he didn't like her. Better leave it that way. They were on different paths. He was ten years her senior. He had a recalcitrant teenage daughter to raise. He would retire and relocate whether he got the job in Van Nuys or not. Yes, he'd leave it alone. No point to it.

The next hour crawled by with the silent tension of the negotiating table on the 38th Parallel between North and South Korea. Finally, he broke the silence. "You want to make a pit stop, or grab a cup of joe?"

"Yeah. Okay." She sighed and visibly relaxed. "Sure."

He pulled off at Hawthorne Boulevard and followed the sign to Denny's. "Will Happy be okay in the car?"

"He won't like it, but we won't be long. Leave the windows down an inch or so." Misty rubbed the dog's head. "We'll be right back, bud."

Hawk pulled open the door when she approached. She didn't look at him and her cheeks pinked. A gust of wind feathered her short blond hair. Feathered his gut, too. "After you, sergeant."

"Smartass."

"That's me." He followed her to the counter. She ordered coffee then excused herself and went to the ladies' room. He ordered two pieces of cherry pie. If she didn't want one, he'd eat both.

Soon as she sat on her stool, he stood. "Be right back."

"I didn't order pie." She pointed to the warm cherries oozing in a flaky crust.

"Don't eat it, then." He needed distance from her. Misty's grumbling followed his back. For some reason it brought a grin to his face. In the men's room he used the head then splashed cold water on his face. This had been a bad idea.

"I'll pay for my own pie," she snarled when he sat next to her.

"Be my guest." He picked up his cup and took a slug of the scalding coffee and nearly choked. "Jesus!" he sputtered. "Where'd they boil this stuff? The seventh level of hell?"

Misty snickered, stirred her coffee and forked a cherry.

"Yeah, go ahead and enjoy my pain, you heartless witch." He gulped ice water to soothe his scorched tongue and throat.

She bumped her knee against his. "Sorry, Hawk. That wasn't nice."

"Eat me."

"In your dreams."

Exactly. In his dreams. The sooner he dropped her at McPherson's the better. Maybe he'd die in a small plane crash tomorrow and wouldn't have to drive her back to San Diego on Sunday. The thought soothed his libido.

She carried a small piece of pie crust back to the car when they left and fed it to Happy. Why was it she could be so sweet and affectionate with the dog, but treated him like a leper?

Because the dog isn't interested in getting in her pants, dickhead!

Traffic had thinned considerably by the time they got back on the freeway. It wouldn't be much more than an hour to McPherson's. Hawk flogged himself mentally for feeling like a sex starved teenager. It wasn't her fault. She'd never encouraged him. Anyway, when they were in Iraq he was married and she was hooked up with McPherson, so what had he expected?

"Don't get out," she said when they pulled into McPherson's driveway. "I'll see you tomorrow. Thanks for the ride." She opened the back door, let Happy out and yanked her duffle off the seat.

"You're welcome. Tell Graciella I should be here no later than six tomorrow."

Beachy waved over her shoulder and stepped onto the front porch. The door opened, McPherson let out a whoop of pleasure and lifted her off her feet then planted a big kiss on her cheek. Cluny waved at Jack as he backed out.

Try and figure out that relationship if you dare, Hawk.

He drove straight to the motel in Van Nuys, checked in, and fell asleep within seconds of his head hitting the pillow. That bitchy little blond exhausted him.

Chapter Three

McPherson home, after dinner, Saturday night

"Leash up Queen and Happy," Cluny nodded toward the dogs. "We're taking a walk in the park."

Santos and Amber scrambled to do his bidding.

Marla helped Mac put on a baby carrier and strapped year-old Declan Dempsey against his chest. "All set, Cluny. You might want to watch out for his binky when you retrace your steps home. He thinks it's great fun to spit it out and watch his adult slaves retrieve it for him."

Mac tickled the chubby boy and kissed his red hair. "I'm your very own Uncle Slave, Dec."

"How do you tell them apart?" Misty's brows drew together watching Graciella set one of Marla's two-month-old twin daughters in the double stroller, while Dwayne did the same for his other girl.

"One's Sylvia and one's Kathleen. That's the best I can do. Bye-bye babies. Have fun." Graciella patted their wispy red hair.

"Thanks, Mrs. M." Dwayne double checked their restraints and tucked the blankets around them. "Sylvia." He patted the head of the baby in the top seat. Let's go, my precious girls."

"God! You people are making me ill." Misty wrinkled her nose. "I can't believe my warriors have surrendered so pitifully." She pointed at Hawk. "You can go with them. You've been on the Daddy Train longer than they have."

Jack Hawk flashed a bite-me look.

They were barely out the door when Graciella asked her, "What's with you and Jack?"

Being left alone in the company of women was like marching in chains toward a court martial. Misty didn't have a clue how to be a *girl*. She liked Marla and Graciella. But they were a separate species. They spoke a foreign language. Face it—they weren't men.

She touched her chest. "Me and Jack? Absolutely, positively nothing. We can barely stand each other." The thought made her teeth ache.

"Why?" Marla frowned.

Misty threw up her hands. "If I knew, I'd tell you." That was a lie. She *wouldn't* tell them even if she understood it. Why would she confide in them? Sharing her feelings was something she'd never mastered. The only person she'd ever trusted with her deepest, darkest secrets was her dead brother. The book on feelings was closed. The End.

"Too bad." Graciella sighed. "The two of you look good together. I've only met him once before, but he seems like a nice man."

Okay. Time to change the subject.

Misty grabbed some plates and pushed back her chair. "Let's get at these dishes. We can have them done by the time the Daddy-Kiddie tribe returns." She eyed Graciella. "You go kick back in Mac's recliner. You've been on your feet long enough." Giving orders—that was what she was good at.

Misty had no experience with pregnancy, but lack of experience hadn't prevented her from noticing how often Mac's wife had linked her hands beneath her bulging belly, or the way Mac frequently watched her with loving concern in his eyes. Mac touched his wife every time they were near each other. Their relationship was worlds apart from what she and Mac had shared in Iraq so long ago. The unmistakable *love* lighting Mac's eyes for his wife, was worlds apart from the look of *like* he'd always had for her.

"I second that." Marla put her hands on Graciella's shoulders and steered her toward the living room. "Take a load off. It'll be months before I'm where you are."

What? Misty carried dishes and silverware from the dining room. She leaned back against the counter and stared at Marla when she carried the last dinner debris from the big table. "You're not, uh, you know, again? So soon?"

"Knocked up?" Marla laughed and shrugged. "This has been my permanent condition since I married Dwayne. Imagine what he'd be like if he had *two* legs. At least when I get him naked he can't chase me.

"Don't look so shocked. This is it. Boy or girl, I'll be back on the pill and any other birth control method it takes. Either that or Dwayne will be making a trip to the urologist for an adjustment."

Misty pressed her lips together and shook her head. "Are we talking about the same Gunny Dempsey? Good luck with that."

"Hmm." Marla sighed and opened the dishwasher. "You rinse and I'll load." They went to work with silent efficiency.

"Ship shape." Wiping up the last drop of water, Misty opened the refrigerator and helped herself to a beer. "I'd offer you one, but I'm pretty sure you and Graciella are on the wagon. How about Sprite?"

Marla carried two bottles of Sprite and followed her to the living room. Graciella's eyes were closed. Misty stopped and held up a hand.

"I'm awake." Graciella rolled her head and smiled. "I'm luxuriating in your pampering. Thank you for cleaning up so fast. Sit. Let's talk while we have the chance."

Misty racked her brain for something to say. Finally, she blurted, "So how's the dad thing working out between your son and Mac?"

"My son?" Graciella chuckled. "I'm a minor league player in my own home. Santos worships the man. He emulates Cluny's every gesture, walks like him, stands like him, likes all the same programs on TV. Overnight he wasn't my little boy anymore. It was bound to happen. He's almost twelve."

"At least he's male," Marla said. "Amber mimics her daddy the same way. She's such a tomboy. I intend to make girlie girls out of our twins. Frilly dresses, Mary Jane's, hair ribbons, doll babies that wet their diapers, the whole nine yards."

"Jack has a teenage daughter." Now why had she said that? Jack had a daughter, so what? She had zilch interest in Hawk—the macho prick. "Not that it's any of my business. I don't even know why I mentioned it."

"Cluny told me she's been difficult to handle since her mother left them." Graciella shrugged. "Sad, really."

"Yes," Marla added. "Dwayne was very lucky his first wife took off when Amber was an infant. He and Cluny did a good job raising her on their own, away from that woman's poisonous influence. So, I shouldn't complain about her being a tomboy. It could have been worse, much worse."

Graciella gave Misty a curious look. "Is she the reason you and Jack aren't...don't..." She threw up her hands. "Forget I said anything. I apologize for asking such a personal question."

"Oh, hell, I don't care. There'll never be anything between me and Hawk, but Ellen would definitely be a stumbling block." She snorted out a chuckle. "Can you imagine me in day-to-day, close proximity to a teenage girl with emotional problems?"

Graciella grimaced.

"I see what you mean." Marla nodded thoughtfully. "No offense."

"None taken." Misty breathed a sigh of relief at the sound of the men, kids and dogs coming in the front door. Reprieve.

Santos flew into the living room like a flaming comet. "Guess what, Mama? Dad said I could keep Happy as my very own dog!" He took a breath. "If it's all right with you. He said I had to ask you." The pleading look in his eyes was downright pathetic, and brought a beatific smile to Graciella's face.

She directed a gaze at Mac. "So, Dad said you needed my permission, huh? Maybe Dad should have talked privately to me before he said anything. What do you think?"

Cluny winced and shoved his hands in his pockets.

Undaunted, Santos soldiered on. "Mama, you promised me I could have my very own dog someday. This is someday isn't it?"

Amber opened her mouth to join in the conversation and Marla made a zip-it frown. The girl rolled her eyes and sidled up to Dwayne. He nodded in agreement with his wife.

Graciella directed her next remark to Misty, who'd been enjoying the fact she hadn't been included in the conversation. "Doesn't the no-kill shelter depend on donations and payments from adoptions to continue their work?"

"Um, yeah, they do." Misty swallowed. Her heart squeezed at the disappointment on Santos's face.

His eyes brightened. "Dad said he'd make a donation." He turned to Mac. "Didn't you, Dad?"

Graciella pressed her lips together, apparently having trouble maintaining a stern face. "Well, in that case—,"

Santos and Amber jumped and screeched gleefully. Queen barked at the outburst. Happy did his happy dance around Santos's legs.

Mac went to Graciella, held Declan tight against his chest and leaned close to her ear. "You're not only the most beautiful mom in town, you're the most wise. Thanks for not putting my ass in a sling, baby. I'll make it up to you." He gently placed his big hand on her belly.

"That's a guarantee." She tipped her face for his kiss, cupped her husband's cheek and smiled at Dec's blue eyes and rosy cheeks before Cluny straightened.

Misty sat close enough to hear every word. She experienced a confused hash of emotion observing their exchange. She wasn't jealous exactly, but the sudden feeling of irreversible loss brought a cold cramp to her chest. Mac was her best friend. She was glad he'd found the love of his life. Graciella was The One for Mac. Dawning realization that she'd never be The One to any man hurt. Why did it hurt? That's the way she wanted it. Right?

Jack Hawk shook hands with Mac. "Thanks for the great dinner and the company. I enjoyed the evening, but I've got another flight and a second interview early in the morning, so it's time for me to make tracks." He kissed Graciella's hand. "Delicious dinner, Mrs. McPherson."

Graciella gripped Jack's hand. "You're welcome anytime, Jack. It was so nice to get to know you better."

"We're in full retreat, too." Dwayne put his hand on Amber's head. "Say goodnight, Amber." He dropped his arm around Marla's shoulder and gave her a squeeze. "Push the girls out to the truck, honey. I'll get Dec in his car seat then strap the girls in. Thank you for a nice evening and a good dinner, Graciella. Next time is on us. Give me a hand, McPherson?"

"Sure. I'll leave him in the carrier and bring him to you. Santos, put the dogs out back then go to the garage and find Queen's old dog bed for Happy. We'll get him a new one tomorrow." He grinned at Misty. "You look tired, Beachy."

"That's always nice to hear, Mac."

He kissed her cheek. "Let me rephrase that. You're gorgeous as ever, girlfriend. Better?"

She shoved him. "Go help Gunny before you step deeper into it." Misty extended her hands to Graciella. "Up you go. Recliners can be a bitch to get out of."

"Thanks. I was going to sit here and wait for Cluny, but your help is welcome. I need to grab a bottle of water before I head to bed. What time is Jack picking you up tomorrow? Will we have time for breakfast? Cluny and Santos are making blueberry waffles. It's their Sunday morning specialty."

Misty followed her to the refrigerator. "Yum, waffles. Hawk's not getting here before eleven. So, count me in." Sitting down to breakfast without Hawk would be nice. He'd be on her nerves all afternoon on the drive back to San Diego tomorrow.

"Good. See you in the morning."

Misty walked to the front window and watched Mac helping Gunny's family load up. She'd set her clock for five, so she'd be up early enough to run with him.

"Help!" Santos banged on the kitchen door. "I locked myself out."

Misty laughed and opened it for him. "Where'd you get that smelly thing? I'll find a blanket to fold up for Happy to sleep on. He'll probably be on your bed the minute the light goes off. Get rid of that ratty piece of trash. Your mom probably doesn't want it in the house."

Santos wrinkled his nose. "It stinks, doesn't it? I'll tell Dad I threw it out."

"Good plan. Where are the extra blankets?"

"Up there." Santos pointed to the cupboards over the washer and dryer.

Misty retrieved a seen-better-days sleeping bag. "This'll do fine. I'll put it in your room, bud. I need to hit my rack so I'll be good and ready for those famous waffles of yours in the morning."

"Dad and I make the best waffles on the planet."

"I have no doubt." She tapped the top of his head and proceeded to the guest bedroom.

* * *

Barely light outside when her eyes popped open, she beat the alarm on her cell phone by seconds, pulled on her running clothes and joined Mac on the front porch steps.

He continued to tie his shoes then looked up. "You're a sight for sore eyes this early in the morning, Mis."

"I figured you could use some other female company besides Queen. Think you can wear me out?"

"I intend to give it a shot." Cluny stood and stretched then he and Queen took off down the sidewalk. "Don't get too far behind."

Misty quickly knotted her shoelace and jogged after him. "Cheaters never prosper, Mac!"

He glanced over his shoulder and grinned. "Since when?"

Forty minutes later they pounded through the back door, laughing and jostling to see who got through first. Misty stopped short when she saw Graciella, tumble-haired and bleary-eyed at the kitchen table while Santos prepared the coffee maker for her morning cup.

"Sorry. Were we making too much noise?" Lame, but that's all Misty could think to say.

"Laughter isn't noise." Graciella cocked an eyebrow. "I'll be human after I've had my first and only cup of coffee. Eight months on one cup of coffee a day is an eternity."

Mac put his hands on her stomach and kissed her neck. "You never looked more luscious, baby."

"That's a demoralizing thought." She reached up and put her hand on the back of his head and tilted her chin to meet his kiss. "Even I can see this early, Macfearsome," she teased, using the name Santos called him right up to the day they were married.

"I'll shower as soon as I feed and water the dogs. You can go ahead, Mis. I installed a bigger water heater so we'd never run out of hot water. My boy and I will get to those waffles as soon as I give my wife a little more mouth-to-mouth. She's in bad shape this morning."

"The coffee's done, Dad. I'll take care of Queen and Happy."

"Thanks, son." Mac kissed the boy's head as he passed by.

Misty had the strange sensation of looking in on a private family scene from an outside window. She'd always known Mac needed this. This warm, loving family home. Something she and Mac never could have achieved together, not that there was any chance of that ever happening at any time in the past decade.

She shook herself. "I'll shower then. KP duty is on me after breakfast. No arguments."

"None from me." Graciella sighed. "I never do dishes on Sunday. It was in the marriage contract."

Mac had prepared his wife's coffee just the way she liked it and set it on the table in front of her. "Back in ten, baby."

He followed Misty down the hall, gave her a sharp swat then dodged away. "You still have a very fine ass, Sgt. Beachy."

Hands on her hips, she glared. "Shut up, you clown. If your wife doesn't shoot you, I will."

Mac's happy laughter trailed behind as he went to the master bedroom at the end of the hall and closed the door. Misty sighed and mumbled to herself, "You married a saint, numbskull."

The Saint had perked up considerably by the time Misty re-entered the spacious, modern kitchen Mac and Gunny had built for the old house. Mac was already busy at the long marble island with Santos, whipping waffle batter.

Santos sorted through a colander of fresh blueberries. "These are full of stems." The kid wrinkled his nose as he held one up for Mac's inspection.

"That's what I have you for, sailor. If we don't want the wrath of Mom, you'll find all of them." He glanced up. "Coffee, Mis?"

"Praise God." She set the mug on the table, smiled at Graciella. "Sure you can't have another one?"

"I'd love it, but this one," she patted her belly, "already thinks he's an Olympic athlete." She pulled her long, wavy brown hair to the back of her head, knotted it, and then pushed up from the table. "He's using my bladder for a trampoline. Be right back."

"He?"

"Yes," Santos answered. "I'm getting a brother. We already have a name, but I'm not allowed to tell it until he's born."

"That's great." She was powerless to stop the grin tugging the corners of her mouth. "Do you know that by the time he's your age, you'll be graduating from college?"

"I'm not going to college. I'm going to be a plumber like Dad."

"We already talked about this." Mac tested the waffle iron. "First a bachelor's degree, then your plumbing contractor's license. After that we'll talk about adding your name to the letterhead. Everyone at management level in my company has a degree." He jabbed a playful elbow into Santos's shoulder.

"You're the only one at management level in Veteran's Plumbing."

"Ah, you've been paying attention."

"I get to go on some jobs with Dad when school's out. I already know how to fix a sink drain and hook up a water heater. Don't I, Dad?"

"Yep, you're my most reliable helper and I can handle your wages. Is the bacon done? Let's get these waffles going. We've got two starving women to feed, not to mention the Olympic athlete."

Graciella returned to the table dressed in stretchy pants and one of Mac's UW sweatshirts with the image of mascot, Pistol Pete emblazoned on the front. "Something smells good in here." She took her seat and smiled at Misty. "You have no idea how much I envy you, Misty."

"Me?" No way did this remarkable woman have anything to envy her about.

"Yes, to be slender and fit like you again will be very hard to achieve."

"I doubt that. Once you start dancing it'll melt away." Even now, Misty would have been prepared to kill for Graciella's long shapely legs and arms.

"From your lips to God's ears."

"How's the student you hired to take over the dance studio doing?"

"She's handling it beautifully."

"After you and Santos met Mac at the beach, he found your studio and wrangled a free lesson from you. Mac is sneaky." Misty asked herself why the story of how they'd fallen in love over a samba lesson was so romantic. She seldom had romantic thoughts. In fact, when she'd first heard the story from Marla, her reaction had been *ho-hum.*

Misty didn't miss the look of contentment in Graciella's face. She couldn't imagine the feeling, loving a man, trusting a man so completely.

Snap out of it!

"When do you plan to go back to teaching?" She sniffed the aromatic coffee and took a bracing swallow.

"Not for about six months. I'm thinking of closing down the school in Chatsworth, and possibly opening up a new location in Simi Valley. The woman who's running the Chatsworth studio for me would like to buy it, but her husband is skeptical. It's in flux. Baby first. Samba school later. I'm enjoying letting my big, strong husband take care of me for now."

Misty glanced at Mac. His wink told her he'd be happy if Graciella stayed home permanently. But knowing him, he'd encourage her to make the decision for herself. She'd danced since childhood in Brazil and had established the school with her own money and sweat equity when she was a young widow with a fatherless baby boy.

A loud rap on the front door interrupted the conversation.

"Shall I get that, Mac?" Misty pushed her chair back when he nodded.

Jack Hawk stood on the front porch, all smiles.

She rolled her eyes. "You got the job."

"Affirmative."

"When?"

"I'll start as soon as my separation papers come through. The owner of the aviation company has a rental apartment for me and Ellen to use until I find a place."

"That you, Hawk?" Mac called.

Misty and Hawk entered the kitchen. "Jack got the job."

"Hey! Good news. You're in time for breakfast."

"I had breakfast at six. Can we call this brunch?"

"Absolutely. Throw some extra bacon in the microwave, son. I'll mix more batter." He filled a mug with coffee and handed it to Jack. "Brunch coming right up."

Chapter Four

Following Tuesday

"WHAT THE HECK IS SHE DOING HERE?" MISTY ROSE FROM HER desk and exited her small office. She strolled rapidly to the security kiosk at the end of the long drive leading into the training facility. Ellen Hawk was in animated conversation with the security guard.

"Ellen? Why are you here?"

"I told her she couldn't come in, Ms. Beachy." The diminutive man shrugged helplessly.

"Ellen, this is a secure government facility. You are only allowed to enter here with prior permission. I'm sorry, but you have to leave." In her ragged jeans and broken down Nikes Ellen looked like a refugee from a homeless shelter. Surely Jack didn't allow her to go to school looking like this?

"Isn't this a school day?"

Ellen's blank belligerent stare was a non-answer. "I don't have a ride." The girl oozed attitude.

Misty glared. "How did you get here?"

"A friend dropped me off."

No wonder Jack has more gray hair every time I see him.

"It's okay, Carlos. I'll take her inside and arrange for transportation."

"You'll need to sign the manifest, ma'am."

"Write down you name, address and home phone and I'll sign you in, Ellen." Misty clenched her jaw. Bad timing. A group of new handlers would be arriving any minute for the first leg of training with their assigned dogs.

Ellen handed the clipboard to her. She scanned it and scratched her signature. "Come with me." She turned her back and didn't wait for the girl to catch up to her.

"What are you so mad about?" Ellen trotted behind Misty and into the small office.

"You know damn well what I'm so mad about. Don't try to play your infantile head games with me. I'm calling your father. Sit down and shut up."

"I can't call Dad at work unless it's an emergency. He doesn't know I'm not in school."

"Well, then I guess it is an emergency. What's his number?" Misty had Jack's number somewhere but didn't try looking it up. Let her squirm a bit. If this was her kid she'd be grounded forever. She had a new appreciation for what Jack had to put up with.

Ellen recited the number, crossed her arms, and sat back in the guest chair with a huff, glaring at Misty.

Jeremy walked in and the girl brightened immediately. He hesitated at the doorway and directed his comment to Misty. "The, uh, the handlers just passed the entrance gate, boss." He raised his eyebrows with a silent question.

"I'll be a few minutes. Escort them to the conference room, please. I'll join you as soon as I can. You can field their questions and pass out the paperwork."

"Will do." He nodded, cut his eyes to Ellen then left the office.

"Can I go with him?" She began to rise from the chair.

"No! Sit down and be quiet." Misty quickly dialed Jack's number at the base. A woman answered. *Damn!* "Yes, this is Misty Beachy at U.S. Customs. I need to speak with Major Jonathan Hawk. Is he available?" She fidgeted when the woman put her on hold.

"Major Hawk will unavailable for the next hour, ma'am. May I take a message?"

"Yes, please have him return my call." She would be out of the office and didn't want to miss his call so Misty recited the number of her cell phone and her office number. She hung up and sat back. What the hell was she going to do with this girl for the next hour? Abruptly, she stood. "Come with me."

"Where are we going?"

"To the kennel."

"Is Happy there? I'm hoping my dad will let me adopt him."

"Happy isn't here."

"Did they—?" Her alarmed eyes bulged.

"He's been adopted by a good family in another county."

Ellen's genuine look of relief broke through her studied façade of ennui. Why did this kid work so hard at being difficult? It must take most of her energy and concentration every breathing moment.

"Come on, I don't have much time."

"What am I supposed to do?

"Keep company with the dogs until I come for you. That's *all* you're supposed to do if you don't want me to put a leash around your neck and drag you around behind me. Got it?"

"Sheesh. Why are you so mean?"

Misty didn't waste her time answering. She pulled open the door to the air-conditioned kennel. The dogs went nuts for attention when they spotted Ellen.

"Oooh." Ellen went down on her haunches in front of the first kennel and let the mutt lick her fingers through the chain link. "You're so cute." She glanced at the name tag in the slot of the gate. "Buster."

Misty hailed a woman dragging a large bag of dry dog food in their direction. "Florine, put this young lady to work. She's not to leave the facility. I'll come back for her when her father arrives."

The woman raised her eyebrows. "If you say so." She motioned to Ellen. "Come with me."

Ellen rose, squinted at Misty, and then followed the woman to the other end of the row. Florine handed her a hose and instructed her to fill the automatic watering tubes outside each kennel.

Crossing her fingers, Misty made her way to the conference room, checked her cell to make sure it was on and willed Jack to call.

An hour later the phone still hadn't rung. She left Jeremy to escort the handlers to the exercise area where they'd be introduced to their dogs and have time to get acquainted with them. Just as she reached the kennel door to check on Ellen, her phone rang. She nodded at Jeremy when he walked in to start moving the dogs.

"Jack? Look, I hate to bother you, but you need to come here and get Ellen."

"Ellen? She's there? What the hell!"

"Yes, she showed up over an hour ago. She said a friend dropped her off and she had no way to get home. I'd have driven her, but I'm totally snowed under today with a new group of handlers transitioning through here."

"Hell! It'll be at least an hour before I can leave." Distress and frustration came through the phone, loud and clear. "I'd ask you to call a cab, but I don't trust her to go straight home. She's supposed to be in school."

She may not particularly like Jack Hawk, but she wasn't unsympathetic to his situation. "Relax, Hawk. I'll keep her here if I have to put her in solitary." She chuckled, but quickly silenced when her joke fell flat. "Sorry."

"Forget it, Beachy. I'll get there soon as I can."

Was that a scuffle? Misty whipped her head around and strode to the kennel door.

"Cut it out! Move away from me!" Jeremy was angry about something.

Misty peeked in the window. He'd just shoved Ellen back against one of the kennels. She yanked open the door and barged in. "What's going on here?"

"He pushed me!" Ellen pointed to Jeremy, an injured and accusing look on her face.

"Yeah, I pushed you, jailbait. Stay away from me. The last thing I need is a child coming on to me. If you think I'd risk my future to make out with a loser like you, you're whacked!"

"Whoa, whoa, whoa!" Misty inserted herself between them.

Ellen sobbed.

Jeremy glared, his jaw clenched so hard the muscles in his cheek jittered.

"Jere, take a breath. Tell me what happened."

"She made a pass at me. Get her out of here or I'm leaving right now."

"No…I…" Ellen gasped. Her face burned deep red.

"Ellen, come with me." Misty took the girl's shaking arm and pulled her toward the door. "You'll wait in my office until Jack gets here. He's on his way."

She glanced back at Jeremy. He slumped back against the chain link and dragged his fingers through his short brown hair. "I'll be right back. Don't start taking the dogs out until I return."

He rubbed his hands down his face and nodded.

Misty yanked open the office door and pointed to a chair. "Sit." She tossed a box of Kleenex. "Blow your nose." She glanced at her watch and picked up the office phone. "Carlos? When does Bill get here? He's here? Good, have him start his shift now and you come to the office."

A few silent minutes passed before Carlos opened the door. Misty realized at his alarmed expression that he thought he was in some kind of trouble. "I need a favor, Carlos. I'm asking you to put in a little overtime for the next hour."

He sighed with relief, removed his cap, and wiped sweat from his forehead with his sleeve. "Sure. Okay."

"This young lady and you have already met. Her father, Major Hawk, is coming to pick her up. In the meantime, she's not to leave this office. You sit here in my chair. Don't talk to her and don't touch her. If she gives you any trouble ring me immediately. I'll be in the training area with the new handlers. Clear?"

Eyes big as Frisbees, Carlos nodded.

Ellen twisted a wad of tissues and stared at her lap.

Misty's sympathy for Jack's situation increased with every step back to the kennel. When she stepped inside, Jeremy seemed to have regained his composure. "Okay, Jere?"

"God, that little bitch is scary. What's wrong with her?" He shoved his hands in his pockets and stared at the ceiling.

"What did she do?"

"She came up behind me and put her arms around my waist. Scared me so bad I nearly crapped. All I could imagine was spending the next ten years in jail for touching her. What is she, sixteen?"

"Fifteen. She's got some serious emotional problems. I don't envy her dad. He'll be here to pick her up in about an hour. In the meantime, I put her in the office and have Carlos watching her." She laid a reassuring hand on his shoulder. "What a day, huh?"

Jeremy blew out a breath and smiled. "Yeah. Let's get these dogs out to the training area and get to work. We're behind schedule, and I have a hot date tonight."

"You gonna get lucky?" Misty laughed when a faint blush painted his dimpled cheeks.

His blush grew deeper. He turned and opened the first kennel. "Come on, Buster. You're starting your real job today." He leashed the mutt and secured it to a hook then opened the next kennel. "You too, Angel. You're a working girl now." He left the kennel with three dogs on leashes.

"I'll bring the other three. We'll get you to your date on time." Misty thought whoever Jeremy's girl was—she'd be the lucky one tonight. The longer she worked with Jeremy the more she appreciated his sweet personality and work ethic. Any girl would be fortunate to claim him as her boyfriend. She wondered if Jack had a ... "Whoa, where did that come from?"

* * *

Jack Hawk wrapped up his paperwork and re-scheduled his separation interview. Ellen was his priority. No question. He was in way over his head with his daughter. Every time he thought they were making progress, she'd pull some rebellious shit like this. The sooner he got her out of Oceanside the better.

She'd screamed bloody murder about being ripped away from her 'friends' and her school, which was no less than he'd expected, but if they were ever going to make any progress they needed a change of scene.

He glanced at his watch. "Shit!" It had been almost two hours since Beachy called him.

He stepped on the gas and maneuvered through traffic, doing all the things he'd warned Ellen about the few times he tried to teach her to drive. That's all he needed–Ellen with a driver's license. Hair on the back of his neck stood erect. His ears rang. "God almighty, what am I going to do with her?" Strangling her was not an option. Neither was sending her to live with his ex-wife. Theresa had made it unmistakably clear that she wanted nothing further to do with him or her daughter.

Marriage for active duty service members was a very bad idea. His stomach had churned the day they'd walked down that endlessly long and surreal aisle. What had he been thinking? They barely knew each other. Blinded by love, *and admit it, Hawk*—lust—he'd proposed to her four days after picking her up at the officer's club. "Jesus, what a night!" Recollection of their hours of wanton lovemaking—downright debauchery—haunted him to this day. He'd been thinking with the little head rather than the big head for sure.

Unfortunately, Ellen was the physical image of Theresa. He had no clue about her level of sexual experience. He prayed she was still a virgin but try as he might he'd never been able to initiate the father-daughter conversation he knew to be necessary. "Godammit!" He pounded the steering wheel then whipped around a slow tractor-trailer.

Misty and Ellen were sitting silently in the office when he walked through the door. Ellen turned in the chair and his heart nearly broke at the look of fear mixed with defiance on her face. She knew she was in trouble but was determined to put an I-could-care-less face on it. The poor kid was a mess, and what was he going to do about it?

"Hey, Jack," Beachy acknowledged his presence. "I'll be in the kennel." She quickly left them alone.

Jack sucked in air. He took the chair next to Ellen but said nothing.

After a few minutes of silence, she faced him and snarled, "What?"

"I think that's my line." He gazed into her rebellious eyes, the only feature she'd inherited from him.

"I hate you!" Her eyes swam with tears she refused to let fall.

"Yeah, well, we've been down that road before."

"You're ruining my life!" Ellen curled her hands into fists on her lap to hide her bitten-to-the-quick nails.

He'd never mentioned them, studiously avoided looking at them. "You need to take a long look in the mirror. You'll see just who it is who's ruining your life, Ellen."

"It's not my fault you and Mom got divorced."

"No, it isn't your fault." Is that what she thought? "Our divorce had nothing to do with you."

"How could it not have anything to do with me? I'm in the middle of it. Mom doesn't want me, and you don't want me!"

Her accusation stung. Actual physical pain gripped his chest. "I want you, Ellen."

Ellen scoffed and deliberately looked away from him. "You don't want me, and you don't love me!"

Jack slumped forward, his elbows on his knees. "For Christ's sake, Ellen," he murmured just above a whisper. "I've loved you since the day you were born."

She remained still. Her knuckles glowed white in the late afternoon light shining dimly between the Venetian blinds in Misty's office. Her breaths came in jerks, jaw muscles bouncing with tension. Jack wanted to take her in his arms, but knew she'd push him away. She'd been pushing him away for the past year.

The door at the back of the office, leading to the kennel opened. Beachy stepped inside and stopped abruptly. "Oh, sorry, I thought you'd left. I was going to lock up."

Jack stood. "We're going to get out of your hair." He took one of Ellen's elbows and urged her from the chair. When she stood, he put his arm around her shoulders. "Come on, sweetheart, let's go home."

He laid a hand on Misty's arm as they left. "Thanks, Mis. See you around."

* * *

Misty's arm tingled where Jack had briefly rested his hand. For two reasons: his gentle softness to his daughter, with no hint of anger in his voice, and because he'd called her Mis. The only other person in the world who'd ever called her Mis was Mac. She wasn't sure whether or not she wanted anybody else to call her that. She slid into her desk chair and dropped her head into her hands. That was the first time Hawk had ever touched her. It didn't mean anything. She groaned.

Jeremy walked in. "You okay, boss?" He opened the top drawer and withdrew his car keys.

She peeked between her fingers and nodded. "That girl wears me out. Poor Hawk."

"Yeah, he's got a handful there." Jeremy sat across from her. "Look, I hate to add to your bad day, but I've been accepted into the aerospace engineering technology program at Cal Tech starting in September."

"Jere! That's great! When did you find out?" Lord, how she hated the idea of losing him, but she knew how hard he'd worked toward his goal.

His grin lit the room. "Yesterday."

"You've known since yesterday and didn't tell me?"

"I was planning to tell you at lunch, but jailbait showed up and ruined my plans. I thought you'd be sad to see me go."

"Don't be an ass. Of course, I'm sad, but I'm thrilled for you. Let's head for Brazos. Mexican food and beer is on me." Goals were important to Misty. She'd achieved many of hers and knew how satisfying knocking them down one at a time could be. "Guess I'll have to look for a new boyfriend."

Jeremy grabbed her when she passed him on the way out the door. He whooped and swung her in a circle. The kid's excitement was contagious. "You'll always be me my first serious crush, boss, but I have a hot date tonight, remember? Can I have a rain check?"

She cupped his cheeks and landed a hard smooch on his mouth. "Anytime, handsome. I'll meet you at the animal shelter in the morning. We've got to find some officer candidates for the next round."

"Maybe I'll call my date tonight for a rain check." He winked and set her on her feet.

"Very funny." She gave him a little shove. "Beat it. I'll see you in the morning."

Misty wrapped up a few details, hopped in her car and drove out of the facility past the security kiosk. To go home was a right turn, but she turned left and decided to go to Brazos anyway. She didn't particularly feel like being alone. Jake was always good for company and conversation, and she'd made herself hungry thinking about their great food.

She parked in front of Brazos and tugged open the heavy oak door. The minute she stepped inside a familiar voice called, "Sgt. Beachy, over here!" The same two young sailors she'd befriended before stood and beckoned her to join them.

She grinned, ordered beers for the three of them and walked to their table. "How are my boys tonight? You behaving yourselves?"

Shy Guy nodded, and Baby Face said, "We are now." They stood at the same time and jostled each other for the honor of holding out her chair.

Chapter Five

Thursday, July 3rd, Misty's office

"YOU SHOULD COME, JEREMY. THEY'RE A GREAT BUNCH OF people. You'll enjoy yourself. Aren't you driving up there tomorrow to move some of your things into your new place?" Jeremy had found an apartment to share with two other Cal Tech students in Pasadena. Even though he wasn't going to move for a month, he planned to get out of his local digs and bunk with his parents in Coronado until a week or so before his semester commenced.

"Any good looking single women going to be there?"

"Other than me, you mean?"

"Yeah, boss, other than you. Like maybe somebody who lives in the general vicinity of where I'll be for the next couple of years." He handed her the preliminary manifest of the new dogs and his assessment of their general nature and abilities. "They all look good, except for this guy. I'll have to keep a close watch on him. He's super smart, but he's not sure he can trust people."

Misty sighed. "I hope he wasn't abused. I don't get animal abuse. Hopefully he was just neglected and hasn't been socialized very well."

"Would you consider taking him home with you at night for the first week or so. Give him some confidence?"

This was something Jeremy had done for a couple of their wards in the past. But now that he was between residences, it was no longer practical.

"I don't want to fall in love with a dog, Jeremy." She pressed her lips together. She didn't intend to fall in love with anything that breathed. She'd avoided love like the plague ever since her big brother got blown up in Afghanistan. The pain of his loss filled her and her parents with cold, endless hollowness. Time had not dissipated it.

"What's his name?"

"Don't laugh. The big, tough looking shepherd mix is named Biscuit."

Misty rolled her eyes and laughed. "You've got to be kidding me."

"Nope. That's his name. It was probably appropriate when he was a fat little puppy."

"I suppose." Using the eraser on the end of her pencil, Misty tapped down the list. "This one's four years old already."

"Yeah, but she's got a nice temperament and aims to please. Her smaller size probably means she'll live for a good many years." He fidgeted. "Sorry, I've got to wrap it up. I promised the guys in Pasadena that I'd get there before dark. I don't have a key to the place yet and they both have plans for a long holiday weekend."

"Okay, beat it. You've got my cell number if you change your mind about tomorrow, call me. I'm sure you'd enjoy meeting all my old Marine buddies and their families." She stood and gave him a little shove. "I'll close up as soon as I talk to Florine out by the kennel. Maybe she'll take Biscuit home with her."

"That's okay," Jeremy, giving her a wink, said over his shoulder. "I'll sweet talk her into it."

Half an hour later, Misty was ready to take off for the weekend. She called Mac's house in Spring Grove. "Hi, Graciella, I just wanted to make sure it was still okay for me to spend the night."

"Yes, we're expecting you. Will you be staying after the party?"

"No, tomorrow night I'm driving up to visit my parents in their new condo in Thousand Oaks. It'll be so nice to have them closer than they were in the Bay Area. Once they get settled in, you'll never have to put up with me again."

"Put up with you? I was planning to put you to work. You can go shopping in my place with Cluny in the morning. The thought of making my way through the supermarket for party supplies, and just generally stocking up is something I wasn't looking forward to. Santos and I'll stay home and cook."

The sincerity in Graciella's voice tamped down Misty's worry. "I'm happy to help. It's my firm belief that men should never be allowed in the grocery store without female supervision."

"You'll be the perfect supervisor." Graciella laughed and Misty felt a new ease developing between the two of them. They should be trusting friends. They both loved Cluny McPherson, albeit in different ways, and Misty enjoyed her son, Santos. A sweet and smart kid, who'd persuaded his parents to adopt one of her dogs.

"When did your parents move south?"

"My dad secured a good job on staff at a local golf club two months ago. He'll be in charge of maintenance and repair of golf carts and greens keeper's vehicles. His retirement lasted less than a year. That's about ten months longer than I'd predicted. Mom's a registered nurse, so she's in demand anywhere. She's taking her time in making a decision about when and where to go to work."

"Your parents sound interesting. I'd like to meet them sometime."

"I'd like that, too. See you in a few hours. I'll eat on the way, so don't even think about feeding me."

* * *

Cluny and Graciella McPherson's home, that night

Misty pulled into Mac's long driveway wondering who he was talking to on the long covered front porch in the dark. Mac's posture, his long legs resting on the low railing, and his gestures were unmistakable, but she didn't recognize the other man. She parked and stepped out of her Jeep.

"Hey, Mis." Mac called. "It's about time you got here."

She grinned and waved. "I stopped for dinner at Cheesecake Factory and picked up a huge Oreo cheesecake to take to Dempsey's tomorrow. I hope Graciella has room in the refrigerator for it."

Mac stepped off the porch. The second the other man stood, she recognized Jack Hawk. *What's he doing here?*

"We'll make room." Mac gave her a hug. "How was the drive?"

"Long. Hello, Hawk." His big lazy smile had her stomach wobbling. Her heart rate ramped up when she remembered his gentle handling of his daughter the day the girl had shown up at the Customs facility. Had she misjudged him all these years?

"Hello, yourself. Need a hand with anything?"

"No, all I have is the cake and my duffle." She dragged the duffle off the back seat.

"Let me get that." Jack took it from her. "You're in charge of the cake, McPherson." Hawk's strange glance at Mac puzzled her. His hooded expressions often puzzled her.

"Got it covered." Mac's expression mirrored Hawks. What had just passed between these two men?

Empty handed except for her small shoulder bag, Misty shrugged and followed the two men into the house. Queen and Happy came running to investigate.

Santos snapped off the TV. "Marine Lady! I taught Happy lots of tricks. Do you want to see?"

"Give her a chance to get in the door, son." Mac nodded toward the kitchen. "Open the refrigerator for me, will ya?"

"What is that?" Santos's eyes rounded when he read the label on the box. "Yum, my most favorite."

"I figured that." Misty put her arm around his shoulders. "You're almost as tall as me. When did that happen?"

"You're not very tall, so it didn't take long. I'm almost twelve."

Hawk brushed past them. "I'll put this in the guest room."

"Thanks." She glanced at his retreating back then followed Mac and Santos to the kitchen. "Where's Graciella?"

"I'm out here," Graciella called from the laundry room off the back porch. She ambled in holding her back.

"I can barely get my arms around you, Mrs. McPherson." The two women hugged when they met halfway. "Why are you doing laundry at this hour?"

"Santos had to have his favorite shirt to wear to the party tomorrow. The one Amber likes."

"Oh, I see. Yes, a very good reason for laundry at ten in the evening. Are we going to be able to get that cake in your fridge? I wasn't thinking about that when I bought it."

"It'll be a tight squeeze after we finish cooking tomorrow, but no problem tonight."

"Maybe we'll have to eat it before the party, Mama."

"You'd like that wouldn't you?" She stepped in front of Mac at the open refrigerator door. "Let me move a couple of things, querido, then you can put it right here."

The cake stored in the refrigerator, Cluny embraced his wife. "I think you should get off your feet. You've been at it all day." He kissed Graciella's forehead.

She nodded. "You're right." Turning to Misty and Hawk she added, "I'm going to excuse myself and head to bed. Santos's, it's time for you to turn in, too."

"Aw, Mom, I wanted to show Miz Beachy Happy's tricks."

"There'll be plenty of time for that tomorrow. Take the dogs out back for a few minutes, then say goodnight."

Mac walked Graciella to the master bedroom. Misty and Hawk stood in awkward silence for a few seconds then he asked, "You, uh, want a cup of coffee or a Coke? We can carry it out to the front porch."

"Okay, sure. Coke please. I'll hit the head and then join you."

By the time she got to the front porch, Mac had rejoined Hawk and they were in deep discussion.

Hawk huffed. "I'm fed up with Pentagon politics. It was a big part of my decision to retire. They're starting to look at us old A-10 guys as dinosaurs. I made the right decision."

"How's Ellen doing, Hawk?" Misty sat on the low railing and he handed her the Coke.

"She's made a couple of friends in the apartment complex and has accepted enrolling in a new high school for her sophomore year. I'm holding my breath."

Mac dropped his big feet on the railing and settled back in an Adirondack chair. "So, what do you think will happen with the A-10? Is it likely they'll retire them in favor of the F-35?"

"I have no doubt the Pentagon politicians are salivating at the prospect of awarding a jillion dollar contract to their cronies at Lockheed Martin and Northrop Grumman for some shiny new toys. They're looking after their own retirement prospects. Every F-35 costs almost twice as much as an A-10, but with overruns it'll cost the taxpayers a lot more in the long haul. Anyway, I'm out of it."

Misty tipped back the Coke and took a long, cold swallow. "All I know is how much we depended on you guys when the Taliban got our nuts in a vise. Nobody listens to the mamzers on the ground. I suppose it's always been like that."

"Mamzer? Where do you come up with some of this stuff, Mis?" Mac's laugh was affectionate. He was often tickled by things she said.

She chuckled. "My dad's always been fascinated with Yiddish. He says there are some things that can only be accurately described in Yiddish. It means bastard, but more."

"We got a new generation of soldiers now." Jack grinned. "They're more into modern technology and whiz-bang weapons. Change comes whether we like it or whether it makes sense or not, Beachy."

She noticed Hawk didn't call her Mis. Maybe that day in her office it had been a slip of the tongue. Just as well. When he said it, it seemed too intimate. Too unsettling.

"Sure you don't want me to inflate the air mattress so you can bed down in Santo's room tonight, Jack?" Mac raised his eyebrows.

"Nah, I've got to get back home. Ellen and her friends should be coming out of the movies just about now." He rose to his feet. "I'll see you both at Dempsey's tomorrow."

Mac and Misty strolled out to the street where he'd parked.

"Where is your apartment, Hawk?" Misty didn't really care. She was just making small talk.

"We're right down the street from the VA Hospital, in what used to be called Sepulveda, now known as North Hills. It's a nice neighborhood." Jack smiled and gave her a peculiar look. Another look she couldn't decipher, but a look that annoyed her.

I'm not planning on dropping in for a visit if that's what you mean, Hawk. "I have an appointment at the auditory clinic there next month."

Mac slung his arm over her shoulders. "You having problems, Mis?"

"Same old crap. I can't hear worth a damn out of my right ear anymore, just the constant whine of tinnitus. I doubt there's anything they can do about it."

He hugged her close to his side. "How's the vision."

"So far, so good."

Jack opened his door and slid into the seat. They backed away from the curb and waved as he drove away.

"I'm ready to hit the sack too, sweet cheeks. How about you?"

"Yes, we need our rest. Your wife informed me she's got a shopping list a yard long for us in the morning."

"Yeah, she's a merciless, whip wielding slave driver."

"I feel so sorry for you, Mac. It just isn't right." She elbowed him in the ribs and raced ahead to the front door.

* * *

Jack pulled into the parking area next to the apartment complex as the city bus stopped and disgorged half a dozen teenagers. They walked in his direction. Ellen saw him and waved. Jack continued up to the apartment and let himself in. No need to hover around and embarrass her in front of her new friends.

"Dad, it's me. Where were you?" The front door clicked shut.

"I dropped in on my old buddy, Cluny McPherson, in Spring Grove. They needed to borrow our gigantic ice chest for the party tomorrow. I'm going to let him keep it."

She cocked her head and put a devilish look on her face. "Oh, I remember him. He's smokin'. So's his little blond girlfriend."

"Friend. He's a happily married man who's about to become a father any day now."

Why did he always take her bait? "Sure you don't want to come with me? It'll be a lot of fun."

"Could I bring Cherry? I don't know anybody there."

"You know smokin' McPherson and smokin' Beachy."

"Come on, Dad. You know what I mean."

"I'll walk over to their apartment and ask her mom. If she says it's okay, and if you can manage to find jeans and a T-shirt without holes, it's a deal." He sniffed. "By the way, which one of the bunch was smoking weed?"

"Derek, the guy who moved here from Arizona with his dad. They live down the block. He likes to hang with us. He tries to impress us, but we just laughed when he fired it up. He's okay." She headed to her bedroom. "Let me know what Cherry's mom says."

Jack walked two doors down the open hall and knocked on Cherry's door. Her mom opened it and scowled. "I know, I already yelled at her about the marijuana."

"That's not why I'm here, Doris. I wanted to know if she could go to a Fourth of July barbeque with us tomorrow. It's at a friend's house in Spring Grove. Mostly retired military and their families. Ellen wants company her own age."

"Oh." The woman looked perplexed. "Would you like to come in?"

Jack stepped across the threshold. "Sure, or you can let me know in the morning. We're not leaving until around noon." The apartment was neat and well furnished. The woman and her daughter always looked well groomed. Cherry had good manners. Jack had liked them from the day they met. It was serendipity that both girls were the same age and would be attending the same high school in the fall.

"That would be best, Jack. I don't want to let her off the hook quite so soon. She needs to think about who she associates with. I'll call you in the morning."

Jack smiled and stepped back. "That's great. You'd be doing me a favor. I don't want to leave Ellen home alone, but I can't force her to go."

"All right. I'll call you in the morning."

Jack thought about the differences between Cherry's mom and Misty Beachy. A few years older than Beachy, willowy Doris had long, dark hair she wore pulled back from her face, dominated by large eyes, dark blue, almost purple. He found her very attractive in a professional-woman way. He sensed she'd be open to his advances, if he'd had any inclination, but he didn't.

He had the hots for Beachy. No denying it. He'd do something about it at the party tomorrow.

Chapter Six

July 4ᵗʰ, Dempsey's Annual Barbeque

JACK CARRIED HIS PLATE ACROSS THE YARD AND SAT ON THE grass next to Misty. He could tell she was miffed by her sour expression and the barely discernable shift away from him. He ignored her reaction, snapped open his napkin and proceeded to cut his steak.

"Why don't you go sit with Ellen?"

"Did you like sitting with your Dad in public when you were fifteen? Look around. It's couples and families, except for the teenagers. I'm single, you're single. We sit together, sit alone or be a fifth wheel."

"Humph."

"Sounds like you agree with me for once." He smirked and put the piece of steak in his mouth. "Dempsey sure knows how to barbeque a steak, doesn't he? Mmm, mmm, mmm."

"God, you're annoying, Hawk."

"You want another beer?" The past half hour while they manned the bar and buffet line, she'd barely tolerated him, pointedly ignoring him. "Beer? Yes or no?"

"Yes, as long as you're going there." She added a grudgingly, "Thanks."

"My pleasure, Sgt. Beachy." He brushed off the seat of his pants, went and opened the big ice chest by the buffet and grabbed two bottles of Corona. He swiped the moisture off and carried them back.

Misty shooed Happy away from Jack's plate. "Beat it, mutt. Go sit in the shade with Queen and DD. Santos needs to teach you better manners." She raised her eyes to Jack and reached for the beer. "You almost lost your steak."

"I knew you'd watch out for me." He grinned, knowing it annoyed her even further. Her answer was a non-committal snort. They ate in silence for several minutes. Misty made a show of looking around the big yard at the various guests as if they were of the utmost fascination to her.

Jack tipped his beer bottle. "That your assistant over there?"

She followed his gaze. "Yes, Jeremy Carter. I invited him yesterday, but I'm surprised he came. He moved some of his belongings to his new shared apartment in Pasadena yesterday. I thought he'd head right back to Coronado."

"Who's the gorgeous brunette sticking to him like Velcro?"

"No clue. Far as I knew he didn't know very many people in the area yet."

"Kid works fast."

Misty was silent for a few beats, then a smile bloomed on her cheeks when Jeremy, sensing she watched him, waved and grinned. He raised an eyebrow and rolled his eyes in the direction of his companion. "Women love Jere. He's never had any trouble finding a date."

"Who does he remind you of?"

She leaned back, chin lowered, eyes squinted. "He doesn't remind me of anybody."

"You sure of that?" He glanced across the grass to the circle of chairs where Cluny and his wife sat with the Dempsey's and another couple. He zeroed in on McPherson.

She caught on fast. "You're nuts, Hawk."

"Am I?" He put down his plate. "Is he the reason you won't warm up to me or any man? Is it because nobody else is Cluny McPherson?"

"What!" She glared. "I don't like *you* because— Are you some shit-for-brains amateur psychologist?" She went silent, her body tight and tense.

Jack thought he saw the faintest light of realization in her furious brown eyes. "Enlighten me." Her jaw clenched so hard vessels in her temples swelled and throbbed. For a minute he thought her vise grip on the beer bottle might break the glass. "Cat got your tongue?"

"You sick bastard. If you think I'm obsessed with Mac..."

"Aren't you? And isn't it about time you got over it? You wear it like armor. I'm not the only one who's noticed. Look at him. He's crazy in love with Graciella. He's a committed family man. Nothing is more important to him than the child his wife is carrying, his child, and the son she brought to the marriage. Get over your twisted teenage self-delusion."

She sprang to her feet. "I swear to God, if you say one more word, by the time you come to you'll be picking glass out of your forehead." Misty marched across the yard, dumped her plate and bottle in the barrel by the buffet table then stormed into the house.

Jack sighed. "That went well."

After a few moments he dumped his trash and wandered across the grass to mingle with a couple of retired Marine pilots his age, who owned a cargo airline in L.A. He'd previously explored the possibility of coming to work for them, but decided the long, frequent absences were out of the question. His first priority was Ellen. She needed to know he would stick close to home from here on out. Needed to be sure he wouldn't abandon her like Theresa had.

* * *

Burning with anger, Misty paced through Dwayne and Marla's house. Afraid she might wake the twins Marla'd put down for a nap before joining the party, she quietly let herself out the front door and strode down the street. Sweat bloomed on her scalp in the afternoon July heat of southern California, but the fire erupting inside like a blazing furnace was the real source of her discomfort.

If anybody thought she was secretly in love with Mac, they were crazy. She did love Mac, but that was light years from being *in* love with him, obsessed with him. "Hawk you're a son-of-a-bitch." He was a master manipulator. His laser eyes bored into hers like he knew her deepest private thoughts—that's what she didn't like about him—his eyes and the way they'd always flustered her. Who the hell did he think he was?

"Hey, boss!" She stopped abruptly and turned to see Jeremy and the brunette approaching.

It took gigantic effort, but she willed herself to calm down and relax. "You leaving already?" She strolled to meet them.

"Yep. Brenda's going to help me with some stuff at the apartment." He drew the young woman closer. "Brenda Brown, this is my soon to be ex-boss, Misty Beachy."

The two women acknowledged each other with friendly nods and shook hands. Brenda's long slim-fingered hand gripped hers firmly. "Nice to meet you. Jeremy's told me so much about you, Ms. Beachy."

"Misty, please, and be skeptical about anything he says." She shifted her attention to Jeremy. "I'm glad you came. Did you enjoy yourself? They have a great view of the fireworks as soon as it turns dark. If you leave now, you'll miss it."

"Yeah, we met some nice people and the food was great, but we have plans for tonight." Jeremy's cheeks dimpled when he flashed the smile she loved.

Misty was pretty sure she knew what plans they had. What "stuff" Brenda would be helping him with at the apartment they had to themselves for the night and all day tomorrow.

Well good for you, Jere.

"Don't be late for work on Monday, or I'll have to fire you." She poked his chest with a school-teacher finger.

Jeremy laughed and tilted his head to Brenda. "She fires me at least two or three times a week." He swooped down and kissed Misty's cheek, tugged Brenda's hand in the direction of his car. "I'll be on time, boss."

Misty watched him walk away. A cold blast of awareness nearly knocked her over.

Oh, my God! Jere is like Mac. He's the same big happy-go-lucky clown. Smart, self-assured, and masculine, with all the gentlemanly qualities women love and men admire. A man to be counted on. A man you could truly be friends with. A man who…

"Oh, shit, shit shit." Misty held her queasy stomach and leaned heavily against a SUV parked in front of Dempsey's house. It couldn't be true. Hawk didn't know what he was talking about. Others noticed? He was deranged. That's what she told herself. That's what she believed.

She had to get back to the party. The last thing Misty needed was for friends to start speculating why she'd left so abruptly, and for Hawk to think he'd hit a nerve. He hadn't. No. Not really.

She returned to the back yard through a side gate, studiously avoiding Mac and the kids setting up the water balloon batting contest. He waved her over. She shook her head and pointed to herself then the women picking up debris. He nodded and grinned.

"Where'd you disappear to?" Marla held a large plastic bag open so Dwayne's sister-in-law could drop paper plates and plastic utensils inside. "You're just in time. I was about to check on the twins. Declan learned to climb out of his crib in the last few days. Daddy went in the house to get him."

Here was her chance to avoid Jack and the turmoil he'd unleashed inside. "I'll get Dec. Dwayne's busy enough." Before Marla could answer she went across the patio and in through the sliding door.

She walked into the room the little boy shared with Amber. Dwayne was about to lay his son on the changing table. "I'll do that, Dempsey. No way am I letting Mac talk me into the water balloon batting cage. Dec will give me cover." She reached for the toddler.

"Thanks. I've been tiptoeing around hoping to not wake the twins. I want Marla to stay off her feet a little longer."

"You already lost that skirmish, Gunny. She's out there with Dylan's wife cleaning up after the barbeque. Good luck getting her to sit for a while."

"Yeah, good luck getting her to do anything I ask." He shrugged and grinned.

Misty smiled because Marla's stubbornness was one of the things that had so intrigued and attracted her husband. They'd butted heads for months at her construction site before he finally broke the ice with her.

"Go on, I've got this." Misty put the safety strap across the lively boy's chest and proceeded to change his diaper. The kid was happy and healthy, and a great source of joy for his parents. At one time she'd thought she might get married, have a couple of children, but for reasons she couldn't fathom, she'd moved farther and farther from that possibility. In fact, Mac was the only man— "Oh my god, Beachy. Stop it!"

Just because Jeremy had many of Mac's qualities meant nothing. Those were qualities she admired in a man. It didn't mean she was obsessed with Mac. Hawk was dead wrong. The man had always put her on edge. She didn't like it one bit when those penetrating eyes of his intruded into her thoughts. Yes, that was the thing about Jack Hawk. It was a major turn-off, making it impossible for them to form a casual friendship. She should turn the tables on him. See how he liked it.

She smiled and poked Declan's fat little belly. "What are you grinning about, huh? You're just like the rest of your species. You love it when you can show your junk to any female." The boy giggled and kicked his legs. "Yeah, I've got your number, pal."

"Mama."

"Nope."

"Nope," he mimicked, giggling.

She was stepping back outside when Ellen approached. "Do you know where the bathroom is?"

"Yes, there's one through the side door to the garage for guests. Dempsey built it last year so kids wouldn't go running through the house when they had a yard party. They won't mind if you and your friend use the one in here, but the twin baby girls are still sleeping, so please be quiet."

Ellen backed up and took Cherry's elbow. "That's all right, we'll use the one in the garage." She stopped. "Whose baby is that?"

"Dwayne and Marla's."

"And they have two other babies? Twins?" Ellen and Cherry wore identical wry, pinched-lip expressions. "We know what they've been doing," Ellen said in a sing-song way.

Her mean-girl comment nettled Misty, but instead of taking the bait, she whispered confidentially. "You think that's funny? They've already got another bun in the oven for next year, and Marla's still nursing the twins." It was all she could do not to laugh at their horrified reaction.

The girls retreated, put their heads together and talked secretively, all the while casting glances at Marla, and at Dwayne's prosthetic leg clearly visible beneath his cargo shorts. They giggled and hurried into the side door of the garage, just as Hawk stepped out carrying two folding chairs under each arm to join the men setting about lining up seating for the traditional military services sing-off, before the fireworks began at the high school down the hill from Dempsey's house. Jack's eyebrows drew together.

"I'm not sure I like hearing that conspiratorial giggling. It's about as clear to me as Sanskrit when girls do that. It reminds me how I'm so far under water as a father."

Misty bounced Dec on her hip. *Why not give the guy a break?* "Phooey, Hawk. You're doing great, and it isn't necessary to know what's going on in your daughter's head twenty-four-seven. She's got a right to her private thoughts."

Just like I do. Get it?

He continued on his way. "You right about that?"

There may have been something he could have done to irk her more, but his parting wink made her want to follow him and aim a swift kick at his ass. The jerk knew exactly what she meant. She wandered across the yard to the far edge where two mature eucalyptus trees cast shade on a few pieces of lawn furniture. Dwayne and Marla sat on the glider. He had his arm around her shoulder, no doubt to keep her off her feet for a bit.

Misty placed Declan on the grass at the base of the chair she'd chosen. DD, Marla's minuscule Yorkie, immediately bounced in the boy's lap and licked his face sending him into fits of happy giggling. Santos's dog, Happy, tried to join the fun, but Misty grabbed his collar and held him back. "No, you don't. You need to learn better manners first. See Queen sitting sedately in the shade?" Mac's service dog calmly observed her surroundings while at the same time keeping a sharp eye on her master.

The big Malinois had the temperament of a teddy bear, but anyone who made the mistake of thinking she didn't know what her job was, hadn't been too observant the past few years. First, she'd been there to save Mac from his PTS nightmares, and then Graciella had been there for Mac. Mac was...

Is it possible for you to get your mind off Mac, you idiot? Is it possible there was a grain of truth in what Hawk said?

As if summoned by some silent signal, she felt Mac's big hands on her shoulders. "Hey, Sarge, aren't you going to help me with the batting contest this year? I need an umpire."

She shrugged him off. "No, when have I ever helped you get soaking wet with all those kids conspiring to drown you? I'm babysitting."

"You're it then, Gunny."

"Nice try, pal. Get a couple of my nephews to volunteer."

"Hah! They're the ones trying to drown me. I'll ask Amber and Santos. They're less lethal."

"Good luck with that." Marla laughed. They all knew how much Amber enjoyed making sure *Uncle Cluny* got a thorough dousing. It was one of the highlights of the annual Independence Day barbeque. The adults enjoyed it as much as the kids.

Resigned to his fate, Mac strolled back to the batting cage across the yard and beckoned to the excited kids. The fun was about to begin, but before he got there he detoured to Jack Hawk.

"Don't tell me Cluny is going to trick Jack into umpiring." Marla shook her head.

"This should be good." Dempsey laughed. "Cluny'll be lucky if Hawk doesn't throw him over the back fence when he finds out what's in store."

It wasn't likely Hawk could throw Mac, a younger, bigger man, over any fence, but it would be fun to watch him try. Misty leaned forward as the smaller kids lined up to take their turn at batting a water balloon.

* * *

"How wet am I going to get, McPherson?" Having second thoughts, Jack dragged his feet. He glanced over his shoulder and noticed Beachy smiling and pointing at them. "Semper fi, Captain."

"I take the hits, Hawk. Don't worry about it. The kids try to out-do one another every year, in a contest to drown me. It's fun." Cluny nodded to the kids lining up in the on-deck circle. He made a face at the pitcher and pointed a warning finger at him.

Cluny went on his heels, in catcher posture, behind the plate. "Batter up!"

Most of the littlest missed the pitches from the teenage boy accidentally, but as the bigger ones took their places a few missed deliberately. The ones who got a hit sprayed everyone within range. Jack noticed that all the adults had moved safely back and were enjoying the spectacle as he and McPherson got wetter and wetter. "Haven't you had enough?"

"Yep, I have." Cluny deftly dodged the next pitch. The water balloon hit Jack in the middle of his chest and erupted, soaking him from his neck to his knees. McPherson laughed so hard he fell on his butt and Hawk caught the next pitch at the belt.

Laughter erupted from the adults watching, and the youngsters who hadn't had their turn at bat. Jack sputtered and glared at Cluny. "I'll get you for this." Then his eyes followed Ellen when she took her turn in the batter's box.

"Having fun, Dad?"

He couldn't help grinning when he saw how much his daughter enjoyed his saturated state. "You'd better get a hit or I'll ground you for life."

"Oooh, the pressure. I'm soooo scared." Ellen took her stance and waited for the pitch. Cluny nudged her as the balloon left the pitcher's hand. Off balance, she took a glancing shoulder blow from the balloon as it whizzed by on its way to Hawk's face.

Ellen shrieked. "It's his fault, Dad! He pushed me! I was gonna hit it, honest."

Misty Beachy's laughter zinged across the yard as Jack sputtered. "Did you and Beachy set me up, McPherson?"

"No, man, I swear." Cluny doubled with laughter.

Jack stared across the yard at Beachy. She stopped laughing and jumped to her feet. He took a step in her direction.

* * *

There was no mistaking the meaning in Hawk's gray/brown eyes this time. They drilled into hers.

Heart pounding she gulped. "Uh oh." Misty took off at a run. Cheers and laughter erupted from the crowd as she bolted through the side gate, Jack's footsteps pounding close behind. She hadn't even made it past the house when he grabbed her. "No, Jack, I didn't do anything!"

"Like hell." He pulled her against his wet body, soaking her shirt and shorts.

She struggled. Even though she'd passed the rigid physical requirements when she'd joined the Marines a dozen years ago, she was no match against his surprising strength. Shocked beyond belief when he held the back of her head and pressed his mouth against hers, she lifted her knee, but he blocked her move easily.

Misty pounded his chest with her fists. He dropped his hand from her head but wrapped it around her upper back. "What the hell do you think you're doing, Hawk? Let go of me right now!"

He grinned and shook his head. "Not yet."

"You bast..." How it happened, she wasn't sure, but she found herself kissing him back. Sinking deeper into him, her mind was inundated, her body burning in places that had lain dormant for more than two years.

Jack's lips melted into hers. He shifted the hand at her waist lower and pressed her tight. She could no longer feel where his body ended and hers began. Her palms roamed his back and shoulders. The small moan she heard came from deep inside her own throat. How had she got to the age of thirty-three without experiencing a kiss like this?

Going still, she pulled back. "Jack, what...?"

"Shhh." He gently held her cheeks, thumbs stroking her earlobes. "Shhh." Kissed her again.

"Dad?" Ellen's voice shattered the moment. "Mr. McPherson said the sing-off is starting in a minute."

"We'll be right there." He dropped his hands, gray/brown eyes burning. "You okay?"

"No." She was anything but okay, not sure she could even walk. Squeezing her eyes closed she sucked in a deep breath.

Jack put his arm around her shoulders and moved in the direction of the gate. "Let's go back."

"Everybody's going to think we've…"

"I don't give a rat's ass about that."

She shrugged him off and walked the rest of the way to the gate without his help. The minute they passed the garage into the back yard, cheers erupted. The heat of her blush nearly floored her. She hadn't blushed since she was a teenager. How she hated Jack Hawk.

Chapter Seven

On the way to Jack's apartment

JACK RUBBED THE KNOT IN HIS NECK AND GLANCED IN THE rearview mirror. Ellen and Cherry whispered in the back seat. He tried to get his mind off the *Kiss* and concentrate on driving. He had steered clear of Beachy for the rest of the party, and she hadn't sought him out. He'd rounded up the girls after the fireworks and enlisted them to help fold and stack chairs. They thanked the Dempsey's and headed home.

He glanced in the rearview mirror. "What's all the whispering back there? Are you planning a bank heist?"

"We were wondering about all the pregnant women and babies there." Cherry giggled.

"What about them?"

"Dad, didn't you notice how many there were?" Ellen gave her Dad-is-clueless snort. "Mrs. Dempsey is pregnant, and they already have three babies."

"And her husband only has one leg," Cherry added.

"Funny. The way he was walking around and cooking steaks all afternoon, I would have sworn he had two." He was pleased to see Cherry blush.

"You know what she means, Dad." Ellen had jumped to her friend's defense. "Mr. Dempsey's…"

Jack shook his head. "I was sure we'd had the how-babies-are-made talk. Did I miss something?" He winked at their embarrassment.

Ellen scowled back at him as they pulled into the parking lot of the apartment complex. "Sometimes you can be such a tool." She did nothing to disguise her disgust at having, like, a totally clueless father.

"Oh, then you do remember the talk." Jack parked, removed the keys from the ignition and opened his door. He stepped out and looked at his watch. "I promised Doris I'd have her daughter home by eleven. We're just under the wire."

"I'm going to Cherry's for a while," Ellen informed him.

"No, it's too late tonight. You've been together all day. I don't know what more you could have to say to each other." He pointed to the stairs. "We'll walk you to your door, Cherry."

He followed them up the stairs and tried not to stare at their womanly backsides. The thought of Ellen's nascent maturity sent sharp pains through his head. What the hell was he going to do to keep her ass out of trouble, keep her from making stupid mistakes? He knew very well what boys her age wanted. What dominated their every breath. He'd been there. Jack had been the bane of one of his early girlfriend's fathers. The man had finally stabbed a finger into his chest and told him if he ever touched his daughter he'd kill him. He'd quickly moved on to greener pastures. God! He hoped no hormone riddled pimply boy thought of Ellen as greener pastures.

I'll never make it through the next few years. Goddamn you, Theresa!

Cherry couldn't find her key, so she rang the doorbell. Jack and Ellen waited with her. Several seconds passed before Doris finally opened the door.

"Sorry. I was on the phone." She stepped back to invite them in. "Where's your key, honey?"

"I must have left it home with my phone. You wouldn't let me bring my phone, remember?"

Doris rolled her eyes. By this small expression, Jack figured Cherry's mom struggled just as much as he did with what to do with a fifteen-year-old-girl. He shrugged and flashed a sympathetic smile. "See you later, Doris."

Her eyes softened with a silent longing. Another dilemma rearing its ugly head. Jack put his hand on Ellen's shoulder and directed her down the open hallway to their apartment.

"Cherry's mom likes you." She turned to look directly into his face. "She must be blind or something. Or like a total desperado."

"Yeah. Must be." He unlocked their door and stepped inside.

"Why were you slobbering all over that dog trainer? Why were you kissing her? She isn't even nice."

Nice wasn't on the same planet with what he wanted from Beachy. "It just happened. I wanted to punish her for setting me up to get soaked. It didn't mean anything." He lied to his daughter because there was no way he could tell her the truth. He was way under water here. It would make more sense to form a relationship with Doris. They had a lot in common. They could share the misery.

"Seriously, Dad. What's with that Dempsey couple? I don't get it. You'd think they'd like to take a break between babies. I know I would. They must be like the Energizer Bunny on crack in their bedroom. They're not exactly young."

Jack couldn't help it. He laughed from deep down. The twenty year difference in age between Dempsey and Ellen was as vast as the Pacific Ocean. He reached back through his memory. Had he thought everybody over the age of thirty was ancient? Maybe some of the men, certainly his father, but he remembered some very sexy and attractive teachers and women friends of his mother. It was probably the difference between boys overloaded with testosterone and girls who just wanted the boys to kiss them and hold hands.

"Dwayne and Marla Dempsey are young! They're in their thirties, for the love of God. I don't imagine they planned to have their children so close together, but they're in love and committed to marriage and family."

Truth be known, Jack found Marla very attractive with her generous Marilyn Monroe curves and wild red mane. As a boy he'd gazed at the Marilyn Monroe calendar his dad had on the garage wall over the tool bench, afraid to gratify his hormones for fear of getting caught. He chuckled to himself. Ellen had probably never heard of Marilyn Monroe.

"If they're so crazy about grabbing each other, why's their daughter ten, and the next kid barely two? What were they doing in between?"

"They've only been married three years. Amber is Dwayne's daughter from his first marriage."

"Did his first wife bail on him like Mom bailed on us?"

His kid didn't miss anything. "I don't know the details. But no two marriages are the same. It would be a lot easier if they were. We'd all be aware of the same rules and danger signs. I only know that he raised his daughter alone until he married Marla."

"His first wife probably left him because his leg was shot off, not because she didn't like her daughter."

"We'll never know, but your mom didn't leave because she didn't like you. She left because she'd had enough of me and the USMC."

"Yeah sure, that's her totally lame excuse why she switched to Air Force. Who's this latest one? Army? Who's next, the Navy, the Coast Guard? You know what I don't get? Why she keeps getting married instead of just sleeping with them."

There were times like this when he hated Theresa for the bitterness in his daughter's voice. "Your mother believes in marriage. She's just lousy at picking husbands."

"Why am I an only child?"

He touched Ellen's cheek. "It just never happened." Another lie. His ex had made it perfectly clear after their daughter was born. She had no intention of ever getting pregnant again. She was too young to turn into a drudge, an old housewife tied down, never to have any fun or adventures. It wasn't fair to lay it all on Theresa. If he'd wanted more children, he could have retired from the military. The bald truth was he didn't want any more children with *her*. Ellen was paying the price of their disastrous marriage.

"What say we call it a night?" He put his arm around her shoulder and gave her a squeeze.

"Dad, are you sorry you were stuck with me?"

"That's crazy talk, sweetheart. You're the most important person in my world."

The pain, mixed with gratitude in her eyes, exactly the color of his own, broke his heart. He turned and embraced her. "Give us a hug.

We both need one." He chuckled. "After all, you're stuck with me, too."

"Oh, right. For a minute I forgot." Her devilish grin warmed him to the core.

* * *

He couldn't fall asleep. He wanted Beachy under him so bad he itched. He imagined the texture of her warm skin beneath his hands; his lips on every inch of her body, the challenge of making her moan and beg for more. Her unique salty scent haunted him. She smelled like she'd just stepped out of the ocean except for the faint musk of her shampoo. Exotic. Incense. Misty's aroma had triggered a memory of his mother's Maja talcum. An old fragrance he wasn't sure was made any longer.

Jesus Christ! My Mother?

Misty Beachy was so far removed from the gentle kindness of his mother that this last thought removed any possibility of sleep anytime soon. He was under no illusion that his parents had anything other than a healthy sex life. Their house was small. He and his two brothers slept in the same room, his sister's bedroom no more than an alcove separating them from the master bedroom.

When he'd been about five, he'd been distressed hearing the noises emanating from Mom and Dad's room. At first, he feared one of them was ill. Once he crept down the hall and pressed his ear to their door, breathing a sigh of relief when he heard his father murmur a muffled endearment and his mother's I love you so much response. They were quiet after that, and before long he could hear his dad's familiar snore.

It wasn't long before he learned from his older brothers that their parents were doing "it." Jack had innocently asked what doing it meant. Brad had taken great pleasure in asking him if he remembered when they saw the neighbor's dog mounting theirs. That's what they do all the time, Brad said. For years after, Jack had a picture of his father on the back of his mother pumping frantically. It made him sick to think about it. He hated his father for doing that disgusting thing to his mom. He couldn't imagine why she would put up with it.

Then, not much later he caught fifteen-year-old Mike and his girlfriend behind the tool shed going at it hot and heavy. The girl was on her back, her legs wrapped around Mike's bare ass, giggling, and demanding, "Harder, Mikey, harder. It feels so good." Mike had looked up when Jack gasped, pulled out, and knocked him to the ground. He'd told him he'd rip out his tongue if Jack ever told Dad. The girl, who was seventeen, told Jack he could have a turn if he'd wait a few minutes, because that's as long as it would take Mikey to blow.

Jack ran like the wind. He didn't stop till he got to the park a mile from home. He climbed as high as he could in a big Norfolk pine and trembled with excitement and disgust. Not understanding why he wanted to do what Mike was doing, and why at the same time he wanted to cry. He could never look that girl in the face again after that day. A couple of years later her family had moved away. He'd wondered what happened to her. As far as he knew she'd had the reputation in school as having done "it" with every boy who asked her, and they all did. Brad and Mike both talked cruelly about her and laughed over what a dirty little slut she was. That bothered Jack.

When they'd all become grown men, his brothers had fallen in love, married wisely, and behaved as good husbands and fathers. Jack had no doubt that neither of them would have put up with the same behavior from their sons or daughters. Everybody was a hypocrite.

If he didn't get to sleep soon he'd end up flying one of his students and the expensive commercial jets he was training them on smack into the ground. He gave himself a good talking to about Misty Beachy. "Stay away from her. She's nothing but trouble. She'll make your life a misery, Jack. The woman has serious hang-ups. Stay away." He expressed a deep sigh, rolled onto his belly and wished with every cell in his body that he had Misty Beachy squirming and panting under him at that precise moment. "Jesus, Jack. You're a sick man, sick."

Chapter Eight

Customs training facility, mid-July

Misty waved at Jeremy's retreating car when it passed through the guard gate. They'd had fun his last day on the job, fun tainted by melancholy. Jere had teased her since the barbeque, saying how much he regretted leaving early because he'd missed catching her and Hot Stick Hawk in a fevered clinch. She fired him several times for repeating it.

She stepped inside her office quickly when the phone rang.

"Sniffer School, Beachy here."

"Marine Lady?"

"Santos? Is everything okay?" A chill slithered up the back of her neck. She couldn't imagine why Mac's stepson would call except for an emergency.

"Everything is fine, it's real good. Dad asked me to call you. He's at the hospital with Mama. She had my baby brother today." His excitement and big grin came right through the phone.

"Hey, that's great! Is your mom okay? When was he born? I bet Mac is on cloud nine." Mac had dreamed of and spoken of having a son. A warm glow tickled her chest, tears formed in her eyes. Mac had his son at last.

"What did they name your brand new brother?"

"Ronan. He was born at two this afternoon."

"I'll bet that was a hard secret to keep." She pictured the adolescent's sweet brown face and thick dark curls. Graciella's son resembled the father he never knew, a Navy SEAL killed in a firefight in Iraq before Santos was born. "Ronan, what an unusual name."

"It was the name of Dad's great grandfather in Ireland. He showed it to me on the family tree he made before he knew me and Mama. Ronan weighed almost ten pounds! Dad said he came out fighting." Santos giggled. "I can't wait to see him. I get to go to the hospital tonight after Mama rests for a while. I get to hold him. When can you come to see him?"

"I'm not sure. It would probably be best if I waited for a while to give your mom a chance to rest. Will she have help after she gets home?" The thought of giving birth to a ten pound infant had spots swimming in her vision. *Holy God!*

"My first father's mom is going to stay here and help for a few days. Grandma Lillian is on her way here. Dad just started a big construction job with Amber's father, but he'll take off early every day. What shall I tell him about when you can come?"

Misty scanned her calendar. "I have an appointment to see the ear doctor Friday, at the VA Hospital up your way. I'll drop by after."

The VA Hospital right down the street from Hot Stick Hawk's apartment.

"Okay, I'll tell him. Bye."

"Bye."

Their short conversation briefly distracted her from nettling thoughts of Hawk, the rat. She had no idea what she would do about him. They'd had no communication since the *Kiss*. Did she expect him to call? Want him to call? Damned if she knew. She regretted the day they'd first met during debrief in FOB Fallujah. The man was a thorn in her foot.

Okay, here's what she'd do. She'd go for her appointment at the ear clinic and afterwards she'd call Hawk. They'd sit down over a cup of coffee and have an adult conversation about what happened between them and agree it had been a mistake. She'd thought about his claim that she was obsessed with Mac. She was not obsessed. Mac was her friend. That's all there was to it no matter what Jack or anybody else thought. She was not in love with Cluny McPherson. She didn't regret their past and certainly never thought of marrying him. Why, the whole idea was ludicrous!

* * *

Her new assistant, a young woman right out of the animal husbandry program at Santa Rosa Junior College, had interviewed well. Jeremy said she'd be great at the job. She was scheduled to start at seven tomorrow morning. Misty rotated her neck and groaned. "Get back to work and return those last two phone calls, Beachy. It'll be a long day tomorrow."

She parked at Brazos an hour later and sat in the car for several seconds before turning off the engine. Then she decided to go in, have a bite to eat and visit with McKillan and his wife before heading home. She needed a distraction from Jeremy's departure, thoughts about Hawk, and Mac's new baby son, Ronan.

The place wasn't as busy as usual. Instead of looking for a table she sat at the bar. McKillan's wife, Lupé, greeted her with a smile and set a bottle of Corona in front of her. "We got special green burritos on the menu tonight, Missy. You try them?"

Guadalupé McKillan had always dropped the *t* from her given name. It amused Misty, and she'd never corrected her. "I sure will. They're just what I'm hungry for tonight."

Jake strolled in from the kitchen. "I've got a letter for you. Those two sailors shipped out for Yokosuka, Japan a couple days ago. They asked me to give it to you the next time you came in." He opened the cash register, lifted the tray, and removed a legal-size envelope with— *Master Sergeant, Ma'am*—scrawled on the front.

She held it in her hand and smiled at the writing. If she wanted to know what Shy Guy and Baby Face had to say, she guessed she'd have to open it. Running a finger under the flap, she pulled out a single sheet of paper and a couple of carnival-booth snapshots of the two sailors. She laughed out loud when she read the short note. The two boys included their Navy addresses with a request to drop them a line now and then. It certainly looked as if Misty had acquired a couple of adopted sons of her own. *Eat your heart out, Mac.*

McKillan wiped moisture rings from the bar. "They showed me the letter and pictures before they sealed it. I told 'em I wouldn't give it to you unless they let me see what mischief they were trying to pull. You made quite an impression on those lonely young sailors, Misty."

She smiled to herself and enjoyed the warmth from the beer and the sweet letter. Unexpectedly, a chill gripped her throat. Feeling old, feeling lonely, feeling empty, she sprang from the barstool and told McKillan in a rusty voice, "I'll be right back."

What the hell is wrong with me?

Leaning her thighs heavily against the sink, she stared in the wavy stainless steel mirror Jake had installed after having to replace the glass in the restroom once too often. The fluorescent light cast an unhealthy yellowish pall on her face. *Who is that?* Jeremy was gone. Mac had found the great passion of his life with Graciella and Santos, and now a new son he'd loved every day since conception.

What do I have?

Misty's brother had been dead since she was twenty, thirteen years ago. She and her parents were unable to talk about him, to face it fully, to this day.

Was this to be her life? Living in San Diego, where she knew very few people, had no real friends, didn't even know the names of her neighbors in the small condo complex? Day in, day out—training dogs? Dogs she refused to form affection for because they were temporary. The knot in her throat was all that held back a sob.

Hawk was right, she *was* obsessed with Mac. Mac was safe to love because he wasn't hers. They would always be close friends and care for each other without the peril of commitment, of inevitable disappointment. There was no gamble in loving him. Cluny McPherson was her shield against heartbreak, against failure. She had no reason to risk loving another man, giving herself fully to a man, because none of them could possibly measure up to him.

She rushed out of the bathroom, hurried to the bar, and told Jake she wasn't feeling well and needed to head home. When she dug in her purse for money, Jake waved her off with a, "Catch me next time."

* * *

For the next two days she threw herself into her job, into training her new assistant, fielding phone calls and queries about their operation, supervising staff, and endless cleaning, sorting and filing. Early Friday morning she'd drive to the VA hospital for her consultation. She didn't need to think about anything else in the meantime. Work, just work. Work was her panacea. Her safe zone.

* * *

Friday evening she left the VA hospital, on an air of exhilaration even though her appointment had been disappointing. There was nothing to be done for the growing deafness and tinnitus in her right ear. The overworked otologist told her the cure for the constant ringing would be when her hearing decreased to less than twenty percent. It wouldn't be long.

What had her excited was the plan forming into her mind for a career change. During the two hours she'd had to wait to see the doctor, she'd wandered the halls of the hospital. Stumbling on the hospice ward, she'd been mesmerized by the therapy dogs visiting terminal patients. One dog in particular, an old gray muzzled yellow Lab, lay on the bed beside a man who was nothing more than skin and bones, an IV drip in both arms. A beautiful smile glowed on his weathered, whiskered face, a ropy veined hand stroked the dog snuggled to his side, head on his belly.

Transfixed, Misty stood slightly back from the open doorway and stared. After a few minutes a woman stepped outside the room and nearly slammed into her. "Gosh, I'm sorry, I didn't see you. Are you here to visit Ralph? I heard he has no living relatives, are you a friend?"

Embarrassed at having been caught snooping, Misty shook her head, looking for her voice. "No, I couldn't take my eyes off the dog."

The woman's face transformed. Eyes shimmery, her smile doleful, she said, "Opal is special. She's the most empathetic dog I've ever owned. There's something deep inside her that comforts even the sickest patients, the ones in the most pain. She's a wonder."

"How did you find her? Did you train her? Do you belong to some kind of veteran's support group?" This was information Misty craved.

The woman handed her a business card. "Opal is my personal pet. I stumbled on the therapy angle when I took her to visit my mother at the Alzheimer's ward of the elder care facility. Mother loved Opal and they allowed relatives to bring pets to calm the patients. Mama knew Opal's name to the last, long after she'd forgotten mine."

"I'm fascinated, stunned really. I train sniffer dogs for U.S. Customs."

"My goodness, we seem to have something in common. I'd love to talk to you more sometime. I do this for a hobby. It's not a business. That's my home phone number on the card."

Misty studied the card. "Thank you…Mary. I'd love to talk to you. How do you know him?" She nodded across the short distance to the man's bed.

"I didn't know him before I brought Opal to make the rounds. He's a Marine veteran of the Korean War. Fought during the bloodiest battle at Chosin reservoir. He's a great old guy and his stories are fascinating."

Misty's heart thumped. Her grandfather had died in that battle. She swallowed. "I'm a retired Marine. I was wounded in Fallujah years ago. That's why I'm here today."

"My, you look far too young." Mary's eyebrows went up so far, they were close to her hairline.

"Thanks." Misty glanced at her watch. "I'd love to talk more, but I want to be there when they call me in to see the specialist."

Mary patted her arm. "You go on then. I hope I hear from you."

"That's a promise." Misty hurried down the long corridor and headed across the huge campus to the auditory clinic.

After her appointment she hesitated, then made the decision to go to the hospice unit to see if Mary was still there. A male nurse fiddled with Ralph's IV's, but Opal and Mary were nowhere in sight.

The nurse spotted her and walked to the door. "You here to see Ralph?"

"No, I, uh, I really don't know him. I was looking for Mary and her dog." She peered at the old Marine. "How's he doing?"

"It's just a matter of time. He might not make it through the night." His warm brown eyes brimmed with compassion. "Mary and Opal left a few minutes ago. Why don't you go in and say hello? He loves it when someone visits."

"Oh, but, I..." This could have been her grandfather dying alone in there. "Do you think it would be okay?"

"Sure, come on. He's partial to pretty girls." He walked to the bed and laid a hand on Ralph's shoulder. "Wake up, Ralphie. There's a beautiful woman here to see you."

The old man's eyes fluttered. "The hell you say."

"True, man. Wait till you get a gander." He beckoned Misty to the bedside.

This was the right thing to do. She walked to the bed and leaned close. "It's an honor to meet you, General."

He smiled beatifically. "I'm no general. Captain is as high as I got." He drew his eyebrows together. "Are you an angel?"

"Hardly." Misty laughed. "I'm a retired Marine Master Sergeant, Captain. I served in Iraq. Opal's the angel, not me."

"She is that." He nodded and covered her hand with his. "Sit awhile, Sergeant. I'm overly fond of beautiful women. Always have been. My late wife teased me about it for fifty years."

Misty pulled a chair close to the bed. "Tell me about her."

An hour flew past without her noticing. They talked about his wife, the regret they'd shared for never having been blessed with children. She told him what she knew of her grandfather's service in Korea. He asked her about her tour of duty and the soldiers she'd served with. She explained why she was at the hospital that day and he shook his head with regret at her injuries. "I got out of that butcher shop over there with nary a scratch. Many good men died in that godforsaken frozen hell."

When his eyes stayed closed longer than they were open, Misty stood and bent close to him. "I have to go, Captain. It's getting late. I'll come back to see you day after tomorrow on my way back to San Diego."

"You do that, Sergeant. Semper fi."

On the bedside table, a framed Medal of Honor stood propped where he could see it. The ribbon still bright blue, the metal burnished. "Semper fi, Captain."

A rising tide of bleakness followed Misty to her car. She'd definitely visit Ralph again. It wasn't right that he should die alone. The weight of deep debt to the old veteran had her hands shaking.

* * *

On the drive to Spring Grove, her heartache lifted, and her excitement grew. She'd meet the new baby boy then bounce her career idea off Mac and see how he reacted. Every mile on the way reinforced the decision to take a new direction in life.

She turned down his street. Unexplained apprehension wormed through her muscles, replacing the elation she'd experienced seconds earlier. She slowed to a snail's pace as she got closer to the McPherson house. Hair on her neck prickled with a sharp chill even though it had barely cooled off after the sun went down. Mature dark trees leaned menacingly in from both sides of the sleepy street. Misty had an overwhelming urge to stop. To turn around. To slink home.

Mac's plumbing truck was in the driveway. He always kept it in the garage at night. Perhaps he had an emergency call and had just got there ahead of her. Graciella's car was parked next to it. It was then she noticed Dempsey's black, Big D Construction, extended cab pickup parked at the curb. Why was he here? Why was the house so quiet? She jumped when a bolt of lightning lit the western sky and thunder crashed down like Thor's hammer on the roof of her Jeep, so close it rocked her from side to side.

Icy sweat seeped from the tight skin on her neck and slipped between her shoulder blades. She pushed her palms out in a futile effort to hold back the dread pressing hard on her.

Something was terribly wrong in the McPherson house.

Chapter Nine

Misty hyperventilated. Fear paralyzed her; the terror greater than anything she'd experienced in Iraq. She could barely breathe. She had to go to the house. She needed to prove that nothing was wrong. This was insane. Nothing *was* wrong. Nothing. They had company. Dwayne and Marla had come to see the baby. They were best friends. Of course they'd be there, even this late.

Still, she couldn't bring herself to open her car door and step out. She had to see Mac, to see his happy face when he showed her his son. There was only one way to do that. Get out of the car and go to the house. *Now!* She put her hand on the door handle, took a deep cleansing breath, and opened the door. Oppressive heat hit her in the face, but she shivered and leaned back against the Jeep.

"Okay, enough!" She strode to the front door and mounted the three low steps onto the covered porch and tapped lightly on the door. A large shadow loomed in the glass and the door opened. "Hey, Gunny."

The stony look on Dempsey's face was a blow to her solar plexus. "Beachy? What are you doing here?" He didn't move aside or invite her in.

What was his problem? "Santos called me. I told him I would be here tonight." Her eyes darted around the dimly lit interior. "Where is everybody?"

Marla, her face tear-ravaged, eyes red and swollen stepped next to her husband. "Santos called you? When?"

"Tuesday. What's going on?" Misty's shoulder muscles tightened hard, like metal straps used to keep wine barrel staves leak proof.

"Oh, God!" Marla slapped a hand across her mouth then gasped, "You don't know."

Dwayne supported his wife with his arm around her waist. "Their baby died. Ronan died."

"What!" Misty screamed, but no sound came from her throat. "Wha...wha...?" She grabbed the doorframe to keep from collapsing.

Dwayne stepped forward. "Stay inside, honey. I'll take care of this." He closed the door behind him. "Their baby died, Beachy."

"No. I don't understand." Why was he lying to her?

"He had a hole in his heart. As soon as they caught it, they rushed him to surgery, but the little guy didn't make it. Things are beyond horrible around here right now. You must go."

"No, I can't...where are they? Where are Mac and Graciella and Santos? Are they here?"

"Yes, they're here. They're together in the master bedroom."

"I need to see them. I need to come in and see them."

"This isn't about what *you* need, Beachy. It's about what they need, and they don't need you right now. They're in deep shock and grief. Trust me on this. You should go."

"But..." A sob ripped from her throat.

Dwayne grabbed her arms when her knees buckled. "Steady. I'll walk you to your car." He towered over her, put his arm around her shoulders and led her off the porch. "Marla or I will contact you when things settle down. We have your cell number. We'll find you." He opened her car door and urged her inside. "Go now, Beachy. We've got this."

He closed her door and stood there, a Minute Man alert for the British invasion. Turgid raindrops splattered on her car and on Gunny's broad shoulders. He didn't move until she started the car and backed out of the driveway.

Her tears and deep wrenching sobs filled every space in her car, her mind, her body. She drove along the rain slicked road, but with no idea of where she was or where she was going. It couldn't be true. This couldn't happen to Mac. Mac didn't deserve this. Mac needed her. She turned around and headed back to Spring Grove. She would demand Dempsey let her in to see him. He of all people knew she and Mac always had each other's back.

Misty neared Mac's driveway when Gunny's harsh words, *they don't need you,* thundered in her consciousness. No! She wouldn't accept that she'd been relegated to the backseat of Mac's life. She hurt so badly for him, but if she was honest, she really hurt for her own loss.

She slammed on the brakes and slid on the slick asphalt. After a minute, she drove and drove, often through rain so heavy she could barely see the road ahead. She didn't know for how long. The tears wouldn't cease.

She smeared cloudy moisture from her eyes at a red traffic signal and stared through the downpour at the VA Hospital. A few blocks later the rain stopped abruptly. She turned into the lot in front of an apartment complex. Hawk and his daughter lived here. She'd spotted the building on her way to her appointment this morning. She didn't even know his apartment number. It was late, very late. She'd been driving aimlessly for two hours. She should have gone straight to her parents. But she'd turned in the opposite direction and was now staring at the front of the building where a man she deeply disliked lived with his teenage daughter.

Arms resting on the steering wheel, she dropped her head forward. The agony of Mac's loss was endless. The last time she'd felt such wrenching devastation was when her dad had opened the front door and they saw the fixed expressions of the uniformed military officers who'd come to tell them her brother was killed in Afghanistan. She'd rather be dead than in this much pain.

The hard, metallic tap of a big flashlight on her window nearly stopped her heart. A burly security guard stood shining a bluish beam of light into her face and motioned for her to lower her window.

"Are you okay, ma'am?"

"No. I..."

"Do you live here? Your vehicle doesn't have the required I.D. parking tag. If you're a visitor, you need to park over there." He gestured to the far side of the lot. "That's guest parking." When she didn't answer, he asked, "Who are you here to see?"

"Jonathan Hawk. I'm here to see Jonathan Hawk."

"What's his apartment number?"

"I don't know."

"It's very late, ma'am. Is he expecting you?"

"No. Something bad happened to a friend. I came to tell him."

The man slid an electronic device from a pouch at this belt. "Spell the name."

"Hawk, H. A. W. K., like the raptor." She shouldn't be here. She'd lost her mind coming here of all places.

"I'll give him a call." The guard tapped a few buttons. "Mr. Hawk? There's a woman in the parking lot who says she knows you. Yes, sir, I know it's late." He listened for a couple of seconds, glanced up at Misty and asked, "What's your name?"

"Beachy. Misty Beachy. I should probably leave."

"Her name's Beachy. Should I send her up?" He nodded as he listened. "Yes, it might be better if you come here. I'll wait."

Misty pushed to open her door, but the man leaned forward. "Stay in your car, miss. Mr. Hawk will be down shortly."

Dying a thousand deaths, fevered blood rose in her face and neck. Jack Hawk was the last person in the world she wanted to see her like this. She lowered her head on her arms again, seeing no way out of the situation.

Footsteps alerted her to Hawk's arrival. He spoke softly to the guard and the man walked away. She raised her head, and tears streamed down her cheeks.

"Mis? What is it? What's happened?" He pulled open her door and leaned close.

"Mac's..." She gasped on a deep sob. "Mac's baby died. He's dead."

"Oh, Christ! No!" He took her hand and urged her out of the Jeep. "Come here, baby. Come here."

She fell into his arms, clutching at him desperately as wracking sobs ripped her. Jack held her tight and rubbed her back. He rested his chin on her head. "Shhh, shhh, take your time." He turned them around so he was resting his back against the side of the car, and he held her. When she took a few breaths and her body relaxed against him, he kissed the top of her head. "Let's get your things and go upstairs. Give me your car keys so I can park you in a guest space. Get in on the passenger side. We'll sort this out, okay?"

Nodding dumbly, Misty did as he asked. He opened the door, lifted her purse off the seat and placed it in her lap when she sat. He slid into the driver's seat and drove cross the well-lighted lot then eased into a guest space and killed the engine. He noticed her duffle bag in the back and easily pulled it between the seats onto his lap. "Let's go upstairs."

"No. Hawk, I shouldn't be here." She looked into his steady gray gaze. Major Hawk had issued an order. "Okay." Misty stepped out of the Jeep and stood still for a minute to get her bearings.

Jack locked the car. Arm around her shoulders, he led her to the stairs. "Up there. Third door to the right." He dropped his arm as she took the first steps without his help, followed her across the open balcony and opened his apartment door. Placing her bag on the floor inside, he led her to the couch. "Sit. I'll get some water."

"Dad? Is somebody here? Who are you talking to?"

Jack called from the kitchen. "It's okay, sweetheart. Sgt Beachy is here. Go back to bed. I'll fill you in in the morning."

"Why is—?" Ellen stopped short when she stepped in the living room, and Misty raised her head. The girl gasped and put her hand over her mouth. "What's happened? Are you hurt?"

Misty closed her eyes and fell back against the couch cushions. She was unable to answer. She hadn't run out of tears and knew if she opened her mouth, the flood would start anew. She opened her eyes when she felt something in her lap. Ellen had placed a box of tissues on her knees. "Thanks."

"Dad, what?" Ellen asked Jack when he walked in with a bottle of water. "Is she...?"

"She'll be fine, Ellen. We just need to give her some space. A mutual friend suffered a great loss. We need to talk about it. I'd appreciate it if you'd go back to your room and give us some privacy. I'll tell you everything in the morning, I promise." He sat next to Misty. "Drink." He handed over the bottle.

Ellen backed away, her young face reflecting concern and worry.

"All right." She turned and fled down the hall to her room and closed the door with a soft click.

Jack moved close to Misty and rested a hand on her shoulder.

Her face crumpled, and she fell heavily into him. He embraced her, his body warm and strong. Hawk's gentle touch dissolved her determination to quit sobbing.

"It's okay, baby. Get it out. I'm here."

* * *

The horror of Beachy's news sent Jack's heartbeat into overdrive. He hadn't known Graciella's due date. She seemed robustly healthy at the barbeque. What could have gone wrong? There was no use questioning Misty until she calmed. He couldn't imagine why she'd shown up on his door.

This petite woman was a mystery to him. He was strangely drawn to her but had very little idea what made her tick. They'd got off on the wrong foot in Iraq. For some reason she'd taken an immediate dislike to him. They barely knew each other at the time, their only connection being his participation in a couple of firefights when he'd been called in for close air-ground support.

He was ambivalent about women in the military but had worked hard to keep it from showing. It was a done deal in today's military services. He wondered if it was possible she'd picked up on his attitude during that first debrief and resented him. She wouldn't be the first woman to accuse him of being a male chauvinist. He couldn't help it. He had natural protective instincts where the female of the species was concerned. They could be a valuable military asset in supporting roles but encountering them in battleground situations had never set right with him.

He'd never expressed disdain toward the many competent female soldiers he'd come across, especially Beachy. He'd been strongly attracted to her that first encounter so many years ago. The stark contrast between her innocent girlish looks and her toughness and fierce determination had proved heady. He was married at the time, with a toddler daughter and dissatisfied wife in the States. He'd put Beachy out of his mind. He was nearing the end of his tour, heading home to Theresa and Ellen, and was fixated on repairing his marriage.

Now, more than ten years later he still felt the same attraction.

Misty quieted, her breathing nearing normal.

"Tell me when you're ready." He smoothed a hand over her disordered short tresses.

As if she'd just realized he was holding her, she stiffened and moved to put some distance between them. She wiped her eyes and nose with a tissue and cleared her throat. "He...the baby...had some kind of rare heart problem they didn't catch in time to save him." Her bleak brown eyes darted away from Jack. "I'm foggy on what Gunny told me. I couldn't believe it. He wouldn't let me in the house. He told me, 'They don't need you.'"

Jack placed his hands on his knees. "I'll call Dempsey in the morning and see if I can learn more. What the McPhersons must be going through horrifies me. My mother gave birth to a stillborn when I was about seven. Mom and Dad's grief devastated the whole family. How much worse it must be to have the child born alive and apparently healthy." Hawk shook his head, his gut twisted when the very old memory became real again.

"I should leave."

"It's after midnight. Where will you go at this hour? Stay here. You can sleep on the couch. Make a decision about your next move in the morning when you've had a chance to digest the shock." He got to his feet. "I'll get a pillow and blanket for you."

"No. I can't stay here." She shook her head.

"Listen to how hard it's coming down." He pointed to the ceiling and a crash of thunder backed up his statement. "Be sensible, Beachy. You can take off at daylight. That's only five hours from now. Stay until morning. Don't leave until we learn more details from Dempsey." He started down the hall. "I'll get that pillow and blanket."

* * *

The downpour thundered. Misty should never have come here, but Hawk was right. It made no sense for her to go out in the deluge, to drive to her parents' house and wake them up in the wee hours. They weren't expecting her this weekend. She didn't tell them she had an appointment at the V.A. hospital. Before she left San Diego, she'd sent her Dad a text saying she might be in the area and would call them. Why she hadn't made it definite she wasn't sure but was in no condition to talk to them. Never mind the weather.

Jack carried a pillow and comforter from what she assumed was his bedroom. "I don't have any clean sheets to offer. Saturday night is when I usually do laundry. Sorry."

His social life sounded like hers. "You know I've slept on a lot of cots without sheets. I'll survive. I feel stupid putting you to all this trouble. You and Ellen probably have plans for the weekend. I'll get out of your hair early, Hawk."

"We have no plans, so don't be concerned. I'm usually up before six. I've set up the coffeemaker to brew at five-thirty. I wish you'd stay until after I've had a chance to find out some of the details from Dempsey. You probably don't want to head south without knowing, right?"

Misty shrugged, plopped the pillow on the end of the sofa and arranged the comforter. "You're right. I haven't been thinking straight for the last few hours." Her chin trembled, and she prayed she wouldn't start wailing again. "Where's a bathroom I can use?"

He tipped his head toward the hall. "First door on the left. It's a small guest bath. If you want to shower you can use the one in my room, or Ellen's after she's up in the morning."

"In spite of what you might think, Jack. I'm low maintenance. I'll manage." She was about as likely to shower in Hawk's bathroom as sprouting wings and a halo. "I appreciate it."

He nodded. "Goodnight then. I'll see you over coffee in a few hours." He locked the apartment and strolled down the hallway to the last room on the right, across from Ellen.

Misty dug through her duffle for her kit. She turned off the overhead light, leaving one lamp in the room burning and found the small powder room. Feeling much better after she washed her wrecked face and brushed her teeth, she tiptoed back to the living room and turned off the lamp. She usually slept in the buff but donned an old T-shirt and left her panties on before she arranged herself under the comforter. Her mind went a mile a minute. She swallowed back tears imagining how destroyed Mac must be over the loss of his infant son. That kind of hurt was an experience she'd never have. By choice.

Marriage and a family were out of the question for her. She was bad news, incapable of compromising a fraction in any relationship. She had issues with loss. Nothing was permanent no matter how perfect it seemed in the beginning. She guarded her feelings. Who needed heartbreak, or betrayal or death? That's always what it came down to. She wasn't willing to take the risk.

She examined her feelings for Jack Hawk. He was quiet and strong. Older than her by about ten years. She had no reason to be snotty with him. What had he ever done really? She didn't know him that well. She'd learned more about him in the past few months than she'd picked up on in the past ten years. One thing she did know— she'd never get used to those penetrating eyes of his. He had a way of making her feel like she'd been caught at something forbidden when he nailed her with the *look*.

She compared Jack to men who were her contemporaries. Men her age and younger who'd served in the Marines with her. Young, strong macho guys for the most part. Mac and his best friend Dwayne Dempsey were big strong guys from Wyoming. Cowboys, if you believed the stories they liked to tell about growing up there. Masculine and confident in spite of their war wounds, determined, hardworking family men, both of them. They were typical of men she felt an affinity for.

But Jack Hawk was a different story. Older, of medium height and build, Hawk had a confident air. An accomplished combat pilot who'd considered making the military his career until his wife ditched them. He didn't display bitterness or behave like a victim. He did what needed to be done. Hawk possessed a razor-sharp mind, and he could fly any aircraft ever invented with confidence and precision. Hawk was compelling, attractive, and sexy. He probably didn't do it intentionally, but somehow in his presence, she always felt on edge, unsure of herself.

Hawk was all man, no doubt about it. If she'd had any uncertainty before the kiss, she certainly didn't have any afterward. She was no babe in the woods, but she'd never experienced such a jolting response to a man's kiss before. She'd been completely unprepared. He'd thrown down the gauntlet and he'd conquered her in that one delicious few minutes. She didn't like the sense of need and vulnerability he'd provoked deep inside. No, she definitely needed to steer clear of any involvement with Jack Hawk. Not that he'd given any indication he was interested in starting anything with her.

Chapter Ten

JACK SMELLED COFFEE AND COULDN'T LIE IN BED ANY LONGER. He stepped quietly along the dark hallway, careful not to wake his daughter or Misty. As soon as it was a decent hour he'd give Dempsey a call and see what he could find out about the McPherson baby.

Glancing in the living room he saw Misty had kicked off the comforter and was sprawled on her stomach with her arm hanging over the edge of the sofa. He got a great view of a very fine pair of legs and an excellent backside. Her T-shirt had rucked up to her shoulder blades revealing her small waist and the edge of one breast. He tore his eyes away and proceeded to the kitchen.

Disgusted at feeling like a voyeur, he grabbed a mug and poured himself a cup of coffee then slumped in a chair. He wished he had the morning paper but wouldn't open the front door and wake her. If he did, she'd be sure he'd been ogling her nearly bare ass. He cursed and grumbled quietly, "You were, Hawk."

"Were what?"

His head snapped up at the sound of Beachy's voice. She'd pulled on a pair of jeans and stood before him scrubbing her hands through her blonde hair. Jack scrambled for an answer. "Unable to sleep. How about you?"

"God, that coffee smells good." She opened her eyes wide and sniffed deeply.

"Help yourself. Use any mug on the counter. Half and half's in the refrigerator." She looked exactly like his fantasy of waking up with her in the morning. Disheveled, no makeup, hair uncombed, eyes heavy with sleep. Devastatingly sexy.

You're walking through a minefield, man.

"I guess Ellen's still sleeping. I scared her, coming here so late last night. I'll try and get out of your hair before she's up. When do you think it'll be okay to call Gunny?" She carried the steaming mug of black coffee to the table and sat across from him.

Jack glanced at his watch. "He's an early riser. It would probably be all right to call him after six, six-thirty."

"I wonder how late they stayed at Mac's. Maybe they spent the night."

"I've got his cell number. I'll find him." He scrutinized her face. "You look like hell, Beachy."

"Thank you, you example of movie-star, breath-stealing handsomeness."

He winked. "I didn't know you cared."

"Pffft! Shut up and let me get this caffeine down."

He got to his feet. "I'm going to get the morning paper."

"Don't be too long or I'll miss you." She raised her hand in a rude gesture.

He returned the favor. "So sweet." Chuckling as he opened the door and shook water droplets off the plastic wrapping on the newspaper, he admitted to himself how much he liked her, how much he'd like to shut her up by kissing her again.

He poured himself a second cup of coffee and sat down. He ruffled through the pages. "Oh look, Macy's is having a gigantic shoe sale. You don't want to miss buying several pair of these ankle strap, F-me, spike heels. Or would you rather read the crime statistics?"

"You're such an asshole, Hawk." She rubbed her hands down her face.

"Thank you for noticing." He shook the paper to deliberately annoy her. "Breakfast?"

"What are you making?"

"Me? There's the stove. There's the refrigerator. Have at it."

"You're this close to hot coffee in the face." A small smile appeared briefly and disappeared quickly.

She felt better. Good. "How about my world-famous oatmeal?"

"Whatever." She pushed back her chair. "I'm going to take a shower."

"About time. I put fresh towels on the side of the tub in my bathroom."

Her mumbled curses would make a hardened Marine blush. *That's my girl.*

He started the oatmeal then placed a call to Dwayne Dempsey. He hoped to get some information while Misty was in the shower. If they got the emotion out of it, they could have a discussion and make some decisions before she went home to San Diego. His brief conversation with Dempsey was heartbreaking. By the time he disconnected he was glad she'd been out of the kitchen.

"There you are, fresh as a daisy, bright as the morning sun." He placed two steaming bowls of oatmeal on the kitchen table.

"Sorry I'm such a bitch." She blew a deep sigh and sank into a chair. "Smells good, Hawk."

"I remember the men in your outfit used to call you Misty Bitchy." He chuckled. "Eat. It'll improve your mood." He pushed a bowl of brown sugar and a dish of raisins closer to her.

"Yeah, they were perceptive. I earned the name. But I had a smooth-running operation the entire time we were over there. Anyway, if I were a man they would have called me authoritative, not bitchy."

"Hmm. I'll give you that." He reached for the coffee pot. "We might as well finish this up. You've got a long drive ahead of you."

"Do you think it's too early to call Gunny?" She picked up her spoon and stirred a heaping mound of brown sugar into the oatmeal but ignored the raisins.

"I called him while you were in the shower." He felt some guilt about that but went on. "The baby had ventricular septal heart defect. It didn't manifest itself until several hours after he was born. By then the damage was done. Dempsey said he died from a stroke during emergency surgery."

Still as a statue, Misty held her spoon above the bowl. Her hand began to shake, and she set it down. She stared at Hawk. Pain clouded her eyes. "It's not fair. Mac didn't deserve this."

Did she think McPherson lived in a vacuum? The way she talked, his wife and her son didn't exist. "Neither did Graciella or Santos, Beachy. McPherson isn't the only one hurt by this."

"You bastard," she spat between clenched teeth, her hands in tight fists. "Don't you think I know that?"

"I wasn't sure. You never mention anybody in that household except McPherson."

She pounded a fist on the table and bolted out of her chair. "Go to hell!"

He followed her to the living room and watched while she slammed her kit in the duffle and yanked the zipper closed. She stormed toward the door. "So," he said to her back, "you're not interested in knowing when and where the funeral is."

She stopped. Dropped the bag. Clutching her arms around her waist, she doubled over. "What's wrong with me?"

Jack lifted her upright. "Your heart is broken, baby." He turned her against his chest and put his arms around her. "It means you're human." He stroked her back. "You are, you know."

He led her to the kitchen and asked her to try and eat. "I'll put this in the microwave and zap it. I don't know about you, but I really hate cold coffee." After twenty seconds, he removed the mug and carried it back to her.

"I don't know what to do, Jack. I have to do something."

"The baby's funeral is Tuesday. We'll go and offer our condolences then do whatever we can to help. It will be very painful all around." His ears perked up. "Come in, Ellen."

"I wasn't snooping, I just stopped when I heard you talking."

"It's okay, sweetheart, take a seat and I'll make you some cocoa." When caught off guard his daughter's innocence and vulnerability weren't masked by her shield of belligerence. She worked so hard at not showing her feelings. She was like Misty in that way. Hawk pulled out a chair and kissed her cheek when she sat down.

Misty set her coffee next to her bowl and nodded to Ellen. "I'm sorry for barging in last night. I know it upset you. I wasn't planning to come here, but next thing I knew I was pulling into your parking lot."

"Something bad happened, didn't it?"

"A friend's baby died. It was awful."

"Whose? One of Mr. Dempsey's?" She was afraid of the answer. Her stricken eyes betrayed her.

"No. Cluny McPherson's." Misty's eyes blurred with unshed tears.

"Oh, no! The funny water balloon man?" She gasped and put her hands over her mouth.

Unable to answer, Misty nodded.

Jack took a seat. "The baby was born Tuesday. You remember Mrs. McPherson from the barbeque? She was pregnant."

Her eyes rounded. "Then it was only…it was only three days old?"

He pressed his lips together and nodded.

"Oh, that's so sad. A tiny newborn baby." The teakettle sounded off. "I'll get it, Dad."

"I'm happy to make it for you, sweetheart."

"I know. I can do it." She poured boiling water into the mug then carried it and the box of cocoa to the table. Astonishing Jack and Misty, she placed her hand on Misty's shoulder. "I'm awful sorry."

Misty gulped coffee and nodded.

Nobody spoke. Ellen measured and stirred cocoa. Her spoon rang against the sides of her Cookie Monster mug. To Hawk's ears it sounded as loud as Big Ben.

"When's the funeral, Jack?" Misty gazed at him. "I know you told me, but my brain isn't working."

"Tuesday. I think it would be best if you stayed here Monday night and we drove there together. Do you have to go home today? If you can get the time off, you can stay here, or don't your parents live in Moorpark now?"

"I have to go home. Jeremy left and I'm training a new employee. I can't leave her by herself for so many days." Listlessly, she picked up her spoon, poked at the oatmeal then took a tentative bite.

"I can see that's a problem. But I really would prefer if you'd let me take you to the funeral on Tuesday. It's too much to drive all the way up here from San Diego early on Tuesday morning. If you drive up Monday night and you don't want to bunk here, I'll pick you up at your parents' place. The service will be at St. Agnes Catholic Cemetery in Spring Grove. They're having a reception at Dempsey's after. I'd feel better if you'd let me do that, Beachy."

Unexpectedly, she agreed, "Yes. That's a good idea. I don't want to do it alone."

Out of the clear blue, Ellen asked, "Can I go too, Dad? He's such a nice man and his stepson is so sweet. I didn't get a chance to speak to his wife. She's very pretty and kind of foreign looking."

Misty commented, "Graciella is from Brazil."

"Of course you can go if you want to, sweetheart, but it will be very sad, and a long hot day." In spite of his being in the military for so long, Ellen had little experience with death and funerals.

"I could do stuff. I could help with the little kids at the reception."

He was touched by her words. "That would be a kind thing to do. I'll let Dwayne and Marla know. I'm sure they'd really appreciate it."

Misty's eyes filled. "That would be great, Ellen."

* * *

After breakfast, Misty thanked Hawk and his daughter. "I'll call my parents and see if they can put me up Monday night, Jack. I wrote down their phone number on the pad by the kitchen phone, but you can reach me on my cell."

"Just let me know where you'll be, and we'll pick you up Tuesday morning."

* * *

She stopped in at the VA Hospital for a brief visit with Ralph, as promised. Misty gave up trying to find a shady parking space in the vast lot and trudged through the blazing morning sun to the entrance.

He was alone in his room and seemed to be asleep, but she went to his bedside and laid her hand on his arm. "Captain." She patted. "Good morning."

A smile lit his face before his eyelids fluttered open. "Ah, Sgt Lovely, you came back."

She grinned at the feisty tenor of his words. "I said I would."

"Beautiful girls don't always keep their promises." He put his hand over hers. "It's good to see you. Have a seat and visit for a while if you have time."

She pushed the chair close to the bed and sat. When she noticed he couldn't see her clearly from his vantage point, she stood again. "Do you think it would be all right if I lower your bed so we can see each other?"

"Go ahead. If they complain I'll tell them I gave you a direct order. I don't think either of us risks facing court martial."

Misty stayed for an hour. They talked of many things. She was interested in his service and he asked questions about hers. She told him about Mac's baby, how broken hearted she was for him—and of course, his wife. Then without knowing why exactly, she confided in Ralph the details of her history with Mac.

"Remember the good things, Sgt Beachy, it's part of who you are, but the past has no place in your life now. You're young, you have so much to do, so many choices to make.'

"It's hard. I thought he loved me." Why was she telling him this?

"I have no doubt he does. You're a fellow Marine. He's probably close to many who were in your outfit, who experienced hard times in war. He's moved on. It's time for you to do the same." The steady look in his eyes reflected regret for the pain his words caused. "You know I'm right."

She covered her face and nodded. "Yes. I know." She stood and raised his bed back to its original height and returned the chair to the side of the room. "Is it okay if I come to see you again, Captain? I have to go back to San Diego now, but I'll be returning Monday evening. The baby's funeral is Tuesday morning."

"I'd like that. There are no restrictions on visiting hours here at the *last tour of duty*. Come in no matter what time it is. I'll see you Monday. You drive safe now."

She leaned close and kissed him on the forehead. "I never kissed a Captain before." She grinned. "But I kissed a Major on the 4th of July." She rolled her eyes.

Ralph chuckled and patted her cheek. "Working your way through the ranks, are you?"

* * *

Misty had hours to think on the long drive home, but organizing those thoughts was harder than grabbing a single raindrop. She'd always had an organized, disciplined mind. Her ability to make the right decisions quickly had been her major strength as an active duty Marine. She'd advanced to Master Sergeant faster than most men. Now with the constant intrusion of Hawk into her thoughts and the death of Mac's baby she sensed she was losing her grip.

She was all the way home by the time she recalled her conversation with Mary about therapy dogs. Her excitement about pursuing something along that line had dimmed. No longer sure that she felt so passionate about a career change.

One thing at a time, Beachy.

First thing she had to get out of the way—contact her new assistant and meet with her tomorrow, Sunday, if possible. The woman deserved more than a rush job on Monday before Misty headed north again. She'd be gone at least two or three days, and doubted she'd make it back to the training center before Friday morning. She could count on Florine to jump into the fray if assistance was needed. Customs frowned on employee overtime, but this was an emergency, she'd had no time to make plans for an absence.

She called Hawk as promised. "I'm home in one piece, Jack."

"What took you so long to get there? I was expecting to hear from you a couple of hours ago." The tinge of annoyance in his voice set her teeth on edge.

"I didn't know I was on the clock. I stopped to visit a friend at the VA Hospital. Sorry I didn't get your permission first."

* * *

Monday morning she called her mother and told her about the funeral and asked if she could stay with them that night.

"You know you don't need to ask permission to stay with us. It annoys me when you do that, Misty. Come anytime. You have a key and you're welcome to stay even if we're not here."

"I know, Mom. I just don't like to assume it's okay."

"You're our only child. Why would we ever deny you or miss a chance to see you? We're your parents. We love you." She expressed a frustrated sigh. "Please don't ever ask permission again. Just come."

Misty smiled. "Okay, Mom. I do need to warn you though. I'll be very late, but we'll have time to catch up on Tuesday morning before Major Hawk and his daughter pick me up. I'm pretty sure I'll be around Wednesday, too, so why don't you and Dad and I plan dinner out, my treat?"

"That would be very nice. I'll tell him not to make any other plans. If we've already gone to bed, let yourself in and we'll see you at breakfast."

"Thanks, Mom. I love you." Until she said the words she hadn't quite realized how much. It had been a long time since she'd told her parents she loved them. From now on she'd tell them every chance she got.

* * *

It was nearing nine in the evening when she pulled into the parking lot at the VA Hospital. She found a spot near the front entrance. Inside the doors the noise level was considerably less than during the day when the waiting areas and hallways were buzzing with activity. She nodded to a security guard. "Hospice visitor."

The man tipped his head. "Do you know the room number?'

"Yes."

"Have a good visit then."

Ralph's room was empty. Dread pounded in her chest.

"You looking for Ralph?"

The man was the same nurse who'd encouraged her to visit the old soldier last Friday afternoon. His brown eyes exuded compassion. "He passed this afternoon."

Misty drew in a sharp breath and clutched her throat. "Oh." She'd known Ralph didn't have long, but she'd blocked that knowledge and looked forward to talking to him again. "I...I'm so sorry to hear it."

"He told me Sgt Lovely was coming for a visit. He left something for you. Will you accompany me to the nurse's station?"

"Sure…but." What possibly could the old man have left for her? His wedding ring, maybe?

"Here you go." The nurse handed her the framed Medal of Honor. A sticky note on it said, in spidery script: *Semper Fi, Sgt Lovely. I know you'll take good care of this for me. Capt Ralph Ferguson, USMC (ret).*

Oh, God, more tears.

She clutched the frame to her chest and lowered her chin. What had brought her and the old Marine together, and why? "Thank you." She turned on her heel and hurried through the endless corridors of the gigantic hospital without realizing that she'd been holding her breath until she stepped outside in the cool evening air.

She drove straight to Hawk's apartment. She heard his voice as she approached the front of the building. He was on the open hallway talking to an attractive woman. She stopped in her tracks, but Jack had spotted her. He made a comment to the woman and started down the stairs. "Are you staying here tonight, Beachy?"

"No. I just came from the VA Hospital. I had to show you this." She'd been hugging the frame to her chest, then held it out to him.

His eyes widened as he studied the medal. "Who is Ralph Ferguson? Is he a relative?"

Her eyes swam. "No." She cleared her throat. "I met him for the first time the day I had my appointment. I visited him a couple of times." Her breath caught again. "I told him I'd stop in this evening. He died today. He didn't have anyone. He left this for me, Jack."

Jack raised those unsettling gray-brown eyes of his to gaze directly into hers. "You must have made quite an impression on him. This is an incredible honor." He placed an arm around her shoulders.

She dropped her head against his neck. "I don't know why he did it. He didn't really know me." The woman on the balcony gazed down at them. "Who is that, Jack? The woman you were talking to when I got here?"

He turned his head. "Doris. Cherry's mother. They live two doors down the hall from us. Come with me, I'll introduce you."

"I should probably just go. It's getting late."

"Don't you think it will look odd?"

"Are you and Doris…?"

"We're neighbors, Misty. Nothing more." He led her up the stairs.

"Doris, this is Misty Beachy. She brought me the tragic news Friday night. Ellen and I will be attending the baby's funeral with other veterans tomorrow in Spring Grove."

Doris' lovely face contorted. "You're a veteran? Of what?"

"The United States Marine Corps." She wanted to sock the ignorant woman but understood her confusion. People often showed surprise when they learned of her service.

Doris closed her eyes briefly and shook her head. "I apologize for asking such a stupid question." Her face reddened. She mumbled, "You don't look like my preconceived notion of a veteran. Really. I'm sorry." She waved and hurried to leave. "Nice to meet you. See you later, Jack."

"Goodnight, Doris." He pressed his lips together and winked at Misty. "You're in your usual top form."

"Go to hell, Jack." She was embarrassed by her behavior and didn't need Hawk to rub it in.

He stuffed his hands in his pockets. "We'll be there to pick you up at ten-thirty." He left her standing on the balcony and returned to his apartment.

Chapter Eleven

Her parents' kitchen, next morning

MISTY GLANCED AT HER WATCH. "IS THAT THE DOORBELL?" JACK wasn't due to pick her up for another half hour. Had she misunderstood the time? She hadn't even dressed yet.

Mom pushed back her chair. "Sure is." She hurried to answer.

Misty followed her and stood in the kitchen doorway. Her mom opened the door and there he was, Ellen at his side. "Hawk, Ellen," Misty said. "You're early."

"My GPS is out of whack. I didn't want to be late." Jack acknowledged her mother and extended his hand. "Jonathan Hawk, Mrs. Beachy. This is my daughter, Ellen. Sorry we're so early. I hope it's not an inconvenience for you."

A big smile bloomed on her mother's face as she gazed at Hawk and Ellen. "Not at all, Major. So nice to meet you, too, Ellen. Sorry it's such a sad day. Would you like something to drink? I have some warm sticky buns that just came from the oven."

"Sure." Ellen glanced quickly at her dad, as if she'd spoken out of turn.

"Thank you. Coffee would be great." He put his arm around Ellen's shoulders. "Coffee for you too, sweetheart?"

Misty approached the door. She fidgeted and held her robe closed. "Um. You can visit with Mom while I finish dressing. I won't be long."

Jack stepped farther into the room just as her dad entered through the back door.

His voice rang through the small house, "I smell something good, Debbie." He stopped short. "Oh, sorry, I was out back and didn't hear your car." He walked forward and held out his hand. "Payne Beachy. You're Major Hawk, and Ellen, is it? Very sad day."

Ellen nodded.

"Nice to meet you, sir. Please call me Jack."

"Glad to if you won't call me sir." The men nodded at each other and shook hands.

Flustered because her parents were fawning over Jack like a long lost best friend, Misty sniffed and headed down the hall. "Be right back."

Dressed in no time, she ran a brush through her short blond hair and smudged her eyelids with just enough shadow to highlight the color of her whisky-brown eyes. Afraid of looking like a horror show freak if she ended up crying later, she avoided mascara. She usually didn't use much makeup. A dab of coral lip gloss finished the job. She stood back from the mirror on the back of the guest room door and made a last check of her appearance in the light brown, knee length skirt and soft yellow blouse. Flat fawn-colored Naturalizers would have to do. She didn't own a pair of heels. She snatched her jacket off the bed post and left the room.

The voices of her dad and Jack drifted from the front. As she entered the living room, her mother and Ellen crossed the dining area. Mom with a steaming coffee pot and Ellen carried a tray of rolls. Misty was wary of her parents getting too chummy with Jack and his daughter. She didn't want them giving her the third degree about them later. She was conflicted enough about her feeling for the Hawks.

"You'll love Debbie's sticky buns," her dad said, the pride in his voice strong. "I married her for her cooking. She was the most beautiful girl in the graduating class. That didn't hurt either."

Misty smiled at the oft-told joke of her father's. The love and trust between her parents was rare and precious. It wasn't likely she'd ever find such a relationship. It was an anomaly of the past, in her opinion.

Her breath caught as she remembered the pure passion in Mac's eyes when he told her how much he loved Graciella and her son, Santos. Her past history with him had threatened his determined pursuit of the woman, until Misty had stepped in and set Graciella straight. Mac's happiness had been paramount. She wouldn't be the cause of them breaking up. She cared for him too much for that to happen.

The mystery was, she'd absolutely believed the love between herself and Mac to be purely platonic. She went to great pains to explain to Graciella that she was no threat to her. She and Mac were good buddies. Sure, they had a brief sexual history when deployed in Iraq, but it had been wartime, it was physical, not love in the romantic sense. Not the kind of love that lasted a lifetime, for better or worse, like her parents. Had she fully believed it herself?

She deeply dreaded today's events brought on by the horrible loss of their infant son. Sudden. Unexpected. Unexplainable. She didn't know what would happen at the funeral and reception afterward. How were they to survive the tragedy? She'd do everything in her power to support the McPherson's, as she knew other family and veteran friends would. She owed Mac that much.

Hawk's eyes met hers when she entered the living room and he shifted sideways on the sofa to make room for her. Ellen sat on his other side and her parents were in the chairs facing the coffee table and couch. She hesitated a split second then took a seat.

"You look lovely, honey," her father said. "We seldom see you in a skirt. You should wear one more often."

Heat rose in her cheeks when a quick glance to the side revealed Hawk nodding his approval. She hadn't dressed to impress him. No way.

She racked her brain for something she could say to Ellen. She felt awkward around the teenager and thought she should break the ice, be friendlier to the girl. She glanced down at her shoes, then Ellen's. "Look, Ellen, you and I have the exact same shoes on." Misty extended her foot.

Ellen's eyes widened. "Your feet are a lot smaller than mine, though. Look how small her feet are, Dad."

Misty cringed. "Thanks, Ellen. They're not that small."

"What size are they?" the girl asked innocently.

Resigned, Misty said, "Six and a half." She asked herself why she was so inept around Jack's daughter.

"Six and a…wow! I wear eight and a half."

Jack turned his attention to her mother. "These pecan rolls are the best I've ever tasted, Mrs. Beachy."

Thank you, Jack. Maybe he'd noticed the corner she'd painted herself into.

The tension in her shoulders eased slightly.

Mom pointed to her husband. "He's Payne and I'm *Mrs. Beachy*? Please, it's Debbie. I'm glad you like them." She leaned forward and directed her next comment to Ellen, "Misty has the recipe. Perhaps she'll show you how to make them for your dad, Ellen."

Misty chose to say nothing about that unlikely possibility.

Five minutes later, Jack tapped his watch. "We should probably get going." He got to his feet. "Thank you for your hospitality, Debbie. So nice to meet you, Payne. I hope to see you again under happier circumstances."

What circumstances would those be, Jack?

* * *

Not more than twenty minutes later they joined the long queue of vehicles creeping down the street to the parking lot of Jensen Funeral parlor. Misty gasped, surprised at the number of cars. It looked as though every friend and acquaintance of Mac and Graciella had come this morning to support them on this tragic day. She recognized a group of kids Mac coached for the park league baseball team, waiting beside their parents. She swallowed the large lump forming in her throat.

"Gosh, Dad, look at the crowd." Ellen's voice trembled. "It's so sad. I hope I don't cry."

"It's okay to cry, sweetheart. Today is a very difficult occasion. I don't expect go to another one like it. I hope McPherson and his wife and son make it through the suffering they must be experiencing." He reached across the seat and covered Misty's hand with his. "You okay?"

"No. How could I be?" She blinked at pending tears. When had she become such a big sob sister?

"I'll be right at your side, Mis." He squeezed her hand and she squeezed back, glad for his rock-steady support. She hadn't thought she needed it, but she did.

Taking a deep calming breath, she whispered, "Thanks, Jack."

* * *

Jack perceived the depth of Misty's distress in her shallow breathing and rigid neck. He pressed her hand again then turned into the large parking lot. A white hearse waited by the front of the chapel to receive the pathetically small coffin it would carry to the cemetery.

The service was brief and dignified. Dwayne Dempsey, his brother Dylan and their father, John, were three of the pallbearers. Jack didn't recognize the tall black man with them right away then realized it had to be Graciella's former father-in-law, Earl Jefferson. He and his wife had stayed close to her after their son was killed in Iraq. She had no relatives in the United States. Earl and Lillian and their daughter were as close as she had to family.

At the cemetery, the priest conducted a brief homily and a short prayer. Cluny stood stone-faced. His beautiful wife, Graciella, clung tight to his arm, her ivory-pale face a mask of dignity and suffering. Young Santos clung to Mac's hand and leaned against his step-father's side, staring into space.

Jack felt his heart crack. This day never should have happened. Not to them. Not to anyone. He and Theresa had suffered the loss of a stillborn son, when Ellen was a toddler. Their marriage bed froze after that. Theresa was terrified of another pregnancy. It was almost a relief when she fled. He no longer had to pretend the lack of intimacy hadn't mattered. He prayed the loss of this much wanted child wouldn't put a chill on the McPherson marriage.

He put his arm around Beachy's shoulders and she leaned into his side as if drawing on his strength. He squeezed her tight and held Ellen's hand. His daughter lowered her head as tears slid down her cheeks. Today was a life lesson she'd not forget anytime soon.

A line formed as mourners waited to express their sympathy to the McPherson's. He lowered his arm and tugged Misty's hand tentatively. "Shall we?"

She nodded. "Yes. We have to. I want to." Without waiting for him, she stepped forward into the queue. He and Ellen joined her.

* * *

Misty carried a tray of canapés through the Dempsey's dining room and strolled among the throng, offering them to guests. The tray emptied quickly and she rejoined Marla in the kitchen for another. "I can't believe these are going so fast. I should have brought more."

"Don't worry. We have plenty. Lillian and I will have the hot dishes on the table in another few minutes." She nodded to Lillian Jefferson who scooped warm finger-food from a tray she pulled from the oven.

"I don't understand how people eat at a time like this," Misty said.

"Eating is life-affirming. It also takes away the requirement for meaningless small talk. Do me a favor? Go out and make sure Cluny and Graciella get off their feet. Take these glasses of iced tea for them and see that they sit down for a while."

Misty faltered. The vacant expression on Mac's face when he'd returned her embrace woodenly at the cemetery had unsettled her. It was as if they were strangers. There wasn't the slightest warmth or recognition in his expression when he'd thanked her for coming.

Time to suck it up, Marine!

"Of course. I'll make sure they're okay, Marla." She nodded to the back yard where Ellen and a couple of Dempsey cousins had taken the children. Amber pushed an unsmiling Santos on the tree swing while Ellen rocked the twin babies on the glider in the shade of a large tree. "Looks like they're doing a good job with the kids."

"That Ellen Hawk is a treasure the way she's taken over. I'm so glad Jack brought her with him today. What a relief it is, not to be running back and forth between the kitchen and the patio to check on the little ones." Marla's hand caressed her abdomen unconsciously. She was beginning to show.

Misty took the small tray with the two glasses of tea and a few napkins. She carried them from the kitchen, through the dining room and scanned the living room to see where Mac and Graciella had gone.

99

She wandered down the hall when she heard Mac's voice and came to an abrupt stop in the doorway.

"Forgive me, baby. I'm trying to be strong for you, but this is killing me."

"I know. I'll be strong for you, querido," Graciella soothed. She glanced up. "Come in Misty."

Mortified to be caught staring at them as they sat on the side of their bed, Misty took a step back. "I…"

"Please, come in. It's okay. I'm sure Cluny would like to talk to you."

"No, I'll leave you alone." Her neck and cheeks were aflame. "Marla wanted me to bring you these and make sure you were resting. I didn't mean to intrude."

Mac's tearstained face lifted. "Mis." He patted the space next to him. "You're my best pal; of course, I want to talk to you. I didn't know you were here today."

Mac had no recollection of her at the funeral or cemetery. Shocked at his lapse, she shook herself. What did she expect? This had to be one of the worst days of his life. She set the tray on a bedside table as a sob ripped from her throat. Mac held his arms open and she fell into them. "Oh, Mac, Mac. My heart is breaking for you."

"I know, sugar." He held her in a firm embrace. His chest shuddered as he lowered his head onto hers and wept. "Our Ronan is gone. I don't know what to do."

She raised her head and ran her hands through his dark curly hair. "You'll get through this, Mac. I know you." She hadn't noticed Queen in the room until the big dog groaned and rested her head on Cluny's thigh. "You'll help him, won't you, Queenie?"

Graciella had left them alone. Cluny gasped a shaky breath. "I love her so much, Mis. You can't imagine how much I love her. We wanted this baby so bad."

Stroking his cheeks, she gazed into his tragic blue eyes. "My heart is breaking for you, my dear friend." She pulled a tissue from the box next to the tray and wiped his eyes. "Mac, you're the strongest, most loving man I've ever known. You'll find your strength for Graciella and Santos. It will come. Give it time."

He flopped back on the bed. "I should go out and talk to people. So many showed up for us today."

"There are no *shoulds*, Mac. Give yourself a break. Lie back for a while. I'll make sure Graciella is okay. Amber is taking good care of Santos." She got to her feet and urged him to raise his legs up onto the bed. "Rest. Everybody understands."

It was so like him. In the depth of grief his concerns were for those he loved. She remembered when he'd taken her in his arms and comforted her during one of the endless mortar attacks at the FOB in Iraq. His ongoing struggle with PTS was testament to how much he'd suffered and hidden it from her over there. Lifting a fringed coverlet from the trunk at the foot of the bed she covered him and let her hand linger on his hip. Queen jumped up on the bed and settled herself against Cluny's back.

She could never love another man as much as she loved Sgt Mac McPherson. Never.

* * *

The evening after the Hawks dropped her off, her mother sat on the back patio with her. They sipped soft drinks and watched the sunset hovering over the distant, rugged Santa Monica Mountains. "It's really beautiful here, Mom. Are you glad you moved?"

"Yes, Payne loves it here. It's also nice to be closer to you, honey."

She gave her mother a sidewise glance and poked her shoulder. "You're dying to ask me about Jack and Ellen Hawk, so go ahead."

"I don't like to intrude into your private life, but I am curious about them."

Misty chuckled and rolled her eyes. "You've been intruding into my private life for thirty-three years, Mom. Why stop now?" The last thing she wanted was for her parents to stop worrying about her. She loved them so much. They'd always been close.

"Don't be a smart aleck. I'm your mother, I love you. It's my job to be concerned."

"I understand, Mom, but if I'm a smart aleck, whose fault is that?"

"You didn't get it from me! You're just like your brother, and both of you took after Payne." She rubbed Misty's hand. This was the first time in years that her mother had mentioned Bill. It took her by surprise.

"It's been years since you've mentioned Billy. I miss him every day of my life. He was my hero. I wanted to be just like him."

"Yes, honey. That's why you joined the Marines after he was killed in Kabul. You were bound and determined to take his place. We didn't want that. The thought of losing you was more than we could bear."

Misty stared at her mother's face. "You never told me that."

"Payne and I talked about it, but it was what you had to do. You have the right to make your own decisions. We always taught you and Bill to think for yourselves. We're extremely proud of both our children."

Misty noticed dampness in her mother's eyes and took her hand. It was true. She and Billy inherited Dad's coloring, his sarcastic humor, and physical characteristics. Misty was small like her mother, but she had her father's blonde, youthful looks and brown eyes. Billy had been tall, like Dad, and just as handsome. He'd been studying forestry and climatology when the Twin Towers were attacked, and had immediately quit school and joined the Marines. The thought of terrorists viciously attacking the nation and killing thousands of innocent people turned him into a determined warrior.

Debbie's expression reflected a mixture of melancholy and happiness. "Do you remember Bill taking you everywhere with him? Even pick-up basketball games with his buddies?"

"He didn't care what anybody thought." Misty swiped her eyes. "I was his little sister. They could like it or lump it." Yes, her big brother carried her around on his shoulders, took her in his car, took her to movies, and took her when he hung out with his friends. He was impervious to teasing where she was concerned.

They sat silently for several minutes, reflecting on the past.

"Misty, I'm afraid you'll be alone all your life. Is there any chance you and Major Hawk could be developing a relationship? He seems such a strong, intelligent man. His daughter is lovely." Her mother's eyes searched hers.

"Mom. I'm not interested in Jack romantically. He's eleven years older than me and too old-school. From the first time I met him in Iraq, even though he never said anything, I could tell he disapproved of women in the military, especially on the front lines. It really miffed me. I was a good officer. I ran a tight operation. I did my job as good as any man." She sighed. "Anyway, even if I were, Ellen is a big complication. She's acting out, making Jack's life difficult ever since his wife walked out on them. He gave up the job he loved and retired early from the Marines, to be a full-time parent for her."

"She sounds like a foolish woman." Debbie pursed her lips and shook her head slowly. "To throw away a man like Jonathan Hawk and her young daughter."

"Mom, you don't even know him."

"I've always been good about judging people, young lady. You can't deny it. Remember Karolee?"

She couldn't deny it. Her mother had an uncanny way of evaluating people, even after a brief encounter. She'd warned her about the girl she'd become friendly with in high school. Misty had brushed off her mother's cautions. She'd trusted the girl who'd turned out to be a treacherous liar, working behind her back to keep her out of a campus social club Misty had wanted so badly to be accepted by. She'd never admitted that Mom had been right all along about the betraying little witch. She sighed, "Sheesh, Mom, this is different."

"Why is it different?" She held up her hand. "No, let me finish. It's time to clear the air between us. Ever since Bill was killed you've closed off part of yourself, built a protective shell around your heart. The only man you've dared to love is the one whose baby just died. It was safe to love him because you'd part company after the war. But instead you've stayed in touch, maintained a friendship with him, and helped him with his ongoing post-war struggles. Now, he's moved on, fallen in love and married, so it's still safe to love him because he's not yours to lose. Don't you see it?"

"First Hawk, now you." Yes, she'd no longer deny she loved Mac, but she'd never mistaken it for romantic, life-long love. Why did they both think she was using Mac to shield herself? She was well aware of her failures for the past dozen years to find someone she thought might possibly be her life partner.

It had nothing to do with Mac. She just hadn't found a man worth the investment in her energy, time and emotion. Maybe she'd never find that man. She told herself again, it had nothing to do with Mac.

"So, Major Hawk agrees with me?"

"Look at it this way, Mom. I live in San Diego. Jack lives in Van Nuys. Geographically, a relationship with him, if I even desired to have one, would be doomed from the get-go."

Her mother gave her a knowing look. "Whatever you say, honey."

Eager to change the subject, Misty asked, "Where's Dad? Did he play golf today?"

"Payne works at the food bank counseling center a couple of days a week. One of his golfing cronies talked him into it. He keeps a special eye on the few homeless veterans who come in now and then. He encourages them to clean up and seek a job. One soldier actually did and he visits your father once in a while." Debbie tapped her temple. "Payne doesn't know I noticed, but the suit the young man was wearing when I met him looked very familiar."

Misty laughed. "I had no idea Dad would be into something like working at a food bank."

"Neither did he, after working for thirty years in the human resources department of McCall, but he loves it." She cocked her head. "I just heard the garage door roll up." She picked up their empty glasses and headed inside. "Come and throw together a salad while I dish up the Crock Pot stew. I'll enjoy the three of us sitting down for a family dinner."

Yes, it would be nice. Now that her parents lived closer, she'd make a point of visiting more often. What else did she have to do on the weekends? Jack and Ellen only lived thirty minutes from here. Maybe she'd drop in on them once in a while, too.

Chapter Twelve

U.S. Customs Dog Training Facility, San Diego

MISTY DROPPED HER BAG ON THE DESK. "SHE WHAT!"

"She quit, Misty." Florine shrugged and raised her hands.

"Why didn't you call me?"

Florine cocked her head. "What were you going to do if I called you? Leave the funeral and rush back here? Relax, everything is fine."

Misty put her elbows on her desk and dropped her head on her clenched fists. She took a big breath then raised her eyes to her longest, most trusted employee. "You're right. Why'd she leave? Did she say?"

"Her boyfriend got accepted at Princeton and they moved to New Jersey right away so she could find another job. She was sorry and embarrassed. She wanted to call you, but I told her we'd manage for a few days until you got back."

"I don't know what I'd do without you, Florine. You're an angel in disguise."

"Some disguise. Are you ready for the other shoe to drop?"

"Crap!" Misty groaned and squeezed her eyes shut. "There's more?"

"Yup." Florine tapped an envelope in Misty's In Basket. "Everybody here got a letter like this one. Before you open it, I'll give you the skinny. The higher ups are closing this facility next month. They're moving the entire operation to Arizona. Your letter might be different, but I and some of the others are invited to relocate to Yuma with no downgrade in pay or in seniority. They cited the reason as 'budget cuts,' the standard reason that doesn't ever explain any details." Florine plopped in a chair across from Misty.

"Are you going?"

"To Yuma? Not a chance. I've lived in the best climate in the U.S. for twenty five years. I can't take the desert heat and my family is here. I'm going to take a long vacation then look for something else. I'm not sure I want to work full time any more. I'm no spring chicken."

Misty had never considered Florine's age. In fact, in any work-place, including the military, age had never been a factor. She'd always judged the people she worked with on what kind of person they were and how they did their jobs. She looked closely at Florine, guessed the woman to be in her early fifties. "You're too young to retire."

Florine laughed. "Thanks, but I'm twice your age and have six grandchildren. When am I allowed to retire?"

"Six grandchildren? How come I didn't know that?" She should have known. She should care more about the people she worked with. She cared, she just wasn't good at getting to know people on a personal level. The same was true in the military. She knew the Marines she'd served with a lot better now than she ever had when they were in tight quarters twenty-four-seven and depended on one another to stay alive.

Florine's eyebrows went up. "Who did you suppose my son's carload of kids belong to? Face it, you're all about getting the job done. You don't leave much time for chit chat outside of our work here. You're a tough but fair boss. We always knew where we stood with you. You don't run hot and cold and keep everybody on pins and needles." She grinned. "I'll miss you, young lady."

Misty leaned back in her chair and smiled. "I'll miss you too, Florine, and Carlos and Bill and the others. I better open that letter and see where I stand. Maybe they're planning to can my ass."

"Not if they share a brain in their collective, bureaucratic skulls." She got up and brushed at a rip on the knee of her jeans. "I gotta get to work. They want us to start shipping out the dogs next week. I never said this, but I'm planning to steal Biscuit. My grandkids have taken a real liking to the big clumsy cur."

"Take him today, before they ask for a full inventory. I'll tell them he flunked out." She waved Florine off and reached for the letter from headquarters.

* * *

Van Nuys Pilot Training Center

Jack Hawk drummed his fingers on the battered desk in his office at the flight school on Roscoe Blvd. He gazed vacantly at the general aviation airport runway. No more students were scheduled for the day. He scowled at the phone. The urge to call Beachy was powerful. His level-headed instincts telling him *no* were just as powerful. He was playing with fire. He grumbled a curse and grabbed the instrument. What the hell was he doing? He didn't know the phone number of her workplace. He'd been given a reprieve from a foolish snap decision. Relieved, he slammed the phone back in the cradle.

The phone rang. Happy for a distraction, he grabbed it. "Hawk here."

"Jack? It's Misty."

His heart thudded so hard he sucked in a breath. "Hey," he managed, and cleared his throat. "How's it going? Everything thumbs up?"

"No, um, I probably shouldn't have called you at work. Is this a bad time?"

He chuckled. "You're not going to believe this. I just had my hand on the phone to call you and thought better of it." His choice of words could've been better. "I mean…I wasn't sure it was a good idea to call you at work." He gritted his teeth and pounded a fist on his knee.

"Oh."

"Uh, you all right?" He should have said something like–I'm glad you called. He could have got that out without breaking his teeth. What was he, a pimply seventeen year-old? This little blond was bad news. He wanted to reach right through the phone and drag her into his lap and devour her. He wanted his hands all over her. It was time to fish or cut bait. "It's nice to hear your voice, Mis. When can I see you again?"

"You want to take me out? On a date?"

He rolled his eyes and rubbed a big hand across his bristly chin. "Is that so hard to imagine? Yes. I want to see you."

"I want to see you too, Jack. I probably shouldn't, but I do. My mother likes you."

"I like Debbie, too, but she's happily married." A hopeful smile pulled at his lips.

"God, you're such an ass! I meant Mom has good instincts and she thinks you're a good guy. Me? I'm not so sure. Why do you want to see me?"

"You first."

"I thought I'd put Mom's instincts to the test and prove her wrong."

A buzz of anticipation zinged his libido. "Living dangerously?"

"It's the only way I know. So why do *you* want to see *me*?"

Speaking of living dangerously, take the leap, man. All or nothing.

"You want the truth? I want to see you because I can still feel that kiss we shared in Dempsey's front yard, and before you deny it—you kissed me back, Beachy. I want to kiss you again, to talk to you, to see if we have anything to work with as far as becoming friends, maybe more. Shall I go on?"

His question was met with silence. "Mis? You there?" Maybe fate *had* intervened and saved him from himself.

"I'm here."

So much for help from fate.

"So?" He waited.

"This is hard, Jack."

"You think that was easy for me to admit? I'm older than you. I have a complicated life. I should know better, but so what? I want to be with you. It's that simple." He'd laid himself bare. It was up to her.

"I am interested in you, Jack. There's something pulling me. Your life is complicated, but whose isn't? Either there's something there or not. I'm *not* interested in a one night stand."

He'd love a one night stand if that's all he could get from her, but in truth he wanted more. "Shall I drive down there, or will you come up here?"

"I'm spending next weekend at my parents'. Could we get together then?"

Was she kidding? "I'll pick you up Saturday night at six. Wear a dress. I like to look at your legs. I'd like to see more, but I'll settle for legs for the time being." He'd already seen a lot more than her legs and liked what he'd seen.

"You're blunt. Most men talk in circles and use tired old pickup lines."

"I'm not most men. I'll pick you up at Payne's and Debbie's Saturday."

"No, Hawk!"

"Yes!"

"No...I mean, yes to Saturday, but I'll drive myself to your place. I have a meeting with Mary, the therapy dog woman, at the VA hospital at five. I'll come to you after."

"Good." He hung up. He wouldn't give her a moment to back out. Now he had to figure out what to do with Ellen on Saturday night. Maybe Beachy wasn't interested in a one night stand, but he'd be ready just in case.

He grabbed his keys and told other pilots lounging around a coffee pot telling bullshit stories he'd see them tomorrow. It was only Monday. He'd be a wreck by Saturday. Yes, he was that pimply seventeen year old, and it felt good. Damn good.

* * *

Heat sizzled in Misty's chest. Her stomach did a cha-cha. Jack Hawk knew how to light a fire. He scared her. She wasn't used to allowing a man to take charge. She was the master sergeant, she gave the orders. Now she felt like a green recruit quailing under the beetle-browed glare of a superior officer. Hawk had a way of putting her on edge, making her feel vulnerable. He threw down the challenge and walked away. Saturday was a long way off, but she needed that time to get her head straight. Time to get back her share of control.

Oh, yes, The Kiss. She ran a thumb along her bottom lip and swore she could still feel the fiery shock of Jack's mouth owning hers, his hands on her. She wanted his kiss and those big hands on her again. She hadn't known that level of anticipation since the last night she and Mac had together in Fallujah twelve years ago. That's how long it had been since she had real desire for a man to touch her. Take her. Own her. Was it too much of a risk? The timing of her job situation further complicated everything.

Her hands shook as she gripped the letter from her supervisor at Customs. She'd read it half a dozen times. They'd not only offered her an all-expenses-paid transfer, but a higher position, a bump up in salary, a path to advancement in the bureau. *Decisions, decisions, decisions.* Dad would be cool and level headed. He'd help her weigh the options, make the right decision. She was nuts to have called Jack. She wished she'd waited until she'd decided whether or not to move to Arizona.

Too late now.

Okay then—she'd go out with Hawk. See where it led. There was no use in lying to herself, she wanted to sleep with him. She was a big girl. He was a big boy. If they slept together and it was clear they had no chance of making anything else out of it; they could part company and no harm done. Who was she kidding? Her traitorous heart told her otherwise.

* * *

Friday evening she had dinner with her parents. She and her mother set dishes and silverware at the umbrella table on the patio while her dad tended steaks and corn on the cob, on the big shiny grill he loved. Misty had stopped at the Cheesecake Factory on the way and bought a Key Lime cheesecake. Dad had nearly swooned. His dramatic heart-clutching had summoned happy laughter from her and Mom. Sharing laughter with them was priceless.

After pushing his dessert plate away, Payne sighed and rubbed his stomach. "Oh, that cake was so good. Do you remember how Bill loved Debbie's Key Lime pie?"

Debbie and Misty nodded. Misty touched her mother's hand. "Billy told me once that all you had to do was bribe him with your pie, Mom, and he'd do anything you asked. He had a super sweet tooth, but he would never let me eat candy at the movies. Popcorn, that was it."

"You were his special project, honey. He was seven when we brought you home from the hospital. Anytime I couldn't find you in your playpen or crib, I knew you were with Bill."

"He was the best big brother in the world, except he scared away every boy who showed the slightest interest in me. He would have been a super dad if he hadn't been..." Misty's lips trembled. "I miss him so much."

"We all do." Dad pushed himself away from the table, stood behind her chair and kissed her head. "Did I ever share with you the last letter he wrote to us from Afghanistan? He told us what he missed the most about being away from home. His baby sister." He squeezed her shoulders. "Debbie and I came in second, but that was fine with us. Wasn't it, sweetheart?"

Misty covered her face with her hands and sobbed. Both her parents held her and cried with her. It tore her heart out, but she was glad they could finally talk about Billy. She suspected they'd avoided mentioning him to protect her. She'd talk about Billy every chance she got. He deserved to be kept alive in their hearts.

* * *

When she parked her car in the lot by Jack's apartment on Saturday night, she saw him pacing on the balcony. She stepped out of her Jeep and waved. Jack said something into his cell phone then hurried down the stairs and met her.

"You look sensational, Beachy." He swept her into a kiss. "We'll take my car." He took her arm and propelled her to his vehicle, opened the passenger door and held it for her. Before she had a chance to get in, he reached for her and kissed her again, this time pulling her tight against his torso.

When they came up for air, she pushed against him and stuttered, "Jack, are you crazy? What if Ellen sees us?"

"She and Cherry are already spying through the curtains in Cherry's apartment. Let's go before I lose all sense of reason, throw you over my shoulder and drag you cave man style up those stairs."

Misty straightened her red silk blouse and slid into the seat. "I'm having second thoughts about coming here, Jack."

He laughed, slammed her door and quickly went to the driver's side and jumped in. "I'm having second thoughts, too. Let's forget dinner and go straight to a motel."

"You are crazy! If you think I'm just going to fall into your…"

He silenced her with a hard kiss. "I'm beyond thinking." He fired up the engine. "Let's eat."

Misty snapped her seatbelt and grumped, "Good idea." She had to slow this down.

Fifteen minutes of sex charged silence later, he pulled under the valet parking canopy in front of a famous old steakhouse in Burbank. This didn't surprise her. Jack wasn't the kind of man who'd romance her at a pretentious French bistro. He was a steak and potatoes guy. The young valet had her door open before she'd had time to touch the handle. "Evening, miss," He ogled her legs when she turned to step out, offering his hand with a gallant flourish.

Jack took her arm and tossed the keys to the valet. As if to put a stamp of ownership on her, he dropped a light kiss on her lips. Fury burned every fiber of her body. Who in the hell did he think he was? He didn't own her and if he thought for one nanosecond that she was going to have dinner with him and then jump into his bed, he was totally whacked. "Stop it," she growled.

He grinned and pulled open the big mahogany door. "After you, sergeant."

She inched away from the hand on her lower back and stepped into the pitch-dark lobby. She couldn't see a damn thing. Why did they keep these old relics so poorly illuminated? A tall, shadowy figure approached. "Good Evening, Major Hawk. I have your table ready, sir. Please follow me."

Misty thought of grabbing the man's coattails to keep from stumbling. She only had one good eye in the dark. Jack stepped to her side and put his arm around her waist. This time she didn't resist. The last thing she wanted was to fall flat on her butt in the middle of the crowded bar.

The host led them to a nice table in the middle of the well-lit dining room. When he smiled and held out her chair she saw he was ancient. At least eighty. He nodded his head of fluffy white hair when she took her seat, shook out a massive, snowy napkin and dropped it in her lap. "Enjoy dinner, folks. Don will be your server this evening."

Misty mumbled a thank you and gave Hawk a hard stare. "How does he know who you are?"

"I was talking to him on the phone when you parked. I told him we were on our way and I was with a beautiful petite blond who'd be wearing a snotty expression. How could he miss?"

She snarled. Resolved to order the most outrageously expensive dish on the menu she reached for the wine list. Jack snatched it from her hand and perused it with a smug smile. Wrinkling her brow, she stared at him and realized he was cultivating a trim beard and mustache. He'd kissed her four times and she hadn't noticed. The whiskers on his chin were black and gray, but mostly gray. She hated to admit it, but he looked very, what was the word? Dashing.

"Good evening, folks. I'm Don." The waiter stepped to their table. Don's name badge identified him as Adonis Petrakis. He hummed approval when Jack pointed to a selection on the wine list. "I'll send the sommelier to you directly, sir."

When the sommelier arrived at their table looking more like a contender in UFC Fight Night than a wine expert, Misty dipped her head to mask a threatening grin.

Jack pointed to the selection on the menu.

The man tipped his head in approval and said, "That's a very nice choice sir, but if I may suggest?"

Jack nodded.

"We just got a case of Nouveau Beaujolais direct from our personal supplier in Burgundy this morning. It's not scheduled for general release for another few weeks. We only have three bottles left."

"Sounds great!" Jack tapped the table. "Bring one bottle and keep one of the other two aside, please." He handed the menu to the big bruiser and winked at Misty.

"Thanks for asking what I'd like before ordering, Hawk. You are beyond considerate."

"If you don't like the wine, we're through. I can't be with a woman with no appreciation for the finer things. He tapped her foot under the table. "Shame on you for always hiding those luscious legs. Definitely two of the finer things in this life."

"I don't know what to do with you, Jack. I have a feeling this will be our first and last date." She buried her nose in the menu. Everything looked good. She was starving.

"You've got a dangerous glint in your eyes, beautiful. Planning on taking me to the cleaners, are you?"

Before she had a chance to reply, the sommelier returned with a bottle of the limited release French wine. He showed Jack the label, waited for his nod of approval, and then whipped out his old-fashioned corkscrew and opened the bottle. In a silly ritual she never understood, he handed Jack the cork to sniff.

"Ah. Yes." Jack watched while the man poured a couple of sips into his glass. Jack tasted the wine. "Great, but before you fill my glass give my lady a taste. I always bow to her approval." He flashed a brief, evil grin her way.

Not in on the joke, the wine steward picked up her wineglass and poured a small amount. He set it in front of her and waited. For an instant she had the urge to toss it on Jack's white shirt as payback for his *my lady* comment, but instead took a very ladylike sip. She held the wonderful, warm red liquid in her mouth a moment and swallowed. It was the best wine she'd ever tasted. "Oh, yes, it's very good." No use denying it. She planned on enjoying a few glasses.

"Excellent, Madame. I was sure you'd approve." He filled their glasses and disappeared.

Jack raised his glass. "Here's to a great first date."

Misty pursed her lips. "I can always hope." They were off to a good start. Jack Hawk was fun to be with. He exasperated her, but he also tickled her sense of humor. She set down her half-full glass and he topped it off immediately. The wine began to flow soft and warm through her blood. Her thighs tingled. Without planning to, she smiled into Jack's compelling, unsettling gray eyes. "Don't think you can soften me up with alcohol, Hawk."

He flashed a speculative, sexy grin.

Several minutes, and half bottle of wine later, *Don* returned to take their supper order. His face registered surprise when she selected the fried calamari appetizer, a small Caesar side-salad followed by a bone-in New York steak with the Jack Daniels demi glaze and a loaded baked potato. Instead of her nerves killing her appetite, she was famished. This man would be impossible to dominate. Was she ready to take a risk with Jack Hawk?

* * *

Jack bit his cheek and smiled. Yes, the little sorceress was taking him to the cleaners. That was okay. He hadn't had such a strong physical reaction to a woman for too many years to count and he felt a decade younger in her company. He'd enjoy every second of it. He nearly fell from his chair when she lobbed a bomb, "Tell me about your wife, Jack." He hadn't seen that one coming.

Chapter Thirteen

"MY WIFE?" JACK TOOK A SWALLOW OF WINE. "YOU MEAN ELLEN'S mother?" He scrambled to shift his brain back in gear.

"Have you had more than one?"

Oh, how he would love to kiss that challenging, smug smile from her face. "Not yet."

"Why'd she leave you?"

"There are two answers to that question. Why she actually left me and why she claims she left me."

"Why don't we start with the first one?"

"Misty," he leaned close, "I didn't invite you to dinner to discuss my ex-wife."

She fixed those sizzling brown eyes on him. "I thought we agreed it would be a good idea to find out if we have anything to work with. How can we do that if I'm in the dark about your marriage? You seem to have no problem voicing your opinions about my ancient history with Mac."

He raised his palms in surrender. "You made your point."

The waiter arrived with her appetizer, apologized for interrupting and set it on front of her with two small plates and two forks. "I brought an extra plate for the gentleman if you wish to share." Not waiting for a reply, he smiled and left.

Jack wrinkled his nose. "I hate calamari. Dig in. Enjoy yourself."

She took a sizeable bite and closed her eyes. "Mmm. So good. You have no idea what you're missing."

He knew one thing he was missing—his previous mellow mood. She had a way of pissing him off with seemingly little effort. This was a bad idea. If he wasn't thinking with his dick instead of his brain, he'd find a way to shorten the evening and consider himself lucky to have dodged a bullet.

Christ on a crutch, what is it about her?

"Okay, chapter and verse." He sat back and watched her devour the disgusting squid. "I was madly, passionately in love and lust with Theresa for a year before she agreed to marry me. Finally, we got pregnant and since she didn't believe in abortion, she said 'yes.' At first, we got along great. I thought we were happy. After Ellen was born, she said she couldn't tolerate being a military wife. She asked me to retire and get a civilian job. Her father offered to hire me to work in his coat hanger factory. Me? Supervising the manufacture of coat hangers? I couldn't believe she was serious, but she was."

Misty snickered.

He snarled and bared his teeth.

"Theresa was pregnant again when I went back to the action. Right after I got my next leave she went into labor. Our son was stillborn. She wouldn't let me touch her, comfort her or sleep in the same bed. I gave her lots of space. My mother went through the same thing when I was a kid, so I understood the depth of her grief and shock. The marriage went cold. The only thing we had in common was our love for Ellen."

Beachy's face softened. She pushed away the nearly finished calamari. Don replaced it with the small Caesar salad. She sighed and lifted her fork.

"Are you sure you want to hear this?"

She nodded. "Uh huh."

"I re-deployed. I didn't find out for years, but every time I left she was screwing around, leaving Ellen with her nutso, gnat-brained mother or various babysitters. Her claim of not liking the military life was bogus. Every man she cheated with was military, most of them married. Finally, she fell in with a recently divorced guy, looking for love in the wrong place, I might add, who begged her to marry him. She met me at the front door when I got home, and two minutes later, she handed Ellen over and walked out with her packed suitcases."

"She sounds like a piece of work, Jack."

Her unexpected sympathy encouraged him. Some of the warm feeling returned and he took a swallow of wine just as their main courses were set on the table with a flourish. "No, Theresa's always been confused. She loves Ellen, but doesn't have a clue how to be a mother. She's re-married four times since then."

"I actually feel sorry for her. I hope she finds what she's looking for."

"I doubt she'd recognize it if she did." He smoothed the napkin on his knee and picked up his fork.

"I have a better understanding why Ellen's so mixed up and resentful. I can't imagine my mother abandoning me. What kid could?"

"You surprise me, Beachy. I detect a crack in your tough, self-possessed veneer."

"You don't think I have feelings?" She put down her knife and nailed him with a dark gaze. "I have feelings! I lost the one man in the world I loved above all others, Jack."

"Oh, Jesus, are you going to start singing the praises of Cluny McPherson again?"

"No! William Andrew Beachy, my big brother. Billy was an Army Ranger. He was killed in Iraq in 2003."

Jack put down his silverware and reached for her hand. "Oh, honey, I'm sorry."

"Billy got killed when he was barely twenty eight. He was working on his doctoral degree. My big brother was denied a life, Jack." Her eyelashes fluttered and a tear dropped on her cheek.

Misty sighed, and let him hold her hand. "I enlisted in the Marines three days later."

Jack got a clearer picture of her. He understood her single-minded defensiveness and dogged determination much better now. She put up a hard front to hide her vulnerability, her fear of risking involvement. He marveled at how hard she worked at being strong and in control. First her brother had been lost to her, and then McPherson. He doubted she and Cluny would ever have been successful as a couple.

They'd both been wounded and evacuated, ending their brief affair. Cluny McPherson was not the man for her. He was the man for her.

She'd stopped eating. "You want to wrap up that steak and take it home? We could go back to my place and talk, watch a movie, relax."

"I didn't mean to spoil the evening." Her rueful smile disappeared quickly. "Okay, so that's not completely true, but I'm fine now. How about having Sasquatch bring out that second bottle of wine?"

Jack laughed. "I won't tell him you said that. You might be able to take him, but I'd be no match for him in a fight." He caught Don's eye and raised a finger. The waiter was instantly at their table. "Would you have the sommelier bring our other bottle of wine?"

"With pleasure, sir. Is the dinner to your satisfaction?"

"Everything is wonderful, Adonis." Misty smiled when his cheeks reddened.

Jack waited until he was several feet away. "You are incorrigible, Beachy."

"One of the things you like about me?"

"Sadly, true." He rose, walked to her side of the table and kissed her on the lips. "Drink fast. I want to get you home where we can talk privately."

Her eyes sparkled dangerously. "Should I be worried?"

"Very."

* * *

Jack cornered Misty in his kitchen and trapped her with her back against the sink. His hands held firm on either side of her. "Quit playing games, Beachy."

"Games? You mean quit playing my games and switch to yours?" She deftly dodged his kiss, but couldn't get away from the bite on her neck. "What do you think you're doing, Hawk?"

"I'm going to kiss you whether you like it or not, so why not make it easy on both of us? Hold still, dammit!" This time he took her head and held her face in his hands. He kissed her, expecting her to struggle, but instead she gripped his torso and pulled him closer. His arousal was swift.

"You delicious witch." He ground out the words against her lips.

Misty's laugh was lost in his mouth. Her nails dug into his back and she matched his tongue thrust for thrust. Jack's knees shook as the sensual storm consumed his body. After a moment he softened his lips and lowered his hands to her hips. He bumped her forehead with his. "What's going on in your devious head?"

She raised her chin and ran her hands over his back and chest. "If I told you, you'd run for the hills, quaking with fear." Her voice took on a sexy, dangerous quality.

"Try me. Tell me what you want."

And that's what she did. Misty told him exactly what she wanted to do to him and what she expected from him in return. He'd never had a woman speak so frankly about sex. It was a massive turn-on. His ribs threatened to crack from the pounding they were taking from his heart. He prayed Ellen would stay at Cherry's overnight as planned, but he'd settle for a couple of hours with this dangerous woman, if that was all he got. He growled, actually growled, as he clamped his hands on her butt and prepared to carry her to his bedroom.

She gently bit his earlobe. "Are you scared yet?"

"Terrified." It wasn't far from the truth. He shoved open the bedroom door and tossed her onto his bed. Pushing her hands aside when she reached for the waistband on her skirt his eyes bored into her smoldering brown gaze. "Hands off. This is part of the deal, or did you forget already?"

"I didn't forget, but I get to go first. That was part of the deal too."

* * *

"You will as soon as I get you naked. I've imagined you naked, on your back, on my bed, for years." He smiled at the surprise in her hot chocolate gaze when he confessed. He undid the zipper on her skirt. Let his fingers drift low on her belly, then pushed them up and over her chest open-handed. "Jesus, Beachy." She wasn't wearing a bra under the dense silk blouse. His hands trembled as he touched her small, perfect breasts and let his thumbs drift gently over her. He slid them from under the soft fabric, unbuttoned it slowly and deliberately, never taking his eyes from hers.

Once he had all her clothes removed he sat back and took his time examining her with his eyes and hands, drinking in her petite perfection. When his fingers drifted down, she grabbed his hand.

"Don't touch." She deftly flipped him off her and onto his back. "My turn." Straddling his legs, she started at his scalp, titillating him with talented fingers. Moving down the sides of his ears and over his neck, her lips followed the trail of electric excitement left in the wake of her hands.

Jack feared he might go into sensory overload. "Christ almighty, you're killing me." He closed his eyes, sucked in air.

"Look at me, Hawk. Don't stop looking at me. That's part of the deal."

Helpless beneath her burning gaze, Jack nodded. This woman was deadly. Dangerous. He stared directly into her eyes, as she proceeded to do to him exactly what she'd laid out like a battle plan. He needed his brain examined if he thought he was a match for her.

"Better." In seconds she had all his clothes off. "Now, Jack, I'm going to do with you whatever I want." Her mouth moved across his chest and shoulders then down his quivering belly.

He groaned. "Use me. Abuse me." He was happy to oblige. He knew what was coming next because she'd spelled it out for him. He prayed he'd last through it. Right now he wasn't sure, and really didn't care. He was living every man's fantasy. A fantasy so intense he'd never imagined being lucky enough to star in his own spine-tingler.

It wasn't as if a woman had never satisfied him, but this had a different quality. Misty methodically, deliberately ravished him, and signaled she clearly enjoyed him, reveled in him. There was no hint of reluctance or obligation in her actions. Her pleasure in his body blew his mind.

She drowned his senses in her satisfied smile. "I enjoyed that. How about you?"

Jack reared up and dragged her face to his. He kissed her brutally, his hands fisted in her short hair. "Let's see how you like it." His mouth was on hers before she could respond. "I want an amendment to the deal."

"Oh, yeah?" She bit the inside of her cheeks and challenged him with her chin.

"Yeah." He tightened his grip on her hair. "I want you to tell me in filthy detail exactly what I'm doing right and why. Show me what turns you on. Deal?"

"Deal." She removed his hand from her hair. "But I'll show you exactly where I want you to touch me and what I expect you to do." She nudged him to her side.

As he watched her hands and read the changing expressions in her face and eyes, he knew this would be unlike any lesson he'd ever had. She narrated how each touch and sensation felt. His breath came in stops and starts.

She smiled and touched his cheek, stroked his lips. "Your turn, Hot Stick."

How in God's name was he going to last? There was no way he could slowly replicate what she'd accomplished on her own. He prayed he wouldn't disappoint, but he had to be honest. "I need to finish this quick, Beachy. I promise I'll take my time later, but right now I can't…"

In reply she stretched sensuously and cat-like, and purred, "Have at it, Marine."

"I think my heart just stopped." He put her small hand in the center of his chest. "Is it beating?"

"Um hum. For the moment."

* * *

Misty stroked Hawk's temples. The moon lit the gray in his hair giving it a silver gleam. She let her fingers drift through his short beard. Her eyes stared into his. "I truly appreciate how you got the moniker, Hot Stick." The muscles of her body were a stick of butter left too long in a warm kitchen.

Jack gently brushed his fingertips over her breast. "Thanks for the compliment, but that's not how I got it."

"Oh?" She wriggled closer to his side, laid her hand on his belly, let it drift downward. "Enlighten me." She grazed his shoulder with her teeth.

"Nope." He grabbed her hand, pulled it to his mouth and brushed her thumb with a soft kiss. "It's a top military secret. I don't know you well enough. You're pure femme fatale. For all I know you could be an enemy spy." He grinned and planted a savage kiss on her open mouth. Open because she was about to express pique over his remark. He rolled on top of her, pinning her down. "I'm willing to work on letting you break me down, little by little."

Misty returned his kiss, deep need for Jack to make love to her again all consuming. She loved everything about Hawk's solid mature *Dad Bod*. No gym created outsized pecs and abs. Every inch of him natural and sexy. Wrapping her legs around his slim hips, she moved beneath him, berating herself for all the time she'd spent resisting her attraction to him.

What a waste. We could have been doing this. She gripped his shoulders. "Again, Jack."

"You read my mind." He smothered her mouth with his and thrust his tongue deep.

She craved the taste of him, the feel of Major Jonathan Hawk, the warm scent of his skin. She was overwhelmed by his ability to send her senses soaring. She struggled to regain control, but gave it up.

The heck with it, let Jack have control. What are you afraid of?

Hawk lifted his head. "I could do this all night, you deadly blond spellbinder."

"God, I hope so." She took some of his chest hair between her teeth and pulled.

"Ow!" He gripped her jaw and challenged her with his eyes. "You want to play rough? Is that it?" His dilated pupils flashed dark and dangerous. He bared his teeth.

"Yes." Misty dug her nails into his shoulder blades. "Please."

Ten minutes later, sweaty, panting and exhausted, Jack dropped on top of her like a felled redwood. Nothing had ever left her feeling so good. She held him tight against her, tears leaking from her eyes. *He didn't hurt me. Where's this coming from?*

"You okay?" He groaned against her ear, gave up trying to shift when she held him tighter.

"Okay can't describe what I am." She ran her hands the length of his back from his shoulders to his butt and back again, memorizing every inch of Jack Hawk.

He tensed. "What was that?"

"What?"

"I heard something." He leapt from the bed, dragged on his pajama bottoms and grabbed the baseball bat next to his bedroom door. "Stay there. Don't move."

"Jack."

"Shhh." He stealthily opened the door and slipped into the hall.

* * *

"Ellen! What are you doing here?" He brandished the bat. "I could have brained you with this."

"I live here don't I?" She nailed him with her pale blue-gray stare.

"You told me you'd be at Cherry's all night. What happened? Why are you sneaking in here at this hour?

"I wasn't sneaking, Dad. I used my key." The look she gave him sent the hair on the back of his neck standing at attention. "Whose purse is that?" She pointed to the small bag Misty had dropped on the sofa.

"It belongs to a friend." He swallowed. "I have company."

"In your bedroom?" She crossed her arms and snarled, "Are you fucking somebody?"

The bat hit the floor. He moved so fast Ellen took a faltering step back. He grabbed her upper arms. "I don't ever want to hear that vulgar word come out your mouth again. Do you understand me?"

Her beautiful young face took on a stony set. Her eyes, genetic duplicates of his, challenged. "Well, were you?"

"I would never characterize it that way." The scorn of his fifteen year-old daughter was harsher than ejecting into an icy body of water wearing full gear.

"So explain it to me, Dad. What would you call it?"

"I don't have to explain myself to you, young lady." He turned at the sound of a door opening and footsteps moving down the hall.

Misty Beachy strode toward them, pulling on her jacket. "I'm leaving, Jack. Goodnight, Ellen." She grabbed her purse.

He put out a hand to stop her. "No, you don't have to…"

"Yes. I do." The front door snapped shut behind her.

"Her?" Ellen dared him to meet her eyes. "How long have you been *doing it*, with her?"

"Shut your potty mouth and stay right there." He poked a finger in her shoulder and followed Beachy out the door. He ran to the parking area just as her Jeep backed up.

"Misty, wait!" He slammed a hand on the hood of the Jeep then the driver's side window. "Open up." He bent to face her. A shock wave went through him when he saw tears dripping from her lower lashes. "Sweetheart, I'm sorry."

Instead of lowering her window she lifted her eyes to the rearview mirror and backed out, waving him off. He knocked on her window again.

Jack stood shirtless and barefoot on the cold concrete. His instinct was to run after her, but it would be fruitless. He had a bigger problem waiting inside. He raked his hair, took a deep breath and went back to the apartment.

Of course, Ellen wasn't where he'd ordered her to stay. He strode to her bedroom door and pounded it. "Open up."

"I hate you! Go away!"

"I said open up. For just once in your life, do as I say. Is that so impossible?" His demand was greeted by silence. He smacked the door with his open hand. "Ellen!"

She flung the door open, turned her back on him and flounced to her bed. An open suitcase on her bed tumbled with clothing and her dresser drawers hung open. She snatched a fistful of underwear and threw it at him. "I hate you!"

"Yeah, I get it. Where do you think you're going?" He dragged a pair of panties off his shoulder and tossed them back to her.

"I'm going to live with Mom. She said I could come anytime I wanted to."

"I'll bet. I noticed she didn't take you with her when she deserted me. Keep packing. I'll call and have her send you an airline ticket. I'm sure her latest husband will welcome you with open arms." He spun on his heel and left her standing there. For good measure he slammed the door.

Jack slumped against the wall feeling lower than dirt.

Chapter Fourteen

Her parents' home, after midnight

MISTY CAREFULLY OPENED THE LIVING ROOM DOOR. THE HOUSE was dark except for a small glow coming from the kitchen. Mom had probably left a light on for her. She went to turn it off and found her mother sipping from a mug and reading, her glasses propped on her small nose.

She looked up. "Hi, honey, did you have a nice dinner?"

"Please tell me you weren't waiting up for me, Mom. I'm not a teenager who violated curfew." She pulled out the chair across from her and sat down with a thud.

Debbie Beachy removed her glasses and scowled. "I happen to be reading a good book and I don't have a mandatory bedtime." She studied her daughter's face and removed her reading glasses. "Oh-oh. What's wrong?"

Misty put her arms on the table and dropped her head on them. She rolled her forehead from side to side and moaned. "Oh, hell, I am so screwed up. I'm totally screwed up. I'm a complete and utter screw-up."

"You are not!" Her mother fingered her hair. "Did he do something to upset you like this? I was sure he was a man to be trusted."

"He? You mean Hawk? No!" She wanted to confide in her mother, tell her everything but bit her tongue instead. She was still so rattled about what happened she probably wouldn't make any sense.

"Well, for goodness sake, what is it then? Did you wreck your car? Did you commit a felony? Did you stub your toe?" She gave her a gentle smack on the head. "You can talk to me you know. I'm your mother, but I'm also a woman who's gained some wisdom in the last fifty-eight years. Why are you so reluctant to confide in me?" The hurt in her mother's eyes jarred her. "You used to tell me everything."

Yes, she did and she missed those conversations. After Billy died she didn't burden her parents with any of her own petty crap. But now she needed to confide. She no longer had Mac to confide in. She sat up and took her mother's hand. "Mom, I love you so much. I should tell you more often. I don't know why you put up with me."

"Oh, cut the drama and tell me what the hell is going on!"

Her mother's response broke the ice, and Misty laughed. Happy tears sparkled in her eyes and she pulled her mom's hand close and kissed it. "I needed that, Mom."

"Yes, I should have said it sooner." She raised her eyebrows. "Shall we talk?" she said in a good Joan Rivers imitation. "Tell me about Major Hawk. What do you think of him after your date tonight? Consider me as your best girlfriend, or a therapist sworn to doctor patient confidentiality, not your mother."

"It's a complicated mess." She swallowed and looked directly at her mom. "Ellen came home unexpectedly. She was supposed to have a sleepover at her girlfriend's house. The girlfriend lives two apartments down the hall from them. Jack and I were in bed together. Poor Jack. I got out of there as fast as I could."

Debbie slapped a hand over her mouth to stifle a shocked giggle. "Oh, dear." She lowered her hand. "Sorry, that's not funny. She didn't actually come into his bedroom did she, when you were, uh, when you and Jack…"

"Mom! No!" Misty took a shaky breath. "Thank God. Jack heard the door open and thought it was an intruder. He pulled on some pants, grabbed a baseball bat and told me to stay put. Then I heard them talking. Ellen was pretty freaked. I got dressed and left. It was humiliating. Awful."

Debbie grimaced. "I would imagine so. Tell me, how did you and he end up, you know, in bed? You were very cool about the idea of going out with him. What changed?"

"I've been lying to you, but the worst part is I've been lying to myself. I'm so attracted to Jack. I don't want to be, but I am. He's the first man who's ever challenged me, dared me to take a risk. I'm no babe in the woods, but every relationship I've been in until now including, I admit it, Mac, has revolved around me being in safe territory. Never risking heartbreak if—when, it fell apart.

"Jack won't take any crap from me. I want to be with him, but his life is so complicated…with Ellen. She dislikes me, and I don't blame her. I haven't exactly been nice to her, treating her like she's a brat. She's vulnerable. She's scared. I'm way under water in knowing how to deal with her. I feel like I have to get out now before all of us get hurt. That's why I wanted to talk to Dad about weighing the options with my job. Maybe I should go ahead move to Arizona and put all this behind me."

"You can't run away, honey. It's impossible to avoid pain in this life by walling off your heart. You tried that with your brother. But just like then, it'll happen anyway, and if you don't have someone to love, someone who's willing to stick by you through rough times, it's even worse. I don't know what I would have done had I not had you and Payne when Bill was killed." She reached for her daughter's hand. "Please don't go to Arizona. I love having you near us."

That was the first time since Misty was in high school that her mother had tried to influence her in making a decision. "I need a job, Mom. I'm too old to live with my parents."

Her mother snorted. "Nonsense, I know you've socked away a good chunk of savings over the years. Your father manages your portfolio. Do you imagine he doesn't discuss it with me? You could go months without jumping into a job. As to living with your parents, you have a valid point. This is a small house. None of us would have much privacy. That doesn't mean we wouldn't welcome you for a time until you decided where to settle."

Misty yawned and pushed back her chair. "Tonight was exhausting. I've got to get some sleep and clear my mind so I can think."

"That good, huh?" Debbie grinned. "Don't deny it. It's clear from your girlish glow."

"Who are you? What did you do with my Mom?" She gave her mother a kiss and dragged her bare feet down the short hallway to the guest bedroom then turned around and came back. "Don't tell Dad. He imagines I'm a pure, uncorrupted virgin."

"Yes. It's a father's curse. Your secrets are safe with me. Now go away, I'm almost to the love scene. I'm going to read it then slip into bed with your father and wake him up."

"Ack! Mom!" Misty slammed her hands over her ears.

* * *

Jack checked his watch. It would be after three a.m. in Onslow Beach. Theresa's latest husband, a Navy SEAL, was temporarily stationed at Camp Le Jeune, no doubt training for some top secret mission to save the world from imminent destruction. She'd only been married to this guy for about four months. He couldn't understand why she kept getting married and divorced. She should just shack up with her latest for a while to see if it was going to work without going through all the cost and legal red tape. This was her fourth marriage since she left him five years ago.

He stared at the cell phone in his hand. *Screw it!* He punched in her number. It rang four times.

"Hel...?" Throat clearing. "Hello?"

"Theresa. Jack here." In the background a man's voice asked who the hell was calling in the middle of the night and it better goddamn well be an emergency.

She told the charmer to shut up. "What's wrong, Jack. Has something happened to Ellen?" The man asked who Ellen was. "My daughter, Harlan!"

"Theresa, Ellen wants to come and stay with you." His statement was met by silence. "Did you hear what I said?"

"Yes...um...I don't..." Mr. Personality told her to hang up and come back to bed. Theresa cleared her throat again. "She wants to come and stay with me?"

The jerk yelled, "I told you, no kids!"

She must have put her hand over the speaker because her response to Harlan was muffled. Then, "Jack, no. She can't, I…"

A red stain of fury flooded Jack's vision. "Fuck you, Theresa!" He disconnected, gritted his teeth, and smacked his phone against the hallway wall. It rang almost immediately. Theresa.

"You mother's on the phone, Ellen." He knocked on her door and opened it. His daughter, in a gloom as deep as the Grand Canyon, sat slumped on the floor next to her bed, head resting on her raised knees. He handed her the phone and walked out of her room, but stayed close enough to hear her end of the conversation, asking himself how much more hurt and disappointment his baby girl could shoulder. He'd tried very hard not to hate Theresa, but it was useless. He hated her. Tonight more than ever.

"Mom?" A long pause. "But, Mom…" A very long pause. "Um, yeah. Okay. Bye."

Jack waited in the hall. He wasn't sure what to do. Finally he walked back into her room and sat on the edge of her bed. Ellen dropped her head on his leg. They stayed like that for several minutes. He stroked her purple highlighted hair. She and Cherry had been experimenting as budding estheticians.

"Dad?"

"Yes, baby?"

"Do you think Mom loves me?"

Her question was a vise-grip on his heart. If the conversation with his ex-wife had taken place in person, someone would have had to hold him back to prevent him from strangling her and beating the snot out of the latest bastard husband.

"Yes. She loves you in her way."

"Her way sucks."

"Yep." He leaned close and kissed her on the head. "Let's get some sleep, okay? We'll talk in the morning. How about going to I-Hop? We'll stuff ourselves with carbs and sugar 'till we puke."

Ellen nodded. "I'm sorry, Dad. What I said about…*her*. I was not expecting you to be…with anybody. With a woman. In your bedroom. I don't hate her."

He pulled her into a hug. "I love you, sweetheart. You're number one, and you'll always be number one."

"But probably not number *only*." She blessed him with a melancholy smile. "Love you too, Daddy."

* * *

Wide awake, Misty crawled out of bed before sunrise. She pulled her sweater tight around her chest and hunched in a chair on her parents' patio waiting for the coffeemaker to do its thing. Fog on the rolling hills slowly burned off. It would be another hot, clear day. She'd slept like the dead in spite of her level of agitation last night. Her parents were still sleeping.

When the coffee was ready, she tiptoed to the front door and retrieved the Sunday paper then carried it back through the house to a wire bistro table overlooking her mother's small flower garden. A jasmine hedge at the side of the house threw off a suffocating sweetness in the early morning air. Misty went straight to the financial pages and checked the stats on the mutual funds and bonds she held in her IRA. *Thanks, Dad.*

"Good morning, honey." Payne Beachy had a suspiciously pleased expression on his face. It no doubt mirrored the one she must have worn after Jack… *No! Nope. Not going there.*

"Hi, Dad."

He took the other small chair. "Beautiful out here in the morning, isn't it?"

"Sure is." They sipped coffee quietly and watched the fragile morning light gradually transform details in the rugged Santa Monica mountains to the west, hiding the Pacific Ocean. They would have been able to see the ocean from here if the house sat at a higher elevation. She gazed at her tall, straight and handsome father. The muscles in his forearms were sexy and tanned. If he had any gray hair, it was difficult to detect because like her, he was blond. Dad was only a dozen years older than Hawk. Her parents were young, healthy, and full of life. Why was it so difficult, so hard to accept, that one's parents were fully human? How did children imagine they'd come into this world if not for their parents' sexuality? It was creepy, that's why.

"So." Her dad ran a hand over his thick hair and yawned. "Have you come to any decision about your job?" Unlike her mother, he'd never come right out and ask her not to move. He'd leave it up to her, even if it ended up hurting him.

"Not really." She folded the paper. "I'll fly to Yuma for the interview and see what I can learn about the new job. The timing is not good. I just locked myself into a condo lease for another year. I doubt the bureau would reimburse me for the loss if I took the Arizona job."

"Surely you can sublet it? There's always a shortage of rentals in the greater San Diego area."

"Sounds like you want me to go, Dad." She bit her cheek against a grin.

"You know better than that. I'm just offering options."

"The idea of being a long-distance landlord is not appealing. You volunteering to manage my condo for me?"

"Hell no, I gave up volunteering when I retired to play golf."

"That's not the way I hear it. The food bank? Job counseling for veterans?"

"I'll have to put a sock in Debbie's mouth."

The screen door slid open. Her mother walked out with the coffee pot, refilled their mugs, and set it on the small table. She pecked her husband's cheek. "I wouldn't advise trying that if I were you."

Before she had a chance to step away Dad grabbed her and pulled her into his lap. He gnawed on Mom's neck, and she squeaked like a blushing bride.

"Not in front of the children!" Misty demanded, but she really enjoyed the display of easy affection between them.

Dad winked. "Maybe you could get lost for a few minutes?"

"Gladly. You people are creeping me out." She grinned and made herself scarce. It was time to hit the shower, dress and get on with her plans for the day. She had a couple of things to take care of before she headed south.

After enjoying her Dad's traditional Sunday special, banana pecan pancakes and bacon, she told them she'd be back in a couple of hours, but wouldn't be staying for dinner. Her mother shooed her out, declaring she needed no help in the kitchen.

Misty backed out of their driveway and turned in the direction of Spring Grove. An idea had entered her head early this morning and it was time to find out if it would fly with Mac and Graciella.

When she turned into their driveway, Mac was lounging on his front porch with his big feet resting on the railing. Queen lay on the floor next to his chair.

She tapped her horn. He stood and waved, a smile of greeting on his beloved face. He stepped off the porch and met her at her car.

"Morning, Mac." She stepped into his arms. "I have something to talk to you and Graciella about." A familiar flood of affection for this man filled her from head to toe. "How are you doing, my friend?"

He tipped his head down to see her face better and she noticed deeper lines around his eyes and mouth. He'd lost weight, but he was a big man, and still young. "We're working on it, Mis." He took her hand as they climbed the few shallow steps and opened the screen door. "Baby! We have company."

Graciella, the tall golden skinned Brazilian wife of her best pal, strolled from the kitchen, as stunning as a Vogue model in a pair of shorts and one of Mac's shirts knotted at her hips. She smiled. "Misty, it's so nice to see you. It seems ages since we've had a nice visit." She embraced Misty, holding it a bit longer than usual.

Tears threatened, but Misty swallowed them back. "Where's Santos?"

"He's playing out back with Happy. He and that dog you gave him are inseparable, and the little mutt has been a godsend at this time." Come, let's sit in the living room and get comfortable. May I get you a cool drink?"

Skeptical when Mac had taken on a widow with a nine-year-old son, Misty now realized she'd been completely wrong. Graciella and Santos had invited Mac into *their* lives. They were the best thing to ever happen to him. The woman and her boy had helped him with their strength and unconditional love in ways she and his other friends could never have done. It was easy to understand the depths of Mac's love for them. They'd make it through the loss of their baby. Graciella would see to it.

"No thanks, nothing for me. I came to ask you a favor."

Mac and his wife exchanged a puzzled look and waited for her to explain.

"This might sound kind of goofy, but I hope you'll let me take Santos back to San Diego with me for a week." When they both reared back in surprise, she grinned. "I told you it would sound crazy, but here's the thing. The Customs Bureau is closing down my location and we're going to inventory and crate all the dogs for shipment to Arizona this coming week. We also have a lot of other things to do before we can close down. A couple of my people have already been transferred. I think it could be fun for Santos and he'd be a big help to me. I'll have him back by Friday, so he'll be home before the first day of school."

They appeared speechless. Misty fidgeted and held her breath. "Am I light years out of line?"

Half an hour later Santos loaded his backpack and a small soft-sided suitcase onto the backseat of Misty's Jeep. He returned to the porch and hugged his parents, and then gave Happy a good ear scratch. "Be a good boy, Happy. I promise not to bring home any competition."

Queen gave the boy a hard nudge, nearly knocking him on his bottom. They all laughed and Santos hugged the big Malinois around her powerful chest, his nose buried in her thick ruff.

Absent were admonitions to Santos to *be a good boy* or *don't give Misty any trouble.*

Mac ruffled Santos's hair and joked, "Go easy on the beer, sailor. Mom and I don't want to drive down there to bail your skinny butt out of the brig."

Wide-eyed, Santos pretended to be shocked. "Dad!"

Mac picked the boy up easily and enclosed him in a crushing hug.

"Have fun with your favorite Marine Lady, son." Graciella gave him a last kiss and waved them on their way.

They slid into the car and buckled their seatbelts. "I have to stop at my parents' house to pick up my stuff and make a phone call before we head out. I didn't tell your folks, but I've got a lot of fun things planned for us. The kennel work will only take about two days."

The child's grin was as wide and his brown cheeks would permit. "Yay! What?"

"I'll tell you on the way. It's a long drive to San Diego."

"Do you love my Dad?"

She nearly drove into the shallow ditch, but recovered quickly. Misty smiled and nodded. "I do. Everybody loves your Dad."

"I know." Santos didn't add anything else just sat silently and gazed out the window until she turned into her parents' driveway. "This is a big house."

"It's actually a triplex. See the garages? My mom and dad live on this end. You're the one who lives in a big house."

"How big is your house?" He unbuckled his seat belt.

"Smaller than this one, buddy. You'll be sleeping on a pullout this week."

"Mom says I could sleep on a bed of nails." He grinned and stepped out of the car.

Her dad opened the front door as she reached for the handle. "Well, hello. Who do we have here?"

Santos held out his hand. "I'm Santos McPherson." He tilted his head back. "You're taller than my dad. Mom says my Jefferson dad was taller. I hope I get tall. My girlfriend is taller than me and I'm a year older than her."

Payne Beachy opened the door wide and stepped aside. "What's your girlfriend's name?"

"Amber Dempsey. She's ten."

"Don't worry, young man. I was a runt until the seventh grade. Then I shot up like a weed." He closed the door. "Debbie, come and meet my new friend."

While her parents entertained Santos, or maybe the other way around, Misty went to the guest room and finished packing her clothes. She left her toothbrush, shampoo and a few other items in the bathroom for subsequent visits. Retrieving her purse and cell phone from the table in the entry, she returned to the bedroom, closed the door, and tapped Jack's number.

"Hawk."

"Jack, it's Misty."

"Where are you?"

She was a bit startled by his abruptness. "I'm leaving my parents' house in a few minutes and heading back to San Diego."

"I can't talk now. We have a situation here. I'll call you later."

"Is Ellen…is she…?"

"Not now." And just like that he's gone.

Chapter Fifteen

Driving south on the San Diego Freeway

"I'm getting kinda hungry," Santos said. "Are we almost there?"

The boy's question shook Misty from her reverie. Troubled by her curt conversation with Hawk, her imagination ran rampant. What could have happened? What did he mean by situation? She patted her jacket pocket, lifted her phone out and quickly glanced to make sure it was on.

"In about fifteen minutes I'm going to take you to Brazos. They make the best burritos on the planet." Misty grinned. "But we'll have to go to the back door."

His eyes huge, Santos repeated, "Why?"

"It's a bar. Your Dad told you to lay off the beer, remember?" Brazos was her favorite place to eat and she hoped Jake and Lupe would serve them takeout from the kitchen. "Every Marine, sailor and navy SEAL in this town loves to hang out at Jake's, but they're not so busy this early on Sunday."

"Did my dad ever go there?"

"Mac?" She checked her side mirrors and changed lanes. "As a matter of fact, the last time he came to visit me, your dad and I and Major Hawk went there for dinner."

"Did he eat a burrito?"

Misty laughed. "I don't recall. It was a long time ago." She remembered the weekend. It was the first time she'd been in Hawk's company since they'd served in Iraq. The three of them had attended the Camp Pendleton Warrior Dog Trials. It was before Mac and Graciella had married. Even then she'd felt the buzz of attraction to Jack Hawk, and her response to him made her edgy and unfriendly. She pulled into the parking lot of the bar and drove around to the back. "Here we are. Wait in the car and I'll order take out."

Misty tried the doorknob on the kitchen entrance and found it unlocked. She opened it and peeked inside. Cooks, busboys and dishwashers were hard at work. She spotted Jake's wife. "Lupé!"

"Meestie! Why you come in back door?" The rosy cheeked woman's eyebrows crunched together.

"I have a friend in the car and we wanted a to-go order. I can't bring him in because he's a minor."

"You bring him into kitchen. Sit over there." She pointed to a rough picnic table and benches used by employees to eat and take breaks. "I tell Jake you're here."

Misty opened the back door and motioned to Santos to join her. He stepped inside and she led him to the table in the corner of the room. A look of wonder covered his face when Jake approached them. He was a big man with red hair and whiskers and a perpetual scowl on his face.

"Who's your new boyfriend, Beachy?" He plopped his big paws on the table and leaned close to Santos for a good look. "What's your name, young man?"

Santos inched away. "Santos McPherson."

"You got I.D.?"

"Cut it out, Jake." Misty smacked Jake's arm. "Santos and I are old friends. He lives north of L.A. I talked his parents into letting me bring him down to help in the kennel this week."

"Well, any friend of this lady is a friend of mine." He extended his hand to Santos.

Misty tugged Jake's bar apron. "We're hungry. Bring us a couple of loaded pork burritos, please."

Santos bobbed his head. "Burritos are my most favorite thing." She'd heard this sweet boy make the same claim about almost anything he ate, and he had a whopper of an appetite.

"I'll have a Corona. Santos, do you want a root beer?" She winked at their inside joke.

"I think Dad would allow me to drink root beer." His smile could melt an iceberg.

"I think so, too." She tipped her head up to McKillan. "So, how about it Jake?"

"Coming right up." The big man went to the line of Mexican cooks and ordered their food, then pushed through the swinging doors leading to the bar. Lupe reentered in a minute and set their drinks in front of them.

Half an hour later Santos groaned and crossed his eyes. "That was the best thing I ever ate in my whole life. I'm stuffed up to here." He leveled a hand below his nose.

Lupe placed two small plates of flan on the table. Santos sat up straight and stared at it. "That looks just like Mama's special pudim. My most favorite thing." He picked up his spoon and eagerly attacked the caramelized milk pudding.

"Hey, bud. I thought you were stuffed."

He grinned through chipmunk cheeks and rolled his eyes.

Misty's phone vibrated and she snatched it from her pocket. A text from Jack: *Call u 11pm. Hawk.* Instead of reassuring her, the terse message increased her anxiety. She pushed her dessert away.

"Can I have that?" Santos wiped the back of his hand across his mouth.

"Have at it." *Where does he put it?*

* * *

By eleven Santos was fast asleep on her pull-out in the small living room and she paced her bedroom anticipating Jack's call. The phone finally buzzed at twenty after.

"Jack?"

"It's me, honey. Sorry it's so late."

"I've been worried sick. Is Ellen all right? What happened?" She heard a whoosh of frustrated breath on his end and waited for his answer.

"This afternoon Ellen and Cherry took an unauthorized joyride in Doris's car. They nabbed her keys while she was in the laundry room and hit the road. They didn't get a mile away when Cherry drove through a stop sign and T-boned a car in the intersection. The other car was a family of five heading home from church. They sustained multiple injuries. Ellen is okay, and Cherry is in the hospital with a fractured neck. What a goddamn mess."

"Oh, my God, Jack. Will everyone be okay?"

"Cherry is immobilized and hasn't regained consciousness. They won't know for several hours if she'll have any lingering paralysis. The family she slammed into has mostly broken bones and bruises. One of the kids is still under observation. Poor Doris is a basket case. I just left her at the hospital an hour ago. Ellen is grounded for life." The defeat and frustration in his voice cramped her heart.

"Jack, I don't know what to say except I'm relieved Ellen wasn't seriously hurt. I'm useless to you from here."

"I didn't expect you to do anything other than listen, honey." He sighed. "It's good to hear your voice. I gotta go. I'll keep you posted, okay?"

"Okay, Jack. Take care." Misty pressed the phone to her chest. How could his life get more problematic? If she'd entertained so much as a flicker of hope they could have any kind of ongoing relationship it was effectively doused by tonight's events.

She set her alarm for seven and opened her door a crack then went to bed. Images of Jack and replays of their verbal jousting looped endlessly in her head. When she smacked her hand to silence the alarm in the early morning she felt as though she'd been running uphill on a rocky mountain trail all night long.

She pulled one of Billy's threadbare T-shirts over her head. It fell to her knees. Dragging both hands through her hair she groaned and stumbled into her kitchen. Santos raised his curly head and rubbed his eyes. "Is it time to get up already?"

"Shut up." She squeezed her eyes closed against the bright sunlight streaming in over the sink, praying she wouldn't feel this crappy all day. "Sorry, I'm in a bad mood. Go back to sleep."

"Okay." He dropped his head on the pillow, rolled over, and snuggled under the blanket.

Good, she thought, a male who knows how to take orders. She patted his shoulder as she passed the bed. "Good man."

* * *

Misty placed Santos under Florine's supervision in the kennel. Florine assigned him to walk and feed the dogs. The day was warm, but not hot. When they broke for lunch he had sweat in his hair and on his face and a huge smile on his lips.

"Looks like Florine put you through your paces." The kid appeared reedy, but he was a strong and willing worker. Bringing him to San Diego with her was her small way of easing the pressure on Mac and Graciella to put on a happy face for their boy. Misty saw how they were suffering and she knew of no other way to help them.

Santos gulped down the icy lemonade and wiped his forehead with his elbow. "You gotta lot of great dogs here. Florine showed me pictures of the one she adopted for her grandchildren. He looks big and scary."

"Yeah, well that's where it ended. Biscuit is confused. He thinks he's a pussycat. Like Happy, all he wanted to do was play and run. He wasn't cut out to be a working dog. He'll make a good family pet." She handed him a large pastrami hero. "Hope you like these. Carlos went out with an order and just brought back a big bag of sandwiches for the crew."

"Oh, wow, yes. They're my most favorite."

Misty laughed and shook her head. No wonder Mac fell in love with this boy. He told her he'd fallen for Santos before he went head over heels for the boy's mother. They gave Mac something that she never could have, and they came along when he most needed them. The new Cluny McPherson family was rock solid. She hoped they'd have more children and wondered if their recent tragedy would dishearten them to the point where that was no longer a possibility.

"Hey, bud. I thought we'd go to a Padre's game on Wednesday night. Looks like they're going to make the division playoffs this year."

He bounced in his seat and raised a power fist. "Yes! I love baseball. Grampa takes me to a Dodgers game once in a while. He even drove me down to Anaheim to see the Angels once when they were playing an exhibition against the Padres. I got to see Tyson Ross pitch."

"I'm pretty sure he's starting on Wednesday. We'll get to the park early and pig out on hot dogs instead of a healthy dinner."

The boy grinned. "You're a bad influence on me, but I won't snitch."

"It's our dirty little secret."

"What are we going to do this afternoon with the dogs?"

"You and Yadi will record them by height, age and weight so we can bring in the proper sized kennels. The truck will be here tomorrow afternoon. We'll kiss them goodbye, load them up and after that, we're off for the rest of the week. You'll have to hang around while I do the final paperwork to close up the office, then we're free."

"I can help you with paperwork. I read all the time. I get all A's in school."

This kid is going to make great husband material one day.

"Fantastic! You can load the files in banker's boxes in alphabetical order. After they're closed and sealed, the UPS truck will pick them up around five."

They settled in to their lunch break. Misty glanced at her phone now and then wondering how it was going on Jack's end. He'd promised to call her with an update but that didn't prevent her thoughts returning to him like clockwork throughout her hectic day.

* * *

Jack enfolded Doris in his arms when she sobbed with relief at the doctor's prognosis. Cherry would suffer no long term damage to her neck and spine from her foolish joyride. His own huge wave of relief brought a welcome calmness. "Thank God, Doris." He rubbed his hand across her back and rested his cheek on her head.

Unable to speak, she nodded into his shoulder.

"How about we send both the girls to a Swiss convent high in the Alps where they'll keep them locked up until they're twenty one?"

His little joke relaxed her. She giggled and stepped back. "You've been a rock through this, Jack. I couldn't have done this on my own."

He ran his hands from her shoulders down her arms. "You'd have found the strength to handle it, Doris." He reached in his pocket for his phone. "I need to make a phone call. I won't be long." The resigned look on her face tugged at him. She was a lovely woman, but she had to know by now. There would never be anything but friendship between them.

She straightened and wiped her face with a tissue. "Sure. Why don't you go to the waiting room and tell Ellen to come on up. She must be sick with worry, down there by herself."

"Hopefully it will be a lesson to her on the consequences of stupid and dangerous behavior." He left the room and walked quickly to an outside door. He'd promised Misty he'd call. It was nearly five o'clock on Tuesday.

She answered on the first ring. "Hawk?"

"It's me, sweetheart. Cherry is going to be fine. We just talked to her doctor."

"What a relief! My mind has been going in circles all day. Thanks for letting me know. How did Ellen take the good news?"

"I haven't told her yet. She can stew a while longer. They could have killed someone, or themselves. She's going to have to face the fallout over this."

"What will you do?"

"I don't know yet. Up to now I've been concentrating on helping Doris cope. I called my sister to see if she could take Ellen for a few days. I've got to return to work. They've been patient about the last two days, but they have a business to run."

"Jack, I'm bringing Santos home in a few days. Would it be okay if I checked in with you?"

He scoffed. "You have to ask?" She was like a hot rock he had to toss from hand to hand so he wouldn't get burned. Somehow he would find the right formula, the right answer on how to deal with her, or at least, God willing, a clue. "I want to see you, Mis."

It took a few seconds for her to respond, but to his relief she said, "Me too, Jack."

"Good. I gotta sign off, give Ellen the news about Cherry, and figure out where to go from here." He clicked off and dropped the phone in his pocket. Staring into the late afternoon sky, he scrubbed his hands over his face and shook himself. "Okay, Hawk, man up."

He strolled to the waiting room. Ellen's head jerked up. The kid was terrified and confused, as she should be. At least she hadn't been the one driving. For that he was grateful, as he suspected she was also. It did little to offset the seriousness of what the girls had done.

"Daddy?" Her frightened eyes implored him.

He stood before her for several seconds before answering. Tears flowed down her cheeks. He put a hand on her shoulder. "Cherry is going to recover. She won't be paralyzed."

Sobs racked his daughter. His instinct was to reach for her, but he wasn't ready to forgive her yet. He'd let this lesson sink in, then they'd talk about it. "Doris would like you to come to Cherry's room. Don't stay long. We need to get home before my sister gets there."

Ellen stood and smeared the tears from her face. "Okay. I'll come right back." She hurried down the corridor to Intensive Care.

Jack flopped down on the plastic covered couch, dropped his head back against the wall and closed his eyes. Beachy's face loomed against his eyelids. Would his pursuit of her tighten the knots on his tangled relationship with Ellen? Knots he couldn't undo? Creating a healthy father-daughter bond was essential, but damn! He was entitled to a life, to some happiness. He'd have it. Damned if he wouldn't! He pounded a fist on his knee.

* * *

Santos looked up from the box he'd finished loading with files. "Who was that?"

"Major Hawk. Do you remember him?"

"Is he the man who Dad tricked at the 4th of July picnic? The one who got soaked with water balloons, and then chased you out of Amber's yard?"

"He's the one." She smiled and handed him the sealing tape. "His daughter was in a car wreck. I asked him to call me when he had news about her friend's injuries. She's going to be fine."

"That's good." He handled the big tape dispenser like a pro. "This is the last one."

"I hear the UPS truck now." She opened the door and signaled to the driver. "Once we get these boxes loaded, we're done."

"Yay! Let's go to the movies tonight, okay?"

"Sure. We can OD on popcorn and sodas to get our stomachs prepared for the ballgame tomorrow night."

"Maybe I'll break up with Amber and marry you instead, Sgt. Beachy."

"You're okay, kid."

The tall UPS driver arrived at the door, pushing a dolly. "Hey, beautiful." He held up his clipboard. "Looks like you've got quite a haul for me today."

"Yep. After this you'll have to find somebody else's heart to break. This facility is closed for the foreseeable future. I'm off to seek the yellow brick road." She'd been on Tony's route for the past five years. They'd had a lovely teasing relationship during that time. Completely hands-off, but deeply flirty. "I'll miss you, good lookin'."

"I doubt it." He laughed and pulled the dolly through the door. "You've left a trail of broken hearts from here to the moon and back. Let's get this loaded up and I'll buy a round at Brazos. Send you off in style."

She grinned and pointed to Santos. "Sorry. I already have a date."

Tony winked. "Watch out for this one, my man."

Santos's grin went from ear to ear. He was having a good time. "I can handle her."

Misty and Tony glanced at each other and broke into surprised laughter. Yes, it was no wonder Mac had fallen for this special kid. Her affection for him increased every minute.

Chapter Sixteen

McPherson Home, Spring Grove, Friday

MISTY AND SANTOS PULLED INTO THE DRIVEWAY. MAC AND Graciella waved and stepped off the front porch. Happy and Queen dashed for the car the moment Santos stepped out of the Jeep. They barked with joy and jumped, knocking him to the ground. The boy and the two dogs rolled around on the grass, celebrating their reunion.

Mac approached her door and grasped the handle. He wore a relaxed smile, almost like the old happy-go-lucky Mac she'd loved for a dozen years. He leaned in and kissed her cheek. "I see you both survived the week."

"Survived and thrived. He's a great kid. In fact, he's thinking of leaving Amber for me."

She laughed and waved to Graciella who stood enclosed in a tight hug from her son. Her smile was happy and relaxed too. Misty hoped she'd been partly responsible for this. If any family deserved happiness, it was this one.

"I'll make sure to disabuse him of that notion." Mac said, pulling Santos's bags from the back seat of the car.

"Some friend you are," Misty teased. "How was your week? You and Graciella seem in good spirits today." She closed the car door and strolled toward the house with him.

"Having a week to ourselves was just what we needed. It gave us a chance to talk freely without worrying about upsetting Santos. I even went back to work yesterday and today. It was good to see my crew, to catch up the schedule. Chief kept everything running like clockwork." He stopped and turned to face her. "We're going to try for another baby. We want to have a family together." His blue eyes warmed when he shared this news.

Misty stepped forward and embraced him. "Oh, Mac, that's wonderful." She turned her head when she heard Santos and Graciella laughing. He was telling her something about their botched attempt to learn windsurfing.

Mac gave her a squeeze. "He's all smiles. Thank you, Mis."

"Hey, I was tempted to kidnap him and run far away."

He dropped Santos's luggage on the front porch. "You want a beer?" he asked.

"Yes, but first I need to use the bathroom. That's a long drive."

"I'll get the beer and meet you out here. We can sit on the porch and talk a while."

"Okay, but not too long. I'm going to drop in on Hawk for a few minutes then head to my parent's house."

Mac wiggled his eyebrows. "Hawk, huh? I had a hunch you two might hit it off."

"Don't play matchmaker, Mac. You know what bad news I am for any man. If you have any feelings for Jack, you'll warn him off."

"Nope. Not me." He gestured to the door. "Get a move on so we have time to talk before you take off."

Refreshed, she joined them on the porch. Mac handed her the cold bottle and tipped his in salute to her. He cocked his head affectionately at Santos as he related another story about his week with her.

"Then we went to the San Diego Zoo to Bai Yun's birthday party. She's twenty-four and they gave her a big applesauce slushy for her birthday, and her presents were boxes of scented hay. She loved it and rubbed the hay all over her face. They had the whole zoo, around her enclosure, decorated for the party. Have you ever seen a giant panda up close? They're big!"

"It sounds like you had a great time," Graciella said. She reached across to Misty and squeezed her hand.

"It was a gazillion times better than summer camp! We even went to McKillan's for burritos and beer." Peering from the corner of his eye, he flashed a feisty grin at his dad.

"Hmm," Mac made a fierce face. "Beer? What brand? Bud Light?"

"IBC," Santos answered, then giggled.

Misty set her empty bottle on the table and stood. "I've got to bolt. My mother is expecting me for dinner in a couple of hours." She tweaked Santos's ear. "Don't get me in trouble, bud."

He jumped up and gave her a hug. "Are you coming to my birthday party? I'm gonna be twelve next month. Me and Amber have our party together because her birthday is only a few days from mine."

Somewhat startled at his affectionate hug and the blurted party news, Misty blinked. "Well, sure, I'd love to come. When…?"

Graciella stood and brushed dog hair off her jeans. "I'll have Mac send you a text message with the details when Marla and I have it ironed out. We'd love if you can join the fun."

Misty remembered something she'd wanted to ask. "Graciella, what did you ever do about your samba studio?"

"Didn't Cluny tell you? I sold it last year. After a while I might go in and give the occasional class, but I hung onto it because it was my security blanket for nine years." She cast an adoring look to her husband. "Now I have a much better security blanket."

They accompanied her to the car and stood arm in arm waving as she backed out. It dawned on her when she looked at Mac and his family; her feelings for him had somehow morphed into those of a loving sister. Mac had filled in the horrible void left by Billy's death. This was the first time she'd come to recognize it. She'd transferred her brotherly love for Billy to her trusted friend Cluny McPherson.

* * *

The sun was rapidly descending in the west by the time she got to Hawk's apartment. She parked and went to his door and pressed the bell, nervous about what may have transpired since she had last heard from him. She stood flabbergasted when a stunningly beautiful brunette opened the door and scowled at her.

"If you're one of Ellen's friends, you can't visit her. She's grounded."

Misty swallowed then tried to speak, "Oh, I'm not..."

Jack stepped up behind the woman. "She's here to see me, Theresa, not Ellen." He stepped around his ex-wife and embraced and kissed Misty. Head whirling, Misty heard Theresa's gasp as Jack stepped outside and closed the door in her face. He pulled her a couple of steps beyond the door and took her in his arms again.

Misty pushed away from him. "Don't you ever do that again, Jack Hawk!" Fury burned in her chest and she bit back the urge to slug him.

"Do what?" Hawk was clearly dumbfounded by her anger.

"Grab me like a caveman and kiss me in front of your ex-wife like I'm some kind of blonde trophy babe!" She shoved against him again.

"Is that what you think I was doing?" He huffed with frustration and stepped back. Hands on his hips he walked in a small circle then faced her again. "I was happy to see you and wanted to show you how glad I was you were finally here."

That stopped her for a moment. No, she hadn't considered it, especially after Theresa's assumption that she was one of Ellen's contemporaries. She'd jumped to conclusions, but wasn't ready to forgive him. "Why didn't you tell me your wife was here, and so... So beautiful?"

"Ex-wife! I know the real Theresa, and trust me, she's anything but beautiful. She's a self-centered, self-indulgent bitch."

"She thought I was Ellen's age. It was humiliating." Against her will, a warm blush rose in her chest and neck.

He squeezed his lips against a small smile. "This is the first time I ever knew a woman who got insulted because someone thought she was younger than her years. Could you explain that to me?"

Misty lowered her head and stared at her feet. Jack was right. She was quick to jump to conclusions with little information to support them. She sighed deeply and raised her eyes to meet his. "I'm glad to see you too, Jack. I hope things are settling down. I didn't come here to make more trouble for you."

"Can't help yourself though, can you?" He put his arms around her and pulled her tight against his chest. "Trouble or not, I need you, honey."

She cared about Jack and it frightened the daylights out of her. She took a deep breath. "I'm here, Jack." She lowered her forehead to his shoulder.

"God, you don't know how good that feels to hear you say it. My life is a mess right now, but having you by my side makes it so much easier." He tugged her toward his door. "Let's go in."

"No!" She dug in her feet. "Please don't ask me to face her. Can we go somewhere else to talk?"

"I'll go in and get my wallet and keys. We'll take a drive."

* * *

Jack went into the apartment and brushed past Theresa, still standing in the hallway, to the kitchen where he'd left his keys. He ignored her flustered and outraged expression. When he turned around to leave, she blocked him, arms folded against her chest.

"Are you sleeping with children now, Jack? No wonder Ellen is such a mixed up mess."

He stepped forward quickly, startling her. "She's no child and it's none of your goddamn business who I sleep with. Got that?" He shoved his face close to hers. "Don't you dare tell me I'm responsible for Ellen's state of mind."

She took a step back. Smugness faded from her face. "Where are you going?"

"That's also none of your goddamn business." He slammed past her and left the apartment.

He strode to Misty, took her hand and led her to the parking lot. "Let's get the hell away from here." He started the engine, backed out and accelerated at an alarming pace into the busy traffic, hands clutching the steering wheel so hard his knuckles were white.

Misty rested her hand on his forearm. "Jack. Take a breath."

The touch of her fingers on his skin was balm to his soul. He eased back on the accelerator and drew in a lungful of air. After a couple of minutes he chuckled. "I don't have the faintest idea where to go."

She pointed ahead. "Look, there's a coffee shop. Shall we get something to eat? I'll call my parents and tell them not to wait dinner for me."

"Are you okay with that?" He gave her a quick glance when he paused at the stop sign.

She tapped her phone. "Dad? I'm going to be later than I thought. No. Everything is fine, I just won't make dinner. I'll see you around eight or nine." She nodded. "Love you too." She put the cell back in her pocket. "We're good."

Jack entered the parking lot of the mini-mall. He found a spot in the far corner beneath some large trees. The second he turned off the engine he reached for her. "Can we neck like teenagers for a couple of minutes before we go in?"

Misty raised a neat blonde eyebrow. "Only a couple?"

* * *

The *couple* of minutes turned out to be more like twenty. They straightened their clothing and went inside the coffee shop. Jack led her to a small booth at the far end of the room and slid over so she could sit next to him.

She motioned for him to change sides. "I can't hear very well out of this ear, remember?" She tapped her right ear and smiled. "Thank you for not remembering my flaws."

Flaws? She was the closest thing to perfection Jack had ever encountered. He slid out, pecked her on the lips and moved across the table. When she sat beside him, he dropped an arm across her shoulder and squeezed. "You have no idea how good it is to see you. It's taken every bit of self-control I could muster since Theresa showed up yesterday."

"I'm not so sure you need me right now, Jack. You have enough on your plate."

Yes, Jack had enough on his plate, but Misty attracted him like a bird flying into the western sun at the close of day, whether or not it was in his best interest. Or Ellen's best interest. If he were honest with himself, her accusation that he'd shown off in front of his ex-wife hadn't been far from the truth. Theresa's anger at him for having a physical relationship with a much younger woman had a nasty ring of truth to it. He told himself he deserved some enjoyment, some fun. He wanted to spend time with Misty and if anyone else didn't like that they could go to hell.

"I do need you, honey. I'm just sorry you're right in the middle of it. We were on a promising path to knowing each other. Finding a way to trust. Don't get me wrong. You're a massive pain in the butt, but for some reason I can't fathom, it's another thing I love about you. Maybe this is going nowhere, but let's gives it a chance."

His use of the word *love* had manifested itself in her wounded facial expression. She couldn't mask it. He supposed she was as afraid of love as with another encounter with white hot shrapnel.

She sighed and rested her head on his shoulder. "Jack, I…"

The waitress set two glasses of water and two menus on the table. "Take your time folks. I'll check back in a minute."

"Whatever you were going to say when she interrupted us? Put it on the back burner for a while. Let's order dinner."

They perused the menus like it was an important major decision. The small place didn't have much to offer but ordinary small coffee shop fare. He'd made her uncomfortable, wary. He placed his hand on her knee and squeezed. He felt the tension in her leg ease. He leaned sideways and kissed her cheek. "Anything look good?"

Misty faced him. "You look good, Jack Hawk." Her eyes were unreadable.

"Wow." What was there to say? He smiled, kissed her nose and went back to the menu. "What looks good on the menu?"

She nodded and pressed her lips together. "I'll have the bacon cheeseburger, curly fries and a root beer float." She snapped the menu shut like a challenge then nearly sent him flying off the seat of the booth when she brushed her fingers lightly across the fly of his jeans.

"Jesus, Beachy!" He grabbed her hand. "Quit it."

She laughed and withdrew her hand. "That's for making me a nervous wreck every time I'm around you. Let's eat and have a serious talk afterward. I have some decisions to make."

What kind of decisions? Decisions about him? Still unnerved, he signaled the waitress. When she got to the table he ordered two bacon cheeseburgers, two orders of curly fries, two root beer floats and a bottle of root beer on the side.

"Did I tell you I took Santos to San Diego for a week? He helped me at work for a couple of days then we spent the rest of the week doing stuff his parents wouldn't approve of. We had a great time. I just dropped him off at home earlier today."

He shook his head. "You are an endless source of surprise. I never thought of you as the babysitter type."

"He's almost twelve. He doesn't need a babysitter anymore than I do. I really did need his help and I wanted to give Mac and Graciella a week alone. It did them good. I could see it in their faces when we got there."

He knew even less about this fascinating woman that he'd thought. He had so much more to learn. He wanted her but wasn't certain why. He asked himself if he just wanted a fling with Misty Beachy. Yes, he did, but what then? He'd ask her about her dreams and aspirations. Possibly, more importantly, what did he have to offer?

"Jack, I need to talk to you about something."

Had she been reading his mind? Had been asking herself the same questions? He answered in a voice he hoped didn't give away his disappointment. "Shoot."

"The Customs Bureau has closed the sniffer dog training facility in San Diego. They offered me a transfer and a promotion to join their location in Yuma. I'm not sure what I want to do."

Don't go. Don't go.

"Okay. When will you decide?" It was over. She was going. It was for the best. A cold fist closed on his heart.

"I'm flying out tomorrow afternoon. I owe them the interview. They've been good to me. I've enjoyed the work. What do you think about it? Since we got together, I'm more conflicted than ever."

He would not put pressure on her or try to influence her decision. His life was in turmoil. He asked himself again what he had to offer her. "I'm in no position to give advice about something as big as this, Mis." The brief flash of hurt in her eyes nearly undid him. "It goes without saying. I'd be sorry if you left California. Make the decision that's best for you."

"I haven't been very good with that in the past." She moved the straw up and down in the root beer float. It foamed over and she grabbed a handful of napkins and set the glass on top of them. "God, I'm a klutz."

"Don't talk bad about my girl." Her put his finger under her chin and turned her face in his direction. "You know how I feel about you."

"Do I?" She sighed and leaned against the back of the booth. "We can't catch any time together before I go because your ex-wife is in your apartment."

"And my eternally grounded teenage daughter." The hopelessness he felt rested in the pit of his stomach like a block of ice. "Ah, God."

They ate in silence for several minutes. He topped off her messy float with a couple of glugs of root beer. Finally, she said, "Jack, is it all right if I call you when I get there and after the interview?"

Instead of answering with words, he placed a gentle kiss on her incredible, delicious mouth. "I expect nothing less. Please call me anytime, day or night."

* * *

As they approached his apartment complex, he took her hand and kissed her knuckles. Her hands were rough and un-manicured. They were the hands of someone who worked hard and lacked vanity. He pulled into an empty guest parking spot next to her Jeep. It was almost beyond him to keep from saying *I love you* when he took her in his arms. He opted for a safer statement, "I'll miss you every minute you're gone, honey."

"I'll miss you too, Jack." She removed her car keys from her small purse and opened the passenger door. "I gotta go."

"I know." He waited until she started her car and backed out, then he drove across the lot to his assigned parking slot. Their relationship, if you could call it that, was a series of departures.

Wearily, he trudged up the stairs to his apartment dreading facing Theresa. He hoped she'd used the few hours he'd been gone to try and talk to their daughter. The place was quiet when he opened the door. There was a light on in the kitchen. He saw a piece of school notebook paper on the table. Ellen had written to tell him she and *Mom* had gone out to eat and might go to a movie.

Yes, Theresa, go sit in a darkened movie theatre with her. That way you won't have to talk to your daughter for two or three hours.

* * *

It was just after nine when Misty parked in front of her parent's condo. During the drive from Jack's apartment in into the darkening horizon of late summer from the San Fernando Valley, she realized how much she liked this part of the state. She'd driven across the Santa Susana Mountains that separated Los Angeles County from Ventura County on the Reagan Freeway. She sailed through Simi Valley where both Dwayne and Mac had their businesses. Spring Grove, where they resided, was tucked closer to the hills behind Simi, but every time she had occasion to go there to see the Dempseys or the McPhersons she appreciated the bucolic beauty of the area. Now that her Dad and Mom retired in Moorpark her attraction to the area had increased.

She considered the difference between here and Yuma. While all of southern California was technically a desert, the climate in Arizona would be drastically different. Who did she know there? Nobody other than a couple of her former employees who'd accepted transfers.

If she stayed in San Diego she'd have to start over again finding a job. Face it, she told herself, Jack was a lot closer to here than Yuma. Could she base such an important decision about her future on where Jack lived? She had strong feelings for Hawk, but doubted they'd be a couple any time soon. He had so much to resolve with his daughter and her mother. At least, Misty'd avoided all those kinds of personal problematic entanglements in her life so far.

She wouldn't make assumptions about what would come about if she stayed with the Customs Bureau. Perhaps they had other things to offer her. Maybe Yuma wouldn't be the place they'd reassign her. Sighing, she stepped out of her car and headed up the front walk, remembering something her grandmother had said to her so long ago about borrowing trouble.

Lights blazed from the front windows and she caught sight of her dad's shadow walking across the living room. Reassuring warmth slowly seeped through her shoulders and back.

Home.

Not the one she'd grown up in, but anywhere her mom and dad lived was home. Instead of using the key they'd given her, she used the door knocker for the sheer joy of seeing one of them open it and beam a loving smile to see her standing there.

Chapter Seventeen

Department of Homeland Security, U.S. Border Patrol Office, Yuma

MISTY STEPPED INTO THE GLARING SUNLIGHT ON AVENUE A IN downtown Yuma. She'd completed her second interview and had one more to go, this time for the Canine Program. She glanced at her watch. *Good.* Time for a quick lunch and a few phone calls before the car arrived to take her to the canine facility, the detection and apprehension training center. She'd call Hawk and let him know when she'd be back. Tiny beads of perspiration dampened her hairline. She hurried across the street and ducked into the small restaurant.

She sighed with relief at the cool blast of air and muted light. The sign at the podium invited customers to take a seat anywhere. She spotted a secluded table at the far end of the room. A sparkly young woman dressed in old-fashioned waitress garb, complete with peaked cap and ruffled apron over her pink dress, approached and set a tall glass of iced water on the table.

"Welcome to Ruffles. My name is Misty. I'll be serving you today."

Misty Beachy did a double-take and stared at the tall brunette. "What is your name?"

"Misty. My mother loves it. What can I say?" She grinned and placed a menu in front of her. "The name isn't heard often, but I don't mind. I like being different."

Misty Beachy shook her head and chuckled. "My name is Misty. What are the chances?"

"You're kidding me!" She smiled and squinted, "I don't believe you."

Misty took her Customs Bureau I.D. from her jacket pocket and handed it to her. "Honest to God."

The two Mistys grinned at each other. Beachy said, "I've actually grown to love it. A man I love calls me *Mis*. Kind of gives the name a double meaning."

The server tilted her head. "The morning fog and my light blue eyes sold the name to my parents. How about you?" Ignoring the fact she was an employee and not a customer, the brunette sat in the chair across from her.

"This is getting weird. Same for me. Except my eyes are brown." Beachy grimaced and shuddered comically.

"Do you live in Yuma?"

She shook her head. "No, I'm just in Arizona for a job interview. Customs closed down the facility where I worked in California."

"If you get the job and stay here we should get together." The brunette took an order pad from her pocket, tore out the last page and scribbled on it. "Here's my phone number." She stood. "Now I better get back to work before Mel has a cow. Are you ready to order?"

Beachy pocketed the note. "I'll have a BLT and iced tea." She handed the menu back. "Nice meeting my namesake." After the woman left she took out her phone and sent Jack a short text telling him she'd call around seven. She paused, her finger hovering over the screen, and then added an X and an O.

Later that afternoon she finished up with the briefing at the canine facility. Customs had fifteen hundred canine teams covering sixty one miles of border between Arizona and Mexico. The dogs were trained in detection and apprehension of illegals, as well as detection and seizure of controlled substances. The latter group not so different from what she'd been training the animals for at the now closed facility in San Diego. The dogs at this location were specially bred for these jobs and were mostly of the German shepherd variety. They reminded her of the war dogs she'd observed with their handlers in Iraq. Not all the puppies bred here qualified to enter the training. The ones who made it were magnificent and fearless.

Misty sighed with weariness. She stuffed the manuals and papers in her briefcase and waited for her return ride to the Comfort Inn. Almost too tired to eat, she ordered from the takeout menu on the desk in her room and showered while she waited. She checked her watch. It was six-thirty. Her pizza arrived and she plopped on the edge of the bed, opened the box and turned on the TV. She wanted to talk to Hawk but it was too early to call him.

Misty ate two pieces of the pizza and nursed her soft drink. She changed into a big baggy sleep shirt, leaned back against the head-board and picked up her phone.

Jack answered on the first ring. "Hi, hon. I've been sitting in my car outside the apartment. I didn't want Theresa breathing down my neck while we talked. How was the interview process?"

"Exhausting. I'll be home tomorrow."

"Have you made any decision about the job?" She detected a hesi-tant note of caution in his question.

"I have."

"Are you planning on letting me in on it?"

Misty pictured Hawk's face when he spoke the words. The two little lines above his nose would be squeezing together and he'd have his thumb and forefinger pressed to the bridge just below them. She marveled that she'd paid that much attention to his expressions, his moods. She clearly remembered his intense gray gaze. Hawk's eyes always held hers while she talked. He listened to her. He was interested in what she had to say. His laser-like scrutiny seemed to penetrate her brain. At first it had made her uneasy, but now more than anything she wished she was looking into those eyes.

"I'm not taking the job." She snatched the phone away from the side of her face when his loud, happy whoop nearly deafened her. "Ouch! That was my good ear, Hawk!"

He laughed. "Sorry, hon, I'm just so glad to hear it. When will you be home?"

"I have a flight out of here at one. Can you meet me at Burbank airport?" He didn't answer. "Jack?"

"Uh, yeah." He hesitated. "I can't. I have a full schedule of flight lessons tomorrow. Sorry."

Disappointment shot through her. "Oh. Um…Okay."

"I'll call you."

"Well…uh bye, then."

"Sweet dreams, baby doll." He clicked off.

She stared at the phone. He was happy she hadn't accepted the job, but didn't suggest any plans to meet. Her heart sank. Ellen, his job, his ex-wife. How would he make room for her?

* * *

The next morning at eleven she stepped out of the elevator and hurried toward the front desk then stopped dead in her tracks, mouth agape. Jack Hawk leaned casually with an elbow propped on the marble counter, his feet crossed at the ankles. His grin was huge and heart stopping. "Jack?"

"You already forgot what I look like? You've only been gone three days." He pulled her into his chest and whispered in her ear. "It seemed like three months." He kissed her soundly. Then again.

"But…what…how…"

He hugged her and chuckled. "I flew here. I'm a pilot. I fly airplanes."

"You flew here?" She repeated his statement like a trained bird. Her brain was mush.

"Did I whisper into the wrong ear?"

Misty relaxed against him and rested her head on his shoulder. "Damn you, Hawk! Why didn't you tell me you were coming? I thought I was having hallucinations." She pounded his chest then laughed.

"That's more like it. Now get checked out and we'll head to the airport. You can be my co-pilot on the way home. Maybe we'll stop at the No-tell Motel on the way."

She bit her cheek. "Check-out here isn't until one. We could…"

He took her arm, picked up her duffle bag and led her to the elevator bank. "Time's a wastin', blondie."

* * *

For the rest of Jack's life he'd remember the look on Misty's face when she spotted him waiting at the front desk. Caught completely off guard, her big brown eyes seemed to take up all the space on her youthful features. Just then, she didn't look old enough for a driver's license. No wonder Theresa mistook her for a friend of Ellen's.

She fumbled with her key card and couldn't get the door unlocked. He snatched it from her and turned it around. The second they were inside the room he slammed the door loud enough to wake the dead and lunged for her. She shrieked and jumped onto him, wrapping her legs around his waist. Her hands fisted in his hair, she kissed him fast and hard. He fell back against the door and slid down landing hard on his butt. He didn't even feel it because he was totally aroused and far too busy tugging at her clothes.

Misty shoved his leather flight jacket off his shoulders. "Wait. Stop." Holding up a hand, she stumbled to her feet and pulled her knitted blouse over her head. When it cleared her face she raised her eyebrows. "Why are you still sitting there?"

Jack laughed and got to his feet. He shoved his jacket to the floor and kicked off his shoes. They were naked in record time. Shrieking with giggles, she ran to the bed and he tumbled on after her. "God'a'mighty, what you do to me, Beachy."

"What do I do to you, Hot Stick? Tell me." She locked her heels behind his knees and dug her fingers into his waist.

Blood roared in his ears loud as the open canopy on a jet. "Let go. I have to get my wallet."

She raised her chin and brushed a hand along his cheek. "I wasn't planning to charge you."

"Funny." He pushed off the bed and picked his pants off the floor and dug out his wallet. Kneeling in front of her again, he said, "We're in business." He watched his hands while he unrolled the condom over his erection. "This is what you do to me. This and a whole lot more."

A tidal wave of passion drenched his senses when she grinned and crooked her finger.

Her eyes blazed hot enough to melt the skin from his bones. He sank into her warmth, drowning himself in her welcome, in her need that matched his own. She breathed his name over and over. "Jack." "Jack." "Oh, Jack."

"Stay with me, honey. Stay with me." The world disappeared leaving only the two of them. He was living his fantasy.

"Housekeeping!" A sharp rap on the door and Jack went still. The knob turned.

Misty gasped and yelled, "Don't come in! I'll be a few more minutes."

"Very sorry. Excuse me." The door snapped shut.

Jack dropped his head on the pillow next to Misty and broke into laughter. "I don't believe it. First Ellen, now the hotel maid." He rolled off her and groaned. "Why? Tell me why."

She snuggled next to him, stroking his chest and giggling. "I don't know, Hawk, but you have to admit it, it's funny."

He gave her a bitter glance from the side of his eye. "Says you." He wanted this complicated woman, but fate intervened to spoil his plans. He blew out a breath. "Let's get dressed and go to the airport. We need to make a Plan B." Jack shifted off the bed and retrieved his clothes. He proceeded to the bathroom and closed the door, a trail of curses in his wake.

* * *

Misty tapped Jack on the shoulder. "Jack, look, have you ever seen anything so spectacular?" They were chasing the sun toward the western horizon. Angled shafts of silver shot down from the clouds like the fingers of God. She sucked in a deep breath.

He answered her over the headset, "Almost every time I come up, honey. It's the perspective on the world that I love the most. Up here is my favorite place." He turned and reached for her. "Almost my favorite place."

She didn't miss the softness in his eyes when he squeezed her hand. Something was happening between them. Her chest filled with warmth at the same time her stomach fluttered with anxiety. She wouldn't kid herself. She wanted a relationship with this special man. She wanted to try at least. Jack Hawk was the main reason she turned down the job offer in Yuma. She had every incentive in the world to accept the promotion in rank and in pay, but those things were not as important to her as Jack. She had no idea how they'd manage. Her track record stank and he had a troubled teenager at home who needed a dad. She closed her eyes for an instant and made a silent prayer. *Please. Please.*

He'd said something she didn't hear. She tilted her head. "What?"

"I said I'll teach you how to fly." His grin gleamed with challenge. "You game?"

"You'll teach me to fly?" Her stomach clenched.

"Is there something wrong with your headset? Yes, that's what I said." He banked slightly north. "We'll be landing in about fifteen minutes."

"Already? It seems like we just took off." Her commercial flight to Yuma seemed much longer.

"It's a one hour flight. General aviation flights are quicker than commercial because we avoid the passenger check-in and security hassle. All that rigmarole makes it seem longer." Jack got on the radio and announced his approximate arrival at Van Nuys airport and requested instructions for landing. He ignored her while he checked his instruments and answered questions. He was all business in the cockpit of the small business jet. A serious professional pilot who'd saved the lives of the men in her unit in Iraq on more than one occasion.

She regarded him while he worked. Even when she'd been annoyed by what she perceived as a patronizing attitude years ago, she'd admired his ability and professionalism. He was sure of himself without being cocky or arrogant. It would take her a long time to plumb the depths of him. There was so much more to this man than she'd ever imagined. Why hadn't she seen him for who he was before now? Years wasted. She made up her mind to try very hard to find some kind of life with him in spite of obstacles. He was worth it. She hoped she was worthy of him.

Jack set the plane down on the runway as smooth as silk then taxied to the flight school hangars. He silently went through all the shut-down procedure like the highly trained and skilled former combat pilot was expected to do.

"How did you talk them into letting you borrow this plane for the day? Do you have something on the owner of the company?" She pulled off her headset and laughed. "I'm spoiled now."

"I only had to talk them into an unscheduled day off." He ran a hand across the controls. "This baby is all mine." The look on his face was pure pride.

"You own this plane?" He couldn't be serious.

"Why do you think I drive such an old clunker?" He led her from the cockpit and lowered the stairs in the door of the small passenger cabin. "I can't imagine not owning an aircraft. It's what I do."

"I have a lot to learn about you, Hot Stick. Now, we'll have to get in that old car of yours and drive to Burbank airport to retrieve my Jeep, otherwise I'm stranded."

"You're at my mercy, Beachy. I expect you to show the proper appreciation." He took her hand and they strolled into the office section of the training facility. Along the way he introduced her to some of his co-workers as *my friend, Misty.* A couple of the men were set back on their heels and didn't attempt to hide their speculation.

She leaned close to his ear and whispered. "Jack, are you showing me off again?"

"Damn right."

He let his hand drift below her waist as they went through his office door. Once they were alone he dropped the blinds on the window in the door and pulled her close. "Let's discuss the details of that appreciation."

"I'm all ears." She raised her chin; ready for the scorching kiss she knew was coming. He didn't disappoint. "Mmm. Want to fire up that jet of yours again and fly down to San Diego? My condo is empty. Nobody around to interrupt my show of appreciation."

He groaned. "Impossible today, but how about next week? Can you get away? I'll make it happen." He went to the desk and retrieved his car keys.

Arriving at Burbank airport parking structure, Jack took a ticket and drove her directly to her Jeep. He carried her luggage to her vehicle, kissed her and waited until she backed out then followed her through the exit. Misty glanced in her rearview mirror and waved goodbye. She turned west and headed to her parents' home. Tiredness seeped through her body now that the tension of the interview process and Jack's unexpected appearance slowly subsided.

Her dad was standing in the front yard when she pulled in. He turned off the hose and came to her car to carry her bags in. "How did it go, sweetheart?"

"It was intense and very tempting, but I didn't take the job. I've been thinking about changing careers. I need to make enough money to support myself, but I want to do something I really enjoy."

Payne Beachy opened the front door. "Around here or back in San Diego?"

"I'm going to try and find a place in this vicinity, and then do some serious planning, weigh my options."

Her dad winced. "Rents in this area are bruising. Be prepared to shell out plenty for even a small one bedroom or studio. The Valley probably has more affordable rents, but this area is much nicer, especially for a single woman."

"Hi, sweetie." Debbie called from the kitchen. "Are you hungry? I'll put on another piece of chicken and a potato for you."

"That would be great, Mom. Do I have time to take a quick shower?"

"Sure, you have plenty of time. We'll watch the Dodger's game while we're eating. They just threw out the first pitch." The sound of the refrigerator opening and pots rattling brought forth a warm memory of her childhood. She and Billy would be in a fierce competition with a video game, ignoring Mom's exhortations to wash up and set the table. They pushed it as far as they could every time. Finally she'd come out of the kitchen and rap them on the head with a wooden spoon to get their attention. Misty and her big brother would groan at the interruption and reluctantly turn off the game and drag themselves to do her bidding.

Mom had exercised so much patience with them, and that would always remain a mystery to her. Every day she became more aware of how fortunate she'd been in the parent lottery.

"I'll set the table when I'm done, Mom."

"Thanks, honey."

Misty's cell phone buzzed when she dropped her duffle on the bed. She didn't recognize the caller, but answered. "Beachy here."

"I'm calling about the sublet in San Diego."

Already? A spark of hope flashed in her chest. This was too good to be true.

"Oh, wow, I just put the ad online. I wasn't expecting anybody to call so soon. I'm up in Ventura County right now, so I can't show it to you, but I'll be back there on Thursday. How much of a hurry are you in?"

"We have a couple of weeks in our current place, but we need to be out by the end of the month." It was impossible to tell over the phone, but the woman sounded middle-aged. Misty preferred to rent to someone other than temporary military.

"Why are you moving?"

"The owner of our building is closing it for a major renovation from rental apartments to luxury condos. If my husband's job pans out we'll be looking to buy a house in a year or so. We want to take time to learn the area before we make that decision. We drove by the location of your rental and like the area. We're prepared to sign a one-year lease."

"What does your husband do?"

"He's a zookeeper at the San Diego Zoo. We moved here from Cincinnati. They recruited him for avian exhibit management. We really love the weather here."

"Um…is it just you and your husband?"

"No, we have our twelve-year-old grandson. Is that a problem? We don't have any pets."

Misty'd had a lot of fun with Santos recently. "I have no problems with kids or pets, but the place only has one bedroom."

"Yes, we know it'll be a tight squeeze, but we can manage."

Misty made arrangements to meet the couple at her condo on Friday afternoon. She hurried through her shower. She needed to talk to her dad about how to handle the sublet. What papers she'd need and how to do a background check. This was a development she hadn't foreseen happening so soon. Forget the idea of her San Diego condo as a secret love nest. She and Jack would have to find another way.

* * *

Bitterness filled Jack's mouth at the thought of having to confront Theresa at his apartment tonight. She'd told him she had to be back home by the time Harlan returned from his deployment and was planning to leave tomorrow. It wasn't soon enough as far as he was concerned. Instead of helping him to come to grips with Ellen, and what to do about her part in the joyride, Theresa had made the atmosphere shakier.

Ellen's face paled when Theresa showed up on their doorstep unannounced. She'd barely reconciled herself to her mother's apparent disinterest in her only to open her bedroom door and find her standing there, tragic and concerned then pulling her into a theatrical embrace and sobbing with relief she hadn't been injured in the wreck. No wonder the poor kid was so mixed up. He wondered how long it would take to reach some sort of normalcy after Theresa left. She no doubt thought she'd fulfilled her motherly duties and had no more responsibility where Ellen was concerned.

For the life of him, Jack couldn't remember what had attracted him to Theresa. He hated to admit he'd been no more than a lust-driven callow jet jockey who hadn't looked beyond her beauty and sexual attraction. If he'd been a civilian the marriage probably wouldn't have lasted as long as it had. He didn't know what made her tick. A little of Theresa went a long way. Like a comet that flared brilliantly and quickly burned itself out, Theresa wasn't there for the long haul. Maybe explaining why she'd been married so often.

On the steps approaching his apartment landing, he wondered if he wasn't the problem. Maybe it was Jack Hawk who was no good for the long haul. He opened the apartment door. Ellen sat alone in front of the TV. Apparently Theresa was not following through on his ban on TV, computer, and social media. What the hell was he going to do?

"Where's your mother?" he asked when Ellen grabbed the remote and switched off the sound. "You are not allowed to watch TV. Turn it off."

Ellen clicked off the power, scowled and crossed her arms over her chest. She didn't look at him. Her mouth set in an obstinate line. "It's off. Happy?"

He threw his jacket across the back of a chair and sat next to her. "Answer me, where's your mother?"

"She went shopping." Ellen held up a note.

"How long has she been gone?"

"I don't know. She wasn't here when I got home from school. What's the difference? I don't care if she's here or not." She cared. The pain in her eyes was a dead giveaway.

"You've been here by yourself all afternoon." It wasn't a question.

"You see anybody else around?" She was hurting and she wanted him to hurt right along with her.

He stood so suddenly, she flinched. "That does it." He strode down the hallway and barged into the room Theresa was using. He grabbed her suitcase and tossed it onto the daybed. He walked across the hall to the bathroom and nearly ran into Ellen.

"What are you doing, Dad?"

Jack picked up the wastebasket and swept Theresa's cosmetics into the empty cylinder. He carried it back to the room and dumped the contents into the suitcase. "I'm saving her the trouble of packing." He removed the few garments she'd hung in the closet and dropped them on top. He checked the drawers in the desk and scanned the book-shelves, finding a few pieces of lingerie and a nightgown and added them to the jumble in the case.

"But her flight isn't until tomorrow afternoon. Where will she sleep tonight?"

"Anywhere but here." He slammed the bag closed, snapped the locks and carried it to the living room where he dropped it next to the front door. "Ellen, sweetheart, go to your room and close the door. You have a book to finish for your report, do you not?"

"Yes, Dad, but what about...?"

He pointed down the hall. The fury on her young face could bring a train to a screeching halt. Ellen flounced to her room and slammed the door so hard a piece of caulk covering a recessed nail-head in the frame blew out, hit the opposite wall and bounced to the floor.

Chapter Eighteen

Misty's San Diego Condo

MISTY AND HER DAD, PAYNE, SHARED CHINESE TAKEOUT OVER her small kitchen table. The sub-lease papers had been signed and her dad told her to hold off depositing the check until he completed the background check. She'd contacted a few movers for estimates to have her furniture and household goods picked up and held in storage until she found a new place to live.

"I'm going to need several boxes for tomorrow for my clothes and computer, and what's left in the refrigerator. We'll take it to your place when we leave here."

"One box will take care of the fridge. There's not enough in there to keep a mouse healthy. You must eat out most of the time. Not good for the finances."

"Face it, Dad. I've never been any good in a kitchen. Santos did the cooking when he stayed with me last week. Maybe I'll hire him as my butler-cook and all-round man of the house."

"I daresay his parents have higher aspirations for him. I'd look somewhere else for your man of the house." He fished with his chopsticks for the last morsel of General Tso's Chicken in the bottom corner of the last take-out box. "I'm still hungry. Let's go get ice cream."

She grinned and nodded. "How about cupcakes?"

"How about both?" He gathered the cartons and dropped them into the wastebasket under the sink. "Any ideas on a new job?"

"I have an interview set up with a large pet food distributor as a sales rep. I'm also exploring openings at the no-kill shelter in Simi. I've been in touch with the owner. We have a meeting next week."

"I hope you find what you're looking for. A position that pays a good salary."

"I want to do something I really enjoy, even if it doesn't include a big enough paycheck to satisfy my financial advisor." She smiled and squeezed his hand to soften her statement.

Payne nodded. "Mmm."

The next afternoon they finished packing up the car and headed north. Her parents assured her they were more than happy to have her stay with them, but she would start looking for her own place right away. She'd searched the internet, and the rents in Simi, Moorpark and Thousand Oaks were shocking. She'd probably have to go over the pass through the Santa Susana Mountains and check the northwest San Fernando Valley. She needed to secure a job before deciding where to settle.

The Valley would be closer to Jack, but it would be more sensible to be close to her place of employment. Her dad told her the pro shop at his country club had a sign up for somebody to drive the ball-retriever-tractor at the driving range. She wrinkled her nose at the thought of driving around while duffers bounced golf balls off the cab's protective screen. Too much like being under enemy fire.

"It would at least fill in the gap and lessen the strain on your finances."

"I'll check it out tomorrow, Dad." She wasn't worried about her finances for now.

Her cell phone chirped. She glanced at the screen. "I'll step outside and take this call."

"Go ahead. I'll clean up the dinner debris."

Misty went onto the small patio and closed the slider. "Hi, Jack."

"Hi, hon. When are you coming back?"

The sound of his voice sent a thrill coursing through her. She was in uncharted waters, unsure of how to handle this developing relationship, because no denying it, that's what it was. "Dad and I hope to leave here late tomorrow. I'm certain that the lease will go through without a hitch."

"We'll have to find a different hideaway." He growled. "I miss you."

"I miss you. What are you up to?"

"I'm taking a break at the office before my student gets here."

She'd never known him to work in the evening. "Isn't it getting kind of late for a flight lesson?"

"This is a night landing exercise. Oh, dammit, the gal's here already. I gotta go, honey."

"Gal?" *Night landing?* Was that an unwelcome twinge of jealousy clogging her throat?

Jack emitted a low, sexy chuckle. "Oh, sorry. Gal isn't PC anymore, is it? I'm conducting a night landing exercise with a woman who's almost ready to qualify for her license. Call me when you get home. I want to plan a night landing with *my gal*." He clicked off.

She stared at the screen for a second, her fingers and toes tingling, and then shoved the phone in her pocket and opened the slider. Dad wasn't in the kitchen so she wandered into the living room. He'd settled on the couch and had turned on a Padre's game.

She sat next to him. "Change your mind about ice cream and cupcakes?"

"Hell no, let's go. I'm buying." Payne clicked off the controller and tossed it on the coffee table. He pulled on his lightweight jacket and held the front door open for her. "How's Major Hawk?"

She grinned and made a face at him.

* * *

Jack liked Betty Hall. "Have dinner with me." His evening was free because Ellen had begged him to let her accompany Doris to the hospital to visit Cherry.

Betty was tall, taller than Jack by about two inches. He had no doubt she could handle herself in any emergency, but she adopted an overly feminine demeanor. Maybe when she'd been a young girl her height was not as popular or desired as it was for young girls and women today. She spoke in what his dad would have labeled a Betty Boop voice. He'd been put off by it at first, but now that tiny voice coming from this Amazon was endearing.

Betty's husband was retired military. She had two grown sons and was a grandmother many times over. Last year during family Thanksgiving dinner she'd expressed a desire to take flying lessons. Her announcement had evoked raucous laughter from her sons and husband. Miffed, she'd never said another word about it. She signed up for lessons at the Van Nuys Airport location where Jack worked. Her original instructor had retired and Jack inherited several of his former students. Betty was his favorite.

"I'd love to." She grinned. "How about Yum Yum's Diner?"

"Sounds good. I'll meet you there."

Hawk arrived at the diner just as Betty's car entered the driveway. They walked inside the popular restaurant, picked up a couple of plastic-coated menus and took a table. "I'm having the cheeseburger and fries."

"Me too."

The waitress set glasses of water on the table and took their order.

"So, Betty, when are you planning on letting the Neanderthals in your family in on our secret rendezvous'?" He laughed. "Aren't they curious?"

Betty sniffed and shook her head. "They're so clueless. I told Will I was going to my book club tonight." She pursed her lips and raised an eyebrow. "I don't even belong to a book club."

He smiled. "So how are you planning on breaking the news?"

"I'll invite the three of them to take a flight-seeing excursion over the Lancaster poppy fields with me in early spring. I'll have all my qualification hours in by then. Then when we're onboard and the plane is buttoned up I'll walk to the cockpit and tell them to fasten their seatbelts. That ought to throw the fear of God into their misogynistic micro-souls."

Jack laughed out loud and nearly choked. He had no doubt Betty loved her husband and sons deeply, but he also knew she was tired of being dismissed like a child. "That'll show 'em." He raised his cup in salute.

"That means you'll have to be the one who taxis the plane to the boarding area and sits in the cockpit as my co-pilot."

"I'd be honored."

After they finished dinner he walked her to her car and said goodbye.

Ellen wasn't home when he got back to his apartment. Visiting hours lasted until nine, so he wasn't concerned. She was safely in Doris's care. He used the opportunity to exercise, shower, and relax while he waited. Around ten he heard her key in the lock.

"Daddy, I'm home. I've got great news! Where are you?"

"I'm here." Ellen seldom called him Daddy. He pulled on a T-shirt and left his bedroom. "What's your good news?"

"Cherry is coming home next week. Her mom's having a traction set-up delivered by the medical supply place tomorrow. If it's okay with you, I want to go over there after school to bring her books and homework so she doesn't get too far behind." She put on her best pleading expression.

Jack kissed her cheek. "Sure. But it's books and homework only. No internet socializing and no Facebook. Understood?"

She rolled her eyes. "I get it, Dad."

"Hey, I brought chocolate peanut-butter cake home from dinner tonight. It's a huge slab. I can't eat all of it."

"It'll be a sacrifice, but I'll help you finish it off." She paused. "Did you and Misty go to dinner?"

"No. It was Betty Hall, one of my students. I really enjoy her company."

"Oh, what about...?"

"What about Misty Beachy?" He put his arm around her shoulder and steered her to the kitchen. "Misty's firmly in the picture. Mrs. Hall is old enough to be your grandmother." He opened the refrigerator and took out the Styrofoam box and placed it on the counter. "Put a couple of plates and forks on the table, sweetheart. I'll bring a knife to cut this monster."

Ellen talked sweetly about her visit with Cherry and was careful to play nice with him. He'd made plain his disappointment and anger still lingering from the car escapade, and she'd worked hard to get back in his good graces, especially after Theresa left. He was sorry she'd had to experience the reality of her mother's detachment, but it was a lesson she needed to learn sooner rather than later.

"Dad?"

"Yeah?" He raised his eyebrows encouragingly.

"I'm glad Mom left. I'm glad she didn't ask me to go home with her. Why did you marry her? I mean…I can count. I was already on the way."

He put down his fork. "I was in love with her. We were never well suited to each other but too immature to see it. I was absent a lot and didn't pay attention to her signs of unhappiness. I'm just as responsible for the failure of the marriage as her. Neither the marriage nor the breakup had anything to do with you. Nothing. Do you understand that?"

"I'm trying." She paused then asked, "Do you ever wish I wasn't born?" The pain in her question was a knife in his heart.

"Oh, sweetheart, no! Never." He reached across the table and caressed her cheek. "You're the best thing that ever happened to me— to me or Theresa. She hasn't realized it yet, but she will someday."

Ellen's gaze dropped to her plate. She made a small nod. "Good cake, Dad."

"Yes." He withdrew his hand and picked up his fork. "Finish up. It's late and tomorrow is a school day."

After Ellen went to her room and Jack loaded and started the dishwasher, he turned off the lights and locked up. In his room he stretched out on his back with his hands linked behind his neck. He was torn. His love and concern for his daughter and his powerful desire to have Misty pulled him in opposite ways.

Jack was forty-three, but still young and healthy. Ellen would be on her own or in college in about three years. Family history said he had a long life ahead of him. He didn't want to live that life alone. He wanted a woman at his side, in his bed, in his heart. He wanted the woman to be Misty Beachy. Was it possible, or was he kidding himself once again?

On the dresser, his phone dinged. He jumped up to grab it. He'd turned down the ring volume, but didn't want Ellen to wonder who'd call him this late. His heart stuttered when he saw caller I.D. *Misty.*

"Hey."

"Jack, I know it's late, but can I come over? Dad and I got back a couple of hours ago. I have things I want to talk to you about, and I know I'll never be able to sleep until I do."

This was tricky. He hesitated.

"Never mind. I shouldn't have called this late."

"No, honey, I want you to come, but I have to tell Ellen first. I need to make sure she's okay with it. I'm not going to sneak behind her back. I don't want that kind of relationship with you." His stomach in knots, he hoped she'd understand what he was trying to say. "Are you on board with me?"

"Jack, it's so awkward. I'm helpless when it comes to a girl her age. I want her to like me, but I don't know how to go about it."

"I'll put down the phone and go talk to her."

"If she doesn't want me to come we'll abide by her wishes. I hate being sneaky, too."

Jack took a deep breath and walked across the hall to Ellen's bedroom. The light was still on. He tapped on her door. "Ellen? It's Dad. Can I come in?"

He heard her giggle. "I know it's you, Dad."

He pushed the door open and stuck his head in. He grinned. "Yeah, who else would it be?"

She stuck a bookmark between the pages of the book she was reading and laid it on her lap. "Is something wrong?"

"Do you mind if Misty comes here for a while?"

She glanced at her clock. "It's after ten. Is everything okay?"

"Yes. She wants to talk to me, but won't show up if you don't want her to."

"Dad." She rolled her eyes. "It's okay with me if you have a girl-friend, but I never expected to walk in and find you…you know."

"That's exactly why I'm asking you now. We want to be in the open about it."

Her eyes got big. "Is she going to spend the night?"

The uncertainty on her face made him smile. "She's not spending the night. We want to talk. In the living room."

Ellen shrugged. "I don't care if she stays. She's okay, I guess. I just don't like feeling like an intruder in our home. You know? Just let me know when she's going to be here. I'm cool with it."

"Okay, thanks." He winked when she rolled her eyes again. "Goodnight, sweetheart." He closed the door and returned to his room.

"You still there, honey?"

"I'm here."

"Ellen is *cool with it*. I'll be waiting."

"I'm on my way."

Jack got dressed and straightened up the living room. He had to lay his cards on the table and quit playing guessing games with her. Either she'd stay or she wouldn't. He'd prepare himself for either outcome.

He looked at his watch for the hundredth time, and stepped outside onto the balcony. He leaned with his forearms on the railing, willing her car to turn into the lot.

In answer to his wish, she drove in and she parked. Jack hurried down the stairs to meet her. His heart bounced when she spotted him then smiled and waved. He couldn't wait another second and closed the distance between them.

"Jack, I..."

He cut her off with a hard kiss. "Shush. Let me hold you for a minute." He dipped his head to kiss her again, and she was smiling. Her arms went around his back. His next kiss was soft and lingering. He sighed when she pressed herself against him.

She pulled back and spoke an inch from his lips. "I know it's out of the question tonight, but I want to sleep with you, Hawk. So much." Her hands drifted down his back to his bottom. "What are we going to do?"

He groaned with frustration as his body responded to her touch and her words. "Between us we should be smart enough to figure something out." He placed his hands on her cheeks and gazed deep into her eyes. "Let's head upstairs. They've got security cameras on the parking lot and front of the building now. I don't want to star in my own porn flick."

"Wait, Jack. I have to ask you something first." There was a note of urgency in her statement.

Jack had a sinking feeling. "What?"

"Is there an us?"

"An us?"

"Yes. A you and me. I want there to be an us, Jack."

He pulled her into a crushing hug. "I hope the cameras are all aimed at *us.*" He kissed her. "This is us, Mis. I want that, too." He let out a deep breath and held her when she rested her head on his shoulder and shivered.

"Good." She relaxed against him.

"Can we go up now?" He held her chin and smiled into her pixie face. It was hard to wrap his mind around the fact that this deceptively small woman possessed the soul of a combat hardened Marine.

She gripped his hand and followed him, but hesitated at his front door. "I'm afraid, Jack. Afraid I'll mess this up. I…"

Shaking his head, he ran a finger down her flushed cheek and pressed it to her lips. "Shhh."

Chapter Nineteen

Jack's apartment, next morning

ELLEN SHUFFLED INTO THE KITCHEN. SHE STOPPED SHORT WHEN she spotted Misty at the kitchen table. "Oh!"

Misty set down the paper. "Sorry. I didn't mean to startle you. You always get up this early?"

Ellen frowned. "Why are you here?" The girl's sleep-tousled hair resembled a fright wig. "Dad told me you weren't staying here last night? Is he still sleeping?"

"No. He left in the middle of the night because of an emergency at the flight training center." Misty looked at her watch. "About three hours ago. He asked me to stay so you wouldn't wake up and find him gone." Misty went to the kitchen counter and lifted the coffee pot. "Do you want some?"

Ellen smoothed down her bed head. She took two mugs from the cupboard and set them on the sink next to the pot. "I can't stand it without half and half. Don't pour mine until I check." She grumbled and closed the refrigerator door. "Never mind. What happened at the flight school?"

"From what I overheard, it sounds like a botched landing on the commercial runway caused a fire. The owner of the flight school called everybody in to help move their aircraft parked nearby. Jack was out of here in five minutes. I hoped he'd call by now."

Ellen plopped into an empty chair. "Oh, man, if anything happens to Dad's planes I don't want to be around when he gets home."

"Planes? He has more than one?"

Ellen nodded with a *Duh!* expression on her face. "He has the Hawker jet, the Robinson two-man helicopter, and the Cessna 150 he uses for lessons."

My god! The man must be in hock to the bank till the end of time! Misty couldn't fathom how a retired military pilot could afford to own three aircraft. She'd been surprised when Jack informed her owned the small commercial jet he'd used to fly her home from Yuma.

"Wow! Three airplanes." She gave Ellen a wide-eyed shrug.

"You didn't know? He loves those planes so much I thought for sure he'd have shown them to you by now." Her eyes swept the kitchen like she was searching for something. "I'm hungry."

Here was an opening. "I have an idea. I've got an appointment with the therapy dog woman at the VA Hospital in about two hours. You like dogs. I bet you'd enjoy meeting her dog and watching her work. I'll take you out to breakfast and we'll head to the hospital from there."

Misty could sense conflicting thoughts flying through the girl's head. Ellen stared at her. "Um…therapy dog? The hospital?"

"Yes. I met her when I went there for my last appointment with the audiologist. I've been toying with the idea of learning how to train dogs for that kind of work. Not as a job, as a hobby."

"You live in San Diego, don't you?"

"Not any more. The facility where I worked closed down and Customs moved the operation to Yuma. I went there to interview for a job and see if I wanted to move. I didn't."

Ellen reared back and gave her a wary look. "You're not going to move in with…"

"What? No! I'm staying with my parents in Moorpark until I find my own place. I came here last night to talk to Jack about the job I'm considering and where I might rent a place." That wasn't the whole truth, but she didn't need to explain to Jack's daughter how much she cared for her dad. That was way down the road and Misty had a lot of work ahead of her. For starters, she had to make friends, or at least reach an understanding with Ellen.

Misty raised her brows. "So, do you think you'd like to go?" She tried for a friendly and encouraging smile.

"I don't need a babysitter. I can stay by myself until Dad gets home." The sulky face again.

"I just thought maybe you'd enjoy it." *Phew. I have my work cut out for me with this girl.* "Leave Jack a text and come with me." She held up the phone sitting next to her coffee cup.

As if she was doing Misty the biggest favor in the world, Ellen shrugged and said, "I guess that would be okay."

"Good. I'll call Mary and re-confirm while you get dressed." She picked up her phone and scrolled down until she found Mary's number. "I'll let her know I'm bringing you."

"Whatever." Ellen shrugged and shuffled out of the room.

That kid is going to have rotator cuff syndrome with all her shrugging.

* * *

Misty pulled into the parking lot at the VA Hospital.

Ellen turned to stare. "You said we were going to get breakfast first."

"There's a good canteen in the hospital. If you know someplace else you'd like to go, it's okay with me."

"What do they serve here? MRE's and other junk?"

Misty sighed inwardly. Jack's daughter was a bigger challenge than the one she'd had with Joey Hamilton in Iraq. Joey was a sweet kid, but he had an alcohol problem and the Marines in the unit gave him the name Boozy. It had started with the Dear John letter from his girlfriend. As Master Sergeant of the unit, Misty worked hard to keep him off the sauce and out of the brig. They couldn't risk him going outside the wire with a snoot full. He'd be a danger to himself and the other guys. Looking back on it after all these years, she thought keeping Hamilton on the straight and narrow had been easier for her than this snarly teenager.

"They serve regular food. It's like an enhanced Starbucks." Her hands gripped the steering wheel. She eased up when she saw her knuckles were white. There was no way she was going to let this fifteen-year-old get the better of her. "Come on inside. We'll go have a look, and if you don't like it, we'll find another place."

Instead of answering, Ellen opened the passenger door and stepped out of the Jeep. Misty took a calming breath and followed her to the main entrance of the huge facility.

They found the canteen, and Ellen took her time looking around. Her decision was made when the cute young barista grinned at Ellen and asked, "What'll you have, gorgeous?"

Ellen grinned at him and pointed to the breakfast menu on the wall behind him. "I'll have the egg and bacon burrito, a medium coffee and one of those blueberry scones, please."

Misty felt ancient when the young guy turned to her and asked, "And for you, ma'am?" She placed her order and he said, "Take a seat anywhere. I'll bring it to you."

Ellen smiled coyly and tilted her pretty head in a provocative manner. "Thank you, David. I'm Ellen."

He winked. "Nice to meet you."

Misty gritted her teeth, paid the check and snatched several napkins, a few individual creamers and took a corner table. Ellen followed her and sat down, but didn't take her eyes off the young man.

"He's too old for you, Ellen."

"There's nothing wrong with a little harmless flirting. Or are you too old to remember back that far?"

"Ellen. Look. I'm no good with girly-girl small talk. When I was growing up I hung out with my big brother and his pals, and then when I joined the Marines I was surrounded by men again. I never had girlfriends who flirted, so no, I don't remember flirting. What have I done to make you so hostile toward me?" She shook her head and sighed. "I'm no threat to you."

Ellen gave her a blank stare.

"Could you explain it to me, please?"

Ellen looked at the top of the Formica table. She opened her mouth to answer when David set a tray down in front of them. He commenced to remove their orders and place them on the table then pressed a folded napkin into Ellen's hand, smiled and retreated.

Misty clutched the napkin in her lap. David had ruined the moment.

They ate in silence for a few minutes. Misty questioned the wisdom of inviting Ellen to join her. She'd give it one more try. "Why don't we just cut the crap and you tell me why you don't like me. Is it me, or is it any woman who shows an interest in your dad?"

"You're okay, but I don't think you're the one my dad should have as a girlfriend."

"What does that mean? Did Jack put you in charge of vetting women for him?"

"It's not like that!" Ellen set her paper cup down and splashed heavily creamed coffee on the table.

"What is it like? Jack Hawk is perfectly capable of choosing his own girlfriend. He chose me. What's the problem? I'm shooting in the dark here, Ellen. Help me out."

"He's too old for you, for one thing. He's forty-three. If he wants to have a girlfriend it should be somebody old like him."

Misty sat back. This surly girl was pissing her off. "What?"

Ellen hissed. "People are looking at us."

Misty gritted her teeth. "Your dad is not old. He's a young man and has a long life ahead of him. I joined the Marines twelve years ago when I was twenty-one. I've known Jack on and off since you were three. We like each other and have a lot in common and several mutual friends. Age is not a factor with us. Jack's a big boy with a fine brain. He can take care of himself."

Ellen crossed her arms. "Are you saying you're not interested in his money?"

That stopped Misty. She must have misunderstood. "His money? What in the world are you talking about? Jack's retired military. You live in a modest apartment. He drives an old car and gives flying lessons for a living."

"He drives an old car because he's stingy. He won't part with a nickel he doesn't have to." She rolled her eyes. "Unless it's to buy or maintain another airplane. He says he's keeping it back for retirement and my education. Like I'm going to get into Harvard. Mom was furious he was such a tightwad."

Misty stared at Ellen's steely gray eyes. Hawk's eyes. She didn't know what to make of this revelation. Obviously, she needed a conversation with Jack. Whatever was going on here was a mystery to her. Her phone vibrated. The canteen was the only place in the hospital where cell phones were allowed, so she grabbed it and punched the talk icon when she saw *Hawk*.

"Hey, Jack. Where are you?"

Ellen reached for the phone and Misty waved her away.

"Ellen's with me. I brought her to the VA Hospital for my appointment with Mary. Yes, the therapy dog coordinator." She listened to him for a few seconds. "We'll be done by eleven. Will you be home by then?" She nodded. "Wait, don't hang up, Ellen wants to speak to you." She handed the phone to Ellen. "I'll be right back." She pointed to the restroom.

Five minutes later she returned to the small eating area to find their table empty, Ellen, the food and her phone gone. "Oh, for the love of—," She hurried out the door and looked both ways down the long hallway then headed for the parking lot. She spotted Ellen and David lounging on a bench outside, smoking cigarettes and laughing.

"Ellen?" She confronted the girl with hands on hips.

David grinned. "It's okay, ma'am. I'm re-warming your breakfast while Ellen joins me on my break."

"David, I'm Master Sergeant Beachy. How old are you?"

David jerked his head at her question. "How old?"

"Yes, I'm asking because Ellen here is fifteen, but I'm sure she already told you that."

He jumped to his feet and jammed his cigarette butt in the sand container. "Wow, look at the time." He pointed to his watch. "Break's over." Turning on his heel he was through the doors before either of them had time to react to his hasty departure.

Ellen stood and shoved her face close to Misty's. "We were just talking!"

Thoroughly pissed by now, Misty shoved her face closer and stuck her finger in Ellen's shoulder. "Get back to the table and finish your breakfast. My appointment with Mary is in twenty minutes. She whirled toward the doors and left Ellen standing alone.

Halfway through breakfast, Misty said nothing when Ellen sat across from her and picked up her burrito. They ate in silence, not looking at each other. Misty didn't know what to say and she suspected Ellen was too embarrassed to speak first. Following her last sip of coffee, Misty picked up the paper plate and utensils and empty coffee cup. "You can come with me now, meet me in the intensive care unit, or wait outside." She stood and dropped her trash in the receptacle by the exit.

Ellen lagged a few steps behind her then caught up. "Hey. I'm sorry, okay."

Misty stopped and faced her. "Sorry about what? Being surly, rude, and uncooperative? Or just a plain pain in the ass?" She punctuated the question with open hands.

"All of it, I guess." Ellen shoved her hands in the pockets of her baggy jeans and averted her eyes.

"You guess?"

"All of it. Don't tell Dad, okay?" When Misty didn't answer, she added. "Really, I am sorry."

"You know what I learned this morning?"

"Huh?"

"Your father has the patience of a saint and I never want to be a mother." She strode down the hall. "Pick up your feet, we're late."

During the session with Mary and her dog Opal, Misty was pleased to see Ellen's belligerent façade fade away. The child clearly loved dogs. Misty had seen this months ago when her class in San Diego had visited the now closed Customs facility. Ellen had been alarmed to learn Happy would be sent to the pound if Misty couldn't find a home for him, and had wanted to adopt the dog herself. That had not been possible at the time, but Happy was now happily ensconced in the McPherson household with Santos.

"I want to learn how to do that," Ellen stated in the car on the way back to Jack's apartment. "Opal is so sweet. I couldn't believe how many of the patients smiled and seemed to forget their pain while she was with them." She turned to stare out the passenger window. "I worry Dad will end up like those other veterans."

"By the time Jack is that far gone you'll be old and gray yourself." This kid was deep. Misty was getting a better handle on how her mind worked. She'd lost her mother and was worried about losing Jack, even though that was far down the road.

I need to be the grownup here and give the kid a break.

"You're probably right, but I can't help worrying about him." She looked straight ahead. "I'm sorry I was such a brat today. I don't want to be one of those mean girls, but sometimes I act like one."

"Look, Ellen." Misty touched her arm. "I'm not a fink and I don't want to get between you and Jack. Your connection with him is untouchable. I accept that. I'm no threat to you. I'm not your enemy."

Ellen sighed, but didn't answer. When Misty turned into the parking lot for the apartment complex, Ellen pointed. "There's Dad's car."

"I'll drop you off."

"Aren't you coming up?"

"No, I have to get home."

"What shall I tell Dad?"

"Tell him I'll call him later. He probably needs to catch some shut eye and I have a job interview this afternoon."

Ellen looked doubtful, but opened the door and slid out. Before she closed it, she leaned in. "Thanks for taking me to breakfast and to the hospital. I don't want to be enemies either." She shut the car door and walked away before Misty could respond.

That evening at dinner Misty talked with her parents about the interview with the pet products company. "The pay and benefits are great. More than I expected. The territory they need covered is Santa Barbara and Ventura Counties. There are twelve mega chain stores and a handful of independent stores to be called on in a regular circuit of checking inventory and supplies, solving customer problems and arranging the shelves for proper placement of product."

"You'd be on the road most of the time, wouldn't you?" Debbie asked. "Do they cover automobile expenses?"

"Better. They provide a Ford Transit Connect van. I wouldn't have to use my car. The van isn't much bigger than an SUV, but it has enough cargo space for product and supplies to hold over the customers between shipments. They also supply an iPad and iPhone for instant communication with all their customer stores and headquarters."

Payne nodded. "Sounds like just the ticket. Are you planning on taking it, or looking for something else?"

"They're still interviewing, so in the meantime I'll keep looking. The woman who owns the no-kill shelter and kennel in Simi Valley has already offered me a job. I'd love it, but the pay is much less so I'm stringing her along for a bit. She gets real busy starting the week before Thanksgiving with boarding and adoptions. I'll have to give her an answer soon."

Her mother got up from the table and began clearing dishes. "Stay put. I've got this."

"I'm happy to help, Mom."

"I know, honey. You go sit with your Dad on the patio. There'll be a beautiful sunset this evening."

Misty and Payne settled down in patio chairs facing west. The sky was taking on a coral hue. End of summer through fall was the time for spectacular sunsets in California. Her dad sipped at a small glass of brandy and sighed with contentment.

Misty laughed. "Dad, you look like a smug and satisfied potentate."

"Life is good."

"Can I ask you something?"

"Always."

"I really like Jack Hawk, but I'm at a loss on how to handle his daughter."

"Ellen seems like a decent young girl, a typical well brought up teenager. What's the problem? Is she belligerent towards you?"

"When we're alone she's rude and obnoxious. She sees me as a threat. I'm not. I don't know how to convince her."

"Have you discussed it with Jack?"

"I plan to, but I don't want to come off as a tattletale. One of the last things she said to me today, after apologizing for her behavior more than once was, 'Please don't tell Dad.'" Misty sighed and shook her head. She glanced at her dad's glass. "Do you want a refill? I'm going to get one for myself."

"No. One finger a night is my self-imposed limit. You go ahead."

She stood and took his empty glass. "I'll have a beer instead. I never acquired a taste for the hard stuff."

"Looks like I fell down on the parenting job," he joked and patted her hand. "Don't be long. Tell Debbie the sunset will be in five minutes or less."

* * *

Jack's phone rang at 9:45 p.m. He'd almost given up on Misty calling him that evening. He stepped out onto the balcony and answered. "Hi, darlin'. When can I see you?"

"Not soon enough." She expressed a small sigh. "How much damage was done at the airport last night?"

"Never got as far as the flight school, so all our equipment was spared. The runway we use most of the time had some severe damage. It'll take a while to fix. We closed for lessons for the next week and will just be open for customers who lease parking space from us so they can come and go. Can you get away for a few days?"

"A few days?"

"I had an itch to fly the three of us up to Jackson Hole for a long weekend. We can spend a day in Yellowstone before they close for the winter. There's an outfit up there that does a covered wagon ride and a cookout. I thought Ellen would get a kick out of. I would, too, for that matter. What do you say?" He threw out the question with his fingers crossed waiting for her answer. He wanted to reach right through the phone connection and drag her into his bedroom.

"Won't that be a little awkward? The three of us?"

"No, honey. I'm friends with the general manager at the Four Seasons. I called him to see if he had anything available on short notice. Nobody's booked into the presidential suite. He offered it to me for practically nothing. It's bigger than my apartment. Has three bedrooms and three bathrooms and a straight on view of the Tetons. Ellen already told me she wants to go."

"I wouldn't even know how to pack for a trip like that. I only own casual clothes." Her words encouraged him. She was considering it.

"Nobody up there wears anything but jeans and boots. Any T-shirt without a logo is considered fancy dress. Come on, say you'll go. I already bought tickets for the wagon train and prime seats at the Pink Garter for the country western revue."

"Sounds like you were pretty sure I'd jump at the chance."

"Will you?"

"I'm packing my bag the minute I hang up."

"Pack light. You won't need anything to sleep in."

"Wasn't planning to get a whole lot of sleep."

"You're my bad girl." Her sultry response had his palms tingling at the memory of her bare skin against his hands.

Chapter Twenty

Jack's apartment, midnight.

MISTY RAPPED QUIETLY ON THE DOOR. JACK OPENED IT FOR HER and put his finger to his lips.

"I think Ellen is finally asleep. You can take the futon in the room I use as my office. We need to be at the airport by six a.m. I already filed a flight plan."

Misty set her bag on the floor and walked into Hawk's arms. "I'll be a zombie at that hour." She tilted her head back and smiled into his gray eyes. "No hanky panky for us tonight."

He waggled his brows and hauled her close. "We'll make up for it tomorrow in the master suite at the hotel. That will by my incentive to fly very cautiously all the way."

She rested her head on his shoulder briefly. "What time shall I set my alarm?"

"Not necessary. My internal clock has me awake at five every morning whether I want to get up or not. I'll wake you with a kiss, Snow White." He picked up her bag and led her down the hall. "See you in five hours, honey."

She pecked his cheek. "Goodnight, Jack. I'll be dreaming about you."

"Good girl."

What seemed like no more than a few minutes after she'd drifted off the door cracked open and Ellen whispered, "Misty? Dad said it was time to get up. Are you awake?"

"Oh, God, already?" Misty yawned and stretched. "I'm awake. I'll be dressed in a flash." What happened to her Prince Charming waking her with a kiss? She threw her legs over the side of the lumpy futon with a ridge down the middle and fished in the dark for her jeans. She'd left her clothes in easy reach and the only thing she needed from her duffle was her toothbrush and comb. Stretching again she groaned, dressed and opened the door to see if the bathroom at the end of the hall was clear. The door stood open, so she hurried down the hall.

Making quick work of it, she went to the kitchen and was soon sitting at the table sipping coffee and stirring brown sugar into a small bowl of oatmeal Jack had set in front of her. She'd never had much of an appetite early in the morning, but had learned in the Marines to eat whenever food was offered.

Jack hummed as he brought the coffee pot to the table and sat down at one end. Misty on his right and Ellen on his left.

Misty made a face. "Is he always so cheerful at this hour?"

Grinning, Ellen wrinkled her nose. "Why do you think I hate to get up early? It's sickening."

"Gee, Jack. This could be a deal breaker." She pressed her lips together and shook her head sadly.

"Maybe, but I have the keys to the car and the jet. Without me you two are stranded."

"He has a point." She raised her eyebrows at Ellen. They exchanged ironic smiles. The day was starting well with the three of them. Misty hoped it was a good sign.

The sun was rising as Jack taxied for takeoff. Ellen sat in the co-pilot seat and Misty took a small fold-down jump seat just inside the cockpit door. She had a good view ahead. She watched with interest as Ellen went through the pre-flight check with her father. She'd done this before, probably for many years.

They lifted off the runway, rolled into a wide circle and headed north. The sky was clear blue and cloudless as far as the eye could see. "We'll be there before you know it," Jack said over his shoulder.

Misty got that *elevator* catch in her stomach when Hawk banked again and gained altitude. She hadn't noticed that flutter when she'd flown home from Yuma with him, perhaps because she'd been next to him in the co-pilot seat that day.

"You can move to the passenger cabin now if you want to," Jack called.

Misty unfastened her restraint and moved to a forward facing seat on the port side of the plane and concentrated on the scenery unfolding below. The cockpit door remained open and every now and then she heard a muffled exchange between Jack and Ellen.

Jack walked through the cockpit door and leaned down to kiss her. Startled, she asked, "Is Ellen flying?"

"She can fly on her own for a few minutes. She's not qualified for takeoff or landing. Don't worry. She had a great teacher." He sat in the empty seat next to her.

Trying to relax, Misty pointed out the window. "Is it my imagination, or does it look like Iraq down there?" She leaned closer to the window. "I can't see anything but desert in every direction."

"Pretty much. We won't see a change until we get closer to the mountains in Utah. Then it gets more interesting." He stood. "You want anything? We have soft drinks in the galley. I came back here to fetch an orange soda for Ellen."

She thought about it for a few seconds and decided she was too tense to drink anything. "No, I'll pass. Thanks anyway." She turned in the seat to watch where he went and noticed the miniscule galley for the first time.

Jack carried two cans of soda toward the cockpit. He leaned down to kiss her again before he left the passenger cabin. "I'll never get enough of that." He winked and took a step toward the cockpit.

She couldn't get enough of him either. If only she didn't mess up this time, maybe they had a chance. Her track record was lousy so far. None of her relationships as a civilian had lasted longer than a month. She wanted it to be different this time. What she felt for Jack was different from the others, special.

Instead of leaving he paused and squeezed her arm. "You think too much. Relax and enjoy the ride."

She watched him hand a soda to Ellen and take his seat. Then she smiled. No matter what it took, she'd make sure the three of them had a fun time in Jackson. She turned her attention to the endless gigantic ocean of sand and scrub.

Several minutes later she felt a change in altitude and a few bumps. Mountains began to appear on the starboard side. Misty switched to the seats across the aisle and peered at the horizon. She got to her feet and poked her head in the cockpit. "Jack? What is that?"

Ellen took off her headset and answered. "It's Great Salt Lake. Want to trade places with me?" Without waiting for an answer she undid her seatbelt and moved from the co-pilot seat. "You can see better from here." She handed the earphones to Misty. "Go ahead. We only have about half an hour to go." She squirmed past her, waited for her to move forward then folded down the jump seat and strapped in.

The girl was making an effort. Misty was grateful. She was aware that Ellen worried how much it would cost to share her dad with another female. "Thanks, Ellen."

Soon, Salt Lake City spread before them, vast and bustling. Jack pointed to a few landmarks as he made a slight turn east. Green earth and mountains replaced the desert. These were tall mountains, but it was hard to tell from so far up. Most of them were dotted with snow at the highest elevations. "It's beautiful, Jack. Do you ever get tired of it?"

Grinning, he glanced at her. "Never."

* * *

Jack adored the look of awe on Misty's face. Her eyes glowed childlike as they flew over the endless Cache National Forest. They'd cross the Wyoming border in minutes after the Uinta Mountains. He aimed the aircraft due north. Jackson was a mere wide spot in the road once they'd cleared the Bridger Forest. And just like that, the Grand Tetons loomed ahead, majestic and fierce. He'd watch her face as he brought the plane down at the base of those same jagged peaks for landing. His thrill would be magnified by enjoying hers. And tonight he'd be enjoying her in other ways.

Misty let out a little squeak at the excitement of brushing along the face of the Tetons when he glided the plane to a perfect landing.

"How you doin', honey?" He grinned at the hands pressed across her heart.

"Jack," She gasped, "that was wonderful. Let's do it again."

He and Ellen both laughed. "No problem, but next time, we'll do it in reverse," he promised.

Once he'd received instruction on where to park he'd lead them through the small terminal. They carried their own baggage off the plane to the rental car counter. But before he picked up the car, they'd grab a quick lunch at Jedediah's right off the main lounge. Jack took the keys to a rental car and they found a table in Jedediah's. Misty ordered a short stack of sourdough pancakes with bacon and eggs on the side. Jack grinned when she dug right in.

Ellen watched with amazement in her eyes. "Aren't you afraid you'll get fat?" she asked Misty.

"Nope. Thanks to good genes, there hasn't been a fat person on either side of my family for at least three generations. I'm lucky, because I do love to eat. I am surprised at the size of these pancakes though. They almost take up the whole plate. What are *you* worried about? You have a perfect figure for a girl your age."

Ellen's face turned red. Jack patted her on the arm. "Misty's right. Enjoy your food. You'll burn it all off by the time the weekend is over. The only rest you'll get is for an hour or so after we check into the Four Seasons. We have to show up for the covered wagon train party by three thirty.

Jack drove the new Cadillac Escalade through the quaint town of Jackson on the way to Teton Village. Their hotel was located by Rendezvous Mountain ski resort.

"This is a very classy car, Jack. You're spoiling us." Misty ran her hands over the leather seats. "Right, Ellen?"

"It's several steps above Dad's clunker, for sure."

"Hey! We can't show up at that super luxury resort in a cheap car. The valet would refuse to park it for me. Enjoy yourselves, but don't get used to it."

Ellen sat forward, reached between the seats and tapped Misty on the shoulder. "What'd I tell you?"

"Um hum. I'm getting the picture."

"What did you tell her, Ellen?" Jack took his eyes off the road for a second and scowled at his grinning daughter.

"Never mind," Misty answered. "We girls are allowed our secrets."

Jack didn't miss the conspiratorial smirks they exchanged. He questioned the wisdom of putting himself at a disadvantage with two scheming females. He chuckled. What was he worrying about? This is what he wanted. The two women he loved to learn to like each other.

The hotel appeared before them like a massive mountain cabin and reflected the ambience of the village and surrounding peaks. The rustic and luxurious lobby was warm and welcoming. Jack approached the check-in desk with Misty and Ellen on either side of him.

"Jonathan Hawk. I believe you have a reservation for me."

The handsome young clerk smiled. "Indeed we do, Major Hawk. Mr. Stimson regrets he couldn't be here to greet you personally and hopes you and your family will enjoy your stay. He asked me to tell you that a two bedroom and loft residence has become available. It's roomier than the Presidential suite and has a beautiful mountain view. I'll be happy to have the bellman escort you there."

"Sounds great." Jack took out his wallet and fished for his credit card.

"That won't be necessary, sir. Just sign in and we'll get you to your accommodations." He handed a brochure to Misty. "This will describe all the hotel amenities, Mrs. Hawk. We hope you'll have time to enjoy some of them during your short stay." He smiled. "On the house, of course."

Speechless, Misty took the slick booklet and held it against her chest. "Um, thanks."

They were whisked to the residence. The bellman opened the door and invited them to enter ahead of him then followed. He spent about ten minutes explaining the amenities, asked if he could do anything further to assist them.

"No, thank you." Jack slipped him a twenty. "We'll call if we need anything."

They stared and grinned at one another when the young man closed the door.

"Wow, Dad! Could we live here?" Eyes agog, Ellen turned in a circle.

"This is a palace, Jack. I can't imagine what you have on the general manager. I feel like Cinderella."

Ellen ran through the place squealing and exclaiming as she looked in every door. She took the stairs to the loft two at a time and shrieked, "Oh, you have to see this! There's a marble bathroom with a spa tub. I don't ever want to leave here! Can I have this room?"

"Take your pick, sweetheart," Jack called, and embraced Misty. He whispered in her good ear, "Cinderella? I was hoping for Beauty and the Beast." He turned and tilted his head at the large coffee table. "Look." A fancy basket of exotic fruit and a gold foil box of Swiss chocolates flanked an ice bucket holding a bottle of French champagne. "I'm beginning to think I don't ever want to leave here either. Shall we?"

"Which one of us gets to be the Beast?" She helped herself to a dark chocolate truffle.

"We'll take turns." He turned and called up the stairs. "Ellen! Want some champagne?"

"Jack?"

"A few sips won't hurt her. For all I know she and Cherry have been experimenting. Better to let her know I don't think it's a kicking-you-out-of-home offense."

Ellen called down from the loft, "No thanks, Daddy. I'm getting ready to take a bubble bath in this badass...er...really neat spa tub. Would you bring my suitcase up while I'm in the bathroom, please?"

"At your service, ma'am." Jack grabbed her suitcase and bounded up the stairs. He set the case inside the door and closed it. When he got back to the sitting area, he lifted the ice bucket and two glasses. "Let's pick a bedroom. We've got two hours."

It took less than two minutes.

Jack closed the door, set the champagne and glasses on a small table and began to remove Misty's clothes, taking brief breaks to kiss her and run his hands over her back and hips.

"Wait, Jack." Misty put her hands flat on his chest. "I have to ask you something."

"What is it?" His stomach gave a little drop. Had he read her wrong?

She shook her head vigorously. "No, it's just—we're friends, aren't we?"

"I thought we were, but you sound like you have reservations. What are you getting at?"

"No...um...I think we're friends, but if this," she waved her hands, "doesn't work out, will we still be friends?"

"As in what? Best pals? Old buddies?" He stepped back and shook his head. "I'm not considering that possibility. The possibility of this," he waved his hands like she had done, 'not working out,' is not on my radar." He turned and walked across the room and stared at the mountain. Shoving his hands in his pockets he marveled at how quickly they'd moved from romantic, sexual excitement to doubt and insecurity. A deep sadness overtook him.

"Jack." Misty put her arms around him and rested her head on his back. "Jack, I'm sorry. I like you so much, but I'm so afraid I'll..."

He stepped away from her. "That's okay. I get it." He poured himself a glass of champagne. "Let's leave it for now. I'm going to catch some zees. Be ready to leave by three."

He opened the locked door, stepped into the hall and entered the third bedroom.

* * *

Heat burned her face and tears sprang from her eyes. Misty slumped down on the side of the bed and dropped her head in her hands. She'd done it again. Just couldn't seem to keep from ruining a good thing. What was wrong with her? What was she afraid of? The answer was clear, she was falling in love with Jack Hawk and it terrified her. Her default solution to every potential emotional pain was to cut off the source before it had a chance to hurt. Except it never worked out that way. It always hurt.

No, she wouldn't allow that to happen again. She dashed the tears from her cheeks, bolted to her feet and followed him to the adjacent room. "Jack?" She tapped lightly on his door. "Jack, can I come in."

"Not a good idea."

"Please, Jack. Let me in."

"Come in for Christ's sake! It's not locked." Anger and frustration were clear in his answer.

She pressed down on the handle and the door eased open. Jack had kicked off his shoes and was lying on his side facing away from the door. The champagne flute on the bedside table was empty. She stepped gingerly on the thick carpet of the vast bedroom. The walk from the open door to the bed where he lay seemed like a mile. She stood at the side of the king bed, unsure of her next move, and then she crawled across the bed and nestled next to him with her knees tucked in the back of his and dropped her arm around his waist.

"Jack. There's something I have to tell you."

He lay stiff and unyielding, his answer a grunt.

"I'm afraid because I love you." She buried her forehead between his shoulder blades. She felt his tenseness ease and a sob caught in her throat when he took her hand and pressed it against his heart.

"I know, baby."

Jack knows she loves him. *Why didn't he say I love you, too?*

* * *

"Dad?" Ellen tapped on the door.

Misty sprang into a sitting position and realized she'd been asleep. Her heart pounded so hard she felt it would explode from her chest. Instinctively she pushed back her short hair and tugged down on her sweatshirt.

Jack rolled on his back and called to Ellen. "Come in. The door's open. What time is it?"

Ellen gave the door a tentative push. "It's three. Aren't we supposed to leave soon?" Her big gray eyes met Misty's. "Oh, you fell asleep." She took a step back.

Jack said, "No that's okay, sweetheart. I'm glad you were watching the time. Do me a favor. Go to Misty's bedroom and take that bottle of champagne and put it in the refrigerator in the kitchen. We'll put our shoes on, and we're good to go."

Misty scooted off the bed and followed Ellen to *her* bedroom. "Good thing somebody was watching the time. I must have gone out the minute my head hit the pillow, Jack too." She retrieved her boots and sat in a small chair to tug them on and pull up the zippers. "I better brush my hair."

"It looks good," Ellen said. "It's not messy at all." She picked up the ice bucket and carried it to the door.

Misty called after her, "The cork for the bottle must still be on the coffee table in the living room."

"I'll find it. I'm ready to leave whenever you and Dad are."

Misty bumped into Jack just outside the bedroom door. "Oh. Jack, can we...?"

"We'll talk later." He put an arm around her shoulders and dropped a small kiss on her temple. "We need to get going. The meeting place is on the other side of Jackson. No time to waste. The wagons will pull out on time whether we get there or not."

Chapter Twenty-One

Covered Wagon Depot, Jackson

ELLEN SCANNED THE CROWD OF TOURISTS WATCHING THE wranglers hitch up the wagons and get them lined up. "Dad, we're the only ones here not wearing cowboy hats. There's a gift shop over there. Do I have time to look for one? I'll pay for it myself."

"Why don't we all get one? My treat." He grinned and hugged her. "We're early. The wagons won't start pulling out for another half hour."

Ellen ran, giggling, to the small gift shop. Misty was sure the prices with this captive audience would be a lot higher than in town. "They're going to cost a fortune in there, Jack. I don't need one."

"Oh? I think you do, cowgirl. Let's see what they've got." He took her hand and tugged her through the door of the small shop where Ellen was already in front of a mirror next to a stack of hats.

Misty picked up one of the nicer hats and gasped at the price tag. "Jack! Look at this. Really, I…"

He plopped the Stetson on her head. "Let me do this, okay?" He turned his attention to Ellen. "Find anything you like?"

Misty settled on a Bullhide Annie Oakley in brown felt, and Ellen picked a Reba Cowgirl in bright pink that matched the streaks in her blond hair. "Do you like it, Daddy?" Jack grinned because she looked so cute and happy with her new purchase. He handed over his credit card and had the clerk snip off the price tags for them.

"Jack, you cheated. That's more Indiana Jones than Western Cowboy."

"Yes, but I look so dashing, and devastatingly handsome in it. I couldn't resist." He winked and sent her a warm look fraught with meaning.

"Hmm. I hate to admit it, but you're right." She reached up and tugged his hat a little to one side and dropped a light kiss on his lips. "There, even more handsome now." She loved everything about this man. Just being with him she felt special and cherished. His penetrating eyes and wise smile prevented her from hiding anything from him, and why should she? He'd given her no reason to doubt him. Whatever happened—happened. There was no good reason to spoil the now for fear of then.

A cowbell clanged and the head wrangler shouted, "Load 'em up!"

Jack took her elbow and Ellen's and steered them outside. "Ellen, you have the tickets. What wagon are we on?"

"Six." Ellen wriggled with excitement and bounced on her toes. "We're on six. Come on."

They climbed into covered wagon six with other laughing pretend pioneers, then watched with anticipation as they pulled from the dusty staging area and headed into a tree lined trail that gained altitude as they moved forward. Progress was slow and gentle. The rumps of the animals hitched to the wagon rolled in dusty rhythm, their shiny hides reflecting the afternoon sun.

A cowboy on horseback rode fast along the line of wagons shouting, "Injuns ahead! Get ready to duck! Guard your women-folk. We're outnumbered!"

Gunshots and blood curdling warrior whoops filled the late afternoon air. Two children across from them shrieked with excitement and alarm when a war-painted *redskin* rode close and reached under the rolled-up canvas flap wearing a fearsome scowl. "Gimme girl!" he demanded.

The girl's father held her tight and her little brother bravely swatted at the fierce re-enactor and yelled, "No! Get away! You can't have her!" The painted warrior gave up and rode away to the cheers and laughter of all aboard.

"Oh, my, God, Jack! This is so much fun." She grinned at him. "I'm wondering, though, would you rescue Ellen first or me?" She gritted her teeth and wondered if her question sounded childish. It felt good to ask though.

Ellen answered for him, "Daddy would rescue me first, and then I'd help him rescue you."

"Good answer, sweetheart. You saved my bacon." Jack tweaked her chin.

The brief battle was soon over and the wagons proceeded peacefully into the foothills. They arrived at a large staging area and the driver asked them to remain seated until the wagon boss gave the go ahead to disembark and head for the chuck wagon chow line.

"Something smells good," Jack remarked. "I don't know about you, but I'm hungry enough to eat a bear."

The *pioneers* were directed to a tented area where they gathered, drank cider from tin cups and milled about talking, laughing and waiting for further instructions. The little kids in the crowd chattered excitedly about the Indian raid and the bravery of the cowboys who drove them off. A grizzled cook stepped to an iron triangle and clanged it loudly with a metal rod. "Come and git it!"

Jack handed big, chipped, porcelain dinner plates to her and Ellen and they stepped into the chow line. Smiling cooks of all ages plopped delicious smelling stew, beans, corn on the cob, and cornbread onto their plates and pointed to the large tent. The last server at the steam table said, "Have a seat inside, folks. There'll be plenty more if you want seconds."

Ellen pointed to the front of the tent. "Daddy, there's empty seats at the table next to the bandstand. Can we sit up there?"

He affected a broad cowboy twang, "Shore we can. Lead the way, little missy." Then Jack tottered bowlegged and tipped his hat. Ellen and Misty laughed so hard they had a difficult time balancing their plates as they stepped through the rustic room lined with long camp tables and benches.

Misty looked back at Jack. "She's having a great time, *Daddy*. Me, too. Thank you for doing this."

"My pleasure, ma'am. Perhaps y'all could show your deep appreciation later?"

"Shh!" Misty hissed, but didn't suppress her grin.

They lined up on the same side of the table facing the bandstand. Ellen sat on the center aisle seat with Jack between the two women. They got comfortable and dug into their camp dinner with gusto. Cooks and waiters circulated with jugs of water and cider throughout the lively meal. Large tubs of butter rested on each table next to baskets of steaming baking powder biscuits and pots of dark molasses.

Misty groaned, "I may never eat again after this."

Ellen leaned forward so she could see her. "I've seen how much you can eat, so I don't believe you." She giggled and went back to her loaded plate. "One of the cooks told me to save room for apple cobbler."

Misty answered loud enough for Ellen to hear, "Your daughter is a smarty pants, cowpoke."

"Takes after the old man, I 'spect." He lifted his cup of cider and toasted himself.

The hubbub quieted as some got up from the tables to get seconds or use the facilities. Musicians, who looked suspiciously like the cowhands who'd chased away the marauders, stepped on the stage and arranged their chairs and instruments. Warm apple cobbler appeared in bowls set before those who indicated they still had room for more food. Ellen took two, compared the sizes then reached across in front of her dad and handed the largest one to Misty. Jack shook his head and raised his hands when offered the fragrant, steaming dessert. "None for me, thanks. I'll take some coffee if you have any."

"Comin' right up. I'll bring a pot from the chuck wagon for all y'all." He reached in his battered apron pocket and dropped a handful of creamers and packets of sugars on the table.

"Jack, how did you know about this?"

"Stimson told me he thought Ellen would get a kick out of it. He said it was schmaltzy but fun, with good food and good music."

"He was right. I'm going to make sure you tell me what you have on that man before the night is over."

He put his hand on her knee and squeezed.

Five cowboys took the stage. "Good evenin' folks. How y'all doin'?"

The audience responded with claps, cheers and expressions of *great* and *fantastic!*

"This here's our last cookout of the season, so we have something real special for you tonight. We're lucky to have here with us this evening Mr. Randy Brooks. Randy and his band, Ice Bison, will be appearing at the Silver Dollar Saloon tonight, so don't miss 'em if you're stayin' over in beautiful Jackson."

A handsome blonde cowboy stepped on the stage and took off his hat to wave at the audience. A loud cheer went up from the crowd, even though Misty doubted few of them had ever heard of him. His clear blue eyes and inviting smile charmed every female in the room, including her. She noticed Ellen, staring, mesmerized.

Misty elbowed Jack's side and nodded at Ellen. He glanced at his daughter and exchanged smiles with Misty. "Ain't love grand," he whispered.

One of the musicians handed a vintage Gibson guitar to Brooks. He bowed low and struck a chord. The audience quieted and the young cowboy began to sing. He had a warm, deep baritone voice and an engaging style. The chuck wagon band members accompanied him and sang backup while tapping their feet and swaying with the music.

Ellen smiled, starry-eyed at her dad. "He's really good, isn't he?"

"Yes, he is," Jack's fingers tapped the table in time with the beat. "This is an unexpected bonus. Stimson didn't tell me this was the last trail ride of the season."

Misty slid a hand around Jack's arm and hugged it against her side. She rested her chin on his shoulder and smiled into his eyes when he turned to grin at her. "I love you, Hawk," she whispered so she could not be heard above the music.

Jack tipped his head and placed a kiss on her nose. "Good. That's the plan."

After several songs, the singer, Brooks, propped his guitar against the keyboard and stepped off the stage while the music played on. Audience members cocked their heads in confusion. What was he doing? He walked directly to Ellen, took her hand and bowed. "Will you join me onstage?"

Mouth open, eyes wide, Ellen stuttered, "Join you?" She looked at Jack as if to ask his advice or help.

"Yes, ma'am, onstage. I won't embarrass you, I promise." He tilted his head toward Jack, "Sir? With your permission."

"Go ahead, sweetheart. Enjoy this." He nudged her shoulder.

Cowboy Randy whispered something in Ellen's ear as they approached the stage. She nodded, her cheeks ablaze. He stepped up and led her to the center. "Folks, this young lady here is Ellen Hawk. A new friend. Why doncha give her a nice warm welcome?"

The audience laughed and cheered when the young man raised Ellen's hand and kissed it.

"Ellen is going to get her very first cowboy dance lesson, then we invite anyone else who cares to join us to please join us on stage." He turned to the band and nodded. They embarked on a familiar country-western number. Brooks took Ellen's hand and positioned himself at her side. He whispered something to her that only she could hear then began to count. They stepped into the familiar rhythm. "This here's called the cowboy boogie, folks. Look at this young lady. Ain't she purty?"

Jack cheered. He grinned at Misty. "I had no idea she knew how to do that!"

"She's a natural. Look at her. She's beautiful." She wasn't exaggerating. Ellen glowed with youthful beauty and happiness. Misty had never seen her like this before. When she dropped her belligerent façade, her true self sparkled like a searchlight at the edge of a dark sea.

Brooks beckoned the audience, "Come on up, folks. Join the fun."

Jack stood and tugged Misty across the bench. "Let's do it."

Her heart fluttered. "I don't know how to do that. I'll take a pratfall the minute we start."

He winked. "And a very nice prat it is. I'm not letting you off the hook."

He pulled her to the stage. Brooks placed himself between Misty and Jack. "Just follow my lead, ma'am. It's fun."

Misty held her breath. The warmth of a blush burned her cheeks. Jack had already taken a couple of pointers from Ellen by the time she got in step with the cowboy. To her great relief, several other audience members stepped onto the stage. Soon, there was little room to move.

When the number ended the room erupted with cheers. The announcer said, "That concludes our show for this evening, folks. We'll start loading the wagons for our return to Jackson in twenty minutes. Happy trails!"

When the others drifted off the stage Brooks held back Jack's family. "I hope y'all will come to my show at the Silver Dollar tonight. We go on at ten." He reached into his shirt pocket and held out three tickets and offered them to Jack. "See you later, little lady." He tipped his hat at Ellen and stepped around the stage.

"Daddy, please say we can go, please." Her big gray eyes pleaded and she clasped her hands under her chin.

Jack laughed and put his arm around her shoulders. "Wouldn't miss it, little lady."

Ellen smiled the entire wagon ride back to the depot, and shyly accepted the compliments on her dancing from their wagon mates. Misty squeezed Jack's hand and took measured breaths to contain the love blooming in her chest for Jack Hawk. Come what may, she would give herself over to him. This time she would not sabotage the affair before it got off the ground. She didn't know whether or not she deserved him, but he deserved the best she could give.

* * *

I'm a happy man. Ellen was enjoying herself. Jack hadn't seen this sweet side of her personality for too long to remember. Misty held his hand and the heated glances they exchanged were filled with promise. He wouldn't rush her. He'd give her plenty of space. But he would find a way to make her a permanent part of his life, no matter how long it took. Her doe-like brown eyes gave her away. She wasn't nearly as tough as she pretended to be. Misty Beachy was fragile and full of self-doubt. He'd find a way to convince her that he was her safe haven, the man who would always be there for her. He'd known this from the day McPherson had brought her along with him to the war dog trials at Camp Pendleton so many months ago.

She'd never been far from his mind since the first time they'd met at the forward operating base at Fallujah for an after-mission debrief. She'd been a newly minted master sergeant at the tender age of twenty-three, and she had the respect of the men in her unit and her commanding officer. She may have looked like a blond china doll, but she'd been a force to be reckoned with. She still was.

He drove them back to the hotel for a rest, refreshing showers and a change of clothes before they headed back to town and the Silver Dollar Saloon. This was Ellen's night and he was determined to see she enjoyed it to the fullest. Tomorrow they'd take advantage of the hotel facilities and kick back until it was time to find dinner and head for the Pink Garter Theater. So far the weekend was going better than he'd dare hope.

"Misty?" Ellen asked from the back seat. "Do you want to go to the spa tomorrow and get the works? I've never had a facial or any of that stuff. It's free and it would be a shame to pass it up."

"I'd love to, Ellen. You read my mind. I treated my mother to a day at the spa for her birthday last year. We enjoyed it so much we thought of making it a tradition. You'll love it, but I warn you, you'll have to marry a rich man so you can continue to enjoy it for years to come."

"I'll start looking right away." She giggled. "One who isn't a tight-wad, like Daddy."

"Hey! Is that any way to thank me for this great trip?" Jack laughed. "Tightwad! I'm no tightwad."

"Skinflint, then." Ellen reached forward and tugged the side of his short beard. She snatched back her hand before he could grab it. "I love you anyway, Daddy."

"Good. It's a long walk back to L.A."

* * *

Jack lay back on the bed; feet crossed at the ankles and eavesdropped on Ellen and Misty making their spa appointments for the next day. They chattered away like two best friends, but he'd temper his expectations on that front. This place, and the excitement of the weekend, was largely responsible for their ease with each other. The conversation dwindled and soon he heard Ellen say she was going to take a walk around the grounds then come back and shower.

A couple of minutes later, Misty shouldered the door open and stood there grinning, a glass of champagne in each hand. "May I join you, cowboy?"

His arousal struck like lightning. He sat up and threw his legs over the side of the bed.

"Lock the door and take off your clothes."

She smirked and rolled her eyes. "That's the most romantic thing you've ever said to me, Hawk." She sashayed the short distance across the room to set the champagne flutes on the bedside table.

She turned to close the door and he grabbed her by the hips and pulled her down on his lap. "The door can wait a couple of minutes. I can't." He held her tight and kissed her ear and neck. "You feel that?"

She moved her hips and slid her hand between them and onto his lap. "Yippee-ki-yay" She pressed down. "I was wondering when I'd be the happy recipient of your *largesse.*"

Jack stood swiftly and kept his arms tight around her waist. He carried her to the door. "Lock it." She did as instructed and he set her on her feet and turned her to face him. "I can't even look at you without thinking about this. I've never wanted anyone as bad as I want you every hour of every day." He lowered his head and planted a hot kiss on her mouth.

Misty tugged his shirt above his waist. "Get out of this. I want to taste your bare chest. According to my watch we have three hours before we need to surface. I told Ellen I was going to take a nap with you. She smiled, said 'okay' and went for a walk."

He couldn't believe his good fortune. "Napping isn't part of my plan."

"I'm so glad to hear it." She bit her cheek and pointed to the bed. "Can we go over there now?"

"That's too far." He tugged her onto the plush carpet at their feet. "Let's start here." Faster than a forest fire in dry brush, they were naked. "Do you have any idea how beautiful and desirable you are, baby?"

"That's how I feel when I'm with you, Jack. Now lie still and let me start showing my 'deep appreciation' for today." She laughed at the blush that lit his chest. "Be careful what you wish for, Marine. I don't want to hurt you." She threaded her fingers through the hair on his chest and gave a little tug. "Then again… maybe I do." She pressed a hand over his mouth. "Let me know if you're about to crack. I don't want to make Ellen an orphan. Not today, at least."

He groaned and relaxed his shoulders. His arms went around her when she moved her mouth over his chest and neck. He gripped her bottom as thrill after thrill raced through him. "Oh, baby."

Half an hour later they sprawled on the floor, leaning back against the unused bed, and sipped their champagne. The front door opened and closed and Ellen's footsteps tapped across the parquet entry then it was quiet again as she went upstairs and closed the door to her loft bedroom.

"What's the story on Stimson, Jack? Do you know something that would put him in a super-max prison for life? The price on this unit is over a thousand bucks a night. If you had to shell out for Ellen's spa day tomorrow it would probably be another grand. What laws did he break?"

"Did you happen to see the note next to the chocolates and wine?"

"No, what did it say?"

"Hawk, you S.O.B. We're even." Jack chuckled and shook his head. "Charlie Stimson is a straight arrow. He and his small contingent of Delta Force operatives got ambushed in Afghanistan. Their JTAC called in air support. I got there quick with my Warthog, and then did several strafing runs and low altitude flyovers, holding off the bad guys until they got reinforcements. They got shot up, but did get all their asses out of there. We've stayed in touch ever since. He's the bastard who stuck me with the call-sign, Hot Stick."

She grinned. "I'm sure he had no idea how right on target he was with that one."

"I liked my former handle better."

"What was it?"

"Raptor." He smirked. "I was Raptor for years before Stimson stuck me with Hot Stick."

She scooted onto his lap and put her arms around his neck. "Wanna join me in the spa tub, Raptor? I'm feeling real dirty."

"I can fix that."

* * *

Silver Dollar Saloon, Wort Hotel

Misty thanked Jack when he held open the door and ushered her and Ellen into the legendary saloon. They shouldered their way to the long silver dollar encrusted bar. It was shoulder to shoulder in the room.

A bearded young bartender decked out in a leather vest and bar apron approached. "What can I do ya for?"

Misty showed him the tickets Randy Brooks had given them earlier in the evening. She cupped her good ear. "We're here to see Ice Bison. It doesn't look like there any seats left." Her eyes swept the jam-packed room. Every chair at every table was taken and revelers milled around the edges of the room holding drinks in their hands while talking and laughing.

"No worry. This crowd is clearing out in the next half hour or so. Only ticket holders will be allowed for the performance. Y'all have guest passes, so your seats will be right up front at that center table. We'll be placing a reserved placard on it shortly. Reckon you'd like something to drink while waiting?" He raised his eyebrows.

Misty nodded. "I'll have whatever's on tap. What about you, Jack? Ellen?"

"I'll have the same," he shouted over the din. "A sarsaparilla for my daughter."

"Coming right up." He reached into a cold case and removed three frosted mugs, filled two from the beer tap, and poured a bottle of Jackson Hole Soda company sarsaparilla into the other. Holding them over the heads of bar patrons, he handed them to Jack one at a time. "I'll run you a tab."

"Thanks, buddy." He smiled at Misty over the rim of the frosty mug and a hot thrill shot up from her knees and settled in her lower torso.

She put her mouth close to his ear. "Stop that, Hawk."

He raised his eyebrows, all innocence, and grinned. "Stop what?"

"Looking at me like that." In truth she never wanted him to stop giving her those heated glances, had never felt so alive, so desired. "That's an order."

"Majors don't take orders from sergeants." His lips brushed her ear and sent a shiver across her shoulders.

"Oh, that's right. Lucky for me."

"Dad. Misty. Our table is ready. Let's grab it." Ellen pointed to the waiter placing a Guest-of-Artist placard on the table. She squeezed past them and wove her way across the room. Misty followed and dropped the tickets in the center of the table where they could be seen. Jack placed himself in the chair between them.

The room filled quickly. Band crew carried instruments and audio equipment to the small riser at the end of the room and quickly set up. "Howdy, folks!" Devilishly handsome, curly blond, Randy Brooks strode in, waved and greeted the audience. "We hope all y'all enjoy the show." He held the hand mic close to his lips, smiled at Ellen and said in a low sexy tone, "Hey, sugar baby. Thanks for coming."

"Hey, Randy." Her sparkling eyes could give merrily winking Christmas lights a run for the money.

Misty noticed Jack shoot a warning glance at Brooks. The cowboy laughed and nodded his understanding. He picked up his guitar and tapped his foot. The ensuing show was great fun. Apparently, Ice Bison was a regional favorite and they got called back for several curtain calls. When the performance ended, Jack invited Brooks to join them for a beer.

"I'd love to, but our tour bus is waiting. We're on our way to Laramie for a big show at U.W. tomorrow." He again picked up Ellen's hand and placed a gallant kiss on her knuckles. "So nice to see you and your folks, sugar. I hope we meet again." He tipped his hat and carried his guitar to the door, enduring back slaps and greetings on the way out.

Ellen, eyes moony and round, sighed. She pressed her recently kissed knuckles to her cheek. "My cowboy prince is leaving and I'll never love anybody else in my whole life."

Misty touched Ellen's nose and smiled. "Wanna bet?"

Chapter Twenty-Two

Stiegler's Austrian Restaurant, Moose, Wyoming

JACK TOOK A SIP OF THE DRY RED WINE. ELLEN AND MISTY WENT on endlessly about their spa day. They agreed they'd both start looking for rich husbands as soon as they got home.

"The good looking man who interviewed me for the pet supply company gave me the once over. I'll do some checking to see if he's rich enough. Then there's one of Dad's wealthy, retired, silver foxes I met at his country club recently. I'm pretty sure he's got gobs of money. There are plenty of women who'd like to get their hooks into him, but I'd have a twenty year age advantage on most of them." She turned to Jack. "What do you think, Hawk?"

"Go for it." Yes, he knew if she really wanted to she could land any number of men. But, the thing was—she was in love with him. He winked and lifted his glass in salute. "Good luck."

Their innuendos went right past Ellen. She scooped a crostini into the dip and took a bite. "This is really good, Dad. What is it?"

"Smoked trout."

She made a sour face. "Eewww. I hate fish. They don't have anything vegetarian on the menu."

Jack forked up some haus salate and nodded. "There isn't a single vegetarian in Austria. Since when are you a vegetarian?"

Ignoring his question, she said, "If I got my grades up and you paid the tuition, I could enroll in North Hills Prep for junior and senior high. A lot of rich kids go there. I bet I could find a future husband who'd love to buy me clothes, an awesome car, and all the spa treatments I want."

Jack grinned and raised his glass again. "Good luck to you, too."

"Dad, let's get serious. You have to buy a house. I can't do what I decided on if we're living in an apartment." She took another big scoop of the fish dip she didn't like and gave him a resolute stare.

When did she start growing up so fast? She'd dropped her snotty attitude—wouldn't that be great if it were permanent?—she came very close to being a lovely young woman. She wasn't Jack's baby any more. He wasn't sure if he liked that or not.

"And why do I have to buy a house?"

"I want to train a reading dog."

Misty grinned. "Ellen, that's great. When did you decide on that?"

"I thought about it a lot after we visited Mary and Opal at the hospital. She gave me a bunch of brochures and some web-links. I also checked with a few libraries and they'd love to start a dog reading program."

He could probably get up and leave and neither one of them would notice. "Would one of you please tell me what in hell a reading dog is? You're going to teach dogs to read?"

Ellen sighed and rolled her eyes, as in Dad-you're-totally-clueless. "It's a dog that kids read to at the library."

"Kids read books to dogs." Maybe he was clueless. He shook his head. "Why?" The rich husband conversation had made more sense to him than kids reading to dogs at the public library. He cocked an eyebrow at Misty. "Help me out here."

Misty smiled and reached across the table to pat his hand. "It's not as goofy as it sounds, Jack. Children who have a hard time learning to read, and difficulty reading out loud, sit in a quiet section of the library, and read to a dog."

"Dogs don't correct or frown at them when they make a mistake. They just listen. It gives kids confidence to keep going. Dogs are nonjudgmental. There is no pressure to be perfect." Ellen said this as if it was obvious enough that even her clueless father should understand it.

Jack was about to answer when the waiter came and set their entrées on the table. Elk Filets Mignon Diane for him and Misty and Chicken Cordon Bleu for Ellen. Ellen wrinkled her nose. "You're both totally disgusting, eating endangered wildlife."

"Elk are not endangered," Jack answered. "They're so overpopulated they decided to reintroduce wolves into the park to get the numbers down."

"Let's talk about something else," Misty said. "Jack, what did you do all day while we were becoming beautiful at the Four Seasons spa?"

"I drove out to Harrison Ford's ranch. We took a look at his elk herd then went fishing for about an hour on the Snake River."

Ellen pursed her lips and shook her head. "You did not."

"Did, too." He grinned and put a big bite of elk in his mouth.

"Harrison Ford." It wasn't a question. "Han Solo. Indiana Jones. You don't know him."

"Do too." He chewed and pointed his fork at her.

"You went to his ranch?"

"Yep."

"Did, not."

"Did, too."

Misty set down her fork. "Come on, Jack. Is that the truth? Do you know Harrison Ford?"

"We go way back."

"He's fibbing, Misty. He doesn't know Indiana Jones."

"I didn't say I did."

"You did, too!" She squinched her face and gave him the evil eye. "He just said it, didn't he, Misty?"

"No, I said I know Harrison Ford. And I do." He tilted his head to the far corner of the room. "He and his wife just took that table over there."

Misty and Ellen stared across the room wide-eyed, mouths open. Harrison Ford smiled and nodded.

Jack raised his chin and returned the smile. "We'll stop and say hello before we leave. He recommended this place. This is some of his elk we're eating."

Misty closed her mouth and blushed to be caught ogling. "How do you know him?"

"He's a fellow pilot. I've bumped into him several times over the years. He's got a helicopter at his place here and he's part of the local search-and-rescue group. Helluva guy." From Ellen's awed expression, he thought he'd been raised a couple of notches on the embarrassingly dorky dad scale. "Eat up, you glamour gals. We need to be at the Pink Garter by nine."

On their way out, they stopped briefly at the Ford's table. Jack introduced Misty and Ellen and thanked him for the restaurant recommendation. When they stepped outside the air had turned sharply cold.

"Brrrr. It's freezing out here, Hawk. I should have worn my down jacket."

"Mr. Ford is old, Dad." Ellen's voice was tinged with melancholy.

"Old enough to be your grandpa."

"He's still hot, though. He has an earring. I liked him a lot." Ellen took Jack's arm and hurried him to the rented Escalade. They only had half an hour until curtain time. She preempted Misty and jumped into the front passenger seat.

Misty shrugged and got in the back. She saw clearly that Ellen's sharing of her father went just so far.

* * *

The next day they made an early start after breakfast and drove north into Grand Teton National Park and continued on to Yellowstone. Stopping at only a few places so they could cover as much of the parks as possible in one day, they carried a boxed lunch Jack had ordered from the hotel the night before.

Ellen insisted they had to come back at another time for a real vacation. She started listing all the places she wanted to go and trails she wanted to hike. "There's a boat that crosses Jenny Lake, Dad. One of the brochures I picked up at the hotel says there's a good trail on the other side."

Jack's thoughts were going in a different direction. Yellowstone would be a great place for a honeymoon. *Slow down, Hawk.* Where had that come from? Misty was so skittish, he was unsure of how long they'd be together, let alone whether they'd ever marry. Perhaps they'd plan a short trip to the park. Just the two of them. He glanced across the seat and saw her excitedly pointing.

"What's the holdup on the road? Everybody's stopping."

"There's a big bison standing on the side. Over there. Can you see him?"

"Yes, now I can. That thing's head must have a two-foot diameter. I had no idea they got that big." She turned in the seat. "Ellen, roll down your window. Take a look at that monster."

"Wow, he's huge!"

A park ranger vehicle was crawling slowly along the narrow road between the parked cars. He stopped and spoke to an Asian couple who'd opened their door and stepped out of their vehicle with cameras. Jack was too far away to hear what was being said, but the couple got back in the car and closed the doors. The ranger nodded and drove on.

"It's hard to believe people don't know how dangerous and unpredictable wild animals can be. They think they can walk right up to them and take pictures as if they were stuffed exhibits in a museum." He shook his head at the naïveté.

The bison stood, shook off a cloud of dust, and took his time strolling across the road then soon moved into the brush. Traffic crawled but they were underway again after the unexpected delay.

"Another brochure I picked up told about the Jackson Visitor Center and museum. They have a taxidermy exhibit of wolves and stuff. I bet that would be interesting. We're definitely going to have to come back here, Dad."

"You're right about that. There's far too much to see in a day or two. We could rent a camper and spend a week and still not see everything." He smiled at Misty and glanced at Ellen in the rearview mirror. "How about next spring, soon as school is out?"

"Really? Could we? We've never been on a vacation longer than four days. I want to go to Grand Canyon, too."

Misty laughed. "Looks like you started something, Hawk."

He raised an eyebrow. "You in?"

Jack knew he was a lucky man to have these two females in his life.

The bright and difficult teenage daughter he loved beyond measure, and the remarkable woman he wanted by his side for the rest of it. It would be a bumpy road, but he had no doubt it would be worth the ride. *You got your work cut out for you, Hawk.*

* * *

Misty nodded, her heart pounding in her throat. *Next spring.* Jack was thinking ahead to next spring. She was afraid to think ahead a month, but he seemed to have no doubt they'd still be together into next year. She swallowed. She could do this. She wanted to do this.

"If Ellen can stand my company, I'm in."

Ellen leaned forward. "We should start making a list of all the places we want to go besides here and Grand Canyon. Do you want to go to Grand Canyon?"

Not only was Jack assuming they'd be together, Ellen was warming to the idea. This came as a surprise to Misty. Her voice unsteady, she answered, "Yes." She cleared her throat. "My parents took me and my brother there when we were kids. We had a great time. We took the train up from Williams but only spent one night. I always wanted to go back."

"It's settled." Jack reached over and squeezed her hand.

"Dad, I'm serious about buying a house. Mrs. Dempsey is a real estate broker and Mr. Dempsey built the house they live in. Maybe she could find a piece of property we like and he could build us the perfect house. You know, a place where I can have a couple of dogs to train."

"You'll only be living at home for a few more years, sweetheart. There's probably any number of houses out there that would meet your criteria." He aimed a serious gray-eyed smile, brimming with secret intimacy at Misty, and followed it with a warm squeeze of her hand.

Did that look mean he was picturing her in the house too? Or was she putting a spin on his remarks he hadn't intended? She tamped down the hope bubbling in her chest.

Ellen squealed, "You mean you'll do it?" She bounced hard on the back seat and grinned when Misty turned and looked at her. "Misty heard you say it, Dad! I'm not letting you back out now. When can we start looking? When?"

"You started something for sure, Jack." Misty laughed because it sure sounded to her like he'd seriously considered Ellen's wish.

"Nah, she's right. I've been tiring of apartment living. Ellen and I haven't ever lived in a house of our own, have we, sweetheart? It's been one military posting after another since before you were born. It's about time I settled down permanently." He glanced at Misty with those penetrating gray eyes she loved so much. Eyes that could pierce her soul one minute and set her on fire the next. "What do you think?"

"I think buying a home is a huge decision and it's between you and Ellen. You don't need my opinion."

"You sure about that?" He cocked an eyebrow. "What do you think, Ellen? Should Misty have an opinion?"

"I guess so. She'll probably be hanging around a lot, won't she?"

"She will if I have anything to say about it." He rolled to a slow stop. "Look over there where people are gathering on the side of the road. I see a mama bear and two cubs fishing in the far stream. Get out the binoculars. This is probably the closest you'll ever get to a grizzly."

"A grizzly?" Ellen gasped and patted around the back seat for the binoculars. "Can I get out of the car?"

"We'll all get out. She's far enough away not to be a clear and present danger. Smokey Bear standing over there isn't stopping people from getting out of their cars. Just be prepared to hightail it back here if he tells us to move." He opened his door and leaned in facing Misty. "Come on, baby. This is a rare sight you won't want to miss."

Misty opened her door and stepped out. She clutched her jacket tight at the neckline. "Jack, Ellen, look, snowflakes. It's only September. No wonder they close the park so early."

"Hurry." Jack waved his arm. "Mama Bear spotted the gathering crowd and she's getting antsy."

They ran to the other side of the road where Misty and Ellen stood on either side of Jack. He wrapped his arms around them to ward off the dropping temperature. Taking turns with the binoculars, they each got a good look at the grizzly family before they disappeared into the woods. "Brrrr," Misty trembled the words from her lips.

"Yep. I think it's time we get back to the hotel and light that big fire." Jack urged them toward the car. "It'll be dinner time when we get there. How about we stop in town and get a pizza to take with us? We'll eat in our unit and order something from room service for dessert."

Misty and Ellen giggled as they rushed across to their car, hugging themselves against the ever increasing snowfall. Misty couldn't remember when she'd last seen falling snow, and never in such a magnificent setting.

On the way back through Jackson, Jack tilted his head to the elk gathering on the vast expanse of the Elk Refuge. "That's a sure sign winter will be here soon."

"You're right, Jack. There are more elk there than when we passed by this morning." Wonder welled in Misty every time she turned her head in this magnificent place. She was afraid of getting ahead of herself, but couldn't help thinking what a great place this would be for a honeymoon.

"Why do they come here, Dad?"

"They feed them all winter. There's a lot of controversy over the feeding program the past several years. Frankly, I think the elk are smarter than the people. They know where to spend their winters in relative comfort. It's a great tourist draw. They have sleigh rides through the herd all winter, and they have telescopes set up in the museum on the hill and at the visitor center."

Jack pulled into the small parking lot in front of Pizza Caldera. "They should have it ready by now. Anything to drink?"

"There's a big stock of soft drinks and beer in the kitchen at our hotel, Jack. I don't think you need to get anything here." Misty hugged herself and directed one of the dashboard vents to blow directly into her face and chest.

"We even have the same kind of sarsaparilla I had at the Silver Dollar. Hurry, Dad, it's getting dark and I'm cold and I'm starving."

Jack grinned. "I have a carload of bossy females. Be right back." He was no more through the door when he was back out again carrying a large pizza box. "Put this on the back seat, Ellen. No peeking or sampling until we get to our hotel."

"Party poop."

Misty laughed. "I second that, Ellen."

"I'm going to hold it on my lap. It's nice and warm."

* * *

Jack put up his feet and stretched back on the loveseat to admire the fine fire he'd built in the river rock fireplace. Misty and Ellen chattered away and rattled dishes, preparing to bring the food to serve on the coffee table fronting the hearth. *I could get used to this. I will, if they'll let me.*

Ellen carried three plates with pizza as deftly as if she'd been waiting tables for years. "Move over, Daddy." She plopped herself down next to him on the small love seat leaving Misty to sit in an adjoining chair.

Misty carried a tray of drinks and stood there with her eyebrows raised. "Feet off the table, Hawk, or I'll put this in your lap." She rolled her eyes in Ellen's direction, and he grinned and shrugged.

They attacked the pizza with gusto and enjoyed the roaring fire.

Misty'd just cleared the plates from the living room when Jack answered a knock on the door. He invited the room service waiter inside and indicated the fireplace. "We'll take it in there. He called into the kitchen, "Dessert's here!" The waiter set up the table and took his leave, smiling all the way out the door after accepting Jack's generous tip.

"What did you order? I smell something spicy and delicious." Misty padded in her stocking feet and resumed her seat in the chair. "Ellen! You better hurry; this sure smells good."

Jack patted the seat next to him. Misty smiled and shook her head. "That's Ellen's spot tonight. I'll be next to you later."

"What are we doing later?" Ellen took her seat next to him.

"Packing." He handed her a thick cloth napkin and set a warm covered bowl in her hands. "Careful it's hot." He removed the cover and handed her a spoon. "You'll remember this, sweetheart."

Her face broke into a big grin. "New Orleans style bread pudding?"

"Yep." He handed a bowl to Misty. "Ever had it?"

"No, but if it tastes as wonderful as it smells, I'm going to love it." She took the bowl from his hands, lowered her face close to the surface and took a deep appreciative sniff.

"Dad took Mom and me to New Orleans when I was little. We stayed in the old French Quarter, went to a Saint's game, and ate a boatload of bread pudding every day. I hope they got the recipe right." She dipped her spoon in and took a small bite. "Oh, my God! It's perfect!"

Jack and Misty laughed at her contented face when she closed her eyes and savored the rich dessert. He took the opportunity to mime a kiss and a wink at Misty. He added a wicked nod in the direction of her bedroom and enjoyed the rosy glow lighting her cheeks.

* * *

The long day wound down along with the flames in the fireplace. The only light in the room was the red glow of the embers. Ellen had fallen asleep with her head in Jack's lap and Misty sprawled languidly on the soft rug close to the fire.

"Ellen, wake up, sweetheart. Time for bed."

She moaned softly and sat up. "Do we really have to leave tomorrow, Daddy?"

It was moments like this, her face unguarded and childlike that filled Jack's heart to bursting with love for his daughter. His baby would be grown and gone soon. He'd missed so much of her precious childhood years. "Yes, we really have to leave tomorrow. So, hop up those stairs and snuggle under that big down comforter and get a good night's sleep. You'll be cranky when I wake you in the morning."

He glanced at Misty. She observed this exchange with smoky brown eyes. A slight smile played across her lips in silent invitation. They'd all be in bed soon, and he wasn't planning to sleep alone in his room tonight. He silently watched her until Ellen's door closed then moved across the short distance and lay next to her. "Hey, baby."

"Hey." She rolled to face him and placed a hand on his cheek.

The fire inside him replaced the waning heat and last glow of the embers. He kissed her softly. "Everything good?"

"Everything is better than good, lover man." She kissed him back and snuggled closer, sighing deeply. "Kiss me again."

She needn't have asked him. He rolled on top of her and granted her wish, again, and then again. There was no way he'd ever get enough of this woman. The heat of his passion built with each touch of her lips, her hands. Her warm breath against his neck and cheek were worth dying for, of that he had no doubt.

"Shall we move this to the bedroom?" he murmured against her ear.

"Hmm?" She giggled and turned her head. "Try this ear."

He abruptly rolled off her and tugged her to her feet then lifted her until her eyes were even with his. A thrill coursed through him as she wrapped her legs tightly around his waist. "Hold on, baby. I've got something special for you tonight."

He closed her bedroom door and took his time removing her clothing, savoring every inch of skin he revealed. His lips worshipped her shoulders and breasts. When she trembled at the touch of his mouth on her navel he grinned with satisfaction. He was so charged with deep erotic passion that he barely noticed her fingers grasping and tugging his hair. "You make me feel like I'm seventeen, baby."

"Make love to me, Jack. I've been thinking of this moment all day. You're driving me wild with wanting."

He sat back on his heels and tugged at the waistband of her jeans. As the rough fabric slipped down her silken thighs he followed with his lips, but said nothing. She didn't know the half of it. He leaned away from her as she stepped out of the pants and panties, wearing nothing but thick white socks. He smiled, stroking her abdomen and legs with his fingertips. "You are so beautiful. Do you have any idea how beautiful you are? Any idea how much I want you?" He stroked the dark blond patch of springy curls at the juncture of her legs, leaned in and kissed her there. "How'd I get so lucky?"

She loosened her grip on his hair. "I'm the lucky one." She gasped and trembled. "I've never wanted anyone so much as I want you, Jack Hawk." She lifted his hands from her hips and placed a warm, lingering kiss on one palm and then the other.

Jack raged with desire, rose, led her to the bed, and swept away the mints left on the pillows by the turn-down service. Lowering her gently he smiled. "I want you too, baby. Now I'm going to show you just how much." He quickly dispensed with his clothes and crawled in next to her. Sweeping his hands over her, he nuzzled his nose into her neck and grazed his teeth along the curve of her jaw, ears, lips and eyelids. She moaned softly under his expert touch on her breasts, a small begging sound, but he wanted to take his time with her tonight.

He pressed a hand between her legs while his mouth tugged at her earlobe. He'd barely penetrated her with his long fingers when she convulsed beneath him in a powerful orgasm.

"Oh, my God, Jack. What are you doing to me?" Her question faded to a whimper.

"Loving you." He positioned himself between her knees. "I want you to come for me again, honey." He shuddered with nearly uncontainable yearning when he sank into her moist warmth, "Can you do that? Can you come for me again?"

"I…I don't know. I've never…" Her trembling fingers dug into his lower back, brown eyes hot and unsure.

"I'll help you, my love. We'll get there together."

Chapter Twenty-Three

Christmas Eve, three months later

MISTY SCANNED THE SPACIOUS LIVING ROOM THAT NOW LOOKED small because of the number of Dwayne and Marla's guests gathered there, and the excited voices of the children. Marla's pregnancy was well advanced, and Misty and Hawk cheered with the others when Mac clapped his hands and said, "I've got an important announcement—Graciella and I are expecting a baby!"

Misty didn't miss the note of melancholy in his eyes when he put his arm around his wife and gazed at her. They still grieved for the baby lost last summer, but had moved on with the business of living. She thought her heart would melt at the shine in Santos's eyes as he stood between his mother and adopted father.

Her eyes teared up and she put a hand to her heart when Mac stood and sang O'Holy Night, to kick off the carol singing. His voice was as strong and clear as she remembered when he'd sung to calm her during a mortar attack on the forward operating base in Iraq. Her love for Cluny McPherson was deep and everlasting.

Across the room by the Christmas tree, Ellen entertained the Dempsey's baby twin girls and joked with Amber Dempsey who was trying to keep track of her toddler brother, Declan. *Why isn't Ellen that happy girl when the three of us are together?* Ellen's acceptance of her in their lives had steadily dissipated.

Jack handed her a cup of eggnog. "Having a good time?"

"Sit next to me, Jack. Mac's singing made me blue, and did you notice that my mother and I seem to be the only women in the room who aren't pregnant."

Jack laughed and pointed at Ellen and grinned. "Not the only ones, thank God."

Misty grimaced. "Oh, yeah, I see what you mean. Are you worried about her? Does she have a boyfriend?"

"I'm always worried about her. If she has a boyfriend, she's not talking about it. You know how busy she's been finishing up the semester at her current high school, and getting ready for the move to a new school and the new house, I don't know when she'd find the time." He put his arm around her and leaned in for a quick kiss.

Misty noticed when Ellen glanced their way at that very moment with a frown on her face. The hopes she'd had for developing a friendly relationship with Jack's enigmatic daughter had deteriorated since their marvelous trip to Jackson and Yellowstone in September. She was at a loss how to handle the girl, and found herself with-drawing from Ellen little by little at the same time she and Jack had grown closer.

Because she'd been so busy with her new job, she still lived with her parents. She and Jack found it increasingly difficult to find time alone. Even if Jack hadn't picked up on it, Misty knew Ellen resented her presence in their lives.

"What's wrong, honey?" Jack's penetrating gray eyes nailed her. He had an uncanny sensitivity to her moods. She loved and feared that quality in equal measure.

"Nothing," she lied. "I'm just a little tired. I had no idea how much work it would be to help set up the pet stores for the season. It's unbelievable how much money people spend on their animals. I didn't get off work until an hour ago, and barely had a chance to shower and change before my parents and I left to come here this evening."

He sniffed her neck and hair. "You smell good enough to eat. You're coming home with me tonight. I'll reenergize you."

"Is that a good idea, Jack? I'm not sure Ellen's willing to share you with me tonight and especially Christmas morning." *Or any other night—or morning—for that matter.*

"Ellen is staying here tonight and tomorrow morning. Marla asked her if she'd help with the babies and the preparation of the big Christmas buffet tomorrow. Kathleen, the Dempsey brothers' mom, has spent a month visiting Donovan and Charlene in Hawaii to get away from the cold Wyoming winter for a change. The three of them fly in tomorrow morning. It will be the first time the whole family has gathered for Christmas in years, and Marla could use the help."

"You're not spending Christmas with your daughter?" This didn't sound like him at all. She had the sinking feeling she was dangerously inserting herself between Jack and Ellen, and it would only lead to more tension.

"Of course I'm spending Christmas with her. We'll be picking her up at three."

"I'm not sure I…"

Her dad stepped in front of them. "How's the house coming along, Jack?"

"Merry Christmas, Payne." He stood and extended his hand. "It's all ready for us. We'll be moving in shortly after New Year's day. What are your plans tomorrow? Misty and I'll be coming back here to collect Ellen at three and we're going over there to do a walk-through. Would you and Debbie like to join us?"

"Knowing my wife, as I should after all these years, she's itching to have a look. Why don't we arrange a time to meet you there? I know right where it is. Nice place."

Misty smiled inwardly at her father's easy acceptance of the fact she'd be going home with Jack to spend the night. She'd felt awkward about the situation at first, almost had the feeling that since she was living in their house she needed to report on her activities to them like she had as a teenager.

"When is Mom planning dinner tomorrow? If you meet us at Hawk's new place, I'll come home with you and help her. Jack and Ellen are going to his sister's tomorrow evening."

Her dad nodded. "Speaking of Ellen, how did she feel about the move to Spring Grove and enrolling in Simi High School? Losing touch with her friends can be pretty traumatic at her age." He turned at the outburst of childish laughter from across the room. "She's turning out nicely, no small thanks to you, Jack. Look how she's managing those three little ones, and enjoying it."

"She's always been great with kids. It makes up for not having siblings, I guess." He nodded in his daughter's direction. "She was anxious about the move for a while, but when her best friend, Cherry, told her she and her mom were relocating to Seattle, and they wouldn't be able to continue their friendship, it was easier for her to make the mental adjustment. She makes friends easy. She'll do fine."

"Dad, wait till you see the beautiful renovations Dwayne's crew made to the interior. Mac and his team did a fabulous job updating the bathrooms, too. You'd never guess the house was over thirty years old." Misty remembered her trepidation when Marla showed them the place for the first time.

Jack told her later that Ellen had been horrified by the dingy and outdated condition of the inside of the house, but the seven acre fenced yard was just what she wanted. The area was zoned for small animals and she was already talking of getting a few chickens and a pygmy goat. Jack's hair had turned a little grayer listening to Ellen's excited plans.

She and Jack had never talked money, a topic she thought best avoided after Ellen's gold-digger insinuations. She'd seen the listing and Marla told her Jack had paid three quarters of a million in cash for it. What he'd spent on renovations, she couldn't imagine. The house layout had two bedroom wings separated by the kitchen, living room, great room and dining room in the center. He'd had two of the five bedrooms converted into a large master suite featuring his and hers bathrooms and dressing rooms. She forced herself into denial over what that meant. Just thinking about it, her breath caught in her throat.

"Tell you what, Payne. When we're on our way there I'll give you and Debbie a call."

"Good plan. We're just about to make our good-byes to our hosts and call it a night. See you tomorrow afternoon."

Jack hugged Misty to his side. "It's time for us to retreat, Sergeant, I can't have you falling asleep on me as soon as I get you to my place."

They made the rounds of Christmas greetings and goodbyes.

Checked to make sure Ellen knew they were leaving, and then found Dwayne and Marla canoodling in the kitchen while restoring order to chaos. Dwayne held Marla from behind and nuzzled her neck. She made small giggling protests and turned off the water, spotting Misty and Jack when she turned.

Jack grinned. "Is this big gimpster bothering you, ma'am?"

Marla smiled and nodded. "Absolutely. Constantly. Endlessly." She gave Dwayne a little shove and drummed her fingers on her prominent baby bump. "You leaving already?"

"Yes, Misty's beat. Thanks so much for inviting Ellen to spend the night. My woman and I need some quality alone time. It was a great party." He shook Dwayne's hand.

Marla smiled at Jack. "No, I should be thanking you. Your daughter is a godsend. She's the best babysitter I've ever had. Amber loves to spend time with her. Santos is staying the night, too. I'm putting all of them to work in the morning." She poked Dwayne in the chest. "You too, buster."

He still held her and rocked her from side to side. "Glad to, after I help you get your beauty sleep, honey."

Misty loved their byplay, but said, "Ick. Let's get out of here. This woman has turned my tough gunny into a...a..."

"Husband?" Jack gave Marla a peck on the cheek and pulled Misty out the door.

The cool evening air was welcome against her face. He'd parked halfway down the block and they took their time strolling to his car, Misty stopped to look at the blanket of stars and a sharp crescent moon hanging in the endless dome of clear sky. "Jack, look how beautiful."

"I am looking."

"You are not." She elbowed him. "You're staring at me." And wasn't that generating a downy blanket of warmth around her heart? She put her arms around his waist. "I love you, Jonathan Hawk."

"And I love you, Misty Beachy." He planted a firm kiss on her lips. "Let's get on home." He picked up his pace and hurried her to the car. When he opened her door he pulled her into another embrace and another blazing kiss.

"Maybe we should just crawl into the back seat, cowboy." She thrilled at the obvious evidence of his passion, and how fabulous it was to be so desired by the man she loved.

"Don't tempt me." He turned her, smacked her on the butt and closed the door once she was inside. "Buckle up. I may have to break a few speed limits."

* * *

It was a wild ride, and she wasn't referring to speed limits on the drive to his place. Jack's urgency for her grew every time they made love. Alone in the apartment, they were uninhibited and vocal. Not only did they enjoy the rambunctious sex, they had great fun laughing at each other. She'd never been so free to express herself without fear of unwanted consequences.

She flopped down beside him on the bed and let out a stream of exhausted giggles. "Jack, you've worn me out. I'm so tired. I have to get some sleep. Have mercy." She laid her hand on his chest and reveled in the way it bounced with his laughter. Rolling onto her side, she threw her leg across his hips and snuggled into the crook of his arm. That's the last thing she remembered.

"Merry Christmas, baby." Jacks lips brushed her neck and ear.

"Jack?" She struggled to open her eyes. Bright sunlight streamed through a crack in the drapes.

"Were you expecting someone else?" He sat next to her and that's when she noticed he was holding a tray and the delicious aroma of steaming coffee filled the air between them.

She rubbed her eyes, ran her fingers through her hair and pushed up into a sitting position, not feeling the need to cover her breasts. "I was expecting Santa, and you're right on time. Breakfast in bed? That was number one on my good girl list."

He set the tray on the bedside table and handed her a mug of coffee, took one for himself and sat next to her. "Lucky for you, Santa has a very broad interpretation of 'good girl.'"

She noticed he was fully dressed. The smell of soap and shampoo tickled her nose. "How long have you been up? I must have been in a coma. I didn't hear the shower." She brushed her fingers through his damp hair. Lord, he was the most beautiful man she'd ever laid eyes on. He smelled good, too. "I'm crazy for you, Hawk. Get back in bed."

He laughed. "It's noon already, 'good girl.' We have things to do, places to go, and people to see. But not before I give you this." He reached in his pocket and removed it with a small box in his hand. She'd never seen such a serious expression in his gray gaze.

Tears sprang to her eyes and her heart thudded like The Little Engine That Could. She nearly bobbled the mug before he quickly took it from her. Hands flew to her mouth. She felt suffocated equally by hope and apprehension. "Jack. I..."

He opened the box, removed the ring and took her left hand from her face. "I love you. Please say you'll marry me. There's nothing more important to me than spending the rest of my life with you, waking up with you, talking to you, laughing with you, sharing meals with you, falling asleep with you in my arms. I can't picture any other life." He slid the ring into her shaking hand and closed her fingers around it. "Please say yes." He raised her fist and kissed it and held it to his lips.

Misty gripped the ring. She struggled to breathe, attempting to stifle the tears. A sob racked from her chest, preventing her from answering him. At last she managed to gasp, "Yes."

Jack sighed, "Thank God," and kissed her forehead. A chuckle escaped him when she wrapped her arms around his neck in a death grip. "Trust me, my darling. I'm not going anywhere."

It took her several seconds to find her breath and gather her thoughts. She pulled up the corner of the sheet and wiped her face and nose. A smile, starting in her heart, bloomed on her lips. "Trust me. I'm not letting you get away."

"Don't you want to look at the ring?" He cupped her face in his hands. "I promise I won't mind if you want to choose a different one."

She let her arms fall and scooted a few inches back. Holding her fist to her chest, not wanting to break the magic of the moment, she mentally counted to ten and slowly uncurled her fingers. "Jack!" She gasped at the ring he'd chosen for her. A glittering diamond big enough to choke a Clydesdale flashed in a wreath of alternating emeralds and rubies. She'd never seen anything so magnificent. Gingerly she picked it up and stared.

"You hate it." He shook his head.

"No! I love it! It's so…Christmas." She handed it to him. "It takes my breath away. Put it on my finger."

Jack took the sparkling promise of his love and kissed her hand before carefully sliding the ring in place.

"Ask me again, Jack. Ask me again so I can say 'yes' again."

"Will you marry me?"

"Yes." She kissed him. "Ask me again."

"Will you marry me?"

"Yes." She kissed him. "Are you sure we have to leave right away?"

"Hmmm," he crooned and eased her back. "We have a little time. But you won't get breakfast."

"You're my breakfast."

* * *

Jack stroked Misty's cheek as they lay face to face. "What do you see when you look at me like that?" Her quiet intense gaze, following their very satisfying lovemaking puzzled him. He looked into her eyes shimmering with tears. "Oh, honey, don't…"

"Shh." She pressed her index finger against his lips then over his eyebrows and sighed. "What I see is my future with the man I love. I see you, Jonathan Hawk." Her finger trailed down the side of his face.

His heart swelled in his chest, breathing became difficult. Unable to form words that adequately expressed his deep emotion at her answer, he kissed her softly, her lips first, and then her eyes and nose, while stroking her satin soft shoulder. When he finally drew breath it came in ragged gulps. She trembled at his touch, and he knew this was the happiest moment of his life.

They stayed like that, quiet and still, sharing each other's breath, two souls blending into one. He never wanted this sense of wonderment to end, but they were out of time. "We have to get up. I'd rather stay here forever, but real life is knocking on the door."

"I know." She rested on her elbow. "I love you, Jack. I'm so happy. I had to tell you again."

"Never stop telling me, baby." He got off the bed and offered her a hand up. "Thanks to you, I have to hop in the shower again. I'll be quick."

Hot water sluiced over his head and face. He looked over his shoulder at the sound of the shower door sliding open. Misty stepped in behind him and slid her arms around his waist.

"I couldn't stand to be away from you." She plastered herself to his back and hugged him. "I'm not in control of all my faculties." She reached for a bottle of shampoo and handed it to him. "I'm incapable of washing my hair. You'll have to do it for me. All of this is your fault."

He barked a laugh and took the bottle. The label said body wash, but he didn't tell her, just turned her around and squeezed a large dollop of it onto her head and proceeded to massage it into her short blond hair. As if under their own power, his hands worked down to her shoulders then her breasts and hips. Her sighing under his touch inflamed him anew, but there wasn't time for that now. He willed his body to obey. "You're killing me."

"Never. I plan to keep you 'till the end of time."

Jack removed the sprayer handle and rinsed her until all trace of the body wash was gone.

"Good as new." He leaned down and nipped her shoulder. "Now get a move on, you sorceress. We have obligations. I fully intend to continue this at the soonest possible moment."

"Promise?"

"Promise." He slid the door open, plopped a towel on her head and stepped out.

On the way to Spring Grove, Jack made a quick stop at an Asian donut shop. That would have to do for her breakfast. He'd promised to retrieve Ellen from the Dempsey's no later than three. Now that they were going to show the house to Misty's parents before driving to his sister's for Christmas dinner, they had no time to waste.

"What did Ellen say when you told her you were going to ask me to marry you?" Misty bit off a piece of a donut and gingerly sipped at the to-go coffee. "How did she react?"

"I didn't tell her yet. We'll share the news on the way to the new house."

She choked. "What! No! You didn't talk about it with her?" She set the coffee in the cup holder and dropped the half-eaten donut in the bakery box. "Jack! What were you thinking?"

"Hell, I don't need my teenage daughter's permission to propose marriage to the woman I love." Hair on his neck prickled. Maybe he should have given Ellen a heads-up.

"Pull over, Jack. We need to talk before we get there."

From the corner of his eye he saw her pull off the engagement ring. She held it in her fist as if she wasn't sure what to do with it. "What are you doing?" He moved into the right lane and steered the car onto a side street and parked. "Why are you taking off your ring?"

She squeezed her eyes shut and held the fist, holding the ring against her forehead. "I can't believe you're so clueless."

Irritation at her dramatics welled up. He bit his tongue against an angry response. "I'm clueless?"

"Yes, you are. This is major. You're expecting her to accept a huge disruption in her life with no advance warning."

"What are you talking about? She knows we're together. She knows how I feel about you." His belly cramped.

"She knows I'm around, she knows we're sleeping together, Jack. She doesn't know you were planning to ask me to marry you. To move me into her home. I didn't even know you were going to ask me." She lowered her head. "God, this is awful. This is a mess."

He smacked a hand on the steering wheel. "Oh, for Christ's sake! Why are you making such a big effing deal about this?"

She whirled on him. "It is a big deal! Marrying you is the biggest deal of my life! And it's going to be pretty damn big in Ellen's life, too. God, I don't believe this."

"Speaking of clueless—did you imagine I *wasn't* going to ask you to marry me? Did you think I only wanted to roll around the sheets with you for the foreseeable future? Is that what you thought when I told you I loved you? I was just saying it to get you to spread your legs for me?"

She glared at him. The muscles in her jaw twitched.

He threw open the door and stormed out of the car. Shoving his hands into his pockets, he uttered a stream of foul invective then clenched his teeth against it. *Women, for God's sake, who needed women screwing up their lives?* He had a bratty, mercurial daughter to contend with, so why did he think it was a good idea to pursue *Misty Bitchy*? Jesus, hadn't he learned anything in all his forty-three years? Unable to master his temper, he walked away from the car and down the street. He needed to put some distance between himself and his *fiancée*. Where he ever got the hare-brained idea to propose marriage to that unpredictable shrew was a question he had no answer for.

* * *

He rounded the corner on the way back to the car. Misty stood leaning against the front fender, her arms crossed defiantly on her chest. This was one angry woman. So what, he was angry, too. He got closer and saw the engagement ring displayed prominently on her finger. Her face wore a don't-start expression. He bit his cheek against a smile, loving her more than ever.

"Get in the car."

"I don't take orders from you."

He faced her with hands on hips, rolled his eyes and spoke with exaggerated politeness. "Would you care to get in the car, please?

She yanked open the door and tossed her head. "You're a world class jerk."

Jack sighed and crossed to the driver's side. He took a breath and slid behind the steering wheel.

They drove half a dozen blocks without speaking. She broke the silence, "Okay, Hawk, we're going to do this your way. I wish you luck." She slammed back against the seat and stared out the side window.

No other words passed between for the next half hour.

Chapter Twenty-Four

Christmas evening, home of Jack's sister, Adele

ADELE'S HOUSE WAS ABLAZE WITH BRIGHT CHRISTMAS LIGHTS. The door flew open the second Jack's finger pressed the doorbell.

"Jonny! Ellen! Merry Christmas!" Adele was the only person who'd ever called him Jonny.

"Merry Christmas, Addi." He gave her a bear hug and a kiss on the lips. He was the only person allowed to address her as Addi.

"Come in, come in. Everybody's already here. We haven't seen you in ages. I'm dying to see how the house turned out. What's been going on with you two?"

Ellen tossed her head and sniffed. "For starters, Dad proposed to the bimbo he's been fu…sleeping with."

Adele's face went white with shock at her niece's blurted statement. Mouth open, she put a hand to her throat.

Jack handed the oversize shopping bag bulging with wrapped gifts to his sister. "Would you put these under the tree? Ellen and I need to step outside for a minute." He gripped his daughter's elbow and steered her out the still open door and marched her back to the car. Adele closed the door quietly behind them.

He spun Ellen around roughly, still holding her arm. "What in the hell is wrong with you!"

"You're hurting me, Dad. You're being a Grinch!" Tears welled in her big blue-gray eyes.

"There's only one Grinch here and we know who it is. You deserve a spanking. I don't care how big you are." He released her arm and ran his hands through his hair, so angry with her he clenched his teeth before he said more. Her reaction when he told her about the engagement had been just as Misty had predicted.

She'd been a sullen little bitch from the moment he'd told her. Curt and rude to Payne and Debbie Beachy with her uncalled for answers like, 'Yeah, whatever." Her open hostility to Misty was apparent to all. Jack was sure Ellen didn't know he'd heard her nasty, 'I hate you," aimed sotto voce at Misty. He'd cut short the house showing and Misty had gone home with her parents, unable to hide her broken heart.

"Get in the car. I'm going in to tell Addi we can't stay for Christmas dinner and presents." He grabbed her shoulders and turned her to the passenger door.

"No Christmas?" Her big-eyed, contrite expression was proof she knew she'd overstepped. "I'm sorry, please, Dad."

"It's too late for that now. Get in!" He waited until she sat. He slammed the door then walked briskly to his sister's front door and let himself in.

Adele was standing in the entry hall holding the bag of gifts. "Jonny, what...?"

"I'm sorry, sis. We're leaving. I'll call you later and explain. Please apologize to Frank, his parents and the kids for me."

Adele was close to tears when she touched his cheek. "Go easy on her, Jonny. She's afraid she'll lose you."

"She's got a helluva way of showing it." He turned on his heel, walked out and went to his car. He hopped in the driver's seat and yanked the door shut. Ellen sat with her face in her hands, her shoulders shaking. Good! Let her consider what she'd done.

* * *

"Ellen spoiled what should have been the happiest day of your life, darling. I'm so sorry." Misty's mother enclosed her in a warm and sympathetic hug. "So sorry."

Her dad stood by helplessly. "How about a drink?" he asked. "I could sure use one after that ordeal."

Misty stood back and wiped her eyes. "Okay, yes. That would be good, Dad. Make it a stiff one. I refuse to spoil our family Christmas together. Jack will sort it out. I have to back away and let him take care of it." She twisted the ring on her finger and worked up a smile for her parents.

"Why don't you go to the living room and sit down with your father? Enjoy your drink and relax. The Christmas tree is especially beautiful this year, thanks to your clever decorating. I'll putter here for a few minutes and put dinner on hold. We could all use a breather." She touched Payne's shoulder. "Make me my usual, sweetie. I'll join you shortly." She shooed them out of the kitchen.

Ellen's hate-filled words rang in her head as Misty accepted the drink, and her dad sat next to her on the couch. He put his arm around her shoulders, and she sighed and leaned in to him. "I miss Billy so much. Especially at Christmas. Remember when I was little? He'd put me on his shoulders and take me everywhere. He didn't care what his pals thought."

She lowered her head on her dad's shoulder. "My funniest memory is the year you gave Billy a BB gun without running it past Mom first. I thought she'd blow a gasket."

Payne grunted. "If you recall, she did when he promptly went out and shot a hole in the neighbor's inflatable snowman. I'll never hear the end of that one." He patted her leg. "I miss Bill, too, but I have you, and I'll always be here for you no matter what." He kissed the top of her head. "Now let me get a good look at that spectacular ring."

She held out her hand and Dad whistled. "Wowee! It's a beaut!"

Debbie joined them. "It's the most gorgeous engagement ring I've ever seen. Jack had it designed especially to symbolize his Christmas proposal. That man is a dear if there ever was one."

Misty's eyebrows drew together. "How do you know he had it designed?"

"Why, I went with him to the jeweler, of course." Mom raised her glass in salute.

"You went… You knew?" She sat forward and faced her father. "Did you know?"

"Not a clue. I'm on a need to know basis with your mother." He winked at his wife and raised his glass. "Good job, honey."

Misty flopped back. "I don't know where to start with Ellen. She gets more difficult to deal with every day. What is that girl's problem?" She wondered again if she would lose the man she loved because of the situation with his daughter. Even if Jack insisted, there was no way she would force herself between him and Ellen.

"Give it time, honey." Dad squeezed her to his side. "Children of divorce have emotional problems they don't understand, let alone the adults around them who try to do the right thing." He held up his glass. "I'm ready for a refill, how about you."

"Why not? I feel like getting totally shit-faced tonight." She handed him her glass. "Merry Christmas."

The sound of her parents' laughter brought a reluctant smile to her face.

* * *

The only sound in the car was Ellen's intermittent sighs and sobs. The long drive back to their apartment seemed endless. Jack's thoughts and emotions were in such turmoil he didn't dare speak. He needed to think. His instinct was to reach out and touch her, to let her know that no matter how angry and upset he was, he'd always love her, but it was too soon. She'd face the consequences of her actions. She had to understand how deeply she'd hurt him. Hurt Misty.

There would be no Christmas when they got home. The presents they'd planned to exchange at Adele's were in the bag he'd handed to his sister. Nothing in the way of a celebratory meal awaited them. Not so much as a Christmas cookie.

He parked in their assigned space and turned off the engine.

"Daddy…" Ellen turned her tearstained face to him.

"Let's go inside." He got out and left her there. By the time he had their door unlocked, she was trudging up the stairs. He went inside and tossed his keys on the hall table, took off his bomber jacket and hung it in the hall closet, and then proceeded to the kitchen.

"Daddy, please, can we…?"

"Go to your room, Ellen."

"But—"

"Now, please." He pointed toward the back of the apartment then turned his back on her and put the teakettle on the stove. He swallowed when her bedroom door closed with a quiet click. "Shit!" What in hell was he going to do? "Shit! Shit! Shit!"

Jack brewed a cup of instant coffee and carried it to his computer. He stared at the screen for a few minutes, closed it, and went to the living room and turned on the TV. After several minutes of flipping through channels with endless choices of old Christmas movies, he found a replay of a college football game. He was unable to concentrate, and if asked he wouldn't have been able to say which two teams were playing or what the score was, but he watched anyway.

An hour passed. His brain swam in a dense fog. Ellen's bedroom door opened.

"Daddy?"

He grunted.

"Is it okay if I fix something to eat? We didn't get any dinner." She'd apparently finished sobbing. Her question was clear, but muted and timid.

"Go ahead," he snapped.

"I'll fix you something to eat if you want me to."

"Do whatever you damn well please, just leave me alone!"

Ellen gasped and ran back to her room.

Pain, sharp as a knife sliced through his chest. *Nice, Hawk. Real nice.*

* * *

What was that? The front door?

Jack bolted upright. It was the middle of the night and the TV was still on. He stepped into the hall and saw Ellen's bedroom door was closed, but the motion sensor light outside the front door was on. A person or an animal had set it off. He hurried down the hall, checked the peep hole and caught a glimpse of Ellen's head bobbing as she descended the steps.

Flinging the door open, he shouted, "Where the hell do you think you're going?" He ran toward her and grabbed her arm just as she waved to the cab waiting at the edge of the parking lot with lights on.

"Get in the house. Now!" He waved off the cab and tugged her arm. She dropped the suitcase she was carrying. He grabbed it and hauled her up the stairs. They went through the still open door as lights came on in the apartment next door to them. Jack slammed the door and dragged Ellen into the living room and sat her roughly down on the couch. "Jesus H. Christ! What am I going to do with you?"

She glared with defiance, her lip curled. "You don't have to do anything with me. I'm going to live with Mom!"

"Like hell you are!" He grabbed handfuls of his hair and paced.

"I called her. She said it was okay if I came." Then in a smaller voice she added, "For a little while."

Jack stopped in front of her. "And then what?" He wanted to break something. Throw something. He clenched his jaw so hard it was a wonder he had any enamel left on his back teeth. "Where's your phone?"

Not quite as defiant as she'd been seconds before, Ellen reached in her pocket. "Here."

"Call Theresa. Tell her you're not coming." He pointed to the phone. "Do it now."

"But she bought me a non-refundable ticket. It's waiting for me at the airport. She'll lose the money if I miss the flight."

"Do you think I give a rat's ass? Call her!" If his headache got any worse he'd probably have a brain hemorrhage. He slumped in a chair and thrust his finger toward her phone.

"What do I tell her?" She held the phone in a shaking hand, fingers still and unsure above the call button, her bottom lip trembling.

He leaned back and crossed his arms. "You created this mess. Figure it out." He gave her a commanding look he'd perfected. It had been very useful disciplining junior officers and airmen in the Marines.

She swallowed, tears shimmering on her lower eyelashes and

placed the call. "Mo…Mom? It's me. Uh…I'm…uh…not coming." She pressed fingers against her lips and nodded. Jack heard Theresa's angry screaming from halfway across the room.

Tears slipped down Ellen's flaming red cheeks. "I know. I'm sorry. I'll pay you back, okay! Stop yelling!" She disconnected the call and threw the phone on the floor. She stood, stomped her foot, retrieved it, sighed and dropped it on the coffee table. She plopped back on the couch cushions. Like a small kid she wiped her nose on the sleeve of her hoodie.

"Get a tissue and blow your nose—and quit acting like the spoiled brat you are. Go wash your face. We're going out to get some breakfast." He tried to harden his heart, but he couldn't sustain his anger after what Theresa had just done to her.

"Breakfast! It's only four-thirty."

"Yeah, I noticed. Go."

* * *

At ten after five a.m. they took a booth at the Denny's on Sepulveda Blvd. in Sherman Oaks. Ellen hadn't spoken a word since she stalked from the living room to wash her face, but her guilty expression gave her away.

A smiling middle-aged woman approached their table, coffee pot at the ready. She held two china mugs in her other hand. "Morning, folks. How about a nice cup of fresh coffee?"

Jack forced a smile and nodded. "Yes, thanks. We need coffee."

She winked. "Looks like you two have had a heck of a Christmas celebration." She took two menus from a wide apron pocket, dropped them on the table and left the coffee pot behind.

Ellen put two packets of sweetener in her coffee and added three containers of creamer. She dared to peek at her father and he caught her eye before she could look away.

"Look at me, Ellen. This nasty acting-out stops now. You'll be sixteen in less than a month, and I've had it up to here with your childish antics." He sliced a hand under his chin. "Are you listening?"

"Yes!" Head bowed, she nodded and stared into her cup. "Do you hate me?"

His guts twisted. He paused and took a tentative sip of the steaming java. Tipping up her chin, he said, "Let's start with you agreeing to never ask me such a stupid question again. Okay?"

She choked on a small sob and nodded.

Jack noticed the approach of the waitress and held up his hand. The woman turned and retreated behind the counter. "Let's talk about love, shall we? If you're under the impression that I have a finite amount of love to go around, and have to portion it out here and there, you're dead wrong. I don't have a love meter that goes from one to ten. You get ten, and then I fall in love with a woman I want to marry, so now she gets six and you get four. It doesn't work that way, sweetheart."

She made a tiny humming sound and nodded.

"Shall we order breakfast? You must be starving. I am."

Ellen started to wipe her nose on her sleeve again, stopped and used the paper napkin under her silverware. "Uh huh."

"Do you know what you want?"

She coughed. "Pancakes and bacon."

Jack caught the waitress' eye and signaled they were ready to order. She wasted no time getting to the table, pad and pen at the ready.

"What'll it be for you this morning?"

"My daughter and I'll each have a stack of pancakes and a side order of crispy bacon. Put powdered sugar and whip cream on hers. I'll have mine plain." He smiled and handed her their menus. "Thanks."

"Wait." Ellen raised her hand. "On the pancakes, not on the bacon."

The waitress laughed. "I got it, hon. Comin' right up." She lifted the insulated coffee pot to judge the amount left, nodded and took their orders to the kitchen pass-through.

"Give me your hand, Ellen." The look in her gray eyes shook him to the core when she tentatively reached for him. "You're my daughter. My only child. There is no limit to how much I love you. I'll admit there are times when I don't like you much, but that can't be helped. I'm human, I'm your father, but I have feelings just like everybody does. You never need to worry that someone else will take your place. There's a special part of me that will always be yours, and only yours. Someday when you have children of your own, you'll understand."

She swiped at her eyes. "Daddy, I'm sorry. I don't know what I…"

"You don't need to apologize to me again, sweetheart, but you will apologize to Misty, her parents and Aunt Adele. Nothing can be resolved until you do."

"I'm so, like…terminally embarrassed?"

Jack nodded and pressed his lips together thoughtfully. "As you should be. I need to understand why you're so hostile to Misty."

"I don't know." She threw up her hands. "I'm afraid of her, I guess."

"You want to know something funny?" He raised his eyebrows. "She's afraid of *you*." When Ellen shook her head vigorously, he raised a hand and added, "Oh, trust me, she is. Not only that, as it turns out she's more in touch with your feelings than I am."

"I'm not sure what you mean, Daddy."

Jack shrugged. "She took off my engagement ring when she found out I hadn't talked to you before I popped the question. She took it for granted I'd tell you first. She was very upset with me."

Her eyes couldn't have gotten any wider as she nailed him with a beam powerful as a Maglite. "Why?"

He shook his head. "She knew instinctively how you'd react. How you'd feel shut out and disregarded. We had a fight over it. She predicted what would happen and she was exactly on the mark."

"She did?"

Jack yanked his hand back like he'd touched a hot iron. "Whoo boy, did she ever." He sighed and took a long swallow of his coffee. "I owe her a whopper of an apology, too." He sat back as the waitress put their plates on the table.

"Anything else for you, folks?"

Jack raised his hand. "We're good."

"Give a holler if you need anything."

Jack reached for his phone. "I'm sending Misty a text. I'll ask her to call me when she wakes up. I want to get this out of the way quick."

"Okay, but I'd rather die." Ellen sighed and dropped her chin in her hand. "Really."

He laughed and dug into his pancakes. "You're not getting off that easy."

* * *

His phone vibrated right when the waitress put their check on the table. Ellen cringed when he answered.

"Good morning, love. Are you up for some company? Yes, me. And Ellen." He listened for several seconds. "No, we're good here. When?" He glanced at his watch. "Sounds good. We'll be there. Uh, huh. I love you too. More than you know."

Jack ended the call and leaned forward on his elbows. "I want to give you something to think about, sweetheart. Don't answer me now, just consider what I'm going to say." He waited for her nod. "Okay, here goes. Misty and I are in love. I *will* marry her. She's the woman I want by my side, to live with me, share happiness and sorrow with me and to grow old with me. I'm very happy and lucky to have her love. My question is: why don't you want me to have that happiness?"

He saw the shine of new tears in Ellen's eyes when he stood and took the check to the cashier.

Chapter Twenty-Five

Home of Misty's parents

MISTY PEEKED THROUGH THE WINDOW BLINDS WHEN SHE HEARD a car door slam. Jack, hands in his pockets, and Ellen, dragging her feet, approached the front door. She nervously twisted the engagement ring and wondered what was in store.

Her mother entered the room. "Are they here?"

"Yes, they just got out of the car. I haven't been this nervous since I was given command of my platoon twelve years ago. I hope I don't throw up. Where's Dad?"

"On his computer. Do you want us to leave?"

"No! I'll need you here to pick up the pieces."

"Honey, relax. Jack loves you. He wants to marry you. This will all be resolved." She glanced at Misty when the doorbell rang. "Are you ready?" Her mom reached for the door. "Shall I open it?"

A sick chill crept down her back. She took a breath and straightened her spine. "Yes. Might as well get it over with." She cupped her hands around her mouth and yelled down the hallway, "Dad! We have company."

Payne strolled into the room just as Debbie opened the door. He briefly patted Misty's shoulder and whispered, "Chin up, my mighty Marine."

Debbie greeted them with a welcome smile. "Hello, Ellen. Jack. Come in and have a seat. Would you like anything to drink? I'd be happy to put on a fresh pot of coffee, or we have soft drinks in the refrigerator."

Jack dipped his head and kissed her mother on the cheek. "Thanks, Debbie. We're fine. Ellen has something to say."

Ellen swallowed and nodded. Her eyes darted furtively around the room. "I…um…I want to apologize for being such a totally, sucky, awful brat yesterday. When Dad told me he was getting married, I…"

"Shall we sit?" Debbie indicated the couch then took the seat next to Ellen. "How are you, dear?"

Ellen took a breath. "I didn't mean to spoil Christmas, I was just so…um…you know, shocked?"

Misty whirled on Jack. "I told you! Didn't I tell you? Ellen, I told your father he was wrong not to give you some advance warning." She made a move to sit on the other side of Jack's daughter. "Scooch over." Not knowing what else to do, she put her arm around the girl's shoulder. "I'm so mad at him. I forgive you. I understand, honey, really."

Ellen raised her ravaged face. "You do?" Her chin trembled pathetically.

Misty stood and took Ellen's hand. "Let's go for a walk, okay?"

Ellen cast a furtive look at Jack. He shrugged and nodded. "Okay," she murmured.

They'd passed three houses when Misty sighed and said, "Look, let me just say it, okay? I've never loved a man the way I love your dad. I never thought I'd find anyone like him, a man who loved me in spite of my weirdness and insecurities. I love him, Ellen."

Ellen stared at the sidewalk and nodded.

Misty took a few more steps. "There's no way I could ever take your place in his heart. I don't want to. I want my own place in his heart; because I know it's big enough for both of us. Can we find a way to share him?"

Ellen stopped and lowered her head into her hands. Misty waited until she got herself together. "Ellen, I don't want to be your mother. I don't have the first clue how to be anyone's mother. The only thing I

244

was ever really good at was commanding a platoon of jock Marines. I would like to be your friend. Can we try that?"

"What I said about you being after Dad's money? That was barf. There was no way you could have known about his grandfather's trust fund. I wanted to get rid of you. I was scared what would happen if he wanted you instead of me."

"What you felt is perfectly normal. You don't ever need to apologize for your feelings. But it would be good if we could talk about them."

"Um…I'll try, okay." She looked up. "I want Dad to be happy."

"Let's go back. My mom just put a pan of sticky buns in the oven."

"Wait, Misty." Ellen stopped. "Can I look at the ring?"

Misty held out her left hand. "It's something isn't it?"

"I've never seen an engagement ring like this. Do you like it? It's kinda—"

"Yes. It certainly is. It's Jack. That's why I love it so much." She linked her hand in Ellen's elbow. "Come on. Shall we let your dad dangle on that hook, or go easy on him?"

"Dangle. He's a guy. Guys are like, ack."

Misty's laugh brought a welcome smile to Ellen's face.

"You know what, Ellen? The no-kill animal shelter is having open house today. All adoptions are free except for the cost of immunizations. I bet we might find just the dog you're looking for. Want to go?"

She gasped, and her eyes went wide with childish anticipation. "Could we?" Her face fell. "Oh, but Dad…"

"We out vote him if we stick together. It's two against one."

Ellen's tentative smile was encouraging. *We can make this work.*

* * *

Jack stopped pacing when Misty and Ellen walked in the front door. *Uh, oh, these two are up to something.* "Hey! Did you smell Debbie's pecan rolls?" He sounded pretty stupid but couldn't think of anything else to say. He put his hands in his pockets then immediately pulled them out and breathed a sigh of relief when Debbie called from the kitchen.

"Get'em while they're hot! Coffee's ready, buns are bubbly."

Payne jumped up. "Oh, boy." He hurried from the room.

Misty's dad had been on tenterhooks just like him while she and Ellen were out. Debbie had left them to stew in silence when she went to the kitchen to check on the rolls. The two men had stared at each other and could find nothing to say to break the tension.

Misty sniffed the delicious aroma. "Come to the kitchen, Ellen. I'm starved. How about you?" Ellen snickered and followed her, leaving Jack standing there like an afterthought. He closed his eyes for a second, then followed them.

I'm toast.

Jack's cell buzzed while they were enjoying Debbie's specialty. He looked across the table at her and said, "Sorry, I should have turned this thing off." He glanced at the caller I.D. "It's my sister. She lives in Palmdale. I'll step out back and take her call." He strode to the slider and stepped onto the small back patio.

He paced and gestured during the short conversation, and then he smiled slightly and ended the call. Opening the slider he stepped back inside and took his seat.

"Everything okay with your sister, Jack?" Misty reached under the table and brushed her hand against his knee. A deliberate direct hit on his libido. He grabbed her hand and squeezed.

"Yes, in fact Ellen and I are going to their place for dinner this evening. I'd like you to come with us. She wants to meet you."

"I'd love to meet your sister. It's about time, don't you think? Does she know about us?"

Ellen spoke up, "I...um...told her. Not in a very nice way, though. We left and didn't get Christmas. Now I have to apologize for it. I want to—really." Her big gray eyes implored Misty. "So, you'll come with us?"

"What time is she expecting us, Jack?"

"Around five."

"Okay, well we better get a move on then. Ellen and I have something important to do first, so we'd better get started. You're coming with us, Jack. Bring your checkbook." She scooted her chair away from the table. "Come on, what are you waiting for?"

Ellen stood, "Come on, Daddy. This could take a while."

"What are you two cooking up? How much is this going to cost me?" They were definitely scheming and it appeared he had nothing to say about it, but was expected to pay for whatever it was. He stood and faced a wall of two determined women. Might as well surrender, he was outnumbered. He cast a helpless look at Payne.

Misty's dad shrugged and held open his hands. "Good luck, my friend. Call if you need backup."

Misty patted his cheek. "Get a move on, tightwad." She stood on tiptoe and kissed him. "This won't cost much. I promise."

"You think kissing me is all you need to do to get me to crack open my wallet?" He couldn't help smiling at the smug expression on her adorable face.

One identical to Ellen's.

Yep, toast.

They piled into his car. Jack started the engine and backed out of the driveway. "Am I supposed to guess where we're going?"

"You want me to drive?" Misty pointed at her chest and cocked her head.

"Not on your life. First my checkbook, and then my car? I don't think so. Just give me directions."

Misty nodded. "Go towards Simi. We'll pick up the 23 Freeway then head east on the Ronald Reagan. I'll give you directions on the way. Trust me, Jack. This won't be too painful. Not that you really have a choice." She turned and winked at Ellen. "Right, Ellen?"

"Right!"

"Oh, for the love of Pete! What do you two have in store for me?"

When they ultimately turned down a busy road in the industrial section of Simi, Jack figured out where they were headed. He'd been here before when Misty brought him to meet the owner of the shelter. She volunteered to work whenever she could. But, why were so many cars in the parking lot on the day after Christmas?

Ellen leaned forward and tapped him on the shoulder. "There's a car pulling out up there, Dad. What a great parking spot. Grab it before anybody else sees it."

"Yes, ma'am. Anything you say, ma'am." He shook his head and surrendered. Whatever they had planned, he was just along for the ride.

With his checkbook.

* * *

When Jack parked in front of his sister's house, Ellen spoke from the back seat, "Aunt Adele is waiting for us on the porch. I want to die right now."

"It won't be so bad, Ellen," Misty turned and gave her a reassuring smile. "Think of it like going on patrol in a warzone. You breathe deep, clear your mind, stay alert and step carefully. Just say what you have to say and it's over and done with." She reached back and patted the big clumsy puppy Ellen held in her lap. "Right, Ace?"

Ellen groaned and hugged the four-month-old yellow Lab.

Jack opened his door. "Okay, troops, forward march. Leave Ace in the car until we get Addi's permission to bring him in."

The three of them walked up the sidewalk to the front door at the same time Adele stepped off the porch and approached them with a lovely, welcoming smile.

Jack embraced his sister. "Merry Christmas, Addi. There's someone I'd like you to meet." He put his arm around Misty's back and urged her closer to his sister. "Addi, this is…"

Adele grinned and finished the sentence, "Your bimbo. I'm so happy to meet you." She gathered Misty into a hearty and warm hug then held her at arm's length. "Nice going, Jonny."

Ellen raised her hands to her face and screamed, "Aaaargh! I hate myself!"

Misty and Adele laughed, and Jack embraced his daughter. "See— you survived."

They were interrupted by a series of desperate, high pitched barks and whines. Adele gaped at the car. "What have we here?"

"It's my dog, Ace. Misty got him for me for Christmas. Can we bring him in the house? Dad said we had to ask you first."

"Of course! Bring him in if you're not afraid your uncle and cousins will spoil him rotten before the evening is out." She grinned at Misty. "What a wonderful gift." She went to the car with Ellen to fetch the puppy before he clawed his way through the window glass.

Jack whispered in Misty's good ear. "Your wonderful gift cost you fourteen dollars and cost me a hundred forty-seven dollars by the time the two of you bought every dog accessory in the place."

She kissed him. "You'll survive, Jonny."

"Only my sister is allowed to call me that." He cocked his head and gave her a stern look, punctuated by his glinting gray eyes.

She tapped his nose. "Until now."

By the time Ellen and Adele had Ace out of the car, the front door opened, and Frank stuck his head out. "What's all the racket out here?" He stepped forward and shook hands with his brother-in-law. "Merry Christmas, Jack." He grinned. "And this must be the bimbo you're engaged to marry. Very happy to meet you, and may I say, it's about time somebody snagged this guy."

"I'm not sure who did the snagging." She shook Frank's hand. "Nice to meet you, Frank. My real name is Misty Beachy. The Marines in my platoon thought I didn't know their private name for me was Master Sergeant Misty Bitchy, so the way I see it, Bimbo is a step up. Perhaps you and I can have a private conversation later and you can give me a heads up on what I've let myself in for."

"Happy to if I can pry you away from Jack." Still holding her hand, he pulled her into a hug. "Just in case he won't let me do this again."

Misty loved Jack's sister and her husband that quick. Adele bore a strong family resemblance to her little brother. Same posture, same chin, same gray eyes. Frank was over six feet with the build of a lumberjack. She was curious to see who their two boys and one girl took after.

"Let's have a toast as soon as we can get everyone in the same room. Adele has dinner ready to go and she's been on pins and needles all day. It'll be hard to pry the boys away from Forza Motorsport 5. They've been at it since last night."

A small redheaded girl peeked through the open door. "Uncle Jack!" She ran into his arms, and he swung her in a wide circle. "How's my favorite niece?"

She patted his cheeks. "You don't got no other nieces!"

"True, but you're still my favorite."

She looked shyly at Misty. "Hi."

Misty smiled and wiggled her hand in greeting. The ring sparkled under the porch light. "Hi."

"Ooooh! Can I look at your ring?"

Misty realized that she'd soon be this adorable child's aunt. She'd never thought of herself in that role, and surely not after Billy was killed. Billy would have put this girl on his broad shoulders and carried her everywhere just like he'd done with her. A sharp pain squeezed her heart, but she smiled at the child and held out her hand.

"Oh! It looks just like a Christmas tree decoration."

Jack winced.

"Yes," Misty wiggled her finger and they watched it sparkle. "Isn't it the most beautiful thing you've ever seen?"

"Uh huh." She kissed her uncle. "Some day a handsome prince like you will give me a ring even more beautifuller than this one."

Jack hugged her. "I don't doubt that for a minute."

The girl squealed and struggled. "A puppy! Daddy, look, Ellen has a puppy. Let me down, Uncle Jack!"

* * *

Jack's eyes swept the living room taking in his sister's family and Ellen and the woman he would marry. Misty had fit in perfectly with them. Dinner was festive and later he'd thank Adele for putting on a second complete Christmas dinner for their benefit. After dinner gifts were exchanged in the living room and Misty went on to beat both of the boys at their X-box game. They were incredulous and embarrassed to be whipped by her, especially because they'd assumed, being a small cute blond, she had no chance.

The two youngest of the family, his red-headed niece and Ace the puppy were sound asleep on the floor under the Christmas tree. Frank rose and gently lifted his daughter in his arms to carry her off to bed. Ellen sat next to Adele with her head on her aunt's shoulder. Addi had asked her if she and her puppy would like to spend the night. Tomorrow they'd do Christmas exchanging. She hadn't hesitated for a second.

Jack squeezed Misty's hand and leaned close. "Time for us to hit the road, beautiful. We both have to work tomorrow. I'll go out and unload Ace's crate and his food while you say your goodbyes. You might want to call your parents and let them know you'll be staying with me tonight."

"That means we'll have to get up well before the sun, you know." She raised her arms in a luxurious stretch.

"You also know that I beat Old Sol to the punch every day. I'll make sure to get you home in time to change and get to work on time."

When they rose from the couch, Adele and Ellen followed their lead. Jack was pleasantly surprised to see Ellen give Misty a good night hug as he went out the door. He heard the oldest nephew shout, "We demand a rematch, Misty!"

"You don't stand a chance, pal," Misty teased.

Jack carried the dog's luggage in the front door and said goodnight to his sister and her husband.

"The boys said to tell you goodnight. I've already sent them off to bed." Frank gathered up Misty for another hearty hug. He and Adele and Ellen walked them out to the car, Ace trailing behind and tugging on his leash.

"You've got your work cut out for you with this one." Adele laughed. "He and that leash don't mix."

"I know." Ellen stooped down and untangled his clumsy feet from the narrow leather strap. He immediately twisted himself up again. Ellen gave up and lifted him in her arms. "What am I going to do with you?" She kissed him between the eyes, his tail whipping wildly with ecstasy.

"I'm taking him over to those bushes, Dad." She kissed Jack. "I'll see you tomorrow night after you get off work."

"Good night, sweetheart."

Ellen turned to leave, then stopped and looked over her shoulder. "Good night, Misty."

"Good night, girlfriend. See you soon." She climbed in the door Jack held open for her and aimed a last wave at Frank and Adele.

Jack closed her door and rounded the car. He got in on the driver's seat and leaned across to kiss her. "Have I mentioned that I love you?"

"Not for hours." She grinned and fastened her seatbelt. "Home, James."

About halfway back, Jack brushed his knuckles down her cheek. "I want you to start packing your things so you can move in the house with us next week. I don't want to spend one single night away from you than I have to."

"I don't either, but there's something you have to do first, and you know what it is."

"Point taken." He smiled to himself and drove.

When he closed the apartment door behind them, he took her in his arms. "I have something different planned for tonight."

She put her arms around his neck and smiled. "I can't wait to hear it."

"I want to do something really bizarre." He ran his hands down her back and settled them on her bottom.

"Am I going to like it?"

"I think so."

"Spit it out, Marine."

"I want to take you to my bed, pull you up tight against me, cuddle with you all night long and dream sweet dreams. You up for it?"

"Have I lost my irresistible allure, fly boy?" Her brown eyes nearly melted his bones.

"On the contrary, I just want to live long enough to enjoy you every way and endlessly."

She kissed his chest and ran her hands down his sides. "You romantic devil, you. At this rate I may lose count of all the reasons I love you."

Chapter Twenty-Six

Hawk Home, Spring Grove, Mid-January.

"Now aren't you glad we did this?" Misty grinned at Jack. Ellen's Sweet Sixteen birthday party was winding down. "I'm glad Cherry and her mother, Doris, helped by supplying the names of half a dozen girlfriends from her former high school." She gave him a smug look. "The timing worked out great as a going away for Cherry's departure to Seattle in a week too."

"I thought you said you didn't know anything about girlie stuff," Jack teased then helped her carry the gifts out to the picnic table on the back patio.

"You did a great job stringing the twinkling lights around the perimeter of the patio and through the trees and shrubs, Jack. Cherry's unique cake is a big hit."

"It was delicious too."

The girls would be leaving to meet other friends for a movie at the Regal Cinema in Simi Valley.

Jack set the packages on the table. "I'm still not comfortable with them meeting kids I don't know and being out so late at the movies in Simi Valley without us chaperoning."

"Don't be such a worrywart. She promised to be home by eleven. It's her sixteenth birthday, my love. This is a rite of passage. She's been so good since Christmas, through the ordeal of moving, and then starting in a new high school. Give her a break."

"You're right, but I know what sixteen and seventeen-year-old boys are like, and don't tell me they won't be meeting boys as soon as they're out of our sight."

"Of course they'll be meeting boys, but there's protection in numbers. She promised they'd stay together. What do you want to do, put her in a convent?" She embraced him. "Come on, Daddy, relax. If it makes you feel any better, Doris told me she was going to shadow them from a distance until they enter the movie theater. She has to be there to take Cherry and the other girls home when the movie lets out anyway."

"Okay, I feel better. I told Ellen we'd pick her up, but she said a new friend who lives nearby would give her a ride home."

His words didn't match the worry lines between his eyes. Misty remembered how her dad looked when she first started dating. He'd ask a gazillion questions, make sure he had the boy's home phone number and the names of his parents, and then he'd call the boy's parents to make sure they'd be home for the evening of the date or he wouldn't let her go.

She supposed men remembered the raging hormones of their youth, and what they'd tried to get away with. There were always compliant girls whose names spread like wildfire through the teenage male ranks. And while the boys may have been sweet on 'nice' girls, they did everything possible to get between the legs of the willing ones.

She'd overheard Billy and one of his friends talking the evening they dressed to take their nice girlfriends to the senior prom. They joked derisively about an adventure they'd shared with one of *those* girls in a darkened park one evening, calling her a slut and worse. She was silently disappointed and angry with Billy for a long time after that. What made them think they weren't the sluts?

"Ellen's not one of those girls, Jack."

"What?"

"She has standards. She thinks too much of herself to go down that path."

"You seem to have forgotten how she was last year when we lived in San Diego."

She waved her hand. "She was rebellious to get your attention. And it worked. She knows what you gave up for her, and she won't disappoint you." She paused and placed her hand on his chest. "Let's call them out to the patio. Once they clear out we'll have a few hours alone before the day is done. I promise I won't disappoint you either, man of mine."

"Alone?" He quirked an eyebrow and tipped his head toward Ace who galloped around the back of the property chasing invisible prey. "He's more trouble than I expected."

"He's just a baby. Ellen and I are making great progress with him. Think of Ace as the only grandchild you're likely to have for many years." She laughed at his peeved expression.

* * *

At ten thirty, Misty rose from Jack's bed and pulled on a pair of sweat pants then grabbed the denim shirt he'd had been wearing, put it on and rolled up the sleeves. "Better get some clothes on, Hot Stick. Can't greet your daughter in your birthday suit." She slipped her bare feet into an old pair of sandals she used as slippers. "I'll meet you in the kitchen. We left a big mess in there."

"I'm right behind you, baby." He threw back the sheet and stood. "You're wearing my shirt."

Misty gave him a knowing smile. "Yes I am. This way you still have your arms around me." She threw him a kiss. He reached into thin air and grabbed it, but instead of putting it on his lips he put it on a part of his anatomy she'd paid particular attention to the past hour.

Feigning shock, she gasped, "You're awful, Jack Hawk. I don't know what to do with you."

"I do." He leered and gave his hips a little forward thrust.

She ran laughing from the room.

* * *

They were putting the last of the silverware in the drawer when she heard Ace barking like crazy. "What's got into him?" She looked through the kitchen window. "Jack, he's spooked about something. He's going to try and jump the gate."

"I'll go see what's wrong." He dropped the dishtowel on the counter and went to the back door.

Misty opened the front door to see if she could tell what had set the dog off. She spotted a car parked at the end of the long driveway. Hair prickled on the back of her neck. Something was wrong. Taking a few steps in the car's direction she hesitated then broke into a run.

A terrified female scream assaulted Misty's ears.

"No! Stop!"

What the hell! Was the bastard trying to kill her?

She reached the car and yanked open the driver's door, grabbed the back of his jacket and hauled him out of the vehicle onto the asphalt. He was on his feet in a nanosecond. His big fist slammed into Misty's face. Everything went black when her head bounced on the ground. His boot stomped her stomach like a pile driver.

Pain screamed through her. *He's killing me. I'm going to die. In the street. In front of Hawk's house.*

"Don't move." The arctic blast of Jack Hawk's deadly calm voice jarred her into consciousness. "Down on your knees. Now! Ellen," he said in the same cool timbre, "dial nine-one-one on your cell phone and hand it to me."

"No. Daddy, wait, he didn't…"

"Do as I say."

Misty struggled to her feet, staggered against the car, her hand cupping her right eye.

"You okay, baby?"

She sucked in a breath to clear the fuzz. Her midsection screamed in pain. "No. But I will be." She hurled her arm forward with every bit of strength she could muster and slapped the bastard, open-handed, on the side of his face, knocking his neck against the barrel of Hawk's big service weapon.

"You bitch!" The guy held the side of his face and sputtered saliva.

"You move one inch and you'll be in a body bag. This is a forty-five in the back of your neck with a round chambered. The clip is loaded with hollow point ammo, but I'll only need one to take off your head."

Ellen stepped out of the car clutching the ripped front of her ruined new blouse. She held the phone across the hood. "They answered."

"Hand the phone to Misty, then go inside. Go straight inside and lock the door." He hadn't raised his voice. Hadn't needed to. "Do not turn on your laptop or your tablet. Do not call or text anyone. Do you understand me?"

Her mumbled *yes* was barely audible.

This time Jack cranked it up a notch. "Do you understand me?"

"Yes." Ellen made a run for it and slammed the door behind her. The bang was a cannon round echoing down the tree-lined street.

Misty's palm stung. The slender cell phone burned her tender skin. "Send a police cruiser to five-four-five Sunkist Trail. We're holding an attempted rapist at gunpoint." She dragged in a lungful of cool air despite the sharp pain in her ribs. "Misty Beachy. The home is owned by Jonathan Hawk. Yes, I'll stay on the line." The pain in her eye mounted, skin burning like fire down the side of her face all the way to her neck. She clutched her stomach.

The Elvis wannabe snarled, "That little cock teasing cunt wanted it. She ..."

Jack shifted the barrel of his weapon to the guy's ear and jammed it home. "Please say one more word. Just one word, asshole. I have a feeling this weapon might discharge accidentally. Wouldn't that be a goddamn shame?"

Misty touched her eyebrow. "I can't see out of my right eye, Hawk."

"Tell them to dispatch an ambulance. Move over here and sit on the curb behind me. I don't want you to end up as collateral damage when I *accidentally* pull the trigger."

"Please, man," the slime-ball whimpered, "that hurts."

Jack gave the forty-five a forward push. "That?"

"Ease up, Jack. I see the strobes. They'll be here in a second." Misty dropped her chin on her chest as two black and whites converged from opposite directions. A young officer, gun drawn, ordered, "Put down the weapon, sir! Put down the weapon and put your hands on your head."

Jack extended both arms, the forty-five dangling from his left index finger. He took a step back, eased into a squat and slowly and carefully laid the gun on the ground.

"Hands on your head, sir." Jack immediately complied.

"That prick tried to kill me," the creep whined. "He—"

"Keep your hands where I can see them and keep kissing the pavement. Do not speak again."

A female officer exited the second cruiser and approached Misty. "Stay where you are, ma'am. You're hurt. The medics are on the way."

Misty's eyes followed the officer's gaze to the front of her shirt. A red blanket of blood covered the denim. She pulled back a hand sticky with blood. The coppery stench assailed her, turned her stomach. Suddenly, she was transported to the day of the ambush and firefight in Iraq. A hard retch racked her throat. Projectile vomit spewed her knees and feet.

"Let me help her," Jack demanded.

"Stay where you are, sir. I've got it."

"Goddamit! She's hurt!" The volume cranked sharply up. Now Jack's rage was unmistakable.

A fire truck and a rescue ambulance rumbled to a stop next to the police vehicles. Residents across the street pointed and speculated. Running footsteps converged on Misty. A fire captain knelt beside her and two other men guiding a gurney hesitated so the female officer could step aside.

The fireman supported Misty's back and his fingers rested lightly on the pulse point of her wrist. The paramedic directed a bright light into her left eye. She winced at the glare. The light swept to her right eye but she could only see a faint glow.

"What's wrong? I can't see."

"Your eye's filling with blood. Don't move if you can help it." He squeezed her shoulder. "Let's immobilize her head and get her on the gurney."

The female officer said, "I need to take her statement."

"Not now." He waved her back. "Ready, Joe?"

"Ready."

"Okay, ma'am. Lean slowly back against Captain Russell. Easy. Easy. Good. We're going to put this brace around your neck and slide you onto the gurney. Easy does it."

"My eye, I can't see." Another wave of nausea hit her and she swallowed against the rising bile.

"Yes. We'll take care of you." He patted her arm. "Okay, good. Raise it up, Joe."

Jack stepped forward, hands still on his head, then stopped. "She was wounded in Iraq. Years ago. Her right eye and right ear. Tell the doctor she has shrapnel fragments in her eye."

"You her husband?"

Misty's hand flopped at her side. "He's my fiancé." She sucked in a ragged breath. "Jonathan Hawk. We're going to be married." The words slipped easily, naturally, from her tongue.

"Come with me, Jack." She couldn't move her head but his face was clear when he leaned close and kissed her gently.

"You need help. I'll get there as soon as I can, but I can't leave Ellen right now, baby. The police need to finish their work." He laid a gentle hand over hers. "Okay?"

Her chin trembled. "Yes, you have to stay and make sure she's all right." Of course, he had to look after his daughter first.

They moved her into the ambulance and secured the gurney. The one called Joe stepped out and closed the back door. He entered the front and put the vehicle in drive then, lights flashing, headed down the dark street.

Jack, she wanted Jack.

* * *

Hawk watched the ambulance move away. He scrubbed his hand over his face and dropped his head back. "Be okay, baby, please be okay."

The female officer asked him to step out of the street and onto the grass. He nodded to her and stood where she indicated.

"Hey, Sanchez!" Another officer held Jack's weapon dangling from the barrel of a pen. "There's no clip, no ammo."

"You fucking son of a bitch!" The garbage on the ground attempted to move, but the officer who'd cuffed him pushed him back down. Two officers lifted him up by the elbows and shoved him into the back of a squad car.

One of them leaned in and recited the Miranda warning then slammed the door.

"Was your fiancée, Miss, uh, spell the name please, the intended victim?" The female officer held an electronic pad in front of her and tapped in the name as Jack spelled it. She then entered his name, the location and the time.

"No. My daughter, it was my daughter, Ellen Hawk. She's sixteen. It's her birthday. Misty saw what was happening. She charged the car and dragged him off of her."

"That bitty thing?" Her skeptical expression told him she didn't believe it. "Are you sure?"

"Yes, I'm sure. She's a Marine." A swell of pride filled his chest. "She's fearless. I saw it happen, grabbed my weapon and ran out here."

"Where's your daughter, sir?" She scanned the area.

"I sent her inside."

"I'll need to talk to her."

"How long is this going to take? I have to get to the hospital."

"Not long. You can give me the preliminaries, then we'll go to the ER and get the rest of your statement when we get there. Take me to your daughter now, please."

He led her to the house. All he could think about was the sound of the guy's fist when it smashed into Misty's face. If he actually kept his weapon loaded he'd probably have shot the bastard. The door was locked. He didn't have his keys, so he knocked. "Ellen, it's Dad. Open up. The police need to take your statement."

His traumatized daughter opened the door. Her crumpled expression gave way to a ragged sob and she flung herself against him. He crushed her in a hug. After a few seconds, he held her at arm's length and looked her over. Ugly red bruises glared like stoplights on her tender young neck and arms. "You need to see a doctor." He turned to the officer. "She needs to see a doctor."

The officer nodded, tilted her chin to her collar microphone and summoned her partner. "We need to take the intended vic to the hospital, Stu. I can get her statement there. Yes. We'll be right out." She faced Hawk. "Gather what you need, sir, and we'll get your daughter to the hospital."

"Can I drive my own car?"

"Yes, follow us."

It only took Jack a minute to find his keys and wallet. He jogged to Ellen's room and grabbed a hoodie off the back of her desk chair, returned to the living room and put it over her shoulders. "Come on, sweetheart."

When they stepped outside he spotted Doris and Cherry in front of their house, wringing their hands, eyes wide. The girls in their car stared like scared rabbits. "Jack, what happened?" Doris' stricken face was pale.

Cherry touched Ellen's shoulder. "I told you not to go with him. Did he hurt you?"

Jack opened his car door. "I'll fill you in later, Doris. We're in a hurry."

"Please call. I don't care what time it is, Jack. I won't be able to sleep until you call me."

Jack nodded and started his car.

On the brief drive to the local hospital, Ellen shrank into herself. Jack cast furtive glances in her direction throughout the trip. He followed the patrol car to the back entrance and parked where the officer pointed with his long arm thrust from the window.

"Stay put," Jack ordered Ellen. He stepped from the car and rounded the hood quickly to open her door and gently help her out. "Easy, honey. Should I carry you?"

She shook her head and brushed tangled hair from her eyes. "No. I'm okay. Is this where they brought Misty?"

"I hope so. I need to find out how badly she's hurt." If anything happened to her he swore to God he'd hunt down that guy and pound the living shit out of him.

"It's my fault he hit her, Daddy. I never should have let him drive me home. I knew better. I don't know why I went with him. I'm sorry."

He escorted her to the emergency entrance. Officer Sanchez waited at the door then directed them to follow her. An intern met them halfway and directed them to exam room three. He put out his arm when Jack tried to follow him, Officer Sanchez, and Ellen inside.

"She's only sixteen. I'm her father."

"Wait here, sir. We won't be long." The young intern nodded to Sanchez and she followed him and Ellen into the room and slid the glass door shut. He had Ellen sit on the exam table and pulled the privacy curtain, blocking Jack's view.

Jack hurried to the busy nurse's station. "Is Misty Beachy here?"

"Ms. Beachy is here. Are you Mr. Hawk?" She glanced at her computer screen. "She's in two, just across the hall from your daughter. The doctor is completing his examination. He has her stabilized and just did a couple of x-rays. We're waiting for the ophthalmic surgeon. If you wait over there you can get an update on her condition before they move her to surgery."

"Surgery!" The word speared through him and twisted viciously. "What—?"

"There's the doctor now. Hurry and catch them before they get on the elevator."

Jack jogged to the hospital bed the attendant and doctor were pushing in the direction of large swing doors that warned anyone but hospital personnel not to enter. "Misty, I'm here, angel." He clutched her outstretched hand and nodded to the doctor. They proceeded through the doors, down a quiet corridor to a bank of elevators. "Is she...where are you taking her?"

"Her eye is engorged with blood. We need to relieve the pressure so we can do a thorough exam. You can accompany us to the waiting room outside the surgical suite."

"My daughter's here in the ER."

Misty's voice was ragged with pain. "Is Ellen hurt? Did he...?"

"No, baby, she'll be fine. I'll stay with you."

"No, Jack! Go to her. The doctor will find you. She needs her father now."

Jack's gaze swung to the harried doctor. He felt like he was being ripped in two.

"The preliminary shouldn't take long. I'll find you."

When they stopped at the automatic door, Jack leaned down to drop a gentle kiss on her lips. "I love you so much, honey."

A sob racked from her throat. "I know. Me too."

He stepped aside and watched them wheel her in. After a brief wave of indecision, he returned to the ER.

Chapter Twenty-Seven

Misty's Hospital Room, next evening

JACK PUSHED OPEN THE DOOR QUIETLY THEN STEPPED INTO THE room. Ellen followed him. She grabbed the back of his jacket. "Daddy, she's asleep."

"Maybe." He went to the bedside and put his hand over hers. "It's me, baby."

Misty's eyelid fluttered open. "Jack?"

He leaned down and kissed her gently. It was killing him to see her like this. Her face was a bruised mess. Right eye bandaged and left eye nearly swollen shut. Nasty discoloration covered the side of her face and neck. He wanted to pick her up, carry her out of there, and take her home so he could care for her night and day. He forced a smile. "Yes, it's me, baby. The man who loves you. How's the pain?"

She licked her dry lips. "Water, please."

He took the pitcher and poured water into the glass and adjusted the straw on her split lip so she could drink. "That's enough. The doctor said small sips only until after the CT scan. When are they going to do that?"

She swallowed. "I just got back. He's looking at the images now." She turned her head. "Is that you, Ellen?"

Ellen stood behind her father. "Yes." Tears ran down her cheeks. "I'm so ashamed, Misty, I'm sorry."

"Oh, honey, it's okay. Did he hurt you? Are those bruises on your neck?"

Ellen's hand went to her neck. "Yes, but I'm fine. Really. You saved me from…" She choked on a ragged sob.

Jack reached back and pulled her forward with his arm around her waist. "We're all going to be fine, sweetheart." He turned his attention back to Misty. "Did you get any feedback from the ophthalmic surgeon?"

"He said they'd take another look tomorrow. He drained some of the blood to relieve the pressure. It feels better, but until they remove the dressing, I don't know whether I can see or not." She touched her bandaged eye for a brief second.

Ellen wrenched with a sob and lowered her forehead to the bed, resting it on Misty's arm. "It's my fault. I hate myself." Her body shook with sobs. Jack patted her back but didn't say anything.

"Jack, would you leave Ellen and me for a while?"

He stiffened. "You want me to leave?"

"Not long. Please, don't worry."

He straightened reluctantly and stepped back. "I'll go get a cup of coffee. I'll be in the waiting room at the end of the hall." Conflicted, he left the room. The darkness of deep dread filled him. Why did she want him to leave?

* * *

"Ellen, lie down beside me, hon." Misty slid over gingerly and patted the space she'd left. "Come on. Nobody will say anything about it. It's hard for me to talk to you otherwise."

"Are you sure?"

"If anyone objects, I'll tell them to butt out. They won't mess with me."

Ellen choked out a giggle and wiped her hands across her face and reached for a tissue from the hospital-supplied box on the tray. "I'm afraid I'll hurt you."

"You won't hurt me."

"Please don't hate me."

"Hating you is not on my radar, Ellen. How could I hate the daughter of the man we both love so much? Life happens. Bad stuff happens." She patted the bed again. "You're part of Jack. You're like him in so many ways I admire."

Ellen's face crumpled, but she kicked off her shoes and crawled up beside her, and sighed when Misty shifted and put her hand on her upper arm.

This poor kid is a mess, but she's trying.

Deep in her heart Misty hoped tonight was the beginning of the end of their enmity. Ellen craved a stable home and only needed the assurance that Misty and Jack accepted her without question as a natural part of their lives. Not confident what was right or wrong for her to say, she kept silent and continued to touch Ellen in a loving way until she'd calmed and relaxed. The way Mac had soothed her during mortar barrages in Iraq.

After several minutes the door opened and the internist entered the room. "Ah, you have company. I'll come back."

"No, it's okay. This is Ellen, I'll soon be her evil stepmother. We don't have any secrets, so she can hear anything you have to tell me. Her father, Jonathan Hawk, may be out in the waiting room. He'll want to be in on this."

Ellen sat up. "I'll go get him."

The doctor smiled. "You stay put, I'll find him." He left the room and soon returned with Jack.

"I've got the results of the CT scan. The good news is there's no rupture or tear of the spleen or any internal bleeding we can detect. The swelling indicates contusions. The not so good news is we'd like you to stay in the hospital for a few days so we can monitor it."

"That's no problem." Jack took in the situation with his daughter reclining on the bed with Misty and smiled. "Her eye surgeon has already told her the same thing. I'm not letting her come home until we get the all-clear from everybody. I already informed her employer she'd be off for a while."

Misty wrinkled her nose. "Who put you in charge, Hawk?" She looked at the doctor. "What about the pain in my left shoulder?"

"As strange as it may seem, pain in the left shoulder is often a side effect of trauma to the liver or spleen. You have no injury there." He checked her chart. "When is Foster planning to take another look at that eye?"

Jack jumped in before she had a chance to answer. She wasn't sure she was okay with him taking over. He spoke directly to the doctor as if she wasn't there. "He's going to do a more thorough examination tomorrow. He hopes to have some good news for us, but we'll handle it, whatever it is. Right, baby?" He squeezed her leg.

Misty felt her annoyance draining away. Jack loved her, treasured her. It was natural for him to want to take over when she was injured. There was no reason she shouldn't be happy about him caring for her. He was being the man of the family. And isn't that what she wanted? A man to depend on, a man to be there for her no matter what? Like Mac and Dwayne. Like her dad.

"Right." She raised her hand and he walked around and stood right beside her. "You and Ellen will take good care of me, even when I'm being snotty. Won't you?"

Ellen sat up and eased off the bed. "Ha! I could give you lessons in snotty. I have an advanced degree in snotty."

Jack and the internist chuckled. He put his pen in his pocket and closed the chart. "I'll check on you again in the morning. If you have any increase in pain, or you think anything doesn't feel as it should, inform the nurse immediately."

Next day, Misty's hospital room

God, how he loved these two women. Much as he hated to admit it, Ellen was a woman, and he was so proud of the way she'd apologized at Christmas and done her best to welcome Misty into their home. He knew better than to kid himself. There was still some lingering uncertainty in his daughter, but in time she'd accept reality and know she was safe with them. Misty had turned herself inside out in her effort to build bridges between the two of them, even though she protested she didn't know a thing about being a girl or how to relate to a teenager, she was doing great. He didn't know how it was possible, but he loved her more every day.

Her face was a kaleidoscope of bruises, but the swelling was diminishing. Deep anger burned in his gut when he relived the moment he'd seen that bastard wallop her then stomp on her when she went down. He was looking forward to testifying against him. If there was any justice in the system, he'd go away for a long time.

"You seem tired, baby. Did they put you through the wringer today?" He noticed the wad of tape on her finger covering her engagement ring. She'd refused to take it off when they'd admitted her, so one of the ER attendants had covered it with about a yard of tape. It would take a magician to get it off her if she was asleep or under anesthesia.

"I thought the VA hospital was bad, but I've spent as many hours here lying in hallways outside labs waiting my turn for every test under the sun. I hope they give me a day off."

"Does it still hurt?" Ellen asked. "Your chest and stomach?"

"Not as much." She smiled at Ellen. "It's not your fault, you know, so erase the guilt from those pretty gray eyes. Bad guys do what they want without caring how much they hurt other people. If what I did saved you from him, it was worth it, believe me."

Jack stood. "I'm going to the nurse's station to see if they can tell me when the eye surgeon will be making his rounds. I don't want to miss him." He kissed her and squeezed her hand.

The doctor approached the nurse's station.

Good timing.

"Do you mind if we have a private word before you visit my wife?"

My wife. Man, it feels so good to say that out loud.

Jack crossed his arms. "She's so damned independent. She keeps everything to herself. Is there anything you can tell me before we go in?"

The surgeon took some time before he answered then shook his head. "Privacy laws don't permit me to discuss her case with anyone. I'll go over my findings with both of you." He motioned for Jack to follow him to her room.

Jack followed Dr. Foster to her room. Misty and Ellen were scheming like two thieves planning a heist. He rolled his eyes heavenward in silent thanks for their little conspiracy, whatever it may be.

"Good evening, Mrs. Hawk. "I have the results of your tests."

Jack noticed the startled looks from both Ellen and Misty at the doctor's greeting. He grinned, raised his hands and shrugged. Misty pursed her lips and shook her head as if to ask, who told this man I was your wife, I wonder?

Misty used her elbows to push herself higher on her pillow. "Jack, would you and Ellen step out while I talk to Dr. Foster?"

"Hell no!"

She blinked. The surgeon glanced from her to him and back to her. Ellen's eyes went wide.

Jack leaned forward, fisted hands at his sides. "We're partners in this, or am I mistaken?"

Dr. Foster cleared his throat. "Would you like me to step out?"

Misty set her lips in a firm line and stared at Jack for a moment. Finally, she sighed and reached for his hand. "We're partners, Jack." Nodding to the doctor she said, "It's okay, my *husband* can hear what you have to say."

Jack squeezed her hand, glad she'd chosen not to fight over it.

The surgeon flipped pages on her chart. "You'll most likely lose most of the eyesight in your injured eye. The only surgery I recommend at this point is extraction of a small cataract to allow more light to reach the damaged retina. The excess blood now present will reabsorb on its own before too long. I found the microscopic fragments of shrapnel, but it's too risky to remove it as long as it doesn't seem to be doing harm. Further surgery wouldn't likely result in any improvement in vision and might damage your appearance. I doubt you'd want that."

Jack's stomach fell with a thud. Icy tingling coursed through his arms and hands, something he'd only experienced while flying combat missions. "That son of a bitch!"

Dr. Foster touched is arm. "Mr. Hawk, the recent injury merely speeded up an inevitable outcome." He faced Misty. "I'm surprised you had a dozen years of fairly good eyesight after your original injury. The eye itself will look perfectly normal to the world at large. I do not see prostheses on the horizon."

Jack expelled a breath through his nose. "Thank God." Misty was very casual about her natural good looks, but he was under no illusion that her appearance was unimportant to her. He smiled. "You know what, baby? You're a trooper, you'll do fine."

Misty tightened her grip on his hand and gave him a wobbly smile. "I will."

"I'll check on you in the morning, Mrs. Hawk." Foster excused himself and left the room.

After the physician left Jack questioned them about what she and Ellen had been up to. "I saw the way you two had your heads together. Am I in trouble again?"

Misty pressed her lips together. "We were planning a wedding, but it seems I've forgotten that I'm already married to you. Must be the blow to the head."

"Could be, but then, what's Ellen's excuse?"

"Seriously, Dad. Now that we're finally done with all the hassle of the move, what's the reason to delay it? It's awkward for me to tell my new friends who come over that Misty's your live-in-fiancée. It would be so much easier to say step-mother."

"I see your point." He looked her in the eye then shifted his gaze to Misty. "So, when am I getting married?" He shoved his hands in his pockets and grinned.

This is what winning the lottery must feel like.

"Ellen suggested Valentine's Day. I could wear a red dress, like the harlot I am."

"I never said that!" Ellen's eyes expanded on her gasp.

"I'm teasing you, Ellen, but when you think about it, red's my best color. What do you have to say, Raptor?"

"Red's good." He pushed out his lips. "Tomorrow would be fine with me, or I could see if there's a justice of the peace available for tonight."

"No way!" She pointed to her face. "What great wedding pictures."

"We can get married tonight and have our pictures taken on Valentine's Day."

Misty wrinkled her nose and shook her head. "Since you have nothing intelligent to contribute to this conversation, why don't you get lost so Ellen and I can talk?" She glanced at her watch. "You can pick her up around nine. She's going to get something from the canteen and eat dinner with me."

He raised his arms and grinned. "Okay by me. Just tell me when and where I need to be and what I should wear, Master Sergeant."

"So, in this case the major is going to take orders from the sergeant?" She smirked at Ellen.

"I know when I'm outnumbered." He snapped off a salute. "See you ladies later. I'll call a *good* friend to share dinner with me."

"Scat." She flipped her hand.

As he strolled out to the parking lot he recited his new mantra: *Life is great. Life is beautiful.*

* * *

"Can I ask you something?" Ellen's face was suddenly shy and unsure.

"Always ask me anything, Ellen. If I don't want to answer or don't know the answer, I'll say so." Misty shifted higher on the uncomfortable hospital bed. Her bottom was beginning to hurt as much as her chest. "So ask."

"Why my dad. You could get lots of guys. Why'd you pick him?" Her cheeks glowed cherry red.

"Ah, your dad." She patted the bed next to her. "Sit, this will take a while." She smiled to put Ellen at ease.

"Major Jonathan Hawk, USMC, retired." Misty smiled at an old memory. "I was attracted to Jack all those years ago in Iraq. He was a mature and confident professional and all business. And he was married and had a kid. Strictly off limits. Our relationship was purely professional from the get-go.

"When I met him again, more than ten years later, I felt the same breathless and disconcerting tug. Mac McPherson and I went to see the war dog trials at Camp Pendleton and met up with Jack. I didn't know Mac and your dad had continued their friendship and were still in touch after all that time."

Ellen shrugged. "I guess I don't get it. He's just my dad."

"Jack is a mensch."

"That's what Cherry's mom says. She's Jewish. She told me it means honorable and manly. She really likes him. I kinda thought they would…" She clapped a hand over her mouth.

"But you got stuck with me instead?"

"I didn't mean it to sound like that."

"I know." Misty smiled and nodded. "I suppose whether their fathers are wonderful or rotten, girls tend to use their dads as some sort of yardstick to measure all the men they meet in adult life. You and I both won the dad lottery." She grinned. "Admit it, Ellen. Every guy you meet from now on will have to measure up to Jack."

Ellen dipped her head, cheeks still glowing. "I guess so. I love him, but I still don't understand what it is that makes you want to be with him *forever*. He's just an ordinary father."

"He's an ordinary father to you. For me he's a mensch, strong, confident, intelligent, reliable, he's got good manners, he's a gentleman, he's virile and he wants me and only me." Ellen's blush increased on the word *virile*. "I love it when he teases me and makes me laugh. It's such a wonderful feeling as a woman to know you are adored by the man you want. I never even came close to that with any man I ever met before, even Mac."

"What's the story with you and Mr. McPherson? He's got such a nice family and he seems so happy with his wife and her son. I know you served together. You're not...?"

"No, Ellen." Misty squeezed her hand. This girl needed to know her father was safe with her, and not some substitute for another man she couldn't have. "It's rare for a man and a woman to be friends, but Mac is my best friend in the world. I love him as a fellow Marine. In a way he's like my brother who got killed in Afghanistan. Mac and I were never *in* love but it's hard to explain how important we were to each other in that godforsaken place. Our closeness over there kept us sane. The love I have for Jack is a world away from my feelings for Mac."

Ellen nodded, but didn't say anything.

"So? Are you going to be my Maid of Honor? Wear a bright red dress with a crown of ribbons and roses in your hair?" Misty was gratified when Ellen's mouth hung open in surprise and she stared back, speechless and wide-eyed.

"You want me?" She pointed to herself.

"Who else would I want?" She grinned. "Yes, Ellen. I'd like you to stand up with me and Jack. I need to know you're there as my friend, that you'll help me make all the right moves, at the wedding, and later, too." She waited for an answer. "Will you do that for us?"

Tears sparkled in Ellen's eyes, prompting Misty to tear up. "I will if you'll teach me how to be a non-bratty step-daughter without killing me first." Her lips quivered, but her gray eyes, Hawk's eyes, took on a hopeful shine.

Misty laughed. "We both have our work cut out for us."

Epilogue

Valentine's Day, the Hawk's back yard. Sunset.

JACK WAITED ANXIOUSLY UNDER THE BOWER SO BEAUTIFULLY decorated with red and white roses. Marla and Graciella had spent hours helping Ellen, Debbie and Misty turn the area into a fairyland, a perfect wedding setting. The florist bill had staggered him.

He turned to the clergyman, "I've never been this nervous." The elderly chaplain nodded reassuringly and patted his shoulder. His best man, Cluny McPherson, whispered, "Relax, Hawk, you're marrying my best friend, you lucky s.o.b."

Groomsman, Dwayne Dempsey chuckled. "I know how you feel, pal."

At last Jack detected soft music from the sound system he'd set up this morning.

Graciella McPherson, Misty's proudly pregnant bridesmaid, floated across the yard, onto the white path between the chairs packed with family and friends. Graciella kissed Jack's cheek and stepped to the opposite side, a joyful smile lighting her exotic face.

Matron of Honor, Marla Dempsey, who still glowed like a bride after four children, followed.

Dwayne nudged Jack, warning, "I'll be keeping my eye on you, pal," and brought a welcome smile to the bridegroom's face.

Jack's breath caught when Ellen stepped on the path and drew near, captivating him in her bright red silk dress. She held a bouquet of white roses with a single red rose in the center. In her natural dark blond hair rested a crown of white ribbons, roses and baby's breath. Her smile couldn't have been wider. "Hi, Daddy."

"Hi, sweetheart." He kissed her cheek and whispered, "You're way too beautiful for your old dad."

Following Ellen came the ring bearers; thirteen-year-old Santos Jefferson McPherson, resplendent in a rented tuxedo; the only *man* in the wedding party not wearing Marine dress blues. At his side, Amber Dempsey, a year younger and slightly taller, sparkled in a fluffy white dress sprinkled with red hearts. Jack smiled at the memory of Santos, at the ripe old age of ten, informing Dwayne he would marry his daughter, Amber, one day. Perhaps he would. Jack beamed at the thought.

Adele's diminutive red-haired daughter followed, haphazardly scattering red rose petals on the white path for the bride to walk on.

The music rose in volume when Misty appeared between her parents. Frank Sinatra belted out *Come Fly With Me,* and the audience broke into laughter and applause. Jack prayed his heart wouldn't stop at the sight of his soul mate in the slim red sheath that ended just above her knees, showcasing beautiful slender legs, shiny red high heels on her feet. A small sheer veil complimented her pixie-cut blond hair.

Thank you, God! Thank you!

Misty smiled brilliantly all the way to the bower. She never once took her eyes from his face. Her honey-brown gaze pledged things words couldn't express. Pure love and trust overflowed from her. His knees wobbled.

Cluny murmured, "Wow, take a gander at our Master Sargeant."

Dwayne chimed in with a soft, "Mmm mmm, who knew?"

Jack drew in a pent-up breath and held his hand out to Misty when Payne and Debbie stepped back, their eyes shining with emotion.

The actual ceremony was a blur. He couldn't take his eyes off her.

He had a vague recollection of reciting his vows and sliding the wedding ring onto her finger. She didn't let go of his hand after she'd slipped on his ring.

The next words he heard were the chaplain's, "Ladies and gentlemen, I have the great pleasure to present Mr. and Mrs. Jonathan Hawk."

He kissed his wife thoroughly to the accompaniment of the clapping and cheers of their friends and family. "I love you, Mrs. Hawk. I'll love you to the end of time."

Tears welled in his wife's eyes. She sighed and rested her forehead on his chest.

THE END

* * *

Don't miss out on your next favorite book!

Join the Satin Romance mailing list
www.satinromance.com/mail.html

Author's Mission

All of us were deeply affected by 9/11. When the wounded veterans began coming home in huge numbers, I wracked my brain to see what I could do to help.

In 2014 I decided to alter course and write my Wounded Warrior Series. Love, hope and family stories of men and women facing the challenge of returning to civilian life after being wounded in service to our country.

I donate 100% of my royalties for the series to help some of these special veterans. Wounded Veteran's Relief Fund provides direct, temporary, emergency cash assistance to veterans facing homelessness and family breakdown. Enough cash to get them and their families back on their feet again. Rent. Car repairs. Utilities. Medical bills, other life essentials.

Buy a book and help a wounded veteran.

THANK YOU FOR READING

Did you enjoy this book?

We invite you to leave a review at the website of your choice, such as Goodreads, Amazon, Barnes & Noble, etc.

DID YOU KNOW THAT LEAVING A REVIEW...

- Helps other readers find books they may enjoy.
- Gives you a chance to let your voice be heard.
- Gives authors recognition for their hard work.
- Doesn't have to be long. A sentence or two about why you liked the book will do.

About the Author

I wrote my first novel at the age of six. It was titled "The Mouse," and was two pages long—including illustrations! My mother saved that *first edition* and every now and then, I take it out and smile over it.

When my beloved husband of many years suddenly died, I'd come home after a long day of work and write. Writing allowed me to pour out all my sadness. Then, the more I wrote, the more I realized I would go on. I would be happy, I had a lot of living to do, and love stories to tell.

I'm published now in Romance novels and an anthology of short stories. But my first two manuscripts still reside on a CD somewhere in my house. I can't bear to erase them because they're mine, they're loved, and like a crazy relative one hides in the attic, they reside in a quiet, safe place.

www.pattycampbell.com
pattycampbellauthor.blogspot.com

f facebook.com/Patty-Campbell-Author-536855299661241

g goodreads.com/goodreadscomuser_PattyCampbell

Also by Patty Campbell

WITH MELANGE BOOKS

Wounded Warriors Series
Love of a Marine
Soul of a Marine

* * *

Novels
Risky Business